KING OF THE ROAD

CHARLIE WILLIAMS

KING OF THE ROAD

PUBLISHED BY

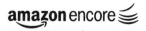

Published by AmazonEncore
P.O. Box 400818
Las Vegas, NV 89140

ISBN-13: 9781935597490
ISBN-10: 1935597493

1

Dear Royston,

Hello. You don't know me, but I knows you. I've always known about you, following your goings on in the paper, picking up this and that from talk in the bar. Keeping up with your antics is one of the easiest things you can do around here, truth be told. You're a famous lad all right, in your own way. And I'm proud of you for it.

I might come across a bit barmy to you, saying I'm proud of you. Well, perhaps I am barmy. But that don't bother us. There's no shame in barminess, Royston, and you'd do well to remember that. But you also got to understand that I do have a good reason for saying what I'm saying. And I want to explain it all to you.

I'm told they're letting you out of there soon. If it's true, and you do find yourself walking the streets of Mangel again before long (or any time), come and see me if you can. I'll be at the Bee Hive, in Norbert Green. I think you knows the place.

Warmest regards,
BF.

Someone were coming so I folded up the letter and shoved him in me back pocket. I could hear the choppy footsteps clacking along the wood floor out there in the corridor. I knew it weren't a screw cos they went slower than that. And the nurses went faster, often as not. So it had to be the Doc.

'Right then, Royston,' he says, opening the door. 'All set, are we?'

'Well,' I says. 'You see, Doc…er, I dunno if…'

'Come now, none of that. Today's the day. Remember how we talked about it in group yesterday? There comes a time when all of us has to go back into the world. This is a place for the sick, Royston. You, my friend, are *cured*.'

He came over and brushed the dandruff off me shoulders.

'Are you not glad, Royston? You can get on with your life now. You can start again.'

I thought about it. I wanted to tell him the truth. No one tells lies in Parpham, see. Telling lies is letting everyone down.

And then I recalled who were waiting for us on the outside. It were brung home to us in that minute how a little someone out there needed us. And the quicker I got my arse out there, the better it'd be for that individual.

'Aye,' I says. 'Open the fuckin' gates, Doc. Blakey is on his way.'

We went off down the corridor, him saying: 'No need for swearing, Blake.'

He were all right, though, the Doc were. He took us out them gates personal, laying on the full VIP bit. Which is only fair when you're talking a feller of my standing in the community. Course, there were no one to meet us t'other side. And I didn't mind that. I knew I'd let folks down here and there and treated some of em bad. But I'd been drifting in me life, back in them days. I used to live day-to-day, not knowing where the fuck I were headed, and thereby not knowing why the fuck I were living at all.

But now I had summat to live for.

'Now, Royston,' says the Doc, turning to face us. Normally I fucking hated it, folks calling us Royston. But coming from him I didn't mind it. See, your doctor is a member of your professional classes. Like your doorman. You lets em get on with it and you don't question em. 'Now, Royston, remember what we talked about in one-to-one. You'll find things strange out there for a while. The world moves on, my friend, and not always for the better. But don't let it overly concern you. Just remember my words, and what we talked about.'

'Aye.'

'And remember that you're not alone.'

'Aye,' I says. But I'd heard all this already. He'd been going on about it ever since I'd been in Parpham. And to be frank with you, me swede were on other matters just now. Mind you, he didn't know about that. I'd kept it from him, just like I'm keeping it from you, for the minute. I hadn't told no one in Parpham cos the bastards'd like as not fuck it up for us. But he were all right, were the Doc.

'Well then,' he says. 'This is it. Have you got your bit of paper saying where you're to go?'

'Aye, aye...' I says, getting it out me pocket and showing it him.

'Good, good.' He stuck his paw out. 'Then this is goodbye, Royston. And remember...'

I shook his hand and pissed off out of it before he got going again.

• • •

I had to wait three hours before a bus came. Seemed that way anyhow, though it were only ten minutes like as not. I had catching up to do, didn't I. I'd missed out on a couple years of the lad's life, and them was years I'd never get back. He wouldn't get em back neither, poor lad. He like as not reckoned he had no father at all, and that he'd have to struggle through life with only his mam to show him woss what. And Sal had let him believe it, like as not.

Mind you, I didn't blame her for that. Like I says just now, I'd let her down a bit. But that were all behind us. Turning over a new leaf now, I were. And to get to where I could do that from, I'd had to do a lot of thinking. I'd done more thinking in Parpham than I'd done in all the years prior. And from thinking comes realisations.

And from them you gets decisions.

Bus driver were a big feller of about forty or fifty, and he gave us a funny look when I got on, like someone had wrote CUNT across me forehead or summat. The look were gone soon as it had came, so I let it go. I went to pay but he shook his swede and pulled into the road. I put the 50p in the tray anyhow and started moving off. But he weren't having none of it, and he left it be. It were shame to waste a good 50p, and if he didn't have it some other fucker would, so I went back and got it.

Now I were a dad, I had to save wedge where I could.

There were only an old granny there at the front and a couple of young lovers on the back row, so I parked meself halfway along and looked out the window. It weren't half odd, being out and about. The bus were haring off down the Deblin Road like no fucker's business, and to be frank with you I wanted it to slow up a bit. Not that I were scaredy nor nothing. I just wanted to ease meself back into things gentle. I were on the verge of coming face-to-face with me own begotten youngun for the first time, and I wanted to get me bearings first. I wanted to have a good old gander at every house and pub we passed, and certain trees and hillocks and all. 'Hoy,' my gob says before I could stop it. It were quite loud and all. And you can't just shout 'hoy' on its own and leave it at that. So I went on, a bit quieter: 'Slow up a bit, will you.'

And he did and all. I dunno why that surprised us. Before going into Parpham I wouldn't bat an eyeball at having to order folks about. There's no time for arsery when you're a doorman, and if you don't say it loud and clear you've got a fucking riot on your hands. Didn't feel right this time though. Just didn't sound like meself. Sounded a bit whiney, if I'm honest. But it done the trick all right. I still had what it takes and that's all that mattered. I set me face out the window and had a good look at the halfway house, which we was going past just then.

'Mong.'

Sounded like 'mong' anyhow. I turned my head about. The lad back there were sat in the middle of the row—legs spread wide, bird draped over the one shoulder with a hand on his chest—and he were staring right at us. There were a smirk across his chops, but I couldn't quite tell if it were friendly or if he were asking for it. I mean, I could have been wrong about him saying 'mong' there. Could have been he'd said summat else that sounded like 'mong' but weren't it. So I ignored him and turned back to me window.

We was skirting the bottom bit of Norbert Green here. I'd always hated going down this way. Better than actually going into Norbert Green though. Mind you, you'd never find a bus driver willing to do that.

'Hoy, I'm talkin' to you, you fuckin' spaz,' says the young feller a minute or so later. 'Turn an' face us.'

The old granny up front turned and gave us a quick glare like this were all my fault. I knew what she meant though. She'd had it with mouthy little younguns and she were looking to me—a figure of authority in the Mangel area—to sort it out. Some folks can't stick up for emselves proper, see, and it's up to others to do it for em.

But, do you know, I didn't fancy kicking up a row with this one here. He were only a youngun, fifteen or so. My own lad would be fifteen before I knew where me arse were, and I'd want him to be able to make mistakes on buses without getting his swede mashed for it.

Gran turned and gave us a quick glare again.

All right all right. Maybe I'd give the lad a face. Sometimes a raised eyebrow is as good as a smack in the gob, resulting in no bloodshed and a lesson learned. So I turned and raised me left eyebrow at him.

And that worked out all right for a bit. Granny up there sat tight without glaring at us no more. The lad and his bird kept it quiet behind us. I looked out the window and wondered how long before I could take little Royston down the gym. And the bus driver pootled along over the bridge, hauling us all into Mangel town centre.

Some shuffling behind us, then the lad's punching us on the back of the head.

'Don't you fuckin' ignore us,' he says after. 'No fuckin' mong ignores us. I'll teach you to ignore us, you fuckin'...'

The bus stopped sharpish, making the lad fall over, and me hit my poor head on the back of the chair in front. The lad were getting up already, rubbing his shoulder and calling the driver bad names.

I were starting to wonder a bit about this young feller here. He wanted teaching, didn't he. And sometimes there's only way to learn em. So I cracked me fingers and started wondering how best to begin our lesson.

Took him about two steps to get down the aisle. It's the driver I'm on about now. You'd not have thought him swift from looking at him sat there behind his big wheel, but he weren't half. The lad didn't even have time to stop scowling at us and look sideways, which it would have been good for him to do. The driver stopped when his shoulder met the youngun's, which is when the youngun started shifting. He flew like a big bird who flies sideways, coming to land half-on half-off the back row and missing his lass by not much at all. He tried getting up again, but the driver feller got him by the boots and hauled, dragging him up the aisle and out the door and ignoring the young feller's protestations. The bird followed em out onto the street, all the while screaming at the driver the kind of bad words a young lass oughtn't to use, really, grannies being present.

I were still rubbing the bumps front and back of me swede when the driver got back behind his wheel and set off again. Not but three minutes later he pulled up at Mangel Central Bus Station.

As I went past him on me way off he says: 'We're right behind you, Royston. Don't you worry.' Then he gave us a wink.

I didn't know what to make of that.

• • •

Mind you, I couldn't let it bother us. I had more important fish to fry. Like little Royston. Not that I wanted to fry him, though. I wanted to get a look at the little feller, pick him up and swing him round, lob him in the air and catch him again, the two of us laughing at Sal, who'd be stood nearby having a go at us cos I might drop him.

'Sal,' I says, 'I won't ever drop our little Royston. Not *ever*.'

I got straight on a bus for South Mangel and gave the driver 30p.

'You're 30p short,' he says.

'You what?'

'It's 60p to South Mangel.'

'Sixty fuckin' p? Gone up, ennit?'

'Aye.'

I went and sat down after paying him. No one else were on the bus, so I got the back row all to meself. I'd be taking our little Royston out for rides now, I supposed. Not on buses, mind. I'd take him out in me Capri. I know Sal said she'd flogged it, but you can't hide a top motor like that in Mangel, and I'd soon have her back again, one way or t'other. And then there'd be no stopping us. Me and little Royston, out and about. I weren't gonna be one o' them bastard dads who don't give a fuck about their youngfolk. My old feller had been like that, and look what happened to him. No, the way I seen it is this: Your youngfolk is the future. And if you don't bring em up right, they'll have you. Look at that lad on the bus back there—reckon his old feller done right by him? Too fucking right he never.

And just cos I hadn't ever seen little Royston in all of his three or so years don't mean I couldn't make up for it. I'd take the lad everywhere with us. Aye, why not? He could sit in a special high chair behind the bar at Hoppers, watching us at work on the door. Maybe he'd be on the door there himself one day, if he studied his old man in action and worked hard at school. A dad can dream, can't he?

All right all right all right. I know—there's no saying little Royston were a boy. But do you know what? I didn't even care if he turned out to be a girl. I'd love her just the same. She couldn't be a doorman, mind. Sal could learn her to cut hair or summat. Girls can have dreams and all, you know.

'South Mangel,' shouts the driver. And I had a feeling he'd shouted it once or twice already.

I got off the bus and found meself stood at the end of our road. It were getting dark now. As the bus pulled away I stood there a moment and took a deep breath. Half a minute later, when I'd stopped choking on the exhaust smoke, I set off towards my house.

I wondered if he'd recognise us. Surely Sal had shown him some pictures of us? She'd fucking better have. But I knew in me heart that little Royston would know us anyhow, pictures or no. I'd dreamed about him night after night in Parpham. Me and him playing footy, watching *Rocky III*, sitting on a bench down by the river eating a bag of chips…And do you know what? I truly believed he'd dreamed them dreams and all.

Me and little Royston, together in kip. He hadn't met us in the flesh, like, but he knew his old man inside out.

No one were out and about in the street, and I were glad of that. No one I recognised anyhow. Actually there weren't much of anything I recognised. None of them old potholes in the road I'd come to know like the tats on me own arms. It were all smooth and black now and not a hole in sight. The path had been pulled up and relaid and all. Plus they'd replaced the old lamppost in the middle there and put in a couple of new uns. All the same houses was there, but they'd all been tarted up slightly in some way I couldn't put me pointer on. All except that one just up the way there on the left, which I knew straight off to be my own. I strolled on up to it, noting with a friendly shake of the head the paint peeling off the window frames and the front door that didn't hardly have no more paint left on it. All right, so Sal had let the old place go a bit. But you couldn't blame the poor old cow, could you? Can't be easy bringing up a youngun on yer tod.

But all that's in the past for her now. Daddy's home.

My heart were fairly busting out me ribcage as I put finger to doorbell. Cos this were it…

Time for little Royston to meet his old man.

Wouldn't have been easy for him, neither, growing up fatherless in a world where a feller's got to be hard else he goes by the wayside. Mind you, you can't get much more tougher than old Sal. Especially with them scars already settling on her face last time I'd seen her. Still, there's no replacement for having a male about the house. Everyone knows lads brung up without an old man turns out arse bandits. No fucking way were that happening to our little Royston.

Fuck all were happening with the doorbell so I knocked instead. I wanted to peer through the little bits of glass in the door, but it might ruin the surprise if little Royston came running up and clocked my big mug looking down at him. Maybe I ought to hide behind one of them cars there, jump out when he stepped onto the path for a gander left and right. Nah, didn't want to put the shite up him. Hard as rock but gentle with it, that's the kind of father Royston Blake is gonna be. I knocked again. *Rat-tatatat-tat...tat tat.*

'They ain't in.'

I stepped back and looked up. Cos that's where the old bird were shouting from.

'All right, Mrs Blatt from next door,' I says.

She didn't say nothing to that, just clocked us up and down and didn't look too happy. But that were just her way. Always been that way to me she had, ever since I'd put a football through her living room window and run off. Fucking cunt across the street grassed us up though, Wossname Davis or whatever his name were. Mind you, he choked of cancer a couple of years later so fair's fair.

'They ain't in,' she says again.

'Oh, all right,' I says.

'They're out.'

'Ah,' I says. 'Where?' Cos it were getting on a bit now, and you oughtn't to be going round with a littlun in the dark.

'Well, she'll be workin',' says Mrs Blatt from next door with a little smirk. 'Like as not.'

'Workin'? What about the lad?'

'Oh he'll be with her. Or nearby. Anyway you, I thought you was locked up?'

'Aye, well...' I didn't like talking about that. Specially not with her. But I ought to get used to it, I supposed. 'Got better, didn't I.'

'Ain't you I'm worried about. It's the rest of us.' She shut the window and pulled the drapes before I had chance to ask where Sal worked. She'd only lie to us anyhow, like as not. Fucking old—

'Welcome home, Royston.'

I turned arse and looked down the street, which is where the hollering were coming from. There, stood in his doorway, were Doug the shopkeeper.

'Oh for fuck sake,' I says to meself.

2

I hadn't even looked at the corner shop on me way past. Hadn't wanted to. The shite that place and its proprietor had brung us in the none too distant had left us not wanting to see the place ever again. And now here he were, the fucking smug-faced old bastard, folding his arms and laughing at us.

'Welcome home.'

But, do you know, he weren't. When you looked at him again you saw he had a proper smile across his chops. And his arms weren't folded but outstretched, reaching out to us.

What the fuck were his game?

• • •

DOCTOR: *So Royston, tell me about this Doug fellow.*
PATIENT: *Doug who?*
DOCTOR: *The, er...grocer, is it?*
PATIENT: *Dunno about no grocer.*
DOCTOR: *Well, something else then. Doug the merchant?*
PATIENT: *Who's that?*
DOCTOR: *Come now, Royston, help me here. Remember what we talked about? Remember what we said about community spirit and helping our comrades?*
PATIENT: *Aye, aye.*
DOCTOR: *So which Doug could I be talking about?*

PATIENT: Well...*could be Doug Croney. He works on the floor at Garsides though. An' I met a feller from East Bloater once. His name were Doug, I think. Down the old market flogging pigs, he were. Aye, had this big pink sow, says he used to give her—*

DOCTOR: *Come on, Royston. Help your comrades.*

PATIENT: *All right all right, fuck sake. Well, there's one called Doug the shopkeeper, but he's a—*

DOCTOR: *That's him.*

PATIENT: *What about him?*

DOCTOR: *Tell me about him.*

PATIENT: *Telled you already, didn't I?*

DOCTOR: *What did you tell me?*

PATIENT: *He's a fucking cunt is what.*

DOCTOR: *OK, now we're back on track. But try to dampen your swearing instinct, Royston. Remember—the ideal word is always there for you, if you look for it. And it's never a swear word. But tell me more about this shopkeeper.*

PATIENT: *What? Fuck sake, Doc...I mean, you're the boss an' that, but ain't we gone over this previous, like?*

DOCTOR: *I'd like to do it again, Royston. I feel there are some truths to be gleaned from this Douglas the shopkeeper.*

PATIENT: *Doug.*

DOCTOR: *What did he do to you, Royston? Ah...Royston? Come on now, hold together. If we don't face up to these things, we'll never move on. Come now, what did he do to you?*

PATIENT: *He...he fucking...*

DOCTOR: *It's all right, Royston. I'm your friend. That's it...*
          What did he do?
PATIENT: *He fucking...he...*
DOCTOR: *Just say it, Royston. The sooner you—*
PATIENT: *He turned our Finney into sausages.*
DOCTOR: *Right, there we have it.*
PATIENT: *What?*
DOCTOR: *Now we can start learning about these truths.*
PATIENT: *What fucking truths? I've told you the truth. He*
          makes bangers out of folks. Everyone knows it.
          There's that young lad years ago, Sammy B—
DOCTOR: *Come now, Royston—we've talked about him, too.*
          He was never made into sausages. You know that
          really, don't you?
PATIENT: *He fucking—*
DOCTOR: *Royston, please. You know it, don't you?*
PATIENT: *Well...*
DOCTOR: *And your friend Finney—the truth about him is right*
          here in the civic records. He died in hospital, long
          before this, er...sausage incident is supposed to—
PATIENT: *Bollocks.*
DOCTOR: *Is it?*
PATIENT: *Aye.*
DOCTOR: *How so? His death certificate is there in the files.*
          The police investigated his death, remember? His
          body was buried.
PATIENT: *I never saw no body buried.*
DOCTOR: *That's because you were in custody at the time.*
          Let's...let's just leave that aside for a moment, and
          look at Doug the...er...shopkeeper. You've always
          known him, right?

PATIENT: *Aye.*

DOCTOR: *And the stories about him…you've always known them, too?*

PATIENT: *Aye, course.*

DOCTOR: *Of course. So do you see what's happening there, Royston? You're looking at something and not quite liking what you see. Maybe it doesn't look friendly, or something is out of place. Then you hear a few second-hand anecdotes about it, from people who have also looked and not liked what they saw. And then you form an opinion that becomes set in stone.*

PATIENT: *Second-hand what?*

DOCTOR: *Er…what?*

PATIENT: *You says second-hand aunty summats.*

DOCTOR: *Ah—anec…er, stories. That's all they are, Royston. Legends, yarns, rumours…call them what you like. They're the lifeblood of a town like Mangel. And they're never—never—the whole truth.*

PATIENT: *No smoke without summat smoking though, is there.*

DOCTOR: *Maybe. Maybe not. The point I'm trying to make here though, Royston, is that…*

• • •

'That's a nice anorak you've got there,' says Doug in a friendly voice that he must have robbed off of someone.

'You what?'

'Anorak.'

'Anorak?' I says, looking at meself and feeling mite confused.

We was in Doug's shop now, about five minutes on. I hadn't wanted to come in, course, but I thought I'd give him a go, what with me being able to look at matters from a new position since coming out of Parpham and all. Plus Doug had promised us a cup o' tea, which were suddenly the thing I needed most in the whole world, now he came to mention it. I had it in my paw now and it were fucking marvellous. Except when a lot of it slopped over the sides, scalding me fingers and messing up Doug's floor.

'Aye, anorak,' he says. 'Nice and warm.'

It were well odd being back in Doug's corner shop. Not that it had changed since I'd last been there. Shelves was still half bare and stocked with only your barest of essentials, like bread and beans and crisps and that. By the looks of it he'd settled into hard times quite nicely and found his natural place there. I were happy to see that cos I didn't especially like Doug, on account of him being the root cause of my public downfall and subsequent time in Parpham. But like I says earlier—I didn't have no particular grudge on him.

'You hearin' us, Royston? Hello?'

'Aye. What?'

'You open yer ears now. You don't listen to the like of me, you'll get nowhere with this mission of yours.'

'Aye, aye. Fuck sake,' I says. Cos he sounded like he were having a go, and I were fed up of folks having a go. 'Mission?'

'Never mind that now. You just listen to this, on account of it bein' of the utmost importitude. Right now you're goin' through what is commonly termed as homesickness. You're out and about in Mangel after a period of four years out of it, and it's gettin' atop you. Specially hearin' that bit o' bad news there. And the thing you wants most of all—though you might not readily admit him to yourself—is to get back inside that there mental asylum, where it's nice and warm and safe. *But...*'

I had a sip of me tea. It were all right, though a bit on your weak side. But what I really could have done with were a smoke. I hadn't had one since coming out, and it were high time I did.

'I'm here to tell you, Royston, you can't go back there, to your asylum. They won't let you back in. You go back and knock on them gates shoutin' for Dr Geldin', they'll bounce you up the road on your backside.'

He didn't have much on his fag shelf, mind. There was some Consulate there though, which were the wise choice for us right then, like as not, me being fresh out of hospital and all.

'So out here you must stay, Royston. Mangel is your final stage, and it is here that thou shalt fulfil thine destiny.'

But you never knew what he had round back in the stock room. 'Hey, Doug,' I says, nodding at the passage behind the counter. 'Got any Number Ones back there?'

His face turned purple and I could have swore a little puff of smoke came out his ears. Fucking hell, I thought, putting me empty mug on the counter. Doug were getting on in years, but he were still liable to get physical. A rumble with him were all I needed. I'd never liked hitting old folks. So it were good news when he calmed down and went over to the front door.

'Walk on, brave warrior,' he says, opening it. 'Walk on, and rest not until thou hast slain the dragon, and chopped his head off.'

I didn't like leaving a corner shop empty-handed, but Doug made it clear that it were on the cards this time. Least he'd gave us a cup o' tea, mind, though I'd had to put up with his endless going on. I mean, for fuck sake. Do you know what he were on about? Should be him in Parpham.

'Ta, Doug,' I says, making a move. Cos to be fair I did feel better for his cuppa, and it had been nice of him to welcome us home and that. I patted him on the shoulder as I went past.

But he got us by the arm. 'I will pay for my bad deeds,' he whispers in me ear. 'Don't you worry about that. I've done folks harm in my time and I'll pay. We'll all pay for what we done, in the end, Royston. But just grant this poor wrongdoer one favour. Grant us all a favour. *Save this town.*'

He slipped summat in me pocket and shut the door on us. I walked out onto the main road and sat at the bus stop there. I had the shelter to meself, and I were glad of it. I'd had enough of folks for a while. I wanted to close me eyes and think about them dreams with me and little Royston. I did just that, sliding paws into pockets to keep em warm. One paw found the thing Doug had slipped in there just now, and yanked it out.

A pack of Number Ones.

And a box o' matches.

I opened em up, trying to get me swede back to them dreams but not being able to. Summat else were in the way of em, see. Summat Doug had said. 'Mission?' I says aloud. I wished I'd paid more heed to the other stuff he'd been saying. But he don't half go on, don't he.

I shrugged and lit a smoke.

• • •

I only started wondering where I were headed when the bus pulled into Mangel Central again. To be honest I hadn't looked past going home and being welcomed into the loving arms of me own family. But now that were out (for the minute) I didn't know. It's an odd thing, being in your hometown and not knowing where to go. I went walkies.

It were nine o'clock or thereabouts and the streets was nice and quiet. Folks was either in pubs or at home, and not much else besides. I got to walk up this road and down the next in peace, save the odd punter passed out in a doorway here and there. Seeing the old places got us all nostalgic about the old times. Over there's the corner where I'd had that fight back then. And that there is where I got arrested for shoplifting the one time. And up there's the alley where I had that bird and she chucked up while I done her from behind.

Ah, the old days.

Only it all seemed to have changed a bit now. Same streets and buildings and that, but different everything else. I couldn't recall exactly what shop were meant to be where, but they all seemed to have moved on and new uns moved in. Half of em I couldn't even work out what it were they selled.

The oddness of it all got to us after a while, and I needed summat familiar. I wanted an old face and a friendly word or two. Plus some scran cos I were fucking starving. And I knew just the place for both them things.

Alvin's Kebab Shop & Chippy.

All right, so Alvin didn't ever talk much. But he had an old face, and he were friendly enough in the way he shovelled chips and took your money and that. I walked back down Strake Hill past the bus station and turned into Butt Road, guts growling like a couple of chained bull terriers. They'd gave us summat to eat before leaving Parpham, but that were yonks ago now. And Parpham food never kept you filled for long anyhow. Alvin's chips did, mind. Alvin's chips is all a man needs to keep ticking, supplying your body with every type of vitamin and that it needs, I'd heard him once say.

I stopped halfway along Butt Road and looked up and down, scratching my head at the problem presented there before us. See, I couldn't find Alvin's. I could see that office place up there, and the betting shop over there, but Alvin's should have been stood between the two and it weren't. Nor were the empty place that used to sit beside it, with boards for windows and half the slates on the roof gone. Instead you had an odd-looking shop in place of the two of em, all done out in shiny red and yeller like it were made out of plastic.

The sign over the entrance said BURGER CITY.

Fucking hell, eh. What's going on here? I stood where I were for a bit, wondering just that. Then me guts started up again and I knew there were fuck all else for it. I went in.

'How much is chips?' I says to the spotty bird behind the counter. She were about sixteen or thereabouts and wearing a brown uniform that hid her good side, if she had one.

'You mean fries, sir?'

'I means chips. How much is they?'

'Regular, large, or extra large?'

'All I wants is me fuckin' chips. Fuck sake…Where's Alvin?'

The bird went blank on us and froze, like she'd fallen akip stood up with her eyes open. I leaned over the counter to give her a poke when a feller comes up beside her.

'Sir, please don't climb on the counter,' he says, sounding like an outsider. 'Can I help you?'

'Aye, I wants Alvin. And how much is chips?'

'There's a price list up there, sir. And there's no Alvin here. If I could ask you to keep your voice—'

'Oh aye? Woss you gonna do, eh? Do you know who I is?'

'Sir, I'm askin' you pol—'

'Fuckin' askin' for it, is what yer doin'. You want some, eh?' I says, showing him me fist. 'Cos I fuckin' got it. Royston Blake's the name. Royston fuckin' Blake. You wanna find out who yer talkin' to first, next time you mouths off. Now shut yer face an' giz me fuckin' chips, you fuckin'...'

While he were doing just that I turned about and clocked the other punters, who was sat at tables and chairs screwed to the floor. 'Fuckin' outsiders, eh?' I says to em, shaking me swede and sighing. 'What can you do with em?'

But none of em seemed to hear us, being as they turned back to their burgers and chips and what have you with nary a word.

I got me chips and fucked off, crossing the road and turning back into Strake Hill. A copper car came roaring up Butt Road, siren blaring, but I couldn't be arsed to go back and see what the trouble seemed to be. Some pissed-up cunt smashing windows like as not. No, I had somewhere else I needed to go. Somewhere I'd been thinking about a lot during my Parpham stay.

I walked on, stuffing chips in me gob and looking at all the places that weren't there no more or had turned into summat else. The chips was shite, to be quite frank with you. Too much salt and not near enough tater. But I couldn't seem to stop eating the fuckers. Halfway down Cutler Road I lobbed the empty bag over me shoulder and went into the offy.

Thank fuck that place were still there. The bloke behind the counter were the same one as ever—the fat cunt with the bald head. Gromer his name were, I think. I bought half a bottle o' whisky and some peanuts off him, me having a thirst on and the chips having done fuck all to keep the hounds at bay. I picked up me change with nary a word to him, same as always. I'd never chatted with this feller over the years and he'd never so much as nodded at us. His reason were that he reckoned us one of the younguns who robbed his shop twenty-odd year ago. Mine were that it were true. But this time he seemed to have put bygones behind him, cos he winked at us.

I nodded a bit and left his premises, walking down the rest of Cutler Road towards Friar Street and Hoppers. I couldn't help but wonder why everyone had been nodding at us and saying odd things to us, and helping us out and that. Not everyone, like, but so far I'd had the bus driver getting that youngun off us, Doug the shopkeeper giving us a cup o' tea and talking shite for five minutes, and now the Gromer feller there winking at us. These is the kind of fuckers who wouldn't normally piss on us if me trousers was ablaze. So what the fuck had happened to change that?

It were fucking obvious, when you used your swede. Reckoned us gone soft in the head, didn't they. Poor old Blakey, the mad fucking spanner. I'd not be surprised if they was doing a whip-round for us right then. I'd show the bastards how barmy I were. Soon as I got meself back on the door at Hoppers, I'd show the fucking lot of em. It weren't so bad though, knowing folks had me best interests at heart. I didn't mind it at all, when I thought about it, and soon I found meself whistling a merry old tune. Mind you, I soon stopped that when I turned the corner and found Hoppers to be not there. And I ain't talking "not there" as in Alvin's Kebab Shop & Chippy. I mean not there at all, mate.

As in not fucking there.

• • •

There were *summat* there, mind. Summat the like of what you ain't ever seen before. I'm talking about a building, of sorts. But not like your typical bricks and mortar structure, like Hoppers were. This were a big fuck-off one made out of pale concrete top to bottom. Down the middle was a big long glass bit where you could see in, though there weren't much light in there just now and you couldn't make much out. At the front of it all was a fucking massive big glass door where you went in. Only I couldn't think why anyone'd want to go in there. Cos do you know what the place reminded us of, the shape it were?

A fucking coffin is what.

Above the doors were a big black oblong wossname that had writing on it if you squinted hard enough, but were too dark to read. I dunno how long I stood there squinting and trying make it out, but the next thing I knows the whisky bottle is empty. In fact the sound of it shattering on the path beside us is what brung us to. I lit a smoke. The perfect length and smooth taste of your Embassy Number One gave us the reassurance I needed at that moment. And fucking hell, didn't I half need reassuring.

'For fuck sake, eh...' I started to say, looking around. Cos you got to speak your mind, ain't you. But there was no one nearby to hear it. I looked up and seen the moon there hanging pink and gibbous in the sky, so I addressed meself to it. 'I mean,' I says, 'I can put up with them movin' Alvin's. Chips is chips, ain't they, when you thinks about it. You can get em somewhere else. And them kebab wossnames and all. But Hoppers?' I were pacing around a bit as I spoke, warming to me subject, like. 'What the fuck's goin' on here? They can't take our Hoppers away, the stupid fuckin' bastards. Who the hell told em they could take our Hoppers away? An' woss they put there instead? A big fuckin' coffin is what. A big fuckin'...'

But what were the point? The moon couldn't hear us. Or if he could, he couldn't answer us. No one were listening and no one gave a toss. They was all fine and dandy, getting on with their lives and business as usual, ta very much. Who cares about old Blakey? Who gives a toss that my Hoppers ain't there no more, that the door I'd guarded me whole grafting life were no longer?

No one, is who.

And didn't I know it.

'Ain't a coffin,' comes a voice. 'Shoppin' mall, ennit.'

I looked up at the moon again. A little bit of cloud were just passing over it, but otherwise you'd not have known it had just spoke. 'You what?' I says to it. Though I still couldn't quite credit me own ears.

'Hoy. Over here, you twat.'

This time the voice came from across the way. The big fuck-off door was open at the front of the building and a security guard stood there clocking us. I went over to him.

'All right, Don,' I says.

'All right, Blake. Nice anorak.'

'Hey?'

'Anorak,' he says, feeling me sleeve. 'Warm, is it?'

'What?' I looked at the anorak where he'd been feeling it. Summat weren't right. But I couldn't be doing with that just now. 'Hey,' I says, 'you'll never guess what just happened.'

'What?'

'The fuckin' moon just spoke to us.'

He said fuck all for a bit. And to be fair on him, what could he say? I didn't even know what to say about it meself. But when he'd recovered from the shock of it all he says: 'Oh aye? What'd he say?'

'Telled us it ain't a coffin, iss a…Do you know, Don, I can't recall what he…'

'All right, Blake…' he says, stepping aside and pushing the door open a bit more. 'Forget the moon for now. Come an' have a gander in here a minute.' When I stayed put he says: 'S'all right, Blake. It ain't a coffin. Hoppers really, ennit, though they build summat else on top of it. Hoppers is still there underneath it though. Always will be. They can knock her down but they can't break her spirit, oh no. Now come on in.'

I put me fag out, took a deep un, and went to go in. But I couldn't do it. It were like a hive of bees were in me head, and they started swarming as I drew close. I stepped back and the bees settled.

'Come on,' says Don. 'I'll look after you.'

'Nah,' I says, backing off a bit more. 'I can't. I gotta…' But I were already off up the street by then and Don couldn't hear us.

The big coffin building seemed to go on forever. I trotted on and on and I couldn't get away from them pale grey walls, like in a dream when you ain't getting nowhere. I knew I were getting somewhere though cos I noticed *Margaret Hurge Twentieth Century Hair Design* going past across the way. Finally I found the corner of the big place and stopped. There was an alley there with the coffin on one side and *Burt's Caff* on t'other. The caff were all that remained of a big long block all the way along Friar Street. It sat there all sad and lonely, like the end of a sausage someone's bit off and spat out cos it's all hard and manky. You could see rough brickwork jutting out from the side wall where they'd knocked next door down. The place didn't look capable of staying up on her tod, to be honest, but stay up she did. For now anyhow.

At the end of that alley I found a big high fence enclosing the area behind the coffin building. I put me face up against it and peered through. Though it were dark I could see it were a loading yard, with a new stretch of tarmac coming up from the Wall Road for the lorries. There was no lorries there right now, mind, only a few skips and a couple of forklifts.

I tried hauling meself up, but the wires of the fence were too thin and cut into me fingers. I walked along the fence a bit more. I wanted to get in there, and I weren't sure why. I turned a corner down by the new service road and found a gate halfway along the next bit of fence. I tried it.

Weren't locked.

I went in and shut the gate behind us. There were a latch on it so I slid that home and walked over to one of the skips. It were full of cardboard, so I climbed in and stamped out a nice flat area and laid meself down. I were fucking knackered, what with all the goings-on of that day. And finding Hoppers to be no longer there had knocked the shite right out of us. I don't need to tell you what that place meant to me. And I ain't just talking sentimental here. If Hoppers weren't there, my fucking job weren't there. What job could I do after manning the Hoppers door for all them years? Nothing matched up to it. Even town mayor were a step down from dooring at Hoppers.

Mind you, it were nice and cozy in that skip. Surprisingly so, I tell you. Specially when I pulled a big bit o' cardboard over meself, shutting out the moon. I knew why I'd wanted into that yard now. Safety, wernit. No one could get in and bother us. It were the first place I'd felt all right in since leaving Parpham that morning.

I fell akip.

● ● ●

I felt well rough when I woke up. That's the hard stuff for you. Whisky treats you that way first time you comes back after a time away. She don't like being neglected, and she won't half give you what for about it. I needed water sharpish. I'd always favoured whisky and water but only with a sunrise between em. I needed a fag and all. I tried to ignore these requirements and get on with the kipping, pulling the covers up high on me face. But cardboard never had done the job of a good blanket, and it weren't on this particular morn. Then the thoughts started rolling in, most notably the thought that I were in a skip. And the thought that Hoppers were gone, and with it my place in the scheme of things.

Mind you, there was always the job the Doc had set up for us. I hadn't gave it much thinking at the time. No need to—I had every intention of going down Hoppers and claiming my rightful place there, whoever the latest owner might be. But hadn't the Doc been going on about a job 'just like your old one in many ways, and a lot better in others'? Sounded all right, didn't it, when you thought about it, which I were now doing.

Summat landed on me legs.

I sat up and looked around the skip. Fuck all but boxes, flattened or otherwise. Then another un came sailing over, landing on me right shoulder this time. I found a little box and tried it on for size. Stank of old vinegar but otherwise it went on me swede perfect. Then I peered over the edge, smiling inside at how good I were at disguises.

There was about ten or so fellers out there, unloading trucks by hand or going round in forklifts, or just standing around smoking and having a laugh. It's them smokers I worried about. Not that I were scaredy of em, oh no. I just didn't want em clocking Royston Blake coming out of a skip is all. I got me head back down and had a think.

I had to get to that gate again. That's where the trucks came in, and it were the only gate I could see. But I'd stick out like a greasy chip in a bowl of porridge if I just waltzed over there. I didn't mind that, cos I'd just tell em to fuck off if they started on us. But it didn't look right, did it. I didn't want em thinking Royston Blake's fallen on hard times. Cos I fucking hadn't, you know. I'd just been kipping in a skip, is all. I looked at me watch.

Half nine. Hadn't the Doc said nine o'clock start?

Fuck.

I had another quick gander over the edge and then stared at the boxes for a bit, trying to think. I picked one of em up and turned it over, weighing up the size of it.

And a plan came to us.

3

DOCTOR: *Tell me about your father.*

PATIENT: *I ain't got no father.*

DOCTOR: *Did you ever?*

PATIENT: *Dunno.*

DOCTOR: *You don't know if you ever had a father?*

PATIENT: *[shrugs]*

DOCTOR: *Well, Royston, I can confirm that you did. His name was—*

PATIENT: *I don't give a toss what his name were. I don't wanna fucking talk about him. Right?*

DOCTOR: *Royston, last week in group we talked about swearing, and the way we let ourselves down when…Can you please take your fingers out of your ears? Royston, please.*

PATIENT: *I ain't interested. You always wants to dredge up old shite I ain't even thought of in donkeys, shite that don't mean nothing no more.*

DOCTOR: *How do you know the past has no meaning? How can you be sure your father, though long dead, does not still exert a major influence on your actions?*

PATIENT: *Because I fucking can, fuck sake. How do you manage to get on me tits so much?*

DOCTOR: *I'm sorry if this is uncomfortable for you, Roys-*
           ton. but there are certain areas I would explore
           with any patient, in this situation. And given
           your background, I...Royston, please sit down.
           Royston? Where are you going? Royston...

· · ·

I didn't like this particular forklift, on account of it being yeller and all the others being red. I preferred red above yeller any day of the week, but a plan's a plan and I were sticking to mine. I thumped the feller in the side of the head. Hard. So hard that the box fell off my head.

I'd been aiming to knock him cold and drag him out of his truck, but he fell out t'other side. I went round there, cursing my bastard luck. But I were all right this time cos there were a pile of pallets hiding the feller from the rest of the yard, and no one seemed to have clocked him on his way down. I dragged him round the other side of the skip and yanked his yellow coat off him. It were a bit tight on us—specially with my own jacket on underneath—but I'd be all right if I didn't have to lift me arms. I left him propped up there. He'd be all right and all. His ear were bleeding where I'd twocked it, and the way his arm were hanging made us feel a bit queasy, but you can't make a fry-up without cracking a few eggs, can you. I put the box back on my head—setting it just right so the eyeholes was lined up—and jumped up into the forklift.

Luckily the engine were still running, so I just had to work out how to get her shifting. There was a heavy gauge spanner on the dash, so I pocketed him and started on the controls. I messed around for a bit, moving the fork up and down and switching lights off and on. Then we got going.

Backwards.

No one seemed to notice when I crashed into the skip, mind. Least I knew which way were backward now. I found the stick and put him forward, setting us moving in the proper direction. Weren't a bad motor actually. Bit on the slow side but nice and high up, and a very smooth ride. I quite enjoyed meself, pootling along in that loading yard, keeping near the fence so no one got a good luck at us. I wouldn't have minded taking her with us, but yellow forklifts was thin on the ground in Mangel and I'd have to paint her, which I couldn't be arsed doing.

And anyhow, I had to concentrate on the job in hand, which were to get meself out them gates with no one noticing us, stop the truck, and fuck off. Cos I were already half an hour late for me new job. The new boss wouldn't mind though. The Doc had said he were all right and knew about us and that, so he'd be understanding.

I were only a few yard from the gate now so I went to stop the forklift.

Only she wouldn't stop.

The fucker wouldn't even slow down when I took me boot of the pedal. 'All right,' I says to meself, sailing past the gate and turning left a bit to go back into the yard. I would have just drove the thing down the service road but a lorry were coming in just then, and I knew I'd come off worse in that kind of prang. 'All right,' I says again under me breath. Cos I knew what to do now: go round again and then pull the keys out when I got to the gates next time. No worries.

I thought about taking the box off me head now. A box would get more attention than a strange head. But I couldn't take no chances. I didn't recognise none of these faces here, but you can bet they'd know me. Everyone in Mangel knew Royston Blake. So the box stayed on.

One or two of the fellers glanced at us, but they was right over the far side and not to be fretted over. No one else seemed to give a fuck about us. I were doing a long sweeping arc on me way back to the gate, but the lorry had turned arse and were just then backing up to one of the loading bays. Number seven by the sounds of it, cos just then a tannoy piped up blaring: 'BAY NUMBER SEVEN INCOMIN'.'

The fucking lorry were blocking me path now, so I had to turn towards the building and go that way. 'Hoy, you fucker,' says a feller in front of us, headed for bay seven like as not. I'd clipped his leg a bit with the fork but I didn't think it were too bad. I turned slightly sharper so the wheels didn't go over him, glancing down at where he were lying as I went past. He were holding his leg but his eyes was open and you could see he had puff in him, so no real harm done there. I kept turning sharp and pointed her straight at the gates. I'd soon be off and on me way to work.

It were a shame really, cos I were quite enjoying meself now.

'Hoy, Kev,' says someone not too far off. I dunno who Kev were but he weren't listening. Maybe he were deaf or summat. Or perhaps he were that feller back there with the clipped leg. Anyhow, couple of secs later the feller says again: 'Kev, woss you doin' with that box on yer head?' Only it were louder now. And closer.

But I couldn't be doing with Kev. Here's them gates again, so all I got to do is pull the keys out and…

'Ah, fuck,' I says. Cos the truck weren't stopping even with the keys out. Plus another lorry were coming in just then, so I had to swerve sharpish and head back towards me skip.

'Hoy, you ain't Kev,' yells the feller, running alongside us now. 'Who's you? Hoy…' He ran alongside for a bit, then stopped and started shouting into a walkie-talkie.

For fuck sake, eh. All I wanted to do were get out of the fucking place and go to work. Why couldn't the bastards even let us do that? I took another bend, aiming to make a good run at them gates.

'INTRUDER IN THE LOADIN' YARD,' says the fucking tannoy. 'LOCK THE GATES.'

I put me foot down and made a run for em. 'Come on, you little tart,' I says to the forklift in a firm but gentle voice. Cos you got to coax em on a bit if you wants em to perform for you. And I swear she sped up a bit at that. But two cunts ran up to the gates and swung em closed when I were still ten yard off.

I turned back into the yard and clocked the forty or so fellers running down from the loading bays.

'I've called the police,' says someone nearby. It were that feller again, running alongside us. 'You might as well just jump down now. You'll never get out of here. And you'll get in less trouble if you cooperate.'

'Fuck off,' I says to him.

He tried jumping into the cab so I knocked him back with a bit of elbow. He were a stubborn bastard and he held on with one hand, swinging out on the rim of the windscreen. Meanwhile all them other fellers was swarming around either side of us, some of em laughing but none of em looking happy.

'You won't...' says the stubborn feller, swinging back in for another go at us. I thumped him in the chest this time, hard as I could. He swung back fast towards the front of the truck then let go, and I didn't see where he fell. I went over a bumpy patch just then and heard a noise under the truck. Some twat had left a pallet lying around, like as not. 'Come on, you little slag,' I says, stroking the wheel. Cos you could tell she hadn't enjoyed them bumps. 'You can't stop now.' Fuck knew where I were asking her to take us though, the gates being shut. Suddenly I noticed that no one were around us no more.

I looked over me shoulder. There was a crowd of em back there, all looking down at summat. I couldn't see what it were. Whatever, it were more interesting than me, being as I were all on me tod now. I turned back to the windscreen just in time to watch meself crashing into the fence.

The engine went off then. The forks had gone through the mesh and the windscreen were right up against it. It weren't half silent in that yard at that moment. I looked back once more. They was all still looking at summat on the floor. Maybe they'd found a nest of giant emmets or summat. Always worth a look when you finds one o' them. Anyhow, I couldn't be doing with emmets meself. I climbed on the roof of the forklift and hauled my arse over the fence.

Running down the alley away from Friar Street, I heard the sirens coming.

• • •

I were halfway along the Wall Road before I recalled having the box on me head and the feller's donkey jacket on. I chucked em over a wall and went up to the High Street, sparking a fag and trying to get me puff back. I had a piss down the little alley by the Volley, sat on a bench by the Igor statue, sparked another one up, and got the bit of paper out me pocket.

Mr Porter
Admin Suite
Porter Centre

I scratched me head a bit, wondering where the fuck the Wossname Centre were. I mean, the Doc had forgot to put the street on, hadn't he. Maybe it were up north on the Barkettle Road. Aye, there was a couple of big pubs up there that needed serious dooring. A bit below me station, but when you falls off the ladder you can't get back on at the top. Mind you, I weren't yomping all the way up Barkettle Road only to find it's in Muckfield or summat. Just then I noticed a young feller coming up the road in a suit and tie.

'All right, Rog,' I says.

'All right, Blake.'

'D'you know where the—'

'Nice anorak you got there.'

'You what?'

'Warm, is it?'

'Eh?'

'The anorak.'

'Oh, aye, aye. What about you? Woss this in aid of?'

'What, the suit?'

'Aye,' I says, feeling the lapels. Nice material it were. 'Off to court, is you?'

'Heh heh…No, Blake,' he says, brushing us off. 'I'm off to work, mate.'

'Work? Thought you worked at the spud factory?'

'Thass a long while back, Blake. I bettered meself since then. I works in a call centre now.'

'A fuckin' what?'

'Call centre. I'm a manager there, like. Got eight lads under us, and four birds.'

'Four birds, eh?'

'Aye. Plus Jacqui the secretary. But I gotta share her with Frank, me boss.'

'Oh aye?' I says. 'So do you both fuck her, then?'

Rog laughed and goes: 'Hey, thought you was in Parpham?'

'Parpham? Got out, didn't I.'

'Oh aye?'

'Aye.'

'Thought no one ever got out of Parpham?'

'Oh aye?'

'Aye.'

'Well I ain't no one, is I. I'm Royston fuckin' Blake.'

'Aye, thass true.'

'And besides, I weren't truly in Parpham. Not for proper like.'

'Oh aye?'

'Aye. I mean no. I mean like I weren't a nutter.'

'No?'

'Course not. Just hurt me head a bit is all, and…you know…'

'Aye, heard about that.'

'Oh aye?'

'Aye.'

'Heard what?'

'You know…pills an' that.'

'What about em?'

'Fuck sake, Blake. I'm just sayin' like.'

'I know. An' I'm just askin'. What about pills an' that?'

'You know, you eatin' loads of em. Didn't yer?'

I could feel meself getting wound up, so I took a deep un and calmed down a bit. Rog were all right, after all. And I had to talk about this shite sooner or later. You know what rumours is like. 'Looks like I did,' I says, nodding slow. 'Can't recall it, mind.'

'And you didn't finish the job off proper.'

'What job?' I says after staring at him for a bit.

'You know. Toppin' yerself, an' that. Hey, get off us. Fuckin' let us go, Blake...'

'You fuckin' tell em, right, you tell em I never topped meself.'

'Why'd you eat so many then? Let go me shirt, Blake, you'll pop a fuckin' button. Me work shirt, ennit? I'll get me wages docked for missin' a b—'

'I never knew they was fuckin' pills, did I.'

He shut up at that. Seemed there was a fair few folks in the street just then, and they all shut up and all. I didn't mind having an audience, mind, cos they needed to hear it once and for all. I'd had trouble with rumours before, and sortin' em out ain't pretty if you lets em get away from you.

'Aye, I took loads o' fuckin' pills,' I shouts, taking in the ten or so punters standing about, or just walking slow and giving us the eye. 'But I thought they was sweets. You know—them joey ones you used to get at Doug's corner shop donkeys back. Honest I fuckin' did. I were hungry and I wanted summat in me gob, and they was there, them fuckin' pills. So I fuckin' ate em. Thinkin' em to be sweets, mind. An', well, it done me head in. Done it in proper. Cos thass what drugs does, you know. Sends you to Parpham.'

No one were so much as breathing now. Couple of cars coming past had pulled up and wound windows down for a listen and all. Even a little sandy dog over there had parked himself on the hard stuff and pricked an ear up.

'So anyhow,' I says. 'I ain't no nutter. Right? Anyone says I is, tell em to fuck off. Or send em to us an' I'll fuckin' tell em. All right?'

They still weren't doing nothing. Five motors blocking the road now and about twenty foot punters. The dog had fucked off though. I wanted em all the fuck off with it. I'd said me piece now and that were that. 'What?' I says. 'Eh? Woss you want?'

I looked from face to face, but none of em would answer us. One or two of your more twitchy uns started moving off, but most didn't.

'Go on, fuck off,' I says. 'The fuckin' dog fucked off didn't he? Now *you* fuck off. Go on.' I ran up to a feller and kicked him up the arse, scattering the crowd on that portion of the street. 'Get out of it, the fuckin' lot o' you.' I turned and moved the other way and the folks there started moving, being sensible. The cars was asking for a bit more coaxing, mind.

'Oh aye?' I says, going up to a silver un. I didn't know what sort it were cos it were a flash new un. Actually they was all flash new uns, apart from a nice yeller Cortina Estate back there. 'Oh aye?' I says again to the silver un. Then I kicked the driver-side front light in. 'Hearin' us now?'

'Hoy, you fucker,' someone shouts. But I were busy now. I got started on the panels, getting in three nice dents before it hared off up the way. The others hared off and all, a bit too sharpish for my liking cos one of em nearly clipped me toes. I jumped back, as you do, and lost me footing on the curb. It hurt quite a bit and I had to rub me ankle for a while. When I opened me eyes again only the yeller Cortina were left. Right in front of us. I couldn't quite see who were in there but it didn't half look like Burt. You know, from the caff. Anyhow, he drove off before I could address him.

I got on me feet. I were feeling a tad light in the head now so I sat meself back down on the bench and sparked another one up, humming a tune. A minute or so later I noticed the bit o' paper still in my hand. 'Bollocks,' I says, flobbing on the path.

'Do you mind?' says an old granny walking past just then.

'Oh…all right, darlin',' I says to her. 'Eh, d'you know where the…er…' I looked at the paper, but it said summat different this time…

KEEP YOUR NOSE CLEAN

YOU ARE NOT ALONE

…in the Doc's handwriting. I turned it over and found the address there. 'Fuck sake,' I says to the old bird. 'Thought I were goin' barmy there for a sec. Anyhow, iss the…er…the Wossname Centre.'

I looked up, only to find she'd pissed off. 'Fuckin' bitch,' I shouts after her for form's sake as she disappeared around the corner up yonder.

'Hoy, you,' comes a nearby feller's voice. 'Woss you sayin'?'

'Oh,' I says, looking up at the copper stood there. 'All right, Jonah.'

'All right, Blake. I heared you was out.'

'Oh aye? Here, d'you know where the, er…the fuckin'…'

'Aye. You could say we all knew you was gettin' out, us on the force.'

Fucking coppers. The one time you needs a favour from em—like getting directions and that—they fucks you about. But I'd promised the Doc I wouldn't get in the shite this time, so I bit me tongue and let the pointy-faced bastard say his piece.

'Well let me tell you this,' he says, standing close and bending down a bit on account of me sitting down and his lankiness. 'An' you'd better flippin' listen to me. Cos I'm gonna tell you, I am. An' you'd flippin' well better—'

'Get on with it,' I says, 'you fuckin'…'

'Go on,' he shouts in me face. 'You fuckin' what? What was you gonna call us? Come on.'

I looked up at him. His face—which looked not unlike five or six large bananas strapped together—was but an inch or two from me own (which looked not unlike Clint Eastwood). With little more than a flinch I could flatten a few of them pointy features for him. And I wouldn't even ask a favour in return. Except him fucking off away from us. And staying fucked off. But I never. I never fucking done it.

Cos I were keeping me nose clean for the Doc.

'You fuckin'...police constable,' I says in answer to his question.

'Aye, well,' he says, quite sensibly letting it go. 'As I were sayin', er...'

'You was tellin' us how I'd flippin' well better flippin' do summat or other.'

'Aye, you'd better flippin' keep your nose clean, Royston Blake. Else we'll have you down that Mangel Jail quicker'n you can say...er...'

'What?'

'Don't take the piss.' He were shouting now, pointing his poky finger at me nose and really fucking asking for it, like. 'You just keep yer nose clean, Blake. Stay away from trouble an' don't wind up coppers. Cos...cos...' I thought his head were gonna explode, spraying us with blood and brains and bananas and that. Actually just blood and bananas and shite, this being Jonah. 'Cos there's folks dependin' on you,' he shouts.

Then he stormed off, me watching his back, scratching me swede. After five or so steps he stopped, stood still chewing his nails for a bit, then came back and goes: 'Have you seen a big feller in a donkey jacket and a box on his head?'

'You what?'

'No, thought not. You wouldn't even see a…er, a giant, er…wossname, if it…er, you know, er…Ah, bollocks.'

Then he were off again.

I sparked another one up, then remembered the bit o' paper. 'Oh for fuck's sake,' I says. Cos I still hadn't managed to find out where this Wossname Centre were. I shut me eyes and did some thinking on the matter. Then the answer came to us:

I just weren't meant to have this job.

I mean, I'd fucking tried, hadn't I? I'd asked and asked and no answer had sprung forth. So fuck it—I'd just have to find a job meself. That's the way it ought to be, really. Feller can't look after himself, he ain't a proper feller, so they says. I didn't need no fucking Doc pulling strings for us, setting us up with this job or that un. I were out of Parpham now, a free man standing on his own two size thirteens. I had to fend for meself, scratching a living as best I could. Sort of like Clint Eastwood riding from town to town across the desert, always on his tod with no mates to back him up, getting by any which way he can, shooting fellers and necking whisky. And shagging prozzies.

Aye, I could do that. Except I wouldn't be going town to town on account of not being able to leave this one here. And I didn't have no horse, nor no transport whatsoever at that moment in time. I could shag the prozzies though. Line em up and watch the master at work, mate. (I ain't paying, mind.) And the whisky weren't a problem.

So I tossed the bit o' paper over me shoulder. The Doc can go fuck himself.

Royston Blake is a free man.

'Ah, Royston,' he says. As in the fucking Doc himself. Cos he were right there in front of us, sat there in his posh motor.

41

'All right, Doc,' I says, getting up and going over. I hadn't ever seen his motor before, and frankly I were not far shy of astonished. See, it were a Granada Mk2 3-litre GL. Like the one in *The Sweeney*, a bit. (Except they had a Mk1 Consul GT in that.) 'How long you had this, Doc?' I says, running a finger along the Ford's smooth lines.

'What? The car? Oh, years. Anyway, Royston, how are you getting on? Is there anything I can do for you?'

'Nah, I'm fine, Doc. How quick do she go?'

'Well…I don't know. Would you mind telling me why you're not at work now, Royston? I believe you were all set up for nine o'clock this morning. Now it's half past ten.'

'Nah, I don't fancy it. Did you know this motor has the same engine as the original Capri 3000?' I says. Cos I'd always found that interesting. I mean I've always loved the Capri, of course. But it's a young man's motor. As you gets more mature you got to think about summat bigger, and possibly automatic. Nice to know you can have the same engine though. Not that I'd ever drove a Capri 3000. My drive of choice had always been your 2.8i, as well you knows. But it's a nice thought, ennit? And I think you can get a Granada with the 2.8i under the hood.

'The Capri…? Royston, do you realise what's going on? The only reason you were released yesterday was because you had a home to go to and a job set up. It's *parole*, Royston. I wasn't able to swing your release without that job approved. By the looks of you I doubt you even slept at home last night, and now you tell me what? You don't fancy the job?'

I stood still for a bit, having a little think. Then I came to a decision. 'You know, Doc,' I says, 'I reckon I'll go for one o' these Granadas when I gets back on me feet. I loves the Capri and that but it's a young man's motor, and I don't mind admittin' I ain't so young no more. Plus I'm a man of class, like yerself. And breedin' an' all. So really I ought to be thinkin' about goin' automatic. Behave himself, do he?'

'What? Who?'

'The auto box. I ain't drove an automatic in donkeys.'

'Oh, er…I'll tell you what, Royston, why don't I show you? Climb in.'

'Nice one, Doc,' I says, smiling at him. I opened the passenger door and placed a boot on the plush floor. The tape deck were playing summat boring with violins and that. The Doc flicked it off sharpish, which must have been him reading me mind.

'The cigarette, Royston,' he says, raising one of his grey eyebrows at me Number One.

'Oh soz,' I says. 'Here.' I got the pack out and chucked it him, saying: 'Help yerself.' Then I climbed in and shut the door. The Doc seemed confused about summat, so I says: 'S'matter Doc? Don't like Embassies?'

'No, I meant…'

He didn't seem to know what he meant, so I shrugged and blew out a big cloud of smoke. It were fucking smart, sitting in that big motor. The wide velour seat seemed designed specific for my own particular style of arse, and I just knew the one on the other side would be even more so. The Granada boasted just about the plushest interior I'd ever seen, what with the placcy wood trim and nice little leatherette touches here and there. The gaping space in front of us seemed to beg for a massive gut to fill it with, and though my physique just then were that of a fight-fit heavyweight boxer in his prime (picture Ivan Drago in *Rocky IV*, but with Clint Eastwood's face), I quite looked forward to growing into it. I blew some more smoke around the windscreen, shaking my head at the sheer fucking splendour of it all.

'You all right, Doc?' I says. Cos he seemed to be choking on summat. I were just thinking about shoving him forward and giving his back a slapping when he let down his leccy window and started getting his puff back. 'Swallered a fly or summat?' I says.

I don't think he heard us cos he let the brake off and pulled away without a word.

Mind you, there's no need for words when you got the Ford 3-litre ticker doing your talking for you. It says everything needs saying about a feller. And as we picked up the pace along the Wall Road, I were thinking how much I wanted it to speak for meself and all.

And, you know, it weren't just the motor. Me going on about top executive models is all well and smart, but the more deeper thinking behind it is where the real interest lies. See, it's the whole fucking kit and kebang I were getting sick of, not just the Capri.

And it's the door work I'm on about here.

That and the life that goes with it—being hard and getting pissed and shagging birds down alleys, and getting up in the afternoon and that. I mean (and I'm stringing you some philosophy here so you better fucking appreciate it) there comes a time when a feller needs a bit more out of life. He wants respect.

And to get that, he's got to be respectable.

Know what I mean? And it's more than just the big motor and the cigars. It's about how you makes a living. Dooring at Mangel's premier nightspot is all good and rosy for a young single feller still in his glory days. But look at me—thirty-six fucking year old, last time I'd counted. Bird and youngun at home and all. I needed a job with more prestige, like…like managing or summat. Or…

'Hey, Doc.'

'Royston?'

'How'd you come to be a doctor?'

'You mean why did I choose medicine?'

'No, I means how'd you get to be a doctor, like? Any fucker can choose some medicine.'

He didn't answer us at first. He were taking a sharp left top of the Wall Road, not even having to change down. You could feel the gears working by emselves and it were frankly quite beautiful. 'I don't think it's relevant, Royston.'

'I'm only—'

'You need to concentrate on your own job, never mind mine. We can talk about it some other time if you're really interested, but for now I want to see you making a good start. You haven't helped matters by being two hours late, but I think I can smooth over that. As long as—'

'It's like I says just now, Doc—I don't fancy it. I got me sights set higher now.'

'You don't fancy…? But I set you up with just the right job. It's perfect for your skills and experience.'

'No offence, Doc, but I've had it with doorin'. Much room in the boot, is there?' I says, craning me neck over that way.

'The…? You've…?'

'You all right there, Doc?'

He stopped the motor. The sound of the handbrake pulling up set me spine a-tingling. 'I'll say it one more time, Royston: you *have* to do this job. If you don't, you're back in Parpham. And it won't be so easy to get out next time. Trust me on that.'

'Nah, I don't fancy Parpham neither,' I says. Cos I had plans now. I had plans of driving a Ford Granada auto like this un. And showing little Royston how important his old feller is. And you don't get that from dooring.

'Look,' he says, brightening up a bit. 'You say you've had it with, er, being a pub doorman?'

'Aye. Beneath us, ennit.'

'Maybe, maybe. But the fact of the matter is, Blake, the job I've arranged for you is not that. You won't even be working in a pub.'

'Oh aye? So where is it, like?'

'Right there,' he says, nodding out my window.

It were even bigger in the daylight and no less ugly. The thing above the big doors had looked like a big black oblong last night when I'd seen Don there, but now it were lit up you could see it were writing, about two yard high, saying: THE PORTER CENTRE.

4

'But why not?'

'I just don't like it, Doc.'

'Why? It's just a building like any other.'

'It ain't like no other. Iss fuck all like no other. Too big, for starters.'

'You don't want to work there because it's too big?'

'Nah, I mean…Fuckin' hell, Doc, I just don't like the fuckin' place.'

'All right,' he says, letting a lot of air out. 'Look, I don't know where you slept last night, but you look rough. Frankly, Royston, you look like a tramp. And that's not going to get you any job, let alone this one. How about we go for a cup of tea and get you cleaned up a bit? What say?'

'I ain't workin' there, Doc. I'm fuckin' tellin' yer now.'

'I know, I know. But don't you want some tea? I promise I won't go on at you.'

I looked him over. He were all right, were the Doc. Bit of a twat, mind. 'Go on then,' I says. Cos I were fucking parched.

• • •

'Hello, Burt,' says the Doc.

Burt stuck his big paw out and they shook. Then the Doc leaned in and whispered summat in Burt's ear.

I thought that odd. First off, Burt's a bit of a mong in that he can't hear nor talk, so you got to let him see your lips if you wants to tell him summat. Second off, what's the Doc doing knowing Burt? He never came into town, the Doc didn't. I hadn't ever clapped peepers on him before Parpham. I were still mulling that over as I says: 'All right, Burt.'

He nodded at us. Which is about all anyone ever gets from Burt. Unless you're the Doc, by the looks of it.

'Er, one cup of tea for me, Burt. And whatever Royston here wants.' He turned to me and goes: 'Royston, I'm going back there to make a phone call. When you've had a quick piece of toast you can go to the gents and clean yourself up a bit. All right? But first, have a little chat with Burt here, you might find it enlightening.'

'What?' I says. 'But he can't...'

The Doc were off. I shrugged and turned to Burt. He went on chopping bacon, looking over at us now and then.

I took a stool and smiled back at him.

He got a cloth and started wiping the counter down, still clocking us every so often.

'Here we are, then,' I says.

He didn't like that by the looks of him, so I shut up and let him go on looking at us and keeping his hands busy. I had a feeling he were telling us summat, in his own special way. Fuck knows what it were, mind. You'd need special powers to know what Burt were trying to say, and I seemed to be the only one in Mangel who didn't have none. Besides superhuman strength, course.

I got a smoke out and lit it, smiling at him. I were fucking starving.

About halfway down the Number One, he gave us a last big look and then nodded once.

'Oh well, fair enough,' I says. Cos that's what you says when someone's gave you some advice, ennit? Even if you never harked a word of it. Then I goes: 'Aye, very wise words. So listen, how about sausage, egg, bacon (streaky), mushies, tommies, black pud, beans, and a few slices. Make it eight bangers. And eight or so rashers. Ten. And a pot o' tea. Eh?'

He gave us a nod. I got a paper off the side and parked meself at a table. It were a *Mangel Informer* and, as well you knows, my habit were to steer clear of that particular rag. I'd read enough shite in there over the years to fill a quarry. But we'd talked about that in group, and it were time to overcome my fear. Not that I were proper scaredy, mind.

'PORTER GIVES MONEY TO KIDS' HOME FOR NEW TELLY,' it says on the front, next to a picture of a grinning beardy bloke in a suit and tie. I flicked to another page. 'READERS RESPOND,' it goes at the top...

Dear Sir,

Mr P Dollock complains about the amount of graffiti defacing the walls of our town of late. But has he noticed where it nearly always turns up?

New businesses, that's where.

Outsider concerns. People coming in from the outside with the sole intent of taking our money, giving us endless 'products' we don't need in return.

Mr Dollock ought to open his eyes and wake up to what's going on around him. Then he'll see that it is these ugly shopfronts and their ugly-minded occupants who are really defacing our town.

The Old Guard.

The front door opened behind us and a parky draft blew in, flicking up the pages and going right up me crack. I turned,

opening me gob to say: 'Hoy, shut the fuckin' door, you fuckin'—'
But then I saw it were a bird so I held me tongue.

She weren't bad as it happens, in a skinny and knackered sort
of way. She must have thought same about meself cos she couldn't
take her eyes off us. I'm used to that though, so I just winked at
her and turned back to me paper, tucking me shirt in round back.

'Blakey?' she says.

I turned about and got another clock of her. Aye, she were familiar, but only like the sister of someone you knows is familiar. I went
through all the sisters of folks I knew, but still I couldn't place her.

'You really don't recognise me?' she says, coming over now
and taking her coat off. She had a faded blue dress on with a
couple of food stains down the front. Everything about her were
slightly faded—hair, skin, eyes. As I says though, she were all
right. Nice tall girl who knew how to hold herself, despite all that
fading. Bit short on tit, mind. She looked down at em, shaking her
head. 'They have seen bigger days, ain't they.'

'Have they?' I says, picturing em bigger. Then it came to us.
'Fuck sake, iss Rache,' I says, standing up and pulling out a chair,
me being a gentleman.

• • •

DOCTOR: *You like women, Blake?*
PATIENT: *Eh? Course I fucking do. Woss you saying? Try-*
             ing to say summat, is you? Cos if you is—
DOCTOR: *Royston, I'm merely talking. These one-to-ones*
             are just ways of exploring issues. Sometimes we
             pick the stone up and throw it in the sea. Some-
             times we pick it up, look at it for a while, and
             then place it back carefully in the sand.

PATIENT: *Oh.*

DOCTOR: *So you're a ladies' man?*

PATIENT: *Aye, if you likes.*

DOCTOR: *Do you like being a ladies' man?*

PATIENT: *Ain't a matter of liking. You either got it or you ain't. I got it.*

DOCTOR: *And how do you feel about that?*

PATIENT: *About what?*

DOCTOR: *Having women respond to you in a certain way. Being able to choose your sexual partner. Having "it"?*

PATIENT: *You being cheeky?*

DOCTOR: *No. Just curious.*

PATIENT: *Well you would be, wouldn't you. You wanna know what it's like, truly and honest? Fucking marvellous. That's how I feel about it. I wouldn't change it for the world.*

DOCTOR: *And has it ever failed you? Have you ever been unable to obtain your preferred sexual partner?*

PATIENT: *You what? You mean do I ever get blown out? Fuck off. Me? Nah, it don't work like that, mate. See, it's how you approach life. You don't see a bird and decide you gotta have her and you won't be happy till she's in the pit with you. Nah, you just leaves yourself open and see what comes to you, as you goes about your business. Like fishing, ennit.*

DOCTOR: *As opposed to hunting?*

PATIENT: *Aye. Except I don't use a pole. You only gets one fish at a time, with a pole. I uses a fucking massive net, trawling up fucking loads of em. I gets me pole out later though, when—*

DOCTOR:	And have you ever been the hunter?
PATIENT:	No, mate, I already told you. Mind you…
DOCTOR:	What?
PATIENT:	Well, there's this one bird…
DOCTOR:	Go on.
PATIENT:	I don't like to say…I mean, she ain't one of your typical…What I mean is, you can't just buy her a pint and cop off with her, like.
DOCTOR:	So how do you know her?
PATIENT:	I works with her. I mean, I did. She's a barmaid, like. At Hoppers. Me on the door, her at the pump. Rache, her name were.
DOCTOR:	And she didn't respond to you?
PATIENT:	No…I mean aye. I mean, she fancied us. I reckon she did anyhow. And I fancied her all right. We just never…Ah, I dunno.

• • •

'How is you, Rache?' I says. 'Sit yerself here, come on.'

She went to sit down but stopped short of it, looking over her shoulder at Burt, who were just then glaring a sack of razorblades at her. She went and hung her coat behind the counter, saying to him: 'Sorry I'm late, Burt. Roy was…'

But Burt weren't having it. He jerked his swede around a bit and pointed at this and that with his elbow while he tossed the eggs.

Rache got to it, and not long later she had an apron on and were coming back over with a teapot and mug. I could have kissed her. And not only on account of the tea, neither. I'd been watching her at work, and although she'd lost summat in the womanly charms department, she still had that way of shifting her hips that had us adjusting meself. Always had got us going, watching her behind the bar at Hoppers. When she put the pot on the table I grabbed her arm. 'Come on, Rache,' I says. 'Sit down a sec.'

She looked over her shoulder again. 'You know what he's like. He don't like his staff talkin'. Only Madge can talk to customers.'

'Fuck him,' I says. Cos he had his back turned while he were slicing some bread, and he couldn't read me lips.

'Well...' She sat down. I offered her a smoke and she took it. After a couple of puffs or so she started relaxing, letting the old Rache breathe. I swear I could see her tits growing.

'Who's Roy?' I says, putting a few spoonfuls in me cuppa. She frowned at us, so I goes: 'You was sayin' about Roy just now. To Burt.'

'Oh aye. Well...' She blushed a mite and watched the spoon as I stirred. 'Roy's me little boy.'

'Little boy? Fuckin' hell, Rache, when'd you have a...? Here, is "Roy" short for summat?'

'No, just Roy. It's me dad's name.'

'Oh, right,' I says, nodding. I dunno why it made us sad but it did, a tad. I'd never fucked her anyhow, so I couldn't expect her lad to be named after us. Weren't as if I hadn't tried though. I'd tried just about every time I'd come into work at Hoppers, clocking her there behind the bar with that big juicy gob of hers and the tits and arse and so on. I mean, if she wouldn't let Royston Blake poke her, who—

'I know what you're thinkin',' she says. 'Who's the father, right?'

'Ain't my business,' I says, shaking me swede and sipping tea. That made the tea go down me chin so I wiped it off with me sleeve, then goes: 'Who is it, though?'

'Thought it were none of your business?'

'That's right, but—'

'That means you ain't interested.'

'I ain't. I don't care who you f—I mean, like, you can make babbies with whoever the fuck—'

'Good,' she says between sharp puffs on the Embassy. She were sitting bolt upright now and the relaxed Rache were a summat of the past, like the Rache with big tits. 'That's all right then, ennit.'

'Aye.' I downed the tea, not giving a fuck how hot it were. Then I looked at the pot, which had a nice pattern on it—the one where the feller runs off with his bird and in the end they turns into a couple of pigeons. 'Who is he, then?'

I were still on the pot, but I felt her eyes hit us like a block of cold lard lobbed hard across a frozen kitchen. Then she started laughing.

I looked at her, lairyness stirring but held off by the sheer fucking shock of it. How dare the cow laugh at us? I were only...

'Look at us,' she goes. 'Half a minute gone and already we're rowin'. Not a lot changes, eh?'

I were laughing a bit now and all. Only a bit, mind, cos it weren't proper funny. You had to be sociable though. And she had a point. 'So,' I says, still chuckling. 'Who is he?'

She shook her head. But in a nice way. She'd cut her hair a fair bit shorter. Shorter than a bird's meant to have it, if I'm honest. But it made her head look nice when she shook it. She looked into me eyes and I saw the old Rache again—not the lairy one but the one who fancied us. 'Oh, Blake,' she says, touching the side of me swede. 'What did they do to you in there?'

'Eh? In where?'

She didn't answer us, just went on touching my head just above the ear. My hair were growing out a bit now and I didn't think the scarring showed. But you'd not have knowed it from the way her fingers was playing around there.

'Hey,' she says, brightening of a sudden. I were glad of that cos I didn't fancy answering what she'd looked like asking. She leaned in all smiley and spoke quiet. 'I got an interview.'

'Why?' I says, keeping me own voice down. 'Woss they got you for?'

'Who?'

'Eh? Who? Coppers, course.'

'No, a *job* interview.'

'Oh. But you works here, ennit?'

'Yeah but this interview is for a proper job. In a shop, like. You know, *clothes*.' She looked over her shoulder and goes: 'I'm tryin' to better meself, Blake.'

I smiled and nodded, cos that's what she were doing. I wanted to ask her woss wrong with the job she's got, but I could see Burt weren't an easy boss to graft for. So I goes: 'Where?'

'This is the excitin' bit.' She looked over her shoulder again. Burt were spooning beans on the plate and looking at the door, which someone were just then trying to come through. Rache squeezed me paw and goes: 'It's in the *Porter Centre*.'

'Hoy, you,' says the old crone just come in the door. 'You get up an' start graftin'. There's a breakfast here wants servin'.'

'All right, Madge,' I says, Rache already up and away. 'I were just tellin' Rache here—'

'I don't care what you was tellin' her. Burt don't like his staff talkin' to customers. Only I talks to customers.'

'Sorry, Madge,' says Rache, already coming back towards us with a plate. 'Won't happen again.' Madge were still going on, addressing her complaints at Burt now. As Rache put the plate down in front of us, I copped an eyeful down the front of her dress, then clocked her eyes on us and the filthy grin on her face. Nearly tore a hole in the front of me strides, that did. 'Don't tell anyone,' she whispers, 'but I did name Roy after you.' Aye, I'm sure that's what she says. Bit hard to hear though.

I had a smile about it anyhow. I sat there with a smile on my chops and a cob in me trolleys. I wanted to reach out and pull her to us. I wanted to tell her about my own little lad, in case she didn't know. But I'd got stuck into the sausages by then and couldn't really do either of them things. There'd be plenty of time later on to tell her about little Royston. Maybe him and her lad could even play together. I got to thinking about that as the scran found its way into me belly. And I got to thinking about the other and all, the things I'd do to her when the younguns was all snug and tucked up in their little pits.

'Right,' says the Doc, coming back out. 'Are we ready?'

He could see I weren't ready so I didn't bother looking up. He sat opposite. I could feel his beadies on us.

'All right, Blake,' he says. 'What do I have to do to convince you?'

'Convince us about what?' I says. But it didn't sound like that like as not, on account of all the scran in me gob just then. More like 'vnffbwoh', or summat.

But it were enough for the Doc to go on. 'That you should take this job,' he says. 'What else?'

'Thwossnshench,' I says. ('At the Wossname Centre?')

'Er, yes. Are you interested, then?'

I chewed nice and slow, glancing over at Rache and catching her eye. It were marvellous witnessing the effect I'd had on her. Gone were the faded nature of her general appearance, replaced by a glowing radiance the like of what Mangel hadn't seen since

Finney torched Hoppers the one time. I winked at her, knowing full well it'd make her fumble the dishes she was just then doing.

'Hey, watch them plates, you,' says Madge to her.

I finished me chewing and swallowed, washing it down with half a mug of tea. Then I looked at the Doc and goes: 'Course I'm fuckin' interested.'

• • •

We headed for the Wossname Centre. I wanted to say me byes to the Doc there and then in Burt's Caff, but he wanted to go with us. And I'll tell you summat—I'd not have gone through with it if he hadn't. As we got closer to the front doors I came to realise that I really didn't care for the place—not only as a place of graft, but as a place just to go into. And it weren't just on account of it looking like a coffin. There were an odd whiff about the place. It were like summat nasty were set to happen there, so nasty you could feel it coming. I looked at the big grey frontage and tried putting me finger on it. Cos sometimes you can see things ain't happened yet, if you tries hard enough.

'Off you go then,' says the Doc as we stopped by the doors. 'And for God's sake, *don't mess it up.*'

I couldn't see it. I couldn't see the shite set to go down. But I could smell it. And I could feel it in me guts. I kept looking until me eyes started watering and I had to close em. And under the lids I could still see the big grey concrete wall, clear as before but with all the sky turned black and the folks gone off the street. And then cracks started zagging all over the wall like little spiders, getting wider and deeper, until blood started pouring out of em and turning the wall red.

5

'Blake? Blake, are you going in or not?'

I were being a twat, weren't I. There weren't no blood on the walls. And there weren't really no stink of shite neither. No more than there was anywhere else in Mangel anyhow. No, I had to put me fears aside and get on with it. Specially with Rache working in there, and her quite clearly being up for it now. And if I didn't like the job I could always pack it in after a bit, find meself a career more befitting to a man of my status.

I took a deep un and looked up and down and both ways, reminding meself how much it didn't look like a big coffin after all, when you thought about it.

'Hey, Doc,' I says. 'Er, will you go in with us?'

He shook his swede slow, then led the way in.

'Mornin',' says the old feller on the door as the Doc went past. He were way fucking old for door work, even if it were only a big shop. But door work weren't my concern now.

'Here, Doc,' I says, catching up with him, 'this job of mine... what is it, anyhow?'

'Ah, well...it's a very important...' But I didn't catch the rest. I were inside now.

Me eyes had been opened.

'Fuck me,' I says. And rightly so.

'Come along, Blake. Don't dawdle.'

The Doc tugged me arm and I started shifting again. But it were against my better instincts, I can tell you. I wanted to stand there for a bit by the entrance, taking the place in, like. I won't trot out the entrails for you because I know you've seen similar for yourself, like as not, you being an outsider. I'll just say this:

1. Shops. Fucking loads of em.
2. Big moving stairs zigzagging right up the middle.
3. Nice shiny floor underboot, the like of what you ain't ever seen before.
4. Floors up above made of glass, so you can see up birds' skirts and that. Except you couldn't for proper on account of em being too far up. But if you had a telescope you could.
5. A fucking waterfall. And I ain't joshing you there. It all spilled out into this big pond a few yard in front of us, surrounded by trees and plants and that. In fact if you looked up through them glass floors you could see gardens and streams and that on the others floors and all, and the waterfall sloshing all the way down from the top.
6. Punters.
7. Fucking loads of punters.

'So, as you can see,' says the Doc, stopping near some funny doors. 'It's not frightening at all, is it?'

'Aye,' I says, eyes going everywhere. 'I mean no.'

'There's really nothing to be afraid of. Just a few bright lights.'

'Bright lights, aye.'

'Yes. So let's just go up, shall we?'

I were looking at the zigzaggy moving stairs when he says that, and I started over to em. But the Doc got me arm and goes: 'No, Blake—this way.' He were pointing at them funny doors, which was just then opening on their tod to reveal a lift. The Doc went in.

'I ain't goin' in there,' I says.

'Don't worry, Royston. Trust me.'

'I know but I ain't goin' there.'

'Are you scared, Blake?'

'Course I fuckin' ain't,' I snaps, and went in.

Doc pressed a button and the door shut. Then we started shifting.

'Oh, Blake…here, let me help you up. Sorry—I should have known. It's just a lift, Blake. Like the one at Parpham.'

'I knows iss a fuckin' lift.' It weren't nothing like the one at Parpham though. The one at Parpham had cage doors around it and you could see out while you're moving. I don't mind them lifts. This were a fucking box, though. I hated them sort. You couldn't see fuck all and you didn't know if it were going up or down or sideways.

But I held firm.

To please the Doc, like.

'Here we are,' he says, box lurching to a stop.

'Nice one, Doc,' I says. But I weren't feeling nice. The doors started opening slow so I got me paws in and gave em some elbow. Soon as there was room I got meself through em and out onto dry land again, where I chucked me guts. I couldn't help it.

'Oh, soz, mate,' I says, looking up at the feller stood there. Cos I'd chucked all over his shoes. Nice shoes they was, except for all the chunks on em. Nice suit and all. And briefcase.

He was looking at them shoes, at a loss for what to say. He gave up in the end and just gave us a look that says: *I'm an outsider and you're a cunt. Being such, chucking over me nice shoes is all I expects of you. You ain't even worth shouting at. So I won't. So get out me fucking way.*

'All right,' I says, wiping spew off me chin. 'Calm down.'

He walked around us and went in the lift. The Doc got me arm and yanked us away from the spew. 'Oh, Blake...' he says.

'What?'

We stopped outside another door. A proper one this time, I'm glad to say. The Doc got a hanky out and started wiping me face.

'Get off...' I says, swatting him away. I think I might have swatted him a bit hard cos he went down. 'Oh, soz there, Doc,' I says, getting him by the elbow and hauling him up. 'I—'

'Yes, yes...' He were swatting us right back. Which were fair play. 'Let's just get on, shall we?'

'Do we have to?' I says. Cos I weren't enjoying meself no more.

'Yes we...we bloody well...'

'All right, fuck sake. Calm down, eh?' I opened the door.

A bird were there, sat behind a desk and tapping away on a fancy typewriter. She looked up and says: 'What's that smell?'

'Ahem...' says the Doc, squeezing past us. 'Royston has an appoint—'

'I said what's that smell?' She were getting up now, coming round the desk and sniffing the air with a face like she's swilling vinegar. Nice-looking blonde bit she were, with decent tits and a pleasing swing to the hip. Bit stuck up, mind.

'Ah yes...' the Doc started to say.

'Feller out there just now,' I says as she pushed past us. 'With the briefcase.'

She stopped in the doorway, clocked the spew, and looked back at us. 'Pardon?' she says all posh.

'Feller chucked up there just now,' I says again. 'Said he'd eaten summat, or summat. Telled us to come and ask you to clean it up. Ain't that right, Doc?'

'Er...'

'Aye. Fuckin' stinks though, dunnit.'

She didn't look so full of vinegar now. She hugged herself with one arm and put the other up to her face, where she squeezed her lip. Looked like a little girl now. A very nice one. I were just admiring the way her arm across her belly pushed her tits up when she went back to her desk and got on the blower.

'Blake,' whispers the Doc, turning us aside. 'I really don't think—'

'Ah, leave it, Doc. I done her a favour. See, birds like her needs a firm hand. Give em a bit of dirty work now and then to—'

'But the gentleman...'

'—stop em gettin' too up emselves. You what? Gentleman? Ah, fuck him. He's just a fuckin'—'

'What this?' says a new voice.

A feller's head were sticking out the door behind the bird's desk. It were quite a small head. So small in fact you'd think it a youngun's, were it not for the ginger goatee on it. Seemed familiar and all, like I'd just clocked him outside.

The bird put a paw over her handset and says to him: 'Oh, Mr Porter...there seems to have been some sort of problem with the pastries. Mr Adam...um...'

'I can smell it from here,' says the little feller. 'Never mind,' he says. 'Get it cleaned up, will you.'

'Yes, Mr Porter.' She got back on the blower and started laying into some poor fucker the other end of it.

'Who's there?' he says, his little head turning to us.

'Er...' says the Doc, shitting himself.

'Who's you?' I says to the little feller.

'Who am I? You're coming in here asking who am I?'

'Ah, heh heh,' says the Doc, stepping in front of us. 'This is Royston Blake, the, er... *security expert* I was telling you about.'

'Ah,' he says, 'so you're this Dr Gelding, is it?'

'Yes. Please forgive Royston, he—'

'Never mind that. Let's get on with it, shall we?' He pulled his head from view, leaving the door open.

'Royston, you must try to curb that tongue of yours. No one—'

'Fuck sake, Doc. S'only a little feller. I ain't scaredy of no little feller.'

'I'm not saying…I'm just…'

'Aye, all right, Doc. You can leave us to it now.' I went over to the bird, who were just then winding down her phone bollocking. 'All right, doll,' I says, sitting on the edge of her desk where I could get a nice gander down her top. She slammed the blower down and glared at us. Didn't half have nice eyes though. 'Hey,' I says, 'you ain't half got—'

'Are you coming in or what?'

We both looked at the doorway, where the hollering had come from. 'Ah well, it'll keep,' I says, winking at her. 'And so will you. Eh?'

She gave us that look again that told us how much she wanted it, even if she didn't know it yet. Instead of facing up to it she started taking it out on her typewriter.

I went in to see the little feller.

• • •

DOCTOR: *What about your work life?*
PATIENT: *What about it?*
DOCTOR: *Do you enjoy it?*
PATIENT: *Do I enjoy being a doorman? Course I fucking does. Who wouldn't?*
DOCTOR: *Well, quite. But…say I didn't know anything about being a doorman…How would you describe the essence of it to me?*

PATIENT: *The fucking essence of it? Manning doors, ennit. You welcome them what's welcome, and send t'others on their way. Simple ennit. But…but… it takes a special feller to do it.*

DOCTOR: *And that's you.*

PATIENT: *What do you fucking think? You could do it, could you?*

DOCTOR: *No, I probably couldn't.*

PATIENT: *Take it from me, mate—you definitely couldn't. It ain't just about being hard, neither. You can be hard as rock and still be a shite doorman. All up here, see…*[taps head]* All in the swede. You know what I says? 'A raised eyebrow is good as a thump in the kidneys,' I says. 'Sometimes.' Mind you, you gotta be hard and all.*

DOCTOR: *And you're hard?*

PATIENT: [laughs] *For fuck sake, Doc…you dunno much, does you? They don't come harder, mate. I'm as hard as they gets.*

DOCTOR: *What about Hoppers?*

PATIENT: *You what?*

DOCTOR: *You've always worked there, right?*

PATIENT: *Aye. S'pose I have.*

DOCTOR: *What would you do if you couldn't work there anymore. If it wasn't there anymore, say?*

PATIENT: *Won't happen, mate. Hoppers will always be Hoppers. An' I'll always have a job there. Long as she got a front door anyhow. They tried burning her down the once, you know. But she came back. There's no stopping her.*

DOCTOR: *But what if she didn't come back? What if Hop-*
           pers was gone for good. And what if there were
           no other doorman vacancies in town? What else
           could you do?
PATIENT: [scratches head for a long time. Does not
           respond to further questioning]

• • •

He were sat behind a desk, rummaging around in a drawer. The desk were so big he looked like a lad at school looking for the flick knife his teacher had swiped off him at playtime. I went over to the other chair and parked my arse on it, taking in the plush surroundings. It were a nice office, I had to admit. He had the tasteful tits painting up there on the wall and everything. Bit too much tasteful and not enough tit for my liking, mind. Still worth a gander though. I turned to the feller.

It were a bit of a comedown, I can tell you. Though his little beard were ginger, the rest of his hair were brown, that dry wiry sort you're best keeping tight to the swede. He'd let his grow out just a mite too much though, and it made him look like a mong. When you looked at his eyes, mind, you saw he weren't no mong. Quite the other, in fact. He had them eyes that was always lairy. Not the lairy of pissed-up pub behaviour though. This feller were on top of his personal grudges, and let em simmer behind his eyes and never flare up. You see that quite often on runts, fellers who ain't happy about the body they've been blessed with. Some of em rises to the physical challenge, going down the gym and learning all the skills and that, and it's them who ends up the ones you want to avoid in a rumble. Most is too weedy and little for that, mind, and they ends up getting a job behind the counter at the post office or summat. But now and then you finds one who's worked out other ways to get his own back on the world. And this here were one of them sort.

I opened me gob and says: 'Nice office you got—'

It weren't a verbal interruption that made us stop, but him turning them peepers of his on us. He left em like so for a bit, letting em do their work. Like any other feller in Mangel, I'm a bit touchy about eye contact and didn't much enjoy this little dose of it here. And normally he'd be on his back for it, the red stuff leaking from his face. But I didn't feel it appropriate right now, what with one thing or another. I marked it up on the ledger, mind.

'Firstly,' he says finally and quite calmly. 'Firstly you don't ever sit on my secretary's desk. And secondly you don't ever—*ever*— be late here again. If it was down to me you wouldn't even have got in the building just now. If it was down to me you wouldn't even be in this bloody town anymore. Mangel is going places, Royston Blake, and those who refuse to pull their weight should get off the train *now*.'

I did some thinking for a bit, then says: 'What fuckin' train?'

'Never mind what train.' He rubbed his forehead with both paws, and when they came away the lairy look were gone from his face and you could see a halfway reasonable feller underneath. 'Look, I'll be straight with you: it's been a bastard of a day, and I could do without new employees turning up late, thank you very much. We've had the police crawling all over the place round back. Three employees were injured by an intruder this morning—one of them seriously.'

'Oh,' I says.

'Yes. We're hoping he'll pull through, but it's a worry. It's a real worry, security is. But never mind that for now…I'll just ask you one thing, Mr Blake. And I want the truth. Are you up to the job?'

I rubbed me chin and considered me answer. 'Depends what the job is, dunnit.'

'Didn't the doctor tell you?'

'No, he just says—'

'The vacancy is for a front-of-house customer flow manager.'

'A what?'

He says it again.

'A manager?' I says, getting interested now. 'Oh aye, I can do that all right.'

'I hope you can. The doctor said you can, but that's no use unless I hear it from you.'

'Oh aye, you'll have no—'

'But I'll make one thing clear, first. I'm taking you on based on your past reputation in the field. I know about your troubles with the law and your mental health problems, and I'm...'

Manager, eh? I couldn't believe me luck. There I were one minute, thinking how I were now worthy of a higher station in life than plain door work. And now look at us: manager of this big place here—bright lights, zigzaggy moving stairs, waterfall, the fucking lot of it. Fate had played us a nice little hand there all right.

'...you don't let me down,' says the little feller, finishing up whatever he'd been saying. 'Do you understand that, Mr Blake?'

'Oh aye.'

'Any questions?'

'Aye. Where's me office?'

He looked a mite troubled at that, and I wondered if that lairy eye weren't due for a comeback, just when I'd got him to cheer up a bit. Then his face cracked into a grin and he says: 'Oh, I see. Good. Sense of humour always helps a man though his day, in moderation. Very good. Well, I'll show you to your, er...*office*, heh heh. But we'll need to get you kitted out first.'

I looked down at meself. He were right: clobber-wise I were far from management material. I needed a suit and tie and a smart pair o' boots. And little boss feller here's offering to get em for us, from one of them flash shops down the stair like as not. I were getting to quite like him, actually.

'Come on then,' he says.

• • •

'Not bad,' he says as I came out of the broom cupboard five minutes later. 'Go on, put the hat on.'

I put it on.

'Good. Highly professional.' He reached up and flicked summat off me shoulder, saying: 'Come along then. I'll show you your office. Heh heh, very funny.'

I followed him into the lift, looking meself over. To be fair it were an all right jumper. Nice and warm, and as colours go I don't mind navy blue. The shirt and tie weren't so bad neither, and you couldn't complain much about the boots. I weren't so keen on the strides, mind. They was made of poly-wossname and clung to me legs like fly paper. And as for the hat...

'Hey, mate,' I says while he fucked around with the lift buttons.

He shot us one of his narked looks, then goes: 'It's Mr Porter, not "mate."'

'All right, Mr Wossname. But...er...'

'What's the matter? Don't like your new kit?'

'Aye, iss all right, ennit. But I looks like...'

'A front-of-house customer flow manager. Yes, you do.'

'No, a fuckin' secu—'

The floor fell from under me feet.

That's what it felt like anyhow. I leaned up against a wall and shut me eyes, praying I wouldn't chuck me guts again. I could still taste it in me gob from just now, and there's fuck all worse than two chunders in half an hour. I don't think the little boss feller liked it neither, cos he goes:

'We'll have to get this lift properly calibrated. Goes too fast. I dunno, you people can't seem to get anything right first time, these days.'

Me knees gave way a bit when the lift stopped, but I stayed upright mostly. I made a big effort and let the little boss feller go out first, then follered. Felt like I were walking underwater for a bit, but I managed to keep up with him as he crossed the floor. And by the time he stopped I were starting to feel all right again. And not a chunk of carrot in sight.

'Here you go,' he says, stood smiling next to the big glass doors I'd come in through. I could see a couple of fellers t'other side of it, facing doorward and chatting. They was both holding summat in their paws but I couldn't make em out just then.

'Here's your new office,' says the little boss feller. 'Heh heh.'

I looked around and goes: 'Where?'

He had a quick word with the old fucker on the door there, who then fucked off. I went up and goes: 'Doorman? You want us to be fuckin' doorman?'

'Don't worry,' he says, getting a paw behind us and pushing us out, all gentle like. I didn't like that but I were powerless to stop it, what all them bright flashing lights starting up just then. 'Nice big smile, eh?'

He'd fucked off by the time I knew what all that flashing and snapping were about. So had the fuckers with the cameras. I stood there rubbing me eyes, getting used to me new office.

6

'All right, Blake.'

I looked around, wiping the slobber off me chin and wondering why things was so quiet. 'Wha?' I says, looking left and right along Friar Street. I could have swore someone had said, 'All right, Blake.'

Must have been dreaming. And there's no accounting for dreams, is there?

I'd never dropped off on me door before. And I hoped to fuck no one had clocked us. It were dark, but you could tell from the hum of traffic in the air that it weren't late, and therefore Hoppers couldn't have seen more than a punter or two pass through her doorway as yet, so I were all right there like as not. I reached up to set me dickie askew, only to find a clip-on tie where it ought to be. 'Eh?' I says, feeling the hat slide off me swede.

'I says all right, Blake.'

I turned arse to find Don stood there, smirking at us.

I must have slipped on a banana or summat cos I fell over, landing arsewise on the path. Don tried hauling us up, but I shrugged him off, preferring to stay like so until I got me bearings.

'Six o'clock, ennit,' he says, still smirking. 'The end o' your workin' day.' Actually Don always had a smirk on his chops, so that didn't mean nothing. I noted that he were carrying a placcy bag. 'This?' he says, noting that I were noting it. 'Your togs, ennit. Boss told us to give em you, says you left em in the broom cupboard or summat. Good day, were it?'

I'd got meself sorted now. The dream of being at Hoppers had
wafted away like a dandelion fairy on the summer breeze, leaving us with hard truth and cold November air and fuck all else
besides. 'No,' I says, getting on me feet and taking the bag off him.
'It were not a good day.'

'Oh aye?'

'Aye. An' I ain't doin' it no more.'

'Oh aye?' he says, offering us a smoke, which I took. 'Can't
be that bad though, can it? I mean you ain't doin' much different
from before, at Hoppers. Doorin's doorin', ennit?'

'No it fuckin' ain't. Doorin's more than just standin' there like
a fuckin' tree while folks files past. Doorin's about takin' care of
situations, ennit, and that.'

'Situations eh?'

'Aye. Argy-bargy.'

'Oh aye. Don't get much o' that here, I s'pose.'

'No you don't, Don. Cos they ain't pissed is why. Folks ain't
pissed, they'll behave. And do you know why they ain't pissed,
Don?'

'You'll have to tell us, Blake.'

'Cos it ain't a pub. A doorman needs a pub behind him else he
ain't a doorman. Or a club. A pub or a club. A doorman without
one o' them behind him is like…er…'

'A pint without a fag.'

'Thass it, Don. You fuckin' knows it, mate.'

'A whisky without a cigar.'

'Fuckin' bang on,' I says, shaking me swede at the sheer poetry
of it.

We looked off up the road, thinking about the fag and pint
and the whisky and stogie. He were all right, were Don. We'd had
our ups and downs over the years but I'd had a lot less shite off

him than most others. That's cos of him being my sort of feller. I could see eye to eye with him, and I can't say same about most folks. And that ain't just his height neither, though he were as high as meself while not so beefy. Weren't his face neither, though you could say he were as close to Sean Connery as I were to Clint Eastwood (which is fucking close).

No, it's about what's up here, in your swede.

Me and him could think thoughts that the rest of Mangel wouldn't come up with, not even if you rolled em all into one big feller and gave him two hundred year to think about it.

'No, I can well see why you wouldn't like it. I wouldn't like it neither,' he says. 'Course, I does the night shift so I gets to move around.'

'Aye, I wouldn't mind that so much,' I says. 'You'd get to nick stuff from the shops.'

'Nah, can't do that. They got cameras.'

'Who has?'

'They has. On the walls, hidden uns. You know, vid cameras filmin' you everywhere.'

'Oh aye?'

'Aye. Only place they ain't got em is the corridors out back, and the bogs an' that. S'where I goes for a kip sometimes.'

'In the bogs? I wouldn't fancy that.'

'I wouldn't fancy kippin' stood up here on the door.'

We had a laugh at that.

'Anyhow, Blakey,' he says offering us another fag, 'some o' the lads is comin' round our's the morrer for cards an' that.'

'Oh aye?'

'Aye, iss me night off, like. Fancy it?'

'Oh aye. Try keepin' us away, mate. I fuckin' loves cards. Nice one, Don.'

'Well, iss more than just cards, you know. I wants you to meet one or two fellers. You knows most of em, but…Anyhow, we got summat goin', me an' the lads. A plan, like. And you bein' Royston Blake…'

'You knows how I feels about plans, Don.'

'How's that then?' he says, narrowing his eyes.

'If there's a plan, I'm yer man.'

'Thass what I likes to hear. See you the morrer then. Bring loads of shrapnel. We ain't rich an' we ain't playin' big money, but we likes a gamble. You knows where it is, right?'

'Bonehill flats, still?'

'Aye. See you then, Blakey.'

'See you, Don. Hey, Don?'

'What?'

'Lend us a tenner?'

• • •

I were a bit happier after that, though no keener on the job. It were degrading for a class doorman like meself to be doing that kind of work, and I weren't doing it no more. The Doc could fuck off. I'd find summat else to do—summat to make Little Royston proud of his dad. And if nothing came along straight off, there was always Don's plan. He hadn't told us what it were all about yet, course, but you could just tell it were a good un. And a good plan means a good payout.

Aye, clever lad, were Don. And I were well chuffed about the cards tomorrer night.

'Evening, Royston.'

I knew who it were without even looking. Talk about the devil and up he pops, so they says. And I ain't on about Don here.

'Doc,' I says without turning me head.

'Get in,' he says, pulling alongside in his Granada.

'No, ta.' Cos I didn't fancy it. I'd had enough of the Doc. And I reckon you has and all.

'Why not? Come on, I'll give you a lift.'

'Leave it, Doc,' I says. Cos I didn't wanna shout at him. Not here in the street.

There was a couple of motors behind him and he had to pull in to let em by. He did that and got out, blocking the bit of path left for us to get past on.

'Just tell me this,' he says, really fucking pushing it now. 'How was your day?'

'My day?' I says, squaring up to him. I'd had enough now. 'My fuckin' day? I'll tell you about my day, shall I? It's the last fuckin' day I does on that job.'

'Come now, Royston—'

'Come now bollocks. I ain't doin' it no more.'

'But you've no choice, Royston. Remember you're on parole. If you fail to—'

'Bollocks,' I says, lifting him up and plonking him to one side. When I set him down he must have slipped on summat cos he went down. 'Soz, Doc,' I says. I didn't mean him no harm, like. I pissed off up the road. I had somewhere to go, and the Doc putting us in a bad mood weren't helping us. There were no place for bad moods where I were headed.

I heard him shouting behind us and tried blocking it out. I thought of a tune to sing and came up with 'Don't Cry Daddy' by Elvis. I sung that for a bit before deciding the words weren't ideal, considering the happy occasion awaiting us. And I couldn't block the Doc out anyhow cos he'd pulled up alongside us again.

'Blake, listen,' he shouts out the window.

I gritted gnashers and pumped pins, wondering how long I'd hold out for.

'I've got a proposition for you. A very interesting one.'

Me gnashers stopped gritting.

Me pins stopped pumping.

'Proposition?' I says.

• • •

I had to give meself a pat on the arse. Really I fucking did. There's businessmen and there's businessmen, and the Doc weren't neither of em.

Royston Blake, by contrast, *were* a businessman. When he wanted to be. And he didn't half show it, that evening down Friar Street, outside the Volley and up a bit. And I'll tell you for why.

In a minute.

First off let me tell you what I went on to be doing shortly thereafter (Cos you won't fucking believe it.) (And I ain't lying.):

I were driving the Doc's Granada.

And what were the Doc doing, I hears you ask?

Yomping home.

That's right: Me in his motor. Him on the soles of his boots. Me cruising along at sixty up the East Bloater Road, feeling the auto box do whatever I asked of it. Him scratching his swede, wondering where he'd gone wrong. But he were scratching in vain, see, cos it were fucking simple:

He'd been outclassed. In the swede department.

And him calling himself a fucking doctor and all.

You're like as not fit for gagging now so I'd better tell you how it had all come to pass. Right, the Doc had asked us to come down the Paul Pry later that evening, to talk matters over and come to an arrangement.

Leaving aside how odd it were to picture the Doc drinking in the Pry, I said no. I told him I'd had it up past me arse with his going on, and I weren't in the market for no more.

So then he starts begging.

And I starts walking.

He starts voice-raising.

I starts hackles-raising. (Still walking, mind.)

He says he's got a couple of fellers he'd like us to meet.

I says I got a couple of fingers I'd like him to meet.

He goes quiet.

I goes round the corner.

He pulls up alongside again.

I pulls me fist out and shows it him.

'Blake,' he goes, 'what do I have to do?'

And do you know where the businessman bit comes in? I reckon you don't, looking at you there, gob agape and tongue hanging out, flob dripping down your chin. Some folks needs it spelling out for em so I'll do that for you, since you're sitting nice and harking us proper. So I'd better do that for you:

I'd have gone and met him at the Paul Pry anyhow. I fancied a gander at the old place. And being with the Doc might come in handy if Nathan the barman tried making out like I were banned (which I were, like as not). But I wanted to push the Doc a bit first, see what I could skim off him.

All right, so I only had the motor till later that night. I had to bring it down the Pry for nine o' clock else he'd call coppers on us. But I only needed it for a couple of hours.

• • •

I pulled up on the grass verge and got out. It were well dark now and a bit foggy out here on the East Bloater Road, so I couldn't see fuck all. But I knew what were out there, if you carried on along the road and went right past East Bloater and didn't look back. I knew it cos I'd dreamed it. Dreamed it lying down and dreamed it standing up. Not so much lately, mind, being in Parpham. But I were out now.

I had a smoke, looking into the darkness. Thinking of the outside.

A minute or so later I got the placcy bag off the back seat and started getting me working togs off. Little Royston were meeting his old feller for the first time in half an hour or so, and I didn't want him thinking us a cunt. I couldn't believe I'd kept that security guard kit on so long anyhow. The shirt were sticking right up me armpits and well soggy in them places, and the strides was clinging so bad you could see sparks when I peeled em off.

I felt good, standing there in the night air in me socks and trolleys. It were cold all right, and me skin responded to that by putting out a few goosebumps. Big uns and all, and so many of em that I looked and felt like a nipple farm. But I could deal with it for a bit. I lit another smoke and walked into the road, scratching me bollocks and thinking about what I'd be doing later, after I'd got reacquainted with our Sal. Before I knows it I had a truncheon on me hands. In me trolleys, to be more precise. So like all good coppers I got it out and felt the weight of it in me hand. I couldn't help it—you try going as long as I had without emptying your sack. You can't. And I couldn't no longer neither. So I had a wank, standing on the grass out by the East Bloater Road.

And that's when a motor swung past out of nowhere.

Fuck me, I thought, squirting fat across the tarmac and watching the tail lights trail off East Bloaterward. Who the fuck were that? And where did he reckon he were going? Cos you can't leave Mangel.

By the time I'd got meself dressed I'd stopped worrying over it. You sees all sorts of things in your time on this planet, and some of em you just ain't meant to understand.

I got back in the Granada.

But I didn't start her up again just yet. I flicked the overhead on and fished in me back pocket for summat. I read the letter over a few times, looking up every now and then to where I'd seen the red lights disappearing not two minutes previous.

• • •

DOCTOR: *So who is Sally?*
PATIENT: *Why's you asking?*
DOCTOR: *Because it says her name here in your notes. It says "girlfriend." Is that what she was?*
PATIENT: [shrugs]
DOCTOR: *So it was a casual thing?*
PATIENT: *Aye, if you likes.*
DOCTOR: *You never talked about marriage?*
PATIENT: *Marriage? Get lost, mate. I been wedded before. Told you all that already. Nah, we was just…She liked a slap and I liked a tickle, and between us we had an all right time, when it suited us.*
DOCTOR: *OK. We've established that you saw other women during this time. Did Sally?*
PATIENT: *What, see other birds?*
DOCTOR: *Other men?*

PATIENT:	No, she…Well, aye, she did. At first, you know.
DOCTOR:	And how did that make you feel, the thought of her with another man?
PATIENT:	[shrugs] I didn't mind it, like. But you got to ignore it. Like I says, we weren't going out official like.
DOCTOR:	And so you turned a blind eye and left it at that?
PATIENT:	Well…no. There comes a time when you gotta put your foot down. Don't there?
DOCTOR:	Are you asking me?
PATIENT:	No, I'm telling you.
DOCTOR:	And this is what you told Sally?
PATIENT:	No. I mean I didn't have to, like. She just stopped. She knew the score, and she stopped.
DOCTOR:	And have you wondered if there have been further…dalliances?
PATIENT:	What's you trying to say, eh, Doc?
DOCTOR:	Nothing, I'm just talking about trust. Do you trust her?
PATIENT:	Course I fucking do. I mean, well…[scratches head for a long time] I mean there's no saying for surely, is there? One minute I'm shagging her and she's shagging other fellers. Next minute she says she's only shagging me ever again. Summat ain't right about that. You just dunno where you are.
DOCTOR:	You would like to feel more in control?
PATIENT:	[shrugs] To be honest, mate, I don't give a fuck either way. Like I says, we ain't getting wed. [scratches head] But even so…

• • •

A feller were walking across the road wearing filthy army trousers, hair all clumped together like old cobwebs. He flobbed on the ground and went into Doug's.

I switched off the motor.

I'd wanted to park right outside the house, me having the Granada and all, but there was motors nose to arse up there and I had no fucking chance. I didn't mind though, cos they'd still get to see the Granada. I planned on taking the two of em out for a ride, see, show em how the old man's moved up in the world. I got out and walked.

I didn't even want to look at Doug's corner shop. Knowing my luck he'd clock us and come out again, going on about all that barmy stuff like yesterday. And I couldn't be doing with that right now. Not with me new life as a dad about to commence. I stopped at the front door of my house.

It were open a bit and light from the hall spilled out onto the doorstep. Seemed odd, that. You never knows when a burglar might walk past, and Sal knew that. Still, at least she were in this time. *They* were in. I pushed the door open proper and went in.

'Hoy,' I shouts. Cos I didn't know what else to say. I were in my own home, but it didn't feel like it somehow. 'I'm back, ain't I.'

I stopped short of shouting, 'Daddy's home,' thinking it better for the lad to meet us proper first.

'Sal?'

The place didn't look no different from how it had always looked. Beer tins on the kitchen table, sink full of dirties, floor none too clean. There's fuck all wrong with that if it's a feller living on his tod, but Sal were living here now, and she were looking after our youngun. I weren't happy about it, I don't mind telling you. And when I shouted her name again I let me aggravation rear up.

Still no answer though.

I went into the hall for a think, noticing all the letters piled up by the blower. I'd never liked letters at the best of times, most of em looking like trouble in my experience and thereby flying binward sharpish, but I had a ferret around these uns here for summat to do, seeing as I weren't getting very far with me thinking. Most of em was addressed to Sal, which stood to reason, her living here now. I also found one with someone else's name on it—Kevin summat or other. Had our address and everything, so someone must have fucked up. I couldn't make head nor arse out of it anyhow, so I put him down and picked up a thick one from nearby, where Sal had started a new pile. This un had my name on it, and contained a little flat box by the feels of it. I opened it and found a tape inside and fuck all else. On the tape box were a white sticky label with the words "FOR ROYSTON—A SONG TO MAKE YOU THINK" scrawled on it in biro. I looked at the writing for a while, wondering where I'd seen writing like that before. And it's then that I heard the noise—a deep rumbling coming through the floorboards overhead. I'd know that sound any place.

I shoved the tape in me jacket and went up.

Sal were there all right, flat on her back like always. She were fast akip, which accounted for the deep rumbling. Always had been a bit of a diesel engine, had Sal, and normally it just took an elbow in the kidneys to hush up her snoring. But I didn't do it this time. It had been fuck knows how long since I'd seen our Sal—mother of my offsprung youngun—and it were a joy near as not to hark her snoring away. I sat down next to her on the bed, just clocking her angelic features. Then I noticed there weren't no straps on her shoulders, so I turned down the duvet for a look at her tits.

They was angelic and all, let me tell you. If angels had big round baps that stay up a bit even when the angel's lying backwise on the mattress, nips poking up like bullets with your name on em. Mind you, they weren't so large as I'd seen em previous. And when I tugged the duvet a mite further downriver I could see she'd lost a curve or two elsewhere. You could slot a loaf of toast between them ribs. But a bird's a bird, and there ain't no arguing with tits and a fanny to a red-blooded feller. Specially when you been locked up for donkeys.

I got me kit off first, then climbed atop her and started giving her that special gift a man gives to a woman, with his tongue. She moaned a bit and spread em somewhat, but carried on snoring. I were a bit out of practice anyhow, so when me tongue seized up I thought it time to give the big feller a turn. If that didn't wake her up I didn't know what. And to be honest I didn't care anyhow. I'd gone without me oats for four long year, and all I cared about now were getting em, any which way. And it didn't take long before I found em.

About ten second.

I pulled out, feeling just a mite irked that she hadn't woke up. She weren't snoring no more though, so I'd had some effect on her. And she were mumbling summat and rolling her eyes under the lids. By the time I'd got me trolleys back on she had one of em open.

'All right, Sal,' I says, doing up the buttons on me shirt and winking at her.

The peeper stayed on us for a bit, not blinking and not yet joined by the other un. Then she pulled the covers up over her, sat up, and kicked us off the bed all in one movement like.

'Hoy, you,' I says. Cos I'd burnt me knee on the carpet.

'Blake?' she says, sounding a bit rattled.

'Course iss fuckin' Blake. Who the fuck d'you expect it to be?'

'Wha...' She lifted the covers and looked down at herself, looking frankly horrified. 'So you, er...'

I were a bit put out by her reaction, to be honest, considering the treat I'd just gave her. But she might have been having a bad dream or summat, so I couldn't go too hard on her.

'So you...um...got out of Parpham, then?'

'Course I fuckin' did,' I says, squeezing her bony leg and trying to make light of it. 'Didn't think I'd stay in there forever, did yer?'

'No, but...' She didn't half look worried. 'I, um...'

'Ah well, surprise for you, ennit.'

Thinking it best to leave her be for a minute, I pulled the rest of me kit on and went out onto the landing. I felt better straight away. It's funny how the need of a shag can set your priorities askew for a while. But I'd got em straight in me head now and I felt all excited again.

'Miss us then, did yer?' I says, going into the other bedroom and switching the light on. No youngun in here. Not even a little bed. Just a load of old junk, same as always. Could be the lad kipped in the front room down the stair though. Aye, that were a good idea from Sal. Cos there were more room in there for his toys and that. I skipped down to it, shouting, 'I missed you,' over me shoulder. For form's sake, like.

'But, Blake...' She were up now and coming after us, pulling on her dressing gown. 'You can't...I mean, things...' Like as not she wanted a proper hug and kiss, now she'd woke up proper and got her head straight. But she'd had her chance for that and turned her nose up, so now she'd have to get back in the queue.

I turned the door handle nice and quiet. Little Royston might be kipping in there, you know. It weren't even nine o'clock of an eve yet, but you got to put em to bed early when they're little, don't you.

'Blake, please...' she were going on behind us. 'You can't be here. You—'

'Shhh,' I says, nodding at the door. I gave her a wink to keep her happy, then pushed the door to and poked me swede inside. Light were coming in from the street lamp outside so I could see all right. After a bit I pulled out and shut the door, quiet as I'd opened it.

I turned to Sal. 'All right,' I says. And I were trying hard to stay calm here. 'All right, where is he?'

'Blake, it ain't like that. It—'

'I says where the fuck is he?'

'Blake, please...You don't understand. I didn't have no choice, Blake. I were lonely and, you know, a woman has *needs*. I didn't know if you'd be back. I...I...they said—'

'Fuck's you on about?' I says. 'Juss tell us where's little Royston?'

She looked lost. Actually she looked like she'd been on the voddy again. This were all I needed—Sal pissed up and confused. I might have known summat were up from finding her in her dressing gown at such an hour as this. 'Little Royston?' she says, face turning from confused to summat else. 'Blake, they did let you go, didn't they? At Parpham, like. I mean you are cured, right?'

I got hold of her stinking gown and pushed her up against the wall. She were whimpering a bit but I didn't give a toss. Only one thing I cared about and it weren't her. 'I'll ask you one more time. Where's my fuckin' son?'

She stopped whimpering and stared for a bit. Then her hand came up and touched my face. Why the fuck did everyone wanna touch my face?

'Oh, Blake…' she says. 'You don't know, does you.'

'Know what? For fuck sake, all I wants is—'

'He's gone, Blake. The babby died.'

I didn't say nothing for a bit. What can you say to that? I didn't think nothing neither. I just looked at Sal, trying to read the lie behind her eyes.

But it were no use.

I knew Sal and I knew her lies. And this weren't one of em. This were the fucking gospel truth, as I could see from the way she looked straight back at us with nary a flicker of the eyelid.

'Died?' I says after a bit.

'Aye. Died.'

'But…'

'He's gone, Blake. I'm sorry.'

'But…how the fuck?'

'He never lived. Never wanted to. Opened his eyes, took one look at the world we lives in, and let go his last puff. I'm sorry, Blake. Doctors couldn't of done nuthin'. He just weren't to be.'

'But…why didn't you tell us?'

'I didn't wanna hurt you, Blake, you bein' unsound an' all. An' besides, you know, I wanted to…'

'What? Come on, you wanted to fuckin' what?'

'Let go us, Blake. It ain't my fault. *Oww*…'

'Come on, you fucker—you wanted to what?'

'I…Get *off* us.' Her knee came up and landed square where I didn't want it to. I should have seen it coming. It were a good one and all, and I slumped to me knees before I knew what had hit us.

But do you know what? I didn't care.

'You wanna know what I wanted?' she shouts down at us. 'I wanted to *forget*. Not just about the babby. I wanted to forget about *you*. Do you know what? All I ever…'

I weren't listening. I closed me eyes and pictured it all like she'd described it—her screaming and bawling…the doctor saying come on and hurry up, we ain't got all day…her pushing a bit harder, sweat popping out her forehead…the lad coming out of her and letting out a little wail…the lad carking it.

'Oh, Blake…' She were sat next to us now. I dunno when she'd stopped having a pop at us and gone all tender, but she had. She sat down and pulled us to her bosom, and we stayed like so for I dunno how long. I can't say it made us feel better, though. How could I ever feel better, knowing my own youngun had lived and died while I'd been in Parpham getting me swede sorted? I bet it wouldn't have happened if I'd been there for him when he came out. I bet, if he'd clocked his old feller on opening his eyes, he'd still be here now. But it couldn't happen that way, could it.

Everything in this town turns to shite.

'Hoy, woss you doin'?' comes a feller's voice from the doorway. 'Yeah you, you fuckin' cunt. Get off her.'

I looked over there but me eyes was misted up, and I couldn't see who it were. Didn't matter who he were.

I went for him.

• • •

It's the screaming what brung us to.

Not screaming for proper, like when a bird opens her kitchen cupboard and sees a cockroach there. But screaming as in Sal having a go.

87

'…big fuckin' bully you are. Look what you done to poor Badger. Go on, get out of it, you big fuckin'…'

The blackness were seeping out me fingers and I were feeling a bit shaky now. And Sal weren't helping. So all in all I didn't know what were what. But I got the upshot of it when I looked down at where Sal were kneeling in the gutter, next to that feller. What'd she call him just then? Ferret or summat? Anyhow, he's the same one crossing the street just now, in them filthy army strides.

'Look what you done to him. *Look*.'

But I didn't wanna. It don't do to see all that blood when you ain't feeling shipshape. I sat down on the hard stuff instead, swede in paws. I felt like shite but I knew it'd pass if I just held steady for a bit.

Then I remembered about the babby.

'Sal,' I says after I'd thought about the babby for a bit. Cos there were so much I wanted to know. But when I looked around for her she were gone. The ferret feller and all. I knew they'd gone back indoors cos I could still feel the echo of the door slamming.

A noise across the street made us look over there. Couple of younguns standing in their front window, having a good gander. Twitching curtains and folded arms in doorways up and down the road and all.

The fucking bastards.

Didn't they know what had happened to us? Didn't they know I'd lost me only begotted son? 'Fuck off, you fuckin' bastards,' I shouts at em. 'Don't you know I lost me only begotted son? One of you ain't worth *five* of him, you fuckin'…'

I closed me eyes and covered me face. But I didn't like it that way cos I could still hear stuff, so I pulled jacket over swede and clamped paws over ears. I could still hear a few things, so I started shouting to drown it all out. After a bit a firm grip took hold me arm and hauled us up.

7

'I'll not say anything.'

Doug were sitting beside us, driving. We was in his little van, pootling down the main road. The diesel engine weren't half loud for such a little van, though not so loud as Doug's voice. But that were all right cos he'd just said he wouldn't be saying nothing.

'No, I'll say nothing,' he says, forking right into Clench Road and pulling up at the red light there. 'Other than to say I'm disappointed.'

A couple of lads walked across the road in front of us, smoking fags and flobbing and swearing. They looked like cunts, hoods up and baggy strides with the bottoms touching tarmac, hiding all but a toe of each trainer. Doug started tutting. 'Just look at em,' he says. 'Our future, they are. When you gets elderly it's them who'll be lookin' after you. *Them*, with their drugs and their loud music, and ill-fittin' clothes. What d'you think about that, eh? Eh?'

I searched meself for smokes but I didn't have none left. And Doug didn't smoke, far as I knew.

'Glove compartment,' he says.

I looked at him. We was moving again now, and he were still shaking his swede about them younguns back there. I opened the glove box and sure enough found four packs of Number One in there. I took one out and started unwrapping it.

'Take em all,' he says. 'You'll need em.'

He were right there—I fucking did need em. I took em all. He were all right, were Doug. I couldn't find me matches though, so I looked at him again. He pushed in the fag lighter. 'Aye, I'm

disappointed,' he says again. 'And I don't mean about that feller back there, you givin' him a hidin'. He's a filthy toe-rag and
deserves all he gets.'

The lighter popped out and I lit me smoke with it. I took a few
deep puffs, watching the glowing metal fade till it looked cold. I
went to touch it.

'Don't be a bloody fool,' says Doug, snatching the lighter out
me paw. 'You've got to look after yerself. You've got work to do.'

We'd stopped at lights again now, halfway up Clench Road at
the junction. Doug clicked the flasher on and started drumming
his fingers on the wheel. A gang of five lads was hanging about on
the edge of the car park not twenty yard off, smoking and having
a laugh. They was hooded or capped and cuntish-looking, just
like them other uns just now. All except the one of em, close-
cropped and trackied and standing out from his herbert mates. At
first I thought it were on account of his reminding us of meself.
He weren't so big as I'd been at that age, but there were summat in
his eyes I knew all about.

He were looking out for himself.

Had his eye open for the main chance, like.

'But it's the lyin' on the ground there, outside your own house,
wailin' like a lost kitten. It's no way to behave, Royston Blake. Not
for any man. Let alone a warrior.'

And then I clocked summat else in the lad that made us see
things a bit more clearer. Aye, he were like meself at that age in
some ways, but it weren't meself I were looking at. It were Little
Royston. I were looking at what me own dead son might have
been like, ten or twelve year down the line. I smiled. But the lad
weren't looking our way. That eagle eye of his was off up the street,
homing in on his prey like a starving buzzard.

'A warrior like yerself must stand tall. We're countin' on you, Royston Blake. We've all been countin' on you for a long while, and now the time has come.'

I were still smiling, dreaming like this were my lad. It were a sweet moment while it lasted. I were a proud father and he were a chip off the old potato. He were a brave warrior, afraid of nothing. He could have anyone.

A slow-moving old crone passed in front of him and his mates, and I closed me eyes for a second, not wanting her to fuck up me dream for us. When I opened em again she were face down on the hard stuff and no lads was there. Across the car park you could see four hooded and capped heads pegging it like billy-o, and another one taking it easy, barely even jogging, swinging a black handbag and adjusting his tracky.

The old bird were still there on the deck and she hadn't budged. I looked at her, scratching my head.

'Aye,' says Doug, eyes set on the lights. They'd just gone green so he took the handbrake off and pulled into the Wall Road. 'The time has come to put our town to rights.'

'Doug,' I goes when we got to the end of the Wall Road, 'where the fuck is we headed?'

He kept quiet until we pulled into the Paul Pry car park, stopping beside a grey Ford Zephyr in quite good condition. He turned off the engine and reached across us into the glove box.

'Salvation,' he says, slipping a monkey wrench into me paw.

• • •

I stopped in the doorway.

'Woss the matter now?' says Doug.

To be honest I didn't know. The Paul Pry were my local, so to speak. I don't mean like I lives near it, but it's the pub closest me heart in the drinking sense, if you follows us. There's many a reason for that, not least of em being the overall quietness of the place. As I've stated many a time previous, a head doorman at a busy establishment like Hoppers requires a bit of tranquility in his off hours. And though I hadn't worked at Hoppers in a goodly old while, I did indeed feel the need for a bit of just that, what with recent happenings and that.

But I couldn't seem to get me boots across the threshold.

Summat weren't right, and I found out what it were when Doug opened his trap again: 'Come on,' he says. 'They're all waitin' inside.'

I knew it. Though there'd been no outward sign of it—like more than a couple of motors in the car park—I'd known there was a bunch of cunts in there waiting for us. And by cunts I don't mean your everyday variety, I'm talking folks setting out to be cuntish to Royston Blake in particular.

'Who's all waitin'?' I says.

Doug gave us one of his looks. He only had three looks and it weren't the workaday grimace, nor the rarely seen air of consti-pation that is actually him smiling. Then he cheered up a bit and showed us them two, resting finally on the constipated un. 'Fret not, brave warrior,' he says. He were fucking barmy, were Doug. 'All friends here, we are.'

It were awful really, Doug smiling. It were like he were try-ing with all his might to shit a pineapple, and loving it. It were so unpleasant I had to close me eyes, only to find summat even worser there, flickering away on the blank telly screen of me eyelids. It were Doug again, but many a year previous, that time when I'd gone up a ladder and clocked him in his sausage-making togs (a red rubber outfit with three little holes for his eyes and gob, and a big one where his tadger came out).

'I gotta go for a piss, first,' I says, shooting into the bogs. And I weren't just saying that to get away from him. I honestly could have filled a bucket.

As I got meself out, I heard the door swing slowly behind us. But it never reached the squeaky bit at the end. Instead it swung open again, and shortly I found Doug the shopkeeper to be standing at the porcelain beside us, getting his willy out.

'Think I'll have one meself,' he says quiet like, the last word swallowed up by the noise of piss hitting china.

I dunno how long we stood there for, him putting out gallons and me holding back oceans. 'Come on, you fucker,' I mumbles, looking down at the broken part.

'Woss that?' says Doug.

'Nuthin',' I says truthfully.

I'd heard of this particular affliction before, but it hadn't ever happened to us. If I wants a piss I has a piss and I don't care who's looking on, long as they ain't an arse bandit. But I just couldn't do it here. He weren't working for us, no matter how hard I strained me bladder. And I knew it were on account of Doug.

I closed me eyes and tried picturing meself fishing barbel on the river. That seemed to work, and I felt the waters begin to shift within us. Then I noticed another angler across the river from us. It were Doug in his rubber gear again. And instead of a rod he were holding his tadger, which were two yard long at least, and had a sausage dangling off the end of it.

I'd lost me chance to put meself away and pretend like I'd done a quick one already, so I had to stand there waiting for the rains to come, him putting out fucking gallons the whole while. He must have been one o' them fellers only goes once a week.

'Forgot how to do it, have you?' says Doug, showing some signs of slowing up finally.

I hung me head.

Half an hour later he's zipping himself up and I'm crying inside. He washed his paws and stood with em under the dryer, saying: 'I'll get you a pint then, shall I?' The door creaked to. And this time I heard that squeaky bit at the end.

I started pissing.

• • •

'Ah, so there he is.'

It were dark in the main bit and there was a fair few folks around, so I couldn't make out who'd said that. But I'd know that voice any place. It were a voice more familiar to me than the lint in me own belly button, if not quite so welcome these days.

'All right, Nathan,' I says out of habit. I wished I hadn't though.

I says there was a fair few folks in the Paul Pry just then, but that ain't the half of it, as I went on to realise when me peepers adjusted. It's *who* they was, not the how many. I'll tell you about that in a minute.

'Go on,' says Doug behind us. He'd been waiting outside the bog door, making sure I never made a break for it. Not that he could have done much about it, course. If I wants a break I makes a break and no fucker can stop us. But I chose not to exercise that right just now. All that'd bring is bother aplenty, which were the last thing I wanted just then. 'Got a pint for you at the bar,' he says. 'That'll loosen yer bladder, eh?'

I could have turned arse and smacked the cunt, taking the piss like that. And some might say I ought to have done that. But

I went on up to the bar and lifted the pint of lager there instead. Like I says, I didn't want no bother nor fuss. I knocked back the pint, remarking to meself how this had been the first lager to pass me lips since Parpham. Didn't half taste different, though. There's lack of practice for you.

'Not that one,' says Nathan, plonking a brimming pint in front of us. 'This un here. That un there were Burt's. You owes him a pint now.'

'Oh,' I says, taking note of Burt perched atop a stool not but two yard to me right. 'Soz, Burt. Didn't see you there, mate.' I slid the fresh pint towards him.

Burt glared at us.

'Burt drinks mild,' says Nathan. 'Not lager.'

'Oh,' I says sliding me pint back.

'You'll have to buy him another.'

I shook me swede slow and put paw to pocket, turning away from Nathan's glare. Burt were glaring at us and all, as were every other fucker in the Paul Pry at that moment, which included:

Alvin (of kebab shop & chippy fame)
The miserable cunt from the offy on Cutler Road
Old Mr Fillery from the ornament shop
Margaret Hurge
Greasy Joe the burger man
Filthy Stan the motor man
Fat Ron
Butcher Fred
Bob Gretchum & Sons Building and Clearance
The bus driver from yesterday
Others

Fair play to em, you might say. A public house is just that—a place where any old fucker can walk in off the street and park his arse for a couple of hours' swilling. But I hadn't ever seen these cunts in the Pry in all me borned days. Not ever. So the question as to why they was here now had us scratching me head like a mangy tomcat. Specially that Margaret Hurge, who, while being a fine example of the fairer sex in advanced years—what with her tits and all—were still a bird when all's said and sorted. I mean, I don't mind the odd bird coming in to brighten the place up now and then, but not mouthy old ones like her. The Paul Pry is a place for your working feller, not birds on their own account and posh folk.

And that had us recalling about the Doc, who were meant to be there and all. But weren't.

And nor were the wedge I'd had in me back pocket.

'Er,' I says, trying all me other pockets. I knew I had a bit left from what the Doc had bunged us. And I could have swore I'd lent a brownie off of Don back there at the old Hoppers. But I'd changed me strides since then, and like a cunt I seem to have left the sheets in the other uns.

'Put it on me slate, Nathan,' I says all casual.

'See that sign?' he says, poking thumb over shoulder. 'NO CREDIT. And even if we did give credit, I wouldn't give it you. You've yet to prove yerself, young man.'

The fucking cheeky fucker, that's all I could say. Not that I said it though. I just thought it. What I actually says were: 'But, er...'

'Aaarrggh,' comes a voice behind us. I turned arse to find the Doc staggering from door to bar, clutching his chest.

'You all right there, Dr Geldin'?' says Gromer, the miserable cunt from the offy.

'It's his heart,' says old Mr Fillery. 'He's havin' heart attack.'

'He's not havin' a blummin' heart attack,' says Gromer. 'Are you, Dr Geldin'?'

'Just shut up, the both of yers.' It's Margaret Hurge now, getting up and pulling out a chair for the Doc. 'Can't you see he's just out of puff? There now, Doctor, you sit yerself here.' She forced him down by the shoulders then turned on the other two again. 'Why don't you help the poor man, instead of dancin' on his poor grave? Heart attack...I dunno where you gets it, really I do not.'

'Don't start on us, Marge,' goes Gromer. 'I—'

'I *told* you to *shut up*.'

The Doc were up again, not looking quite so rough now. 'Many thanks, Mrs Hurge,' he says, 'but if you'll excuse—'

'You'll stay there till you starts breathin' proper,' she says, shoving him back and tugging off his jacket.

'But I just need to go to the, er...the gents. If you'll pardon the, er...'

'I told you to—'

'Leave him, Marge.' This were Nathan, stood arms folded by the peanuts, making his will be known. And it done the trick and all, Marge backing down and the Doc slipping all quiet bogward. Mind you, I hadn't ever known it not to come to pass, Nathan's will.

I heard the bog doors creaking shut, then noticed a little movement from Nathan in me peripherals. As I gave him my attention Burt banged his fist down on the bartop, knocking me pint over. Most of the lager went behind the bar, while the empty vessel rolled the other way and smashed on the floor in front of us.

I looked at him. He were still giving it the big one, but it weren't working now. Summat had woke up in us and I didn't feel such a wanker no more. Cos that's what I'd been, letting him and Doug and Nathan push us around. A fucking wanker.

But not no more.

They was dealing with Royston Blake, hardest pound-for-pound doorman in the Mangel area. And it's time I reminded em of it. So that's what I done, saying to Burt:

'You stupid fuckin'—'

Burt had us pushed back over the bartop with his paws on me throat before I could call him what I'd had in mind. He were a swift mover for an older feller, and I were happy this weren't coming to pass in his caff, him with one of his chopping knifes. He were handy all right, but so were I. And I were lairyer than him and all. You don't get lairyer than I were, just then.

I gritted me ivories and swung a left on Burt's ear.

It didn't make hardly no difference, other than to make him blink a bit. I couldn't fucking believe it. All right, it weren't an ideal thump from that angle but it were still one of mine. I roared and threw meself sideways. He tried keeping hold me throat, but I bent over, feeling his nails scratch me skin as he lost grip. I turned sharpish, glass crunching underboot. He'd not get another chance like that.

I fucking had him now.

'You won't get another chance like that,' I says. 'I fu—'

He were at us again, bearing down fast with his big arms open like a grizzly bastard. He put em around us, pinning me left arm down before I could get it up. Being a big feller meself I didn't have much experience of getting hugged hard, but let me tell you, I were making up for it now. His arms worked like a big jubilee clip, getting tighter and tighter with no chance of a let-up in sight. His big face were right up against mine and all, lips peeled back and gnashers on parade. So all in all it were well fucking lucky, Doug slipping us that monkey wrench just now.

I got it out me right pocket and twocked him.

His face changed but his arms took a while to go slack, and when they did he sort of leaned against us instead of going backwards, like I'd have preferred him to in an ideal world. But he went down, whatever way you paints it.

The Paul Pry were silent. You could have heard a mouse scratching his bollocks. Everyone were stood up, looking down at Burt. One or two of em chucked a quick eyeball in my direction and all, but nothing to latch onto.

After about a minute Nathan the barman rubs his chin and goes: 'Hmmmm.'

• • •

DOCTOR:	*You've been in trouble with the law, quite a few times.*
PATIENT:	[does not respond]
DOCTOR:	*It's not unfair to say you have a disregard for authority, is it?*
PATIENT:	[does not respond. Seems more interested in his fingernails.]
DOCTOR:	*You're a criminal.*
PATIENT:	*Fuck off.*
DOCTOR:	*You don't like being called that, a criminal?*
PATIENT:	*It's cos I ain't one, not cos I don't like it.*
DOCTOR:	*How aren't you a criminal? Your police record is enormous. Theft, burglary, assault, murder...*
PATIENT:	*Fuck off—I ain't done no murder.*

DOCTOR: *That's right—no murder convictions. I apologise. But you've been involved in murder on more than one occasion, even if you never actually committed it, or were never convicted.*

PATIENT: *So what? Loads of fellers is.*

DOCTOR: *Involved in murder?*

PATIENT: *Course. Folks gets killed. Other folks is near em when it happens, so...*

DOCTOR: *Is that what happened with you? You were nearby when people got killed?*

PATIENT: *Aye.*

DOCTOR: *That's unlucky.*

PATIENT: *You're telling me, mate.*

DOCTOR: *Royston, you can tell me the truth. Whatever you say to me in here—in this soundproofed room—will remain forever a secret.*

PATIENT: *Oh aye.*

DOCTOR: *It's true. I'm legally bound to ensure absolute confidentiality, as long as it's something you tell me about in here, as part of our one-to-ones.*

PATIENT: *Don't care. I told you the truth already.*

DOCTOR: *Come on, Royston. It must feel good, getting away with all those major crimes. It's not as if anyone innocent was hurt, after all. It's not as if you did wrong. You were just doing what you had to, were you not?*

PATIENT: [nods briefly, then quickly turns it into a shrug]

DOCTOR: *Well, I wish I had the wherewithal to do what I know I should do, sometimes. The fact is, Royston, most men are just not up to it. I think it takes a certain kind of man.*

PATIENT: *You're right there, Doc. And it takes a certain*
             kind of shite-for-brains to talk about it to the like
             of you.

• • •

'See?' I couldn't see him, but I knew it were Doug who says that.
I'd know his voice in a barn full of distraught cows. 'You see now?'

'I ain't convinced,' says Gromer. 'He used an implement. Anyone can use an implement. Can't they, Alv?'

'Right you is, boss,' says Alvin.

'All he done were make the most of his resources,' says Doug.
'I told you he were up to it, and now there's yer proof.'

'I still ain't convinced,' says Gromer. 'What about you,
Nathan?'

'Hmmm.'

'There's no hmmmin' about it,' says Doug. 'The man's a warrior, just like the prophecy says. Ain't he, Alv?'

'Right you is, boss,' says Alvin.

Marge spun in her chair and pointed at him, hissing: 'Shut
up, you.'

'Iss no use pointin' yer finger at Alvin, hissin', "Shut up, you,"'
says Doug. 'He's speakin' plain truth. And Berty would have
agreed with us and all, if he'd—'

'Shush it,' says Nathan, nodding up the way.

The Doc were coming back, rubbing hands on trousers. 'The
hand dryer seems to be...er...' He stopped a couple of yard short
of Burt and goes: 'What's the...um...'

'Fell off his stool,' says Nathan.

'Doctor,' says Marge, hauling him the last couple of yard and
shoving him Burtward. 'Have a look at him, will yer? We think
he's had a bump. The rest of you, come over here.'

They all follered her over the far side of the Paul Pry and huddled in the corner, leaving the Doc, Burt, Nathan, and meself in the bar vicinity.

'Hmmm,' says Nathan as he came from behind the bar and went to join em.

The Doc weren't happy about summat. 'Er...' he says looking over at them others. 'What are you—'

But they couldn't have heard him. Or perhaps they weren't arsed about him. Anyhow, they ignored him. He let his shoulders drop and moved towards Burt, still eyeing them up t'other end and saying: 'Most odd, most odd.'

I sat meself stoolwise and put elbow to bartop. I wanted a pint summat chronic. Specially since finding out I'd been drinking mild just there. I fucking hated mild. Me old feller used to drink it, and he were a cunt. But there were no Nathan there to serve us just now. And if he were there he wouldn't even give us a pint o' piss, unless I paid him.

'Doc,' I says.

He looked up from fiddling with Burt's eyelids and goes: 'Huh? Oh, Royston. I'll, er...I'll explain it all to you in a—'

'Nah I'm just sayin' like—'

'Please, Royston. Now is not the—'

'But—'

'Oh, all right,' he says, leaving Burt's eyelids be. He got up slow, like old fellers do, and parked himself on a chair. All the while he's saying: 'You wanted to know why I encouraged you to come here tonight, yes? Well, *they* came to *me*, these people. Several weeks ago. I knew I had to get you into a reputable job if I was going to release you, but I had a torrid time finding one for you. People just aren't interested in rehabilitating their fellow citizens, Royston. It's a terrible state of affairs, and it makes me ashamed to be a human being, it really does. But anyway, I received a call from this, er...'

He dropped his voice, looking over his shoulder and finding them others to be huddled together and conversing quite happily, except for the shouting.

'Yes, I was called by the gentlemen over there, introducing himself as "Nathan the barman." And he said...he said, er...ah yes, he said that, like me, he had your best interests at heart. He said there were a good number of people concerned about your future, you being a former pillar of the community, fallen on hard times, and so on. And to cut a long story short, Royston, they, er...'

'Aye all right, Doc,' I says. 'But can you lend us a twenty, like?' Cos Nathan were coming back now and I were fucking gasping for a pint.

The Doc rubbed the sides of his head, squeezing his eyes shut. Then he says: 'What?'

'Twenty,' I says, a bit quieter now on account of Nathan being earshotwise, and me having pride. I went over to the Doc and whispers: 'Ten'll do if you can't manage it.'

'Oh...yes. Er...' He got his wallet out.

'So how's this un here?' says Nathan, toe-poking Burt in the thigh. Marge glared at him. But not even she were so barmy as to have a go at Nathan.

'What?' says the Doc, looking up. He had a few notes out so I swiped em out of his paw before folks noticed. Seventy sheets—not bad. 'Oh yes, this injured gentleman here. Well, I can't seem to—'

'Fer cryin' out flamin' loud, Doc,' says Nathan, losing his rag a bit. 'Is you or is you not a medical man? Flippin' heck...'

'Well actually...'

Nathan were behind the bar now, pulling a pint. He plonked it full of lager right in front of us. 'Blakey? This un here's fer you, to say no hard feelin's.'

I sunk it in one and says: 'Can I have another?'

'Comrades,' he shouts, making us nearly drop me empty. The others had been murmuring amongst emselves just now, but they stopped and harked what the barman, Nathan, had to say.

'We all knows why we are gathered here today. This ain't the first time we've assembled thusly in this here tavern. No, there's been many an evenin' of late where we've argued hither and thither about the troubles our town has been havin', and to be fair on ourselves we have indeed come to one or two conclusions. And then there's the evenin's after that, when we tossed it to and fro as to what ought to be done about them aforestations. And now here we are in the present day, gettin' summat done at last. Which brings us to young Blakey here.'

'Nathan,' I says, leaning on the bar and waving a twenty. 'Can I have a pint o' lager, mate?'

'We've all had our doubts,' he ploughs on, ignoring us. 'Reasonable doubts, I might say. Iss plain to see the kind of a man Blakey here is, the things he's got up to and sullied his character with. But prophecies is prophecies, and there's no arguin' with em. And now we've all decided—up yonder in that corner just now—that we'll go with em. And it's the prophecies I'm on about there. So—Royston Blake is indeed our man.'

I got a smoke out and lit it, eyeing the row of optics behind Nathan and deciding—quite rightly—that whisky were the only one of em for me. Lager and whisky fulfils all a feller's needs in terms of drinking. He goes for one or t'other depending on which way his flag is flying—up or down or left or right or arsewise. Just then, what with one thing or another, I truly felt mine to be flying every which way at once. But mostly arsewise, what with the tragedy that had befell our little Royston, and me hearing about it only just now. 'Hey, Nathan, can I have a—'

'We've got work for him to do,' he announces to everyone but meself. 'That's what this comes down to. Hard graft is the only way we'll get this town of ours back to where she ought to be.'

'And valour.'

'Eh? Who says that?'

'Me,' says Doug. 'Hard work and valour, I were sayin'.'

'You say what you likes in your own place of business. This here's mine and I'll do the talkin'.' Nathan had got a mug of tea from somewhere and he took a sip of it, shooting eye piss at Doug all the while. 'Anyhow,' he says, wiping his tash and turning the piss tap off. 'Like I were sayin' just now before wossname over there, it's hard work and valour that'll get Mangel straight again. And Blakey here is our man fer the job. A job which, fer the moment, entails keepin' door at the Porter Wossname Centre, or whatever they—'

'I ain't doin' that no more,' I says.

That shut the bastard up. He stopped talking his shite and gave us his full and undivided, which were rightfully mine anyhow, me being a punter and him a barman.

'Pint o' lager an' a large whisky, please,' I says.

Nathan glared at us and kept his counsel for a bit, then picked his mug up and had a sip.

'Give him his malt,' says someone behind us.

Another goes: 'Not the other, mind.' I think it were Doug. 'Ale is the fruit of hard labour, and he ain't done none yet.'

'Some say he never will.'

'Aye.'

'Aye.'

'Shut up, the lot o' yers,' hollers Nathan. 'Blake, explain yerself.'

I shrugged at him. It really were quite simple. 'Well,' I says, 'I wants a pint with lager in it, an' another glass…a smaller un—'

'Not that, you fool. The other. Woss that about not keepin' door?'

'Oh, aye. I ain't keepin' no door no more, at that place,' I says. 'I fuckin' hates it.'

'Ah yes,' the Doc pipes up. 'This is as I told you, and why I, um…'

Nathan started pointing a finger but put it down again. 'All due respect to a medical man,' he says instead. 'But kindly mind yer own, which this ain't.'

'Look,' I says. Cos I'd fucking had enough of this. 'I ain't keepin' door at no wossname place no more. I tried it an' I hates it. Now, is you servin' us here or what? Cos I'm dry as a fuckin' lime basket, an' if you ain't servin'—'

'Mind yer language, ladies bein' present.'

'Right,' I says, sliding off me stool. 'Fuck this, I'm off.'

I turned and went to go, but they was all blocking me passage, glaring at us like I were a naughty youngun and they was wanker teachers. 'Raaagh,' I roars, showing em me fists. That done the trick all right, and a causeway opened up to take us right through to the back door. 'Ragh,' I goes again as I went past em, making Gromer flinch, and shite himself like as not. And not one of em dared so much as open his gob.

All except the one, just as I put paw to handle.

'Blakey,' says Nathan. 'I'll do you a deal.'

I stopped. You had to stop if Nathan addressed you, him being him. 'Oh aye?'

'Aye. A good one. An offer you can't very well naysay, as the sayin' goes. Now, come back here.'

'I can hark you from here. Spill it.'

'Come here.'

There comes a moment in every man's life where he goes one way or t'other. And depending on which he goes, he's either fucked or flying, henceforth. This here were my moment, I can see now, looking back at it. I could have:

1. gone back to hear Nathan's offer, or
2. went on out into the cold Mangel night air.

'Go on then,' I says half a minute later, sliding back on me stool. 'Woss this offer?'

Nathan screwed up his eyes. He looked at us so hard I could smell me eyelashes singeing. Then he done same to the Doc, who were a speccy feller so his lashes was protected, like. Then he looks at us again, licking his tash.

'So you admires a Ford Granada, does you?'

8

PORTER CENTRE: "A CARING, SHARING PLACE"

by a staff reporter

[pictured: Cecil Porter, managing director of the Porter Centre (left), with Royston Blake]

It was all smiles at the Porter Centre yesterday as Managing Director Cecil Porter introduced his latest employee, Royston Blake. Perhaps more familiar to Informer *readers for his involvement in several high-profile crimes over the years, Blake has spent the past four years sectioned at Parpham Mental Hospital, recovering from severe drug-induced psychosis. He was released back into the community only days ago, and has just been recruited as the Porter Centre's front-of-house customer flow manager.*

"I wanted to send a message to the whole of Mangel," said Mr Porter. "The Porter Centre is very much a part of the Mangel community. We are here for everyone, as a service and an employer. Royston here has been through some tough times, and people may have made judgements about him. But we at the Porter Centre are not here to judge. Our job is to welcome one and all—including Royston."

Mr Blake declined to comment.

I had to admit, it were nice hearing the jangle of keys in me pocket again. Even if it did mean I'd have to go to work on the morrer. I could drive there, couldn't I. I could drive to work in a plush executive motor, even if I had to stand on the door of a big fucking shop all day, like a cunt.

A cunt with a Ford Granada Mk2 3-litre GL, mind.

There'd been a bit more to the deal and all, other than staying on as doorman at the new place. Nathan had mentioned summat about being ready to stand up and be counted on a particular day in the none-too-distant, date to be confirmed. The fucker wouldn't give us no more details. 'Wouldn't want to worry your ugly head,' he'd said with a wink at the time. Aye, they all found that amusing, besides meself. Fuck em though, cos I weren't interested in knowing anyhow.

I thought about all that as I smoked fags and yomped homeward up the hill, and for a while it kept me swede away from them other thoughts. And you knows the ones I'm on about there. My hopes and dreams of being a family man, tore up to ribbons and tossed in the gutter with the dog muck and used johnnies.

Poor little Royston.

I couldn't get over it, no matter how much I told meself fate had dealt the lad a lucky hand really, getting him out of the game sharpish while the rest of us grinds on and on, knowing we'll always get beat in the end. I couldn't believe the seed I'd planted on this here earth of ours had withered up and died on us. And the worst bit of it were that there was no one to blame. The poor bugger had coughed and carked it of his own accord.

And there ain't no arguing with that.

As I neared our road, flicking me fifth fag butt at a passing cat, I tried gearing meself up for the big moment when I turned key and fired me own engine up. Cos make no mistake, mate—this were a landmark moment in the history of motoring in Mangel. I could see the headline in tomorrer's paper:

BLAKE IN "NOT A FORD CAPRI" SHOCK

Royston Blake, local legend and former head doorman and manager of Hoppers Wine Bar & Bistro, has been spotted in town driving a car that is not a Ford Capri. The sensational news was first reported by PC Jonah of Mangel Police Force, and later verified by his boss, Big Bob Cadwallader. They claimed to have seen Blake driving a Ford Granada, which is at the top end of your executive motor market.

The news was so extraordinary that both coppers were subjected to a breath test, administered by police scientists Dr G. Gumb and Dr B. Wimmer. 'Bri here saw Blake in the Granada as well, on his way in this morning. Didn't you, Bri?'

'No,' replied Dr Wimmer.

'That's right. So we knew the two coppers hadn't been lying. But they both failed their tests anyhow, so we've had em locked up.'

Blake, who is now a top executive who smokes expensive cigars and has a healthy young son called Royston Blake Junior, was far too busy to comment.

I snapped out of it when I noticed I were at the end of our street. The Granada were still there and I were pleased about that, cos there's no saying for how long a motor will stay put in the Mangel area. But no matter how hard I tried telling meself otherwise, I couldn't get excited over it. I went over to it and let meself in, sliding meself for the first time into that big driver's arse bucket and not giving much of a toss about it.

I sat there for a bit, looking up yonder at the front door I used to call me own. It were still mine in the eyes of the law, course. But not in the eyes of Royston Blake. I couldn't see meself going in there ever again, not even to kick our Sal out. And, to be honest, I weren't sure why. It took two fags before the answer came to us:

I'd lost me own son on account of that house. All I'd ever wanted were a boy in me own image, a lad who I'd lead up the correct path and watch him blossom into a strong, rock-hard young feller who took shite off no fucker, and could have anyone in a fight. And that had been took away from us, cos of that house.

How so? I harks you saying.

I'll tell you how the fuck so.

The ways of the world is a finely balanced state of affairs, and a conker falling here results in a pigeon taking off somewhere else. See, I'd knocked off me old feller, hadn't I, in that house over there. I'd put me boot on his shoulder and sent him down the stair, him landing headwise and thereby taking his leave from this world. Long time previous, but such things as that don't get forgot, and when the time comes, the balance will be righted.

I tops an old feller, I loses a young lad.

The world goes on, happy as Larry.

Meanwhile Royston Blake ain't going in that house ever again.

Cos when you thought about it, right, every piece of shite ever happened to us had been spawned out of that house. I'd took a wife into it and then lost her, bless her charred remains. I'd hid a dead body in there the once and some cunt comes along and swipes him, thereby fucking it all up and kicking up a storm of shite somewhere else, headed for you-knows-who. There's also the tale of them little sweets I ate the one time, a sad story what ended in yet more heartbreak.

So no, if there's one thing I were set on doing, it's steering clear of that there abode. A cursed house, it were. And I'd had enough of curses.

I were brooding on the whole affair when that selfsame door opened, and out comes the feller from earlier—the one I'd done over.

• • •

DOCTOR: *I'd like to try talking about your dad again. I really think this is an area worth…Royston? Royston, where are you going?*

• • •

Ferret, I think his name were.

I'd forgot all about him at the time, things overtaking emselves, as they is so liable to do at such moments. So, Sal had got him kipping in my pit and giving her one while I'd been in the ozzy, had he?

The fucking slag.

I ought to go up there and kick her out is what I ought to do.

But I never.

Summat stopped us. I couldn't see what it were at the time, but it came clear a bit later. (And I'll tell you about it when I gets to that bit.)

Instead I watched the Ferret feller climb into a pissy yellow Viva Estate and turn her over for half a minute until she caught. He pulled out and I ducked before his headlights hit us. Sticking me swede up again I clocked him turning left towards town. Then I put key to slot and fired up the Granada. Ah, the rumble of your own V6 ticker. A satisfying sound like no other. And here were the perfect opportunity to give her a test run.

I went after the Ferret.

Fuck knows where he were headed. For a while there, when he struck the Barkettle Road and kept on it, I thought him bound for Hurk Wood North. That had us thinking all kinds of dire thoughts, that place having played a pivotal role in my own personal history prior to this bit of it. And then I got to considering him as a true ferret. A proper furry one, like. It got so I were picturing him stopping Hurkside and scuttling off into the undergrowth, hunting for small woodland varmints and that. By the time I'd put a stop to that line of thinking—by slapping meself hard quite a few times—I noticed he were gone from his position two cars up from us. And it were only by chance, sailing past Beaver Lane, that I clocked the telltale flash of piss yellow under a street lamp down there.

I went to pull a U-ey but a fucking Avenger coming the other way blocked us. I stopped just in time, and it's lucky I still had me driving reflexes after all the time away from the wheel. The other feller weren't so sharp, mind you, and he swerved late and ploughed into a bus stop. As I went past I let down me leccy window and told him how you never ought to swerve, cos swerving in traffic is for birds and arse bandits. Use your brakes next time, and grow some bollocks, you fucking poof. It were too dark to see the driver and he didn't say nothing back, but I knew he'd harked us, and he knew I were right.

Other motors was honking us now, so I flicked em a big V out the window and pulled into Beaver Lane. I'd lost Ferret now and I were well pissed off. There's always a cunt to get in your way, no matter how careful you is. But he couldn't have got far. Beaver Lane and the few other streets adjoining made up the Danghill district, and there were nowhere leading off it. So all I had to do were go up and down, keeping me peepers open. It were odd that he'd come here though. Danghill were the poshest bit of Mangel. Only your community pillars lived out this way. And what would a piece of shite like him be doing fraternising with them? As I turned into Chugg Avenue, scratching me swede, I clocked him.

He were in a phone box on the corner there, handset to ear. His back was to us so I turned round a bit further up and pulled in behind a Jag (which were the only motor roadside, Danghill being a neighbourhood of driveways and garages and that). He couldn't see us but I could see him, what with the lamppost there on the corner. His right eye were swelled up summat chronic, and you could see how knacked his hooter were from thirty yard off, which is the distance between him and meself, or thereabouts. Fuck knows how many times I'd hit him back there, but he looked to have had a good battering, which I found to be quite a pleasant thought. But the pleasure in admiring your own handiwork wears off after a bit, and soon I were looking at me watch and trying to ignore the whining coming from me guts, me having had no dinner. Cos I didn't really have to be here, when you thought about it. I'd already slapped him about for poking our Sal in my absence, and I couldn't see how more of the same would help. But just as I went to fire her up again things started hotting up in the phone box.

Ferret were sort of jabbing the air. Looked a bit odd at first it did, then I heard him shouting and realised he were having a go at someone down the blower. The hollering weren't so loud that I could pick the words out, apart from a couple of unmistakable uns like 'wanker' and 'cunt.' But it sounded good anyhow, and it's against a doorman's nature to walk away when bother's up. After a bit he slammed the blower down, sparked a fag, and came out of the box.

He didn't look half so aggravated now. Looked proper smug with himself as it happens, smirking and looking up and down the road and blowing smoke out into the cold night air. And you had to admire him in a way, smiling on while his face were all bust up from only a few hours prior. You couldn't admire him too much, mind, cos when you looked at him for a bit he did actually look a lot like a ferret. And anyone who bears a resemblance to a rodent cannot be trusted, in my book. Nor no one else's.

After he'd had a good look left and right and everywhere else he turned arse and carried on up Beaver Lane, like as not to where his motor were parked. I were glad of that cos me guts was nigh on eating emselves, and all the while there's seventy quid and change smouldering away in me pocket, awaiting expenditure. I went to fire the Granada up.

Then I harked summat.

A garden gate clanking shut, a little ways behind us.

I went like a statue. I were pleased about that cos it were the old reflex kicking in. I'd been out Danghill way many a time previous but only on robbing trips, long long ago. The place were a big burglary centre, far as I gave a toss, huge detached houses every which way and each of em like a big present waiting for the unwrapping. And the first thing you learns on the rob is to go statue-like if you harks summat. You can move your eyes and your innards but fuck all else besides. I moved mine to the right. (Me eyes, not me innards. But the way they was grinding and grumbling I wouldn't be shocked to find them going sideways and all.)

I kept them peepers pointed roadside, hearing the slip slap of a feller coming up the way over there. You can tell a lot about a feller from his footslapping, and this one here weren't an old cadger out with his Jack Russell for a Woodbine and a piss up the wall. This feller weren't old, and it were more of a click clack than a slip slap, like he were narked about summat. I kept me eyes straining to the right until he became visible, clacking right past us in his boots and dressing gown and jimjams. And fuck if it ain't the little boss feller from earlier—how'd he call himself again?

He walked up to the corner where Ferret had been just now. Couple of yards this side of the phone box were a rubbish bin. He stopped next to it, looking all over and reaching inside his nice tartan dressing gown. He pulled out a big brown envelope, dropped it in the bin, and fucked off. Three strides away he turned and went back to the bin, flobbed in it, and stomped homeward with a face like a cobblestoned road surface.

Well, I thought. Who's I gonna see next? I'd only been here ten minute or so and already I'd clocked two faces known to us. All right, Ferret didn't count cos I'd followed him here. But the little boss feller there were pure chance, a genuine turn-up for yer trousers, like. And what the fuck were his game, dropping gear in public bins? Didn't they have their own bins in them posh houses? And what's the flob all about? Don't posh folk flob on the floor like everyone else?

I ain't thick, you know. I knows he'd come out here because he had summat to offload that he didn't want folks in his own house finding. An old grot mag, like as not. Aye, it had to be that. In fact I'd not be surprised if it were one o' them filthy uns, with the whips and chains and that. I'd heard about them. Others and all, worse uns. Finney'd told us about one he'd found in a skip once with folks pissing and cacking on each other in it. How about that, eh?

I stubbed me fag, thinking how lucky I'd been here. You can't beat a bit of filth on the boss. And if I played me cards right I'd have him promoting us to a proper managerial position before you knew it. And it had all come from tailing the ferret out here.

That's how your providence works, sometimes. You goes down a road cos you can't be arsed doing otherwise, and lo and behold—there's a crock of gold at the end.

Or an old grot mag your boss has dumped, pages stuck together and everything.

I went to open the door, hoping it wouldn't be a mag with arse bandits in it cos I didn't wanna even see such a thing, much less pick it up. But me fingers froze on the handle. I could hear someone coming along behind us again. And it were different this time. Not the narky clacking of wossname just now but your more typical slip slapping, like a feller out for a stroll. A bit later he pulls alongside and it's Ferret again, gone round the block like as not. He stopped by the bin and reached into it, picking up the envelope and grimacing at the flob on it. He wiped the envelope on his strides, then opened it up for a peek inside. A flash of smirk and he's off again into the Beaver Road, tucking the envelope into his coat.

I sat scratching me swede and smoking for a bit. Then I got out and went over to the bin. As I were peering inside, still swede-scratching, his Viva went past on the Beaver Lane headed town-ward. I ran back and went to fire the Granada up, but she fucking stalled on us. By the time I pulled into the Barkettle Road he were long gone.

• • •

'I'm just disappointed.'

It were nice to have someone to talk to for a change, but I just wished it weren't the Doc. I were grateful for him giving us

117

his motor and all, but I were getting well sick of him. Plus I were in public now, on show, like. Everyone going in and out of the Wossname Centre knew Royston Blake. And like as not they knew where I'd spent the four years previous. So it didn't look good, me standing there getting an earful from the medical man. It were like I were still his patient. And I weren't.

I were a free man. And the only reason I were still doing this shite job is cos of the Granada.

'Half an hour late is not good enough. You'll get in trouble. And you *must not* lose this job, Royston. Not after the sacrifice I made. I gave you my car, Royston. Do you realise what that—'

'Fuckin' calm it,' I says to him, looking over his shoulder at a well-fit housewife coming through the doors just then. I could have swore I'd shagged her going back a while, but she were pushing a pram now. I winked at her as she went past and had a gander in the pram.

'Get away from him,' yelled the bird at us, slapping me paw off the pram. 'Don't you come near us, you…you…'

'All right, doll,' I says. I couldn't quite recall her name, but it didn't matter cos she weren't so fit close up anyhow. And her youngun were just a young babby, no more than a year old. Been seven year back at least when I'd poked his mam, so this un here couldn't be mine. And I think she'd made us wear a johnny anyhow. 'Just meetin' an' greetin' like.'

'Fuck off,' she says over her shoulder.

I watched her storm off into the tog shop over there, wondering what I were meant to have done.

'And look at the state of you,' goes the Doc. 'What happened to your trousers here?'

'Get off us,' I says, swatting him away. I can't abide folks messing with me togs. The Doc ought to have knowed that. 'Oh, soz, Doc,' I says, helping him onto his feet again.

'Never mind that,' he says, swatting us right back. And fair play to him. 'I'm quite used to your lack of muscular restraint. But you must understand—you've got to smarten yourself up for a job like this. You're the first person a customer sees when they come here.' He looked behind him then says, voice low: '*Please*, Royston. I'm just trying to help you. I just want to see you getting on, because...I...'

'Aye, all right, Doc,' I says, getting me fags out.

'Put those away,' he says as I went to get one out. 'You can't smoke here.' The Doc never stayed pissed off for long, and sure enough he were soft as cushions a moment later. 'Look, I don't want to keep on at you, but could you just tidy yourself up before coming in tomorrow? See about some new trousers, too. And lay off the tobacco whilst on duty. You know what the deal is, Royston—if you want to keep the car you must stay in the job. That's not so hard, is it?'

'Nah,' I says with a smile. 'Piece o' piss.'

'Good man,' he says, slapping me shoulder and heading off.

'Fuckin' tosser,' I says, sparking one up. How'd he expect us to tidy meself up when I were dossing in a motor? Mind you, the Granada weren't half spacious as a temporary place of abode. I'd kipped in the old Capri once or twice, and let me tell you, the Granada's like a hotel by comparison. Still didn't have a sink though. Or a bog. I'd parked her up by the river last night and gone for a morning dump in the trees there. Far from ideal, but at least I got to splash me face in the water, although I fell in a bit and me boots was still wet and stony cold.

'Hiya, Blake.'

'Ah…all right, Rache.'

I forgot about all me cold feet. Rache looked bloody marvellous. Watching her walk up to us like that—all swinging hips and nice clothes and pretty smiles—were like coming out of a stormy winter's night into a warm house, with a table laden full of scran and ale, a fire blazing, and Bing Crosby singing 'White Christmas' on the record player. I smiled right back at her. To be honest I wanted to take her in me arms and give her a big kiss. But it were early days for that and I didn't wanna push her.

'I'm all in a flap,' she says.

She didn't look in a flap. 'A flap?' I says.

'Aye, got me interview in a minute. I couldn't get away from the caff. It's a nightmare there this mornin'. Burt's off sick, see.'

'Burt?' I says. 'Off sick?'

'Aye. He's at the hospital gettin' his head patched up. Madge says he walked into a door last night and split it open.'

I frowned and goes: 'Split the door open?'

'No, silly. The head. He split his head open.'

'Oh.' Poor old Burt. First I knocks him out in the Paul Pry, then he goes home and walks into a door, cracking his swede. 'Poor old Burt,' I says. 'One thing after another with him, ennit? And they says them things happens in threes.'

'Threes? Why, what else happened?'

'Ah, well…'

My sharp mind kicked in and I stopped meself there. Wouldn't do no good going into the happenings of last night, in the Pry. I'd tried thinking about em meself this morning while I were having the dump, and I couldn't make head nor arse of em. From where I'd been stood, everyone in Mangel had gone barmy. But telling all that to Rache would just confuse the poor girl, her all set for her interview and that. And Burt wouldn't appreciate us telling everyone I'd floored him.

'Oh, nuthin,' I says instead.

She looked at us funny, then says: 'Anyhow, I gotta go, else I'll be late. And I can't be late for this. I really want this, Blakey.' You could see she were well nervous but still smiling, which overall didn't half look good on her. 'Wish us luck.'

'I can do better'n that,' I says, leaning in and giving her a peck on the cheek. I felt like doing a lot more. Specially when I got a whiff of her perfume and a brush of her soft skin. But like I says—I didn't want to push her and spoil it. Not just yet anyhow.

She went to bat us away but gave us that smile instead.

'I'd give you a job all right,' I says, winking at her.

'Oh yeah? Doin' what?'

I looked around to make sure no one were listening, but when I turned back she were off. 'Tell us later,' she says over her shoulder.

'Don't you worry about that,' I says all quiet. Me cock were starting to throb a bit so I put a paw in me pocket to pin him sideways. 'Good luck,' I shouted after her. But it were too late and I'd already lost sight of her.

I leant on the wall and looked at a half-starkers dummy in the window of that tog shop up there, thinking about Rache and rubbing meself.

9

'You fuckin' what?'

I already told you how much I hated this job. And the reasons is plain obvious. Weren't cos I saw it as a comedown. It weren't a comedown, when you examined it. See, I'd been front door security at Hoppers all me grafting life prior to then. And, Hoppers being by tradition Mangel's premier night spot, you could truthfully say I were at the centre of things of an eve, and the happiness of the entire Mangel drinking community was dependent on my yay or otherwise. And it weren't so different here, once you spent a while clocking all the faces going in and out the Wossname Centre. See, the place were quite clearly still the centre of things. But in a different way now, and at a different time of day.

And here I were again, controlling it all.

'I says you ain't gettin' in,' I says. 'You deaf or summat?'

But like I says, I simply fucking hated the job. And I'll tell you for why:

No action.

What's the point of being a doorman if you can't get a bit of exercise? All I'd done so far is stand there like a wanker, nodding off every now and then. There's no call for my services cos no one fucks about in the usual way. No fights to break up, no pissed-up lads to turn out, no one having a go. To be frank with you, I couldn't see the point in us being there.

Which is where Danny here comes in.

'Fuck off, you,' he says, trying to get around us. 'I'm comin' in. Move aside.'

Danny and meself had a bit of history, see. He'd fallen foul of my own particular brand of doormanship, you might say. I can't recall when it were, but one evening he were in Hoppers giving Rache some grief (her being head barmaid back then). I heard the row behind us and, it being otherwise quiet just then, tuned meself in to it. He were saying how he'd gave her a twenty, when Rache were calling it a tenner. It's an old favourite, and I've pulled it off meself many a time over the years. The secret is keep your peepers on theirs and don't back down. That's *your* twenty sheets you handed over and you ain't shifting for no fucker till you gets your rightful change. Aye, it's a nice little scam all right.

But not in Hoppers it ain't.

I gave him a chance. If possible you should always give em a chance. I went up to the bar all casual and friendly like, and quietly put a paw on his shoulder, saying summat like: 'You all right there, pal?'

'Aye I'm all right. Iss *her* though. She fuckin' robbed us, the cow. I wants me—'

No one calls our Rache a cow. Rache were the best pound-for-pound barmaid in the whole of the Mangel, and she weren't no cow. I got Danny by the hair and dragged him out. When I got him outside I gave him a slap and banned him for life.

'Woss you on about?' he says, back in the present day, outside the Wossname Centre, after I'd reminded him of all this. 'I ain't banned. I ain't even been here more than once or twice. This ain't Hoppers no more, you know.'

'Go on,' I says, pushing him away gentle. 'Get out of it.'

He must have trod on a lace or summat cos he went down, landing in the gutter and making a passing cyclist swerve and fall off.

I ignored all this, preferring to spark up a fag. I had a job to do, didn't I. A crowd was gathering so I stepped towards em, saying: 'Come on, shift.' They was birds, by and large, so I knew I wouldn't get no aggro off em. I hadn't accounted for the verbal sort, mind.

'You oughta be ashamed of yerself,' the one says, a plump blonde lass not much older than meself, though I'm sure I'd never shagged her cos she had a dimple in her chin making her look like Kirk Douglas, who I don't fancy. 'He never touched you.'

'He's banned,' I says, though you couldn't hear it cos Danny were bawling there in the gutter. That didn't stop the ladies though cos they can make emselves heard atop the loudest of dins. You could set a big bomb off and not miss a word from em.

'He's fuckin' banned,' I says again, louder this time. 'The cunt tried gettin' in just now so I stopped him.' You got to nip this kind of talk in the bud sharpish, see. I'd had problems with backchat in the past, and I weren't letting it get us again.

'Woss he banned for?'

'Never you mind. Come on, clear off. Get inside if you wants the shops, else fuck off. Go on…'

'Don't you swear at me. Did you hear him?' she says to her neighbour, a grey-haired bint in a beige raincoat with one o' them two-wheeled trolleys. 'The filthy tongue on him.'

'I know. I know,' says raincoat. 'Mind you, he only got out of Parpham not long ago, I read in the paper. What can you expect?'

'It's a scandal, employin' folks like him. Did you hear what he done before they sent him to Parpham?'

'I know. I know. Should have put him in proper jail though, shouldn't they.'

'Call an ambulance,' says another, a four-eyed bit with greasy brown hair who could have made a lot more of herself, if only she tried. She were kneeling beside Danny and the old feller who'd fell off his push-bike.

'Fuck off,' I says to her. 'They're all right. Leave em.'

'I think he's twisted his ankle,' she says. 'An' the elderly gentleman here can't get up.'

'For fuck sake,' I says, going over. 'I gotta do everythin' me fuckin' self, have I?'

I grabbed the old feller's arm and got him on his pins again in one crisp movement. The key is to do it before they're ready, see, else they'll pretend they can't stand up and make a fucking meal of it. But he were standing now, so he had to stay stood.

'Um…' says the speccy lass, 'I really don't think you—'

'I told you to fuckin' stay out of it.' Danny were still bawling like a cow watching her calf herded onto the truck. It were doing me head in, so I might have been just a touch rough with him. But then again I might not have. Anyhow, I got a two-pawed grip on his arm and yanked hard. That got him up all right, but his arm didn't half look funny. 'Hey,' I says to the speccy lass, pointing at Danny's arm and laughing. 'Look at his arm. It don't half—'

'You've dislocated it,' she says, though I couldn't hardly hear her cos Danny were sounding like the whole fucking herd of grieving cows now. 'Why didn't you just leave him be? You'll definitely have to call the ambulance now.'

'Bollocks,' I says, watching Danny go down again. 'He's fuckin' havin' you on. I hardly touched—'

'I'm a nurse. I know a popped shoulder when I see one. Are you gonna get the ambulance or not?'

'I already called one,' says a bird stood just behind us. 'On me mobile.'

'Yer what?' I says.

'Called coppers an' all,' she says, backing away from us.

'Oh for fuck's fuckin' sake,' I says. I couldn't have the coppers here. Danny and the old feller would tell fibs about us for surely, saying I'd knacked em on purpose. Then I'd lose me job and me new motor. And me freedom, like as not, the Doc telling em I'm on parole.

If I could only think straight I knew I'd be all right, just like all them times at Hoppers when I'd stopped a riot with a word here and a gesture there. I got a smoke out and lit it, trying hard to block out the row going on all around and concentrate on the matter in hand. Coppers, she'd said. She'd phoned the fucking coppers, the stupid fucking slag. I turned and glared at her, still thinking. It wouldn't do no good to chastise her now. What's done were done, and I had to handle it.

And I knew just how.

First I dealt with the old feller, who were still on his feet but teetering a bit. I hauled his bike upright and got him on it. Weren't easy cos his leg were well stiff and wouldn't go up very far, but I gave it a good yank and got it over. 'You're all right, mate,' I says to him in a soothing voice, planting his paws on the handles for him. His face were a picture, all watery eyes and gob agape. I think he might have had some specs before but I couldn't see em nowhere, and I didn't have time to fuck about with that anyhow. 'Here we go then,' I says, pushing him along a bit. 'Go on—pedal, you lazy fucker.' I'm always happy to help, but I expects the other feller to do his bit and all. 'Thass it, like that.' I were still holding him up and going at quite a pace now, and I knew I couldn't keep it up much longer. And besides, he were all right now. I gave him a last push and off he sailed, happy as fucking Larry. He were wobbling a bit and slowing down, so I yells after him: 'Push the fuckin' pedals.' And that saw him round the bend there and out of sight.

'See?' I says, going back to the crowd of birds. 'See? There's no fuckin' problem.'

I'd hoped seeing the old feller all right would make the birds happy enough to piss off, but it weren't happening. And I could see now that it wouldn't be happening until Danny here were sorted. He were wriggling on the deck and making a row like no other, speccy bird trying to keep him still. I stood over him, working it out.

'All right, love,' I says to the lass, nice and loud so the others could hear how polite I were being. 'Stand back.'

'But he—'

'Now now,' I says rolling him onto his side. 'I'm a trained professional.' And I were and all. First aid is a vital part of good doormanship. A lot of injuries can take place in pubs and clubs and there's no nurse or doctor to deal with em, so it falls to like of me. I'd dealt with all sorts over the years, right down to a lass who went into labour and popped a sprog right there in the birds' bogs at Hoppers. I didn't help with pulling it out, like, but I stood outside making sure no one else went in, so she could deal with it in peace. I let Rache in though cos she were staff, and I didn't want the bird damaging our bogs nor nothing. And afterwards I brung a nice pint of lager and lime, knowing how gruelling an ordeal sprogpopping can be. When I'd necked that I went and got half a cider for the lass. Mind you, I got another female to take it in cos it weren't half a mess in there, and a feller oughtn't to see that kind of mess.

Sprogs aside, I'd helped injured folks in all sorts of ways. And I knew just what Danny here required. I got his arm and pulled backwards on it with all me might, which is a considerable amount, I can tell you. Danny screamed to wake the dead, but I weren't letting that put us off. You can't break a chicken without making some eggs, after all, can you?

The speccy lass were shouting summat and all, which didn't help. Frankly I were surprised at her, cos a nurse ought to know not to interfere with a surgeon at his work. I told her as much, then went on pulling. I could feel a little give on the arm now and I knew I'd have it back in place soon. Speccy put her paws over Danny's gob to give us all a bit of peace, which I thought were a nice touch, and raised her in my estimation just a bit. But before I could tell her as much she hollers: 'It's his other arm. You've got the wrong arm.'

I stopped tugging and looked at it. 'Why didn't you fuckin' tell us?' I says, turning him over and starting anew. I were well narked about that. 'I could have bust his good arm, an' it would've been *your* flamin' fault.'

While I ticked her off the arm slotted home with a nice dull click. 'There you go—good as branny,' I says to Dan, pulling him arsewise. 'Now, less have a gander at this leg.'

But I knew I didn't have time. I could hear sirens in the distance and I still had all them women hanging about, which I didn't want. Plus Danny were still bawling. I slapped him hard and goes: 'One more peep an' I'll knock yer fuckin' teeth out, right?' Which shut him up finally.

Then I leaned down and whispered summat in his ear.

He took a couple of secs to think about it then nodded, as I knew very well he would. Then I helped him up. As expected, he were able to walk without falling over, though he weren't hardly putting no weight on the dodgy ankle. I didn't give a toss about that though, long as he did as told. And he did. I watched him go through the glass doors and stagger off towards them moving stairs. Then I turned to the birds.

There was about eight or so of em, all in a group roadside. They was quiet now, staring at us like I'd just done a miracle or summat. Which I had in a way, what with healing the lame just now, and that. But I couldn't have em there causing trouble for us when the coppers got here, which they'd be doing in just a moment, going by the sirens.

'Shift,' I says to em. 'Yer causin' an obstruction.' That didn't work, so I got me monkey wrench out and ran at em, going 'Raaagghh.' It were shite or bust, cos if they stood their ground I'd have to twock em, which I didn't wanna do. But I didn't have to face that difficult question cos they started squealing and scarpering, one or two into the Wossname Centre, the rest up the Friar Street. I chased these uns along a bit, roaring and swinging at em, until the raincoat bird dropped her trolley and I tripped over it. By the time I got meself up again they was gone.

'All right, officer,' I says back at me door a short while later.

'Where's this trouble then?' he says. I hadn't seen this un before and he were quite young.

'I says "All right, officer."'

'I know, I heard you. An' I says "Where's this trouble then"?'

'If you ain't gonna be polite to us,' I says, sparking up a much-needed smoke, 'I ain't gonna tell you where the trouble is.'

'Oh for fuck sake...Hey,' he says over his shoulder to his mate who were still in the motor, talking on the radio. 'We got a right one here.' He turned back to us with a grin across his chops and goes: 'Woss your name, son?'

I could have lamped him. Truly I fucking could. He knew who I were. Every fucker know who Royston fucking Blake were. 'Every f—'

'Oh, I knows you. You're that Roy Blake, right? There can't be many walkin' round with a scar like that,' he says, looking at the side of me head where the hair hadn't growed back yet. 'Aye, I heard all about you.'

I stared at him for a bit, and he stared at us. We stared each other out, you might say. We was doing quite well and all, not one blink apiece and nary a drop of moisture in the eye. Then the other copper shouts: 'Hoy, Nige, get in. We got on an RTA up there on Friar an' Clench.'

'You fuckin' what?' says Nige, looking away and thereby making me the winner.

'Aye, truck's gone over an old bloke on his bike up there. Poor old bastard just sailed into the traffic, so they says.'

Nige pointed a finger at us as he backed off and got in the car. As it pulled away I coughed up a big a chewy one and sent it skyward, landing on the back window. Then I flicked em a V and allowed meself a little smile of satisfaction.

This job weren't so bad after all.

'Come on then.' It were Danny, crept up behind us with his manky pin and his outstretched paw. 'Giz it.'

'Giz what?'

'Eh? Giz what? Fuck off, giz the seventy fuckin' notes.'

'What seventy notes?'

'What sev…The seventy fuckin' notes you promised us just now. Come on, cough up. "Get up an' walk into the shop," you says, "and I'll give you seventy fuckin' notes." S'what you says just now.'

'I fuckin' never.'

'You fuckin' *did*, you fuckin'—'

'I never,' I says, blowing smoke in his red face. 'I says "fuck all," not "seventy notes."'

'You…you…' He went a bit redder, then started going back to his typical skin colour, which were pink with a few blackheads here and there. When he'd got a hold himself he went to say summat, then just shook his swede and limped off.

I started whistling. "King of the Road," I think it were. Cos that's what I felt like.

King of this particular road anyhow.

• • •

DOCTOR:	*You were married, then?*
PATIENT:	*Aye.*
DOCTOR:	*To Elizabeth.*
PATIENT:	*No. Beth.*
DOCTOR:	*She preferred Beth?*
PATIENT:	*I preferred Beth.*
DOCTOR:	*Why?*
PATIENT:	*Cos.*
DOCTOR:	*All right…So the marriage ended when she died in a fire. How did you feel about that, at the time?*
PATIENT:	*Dunno.*
DOCTOR:	*Were you sad?*
PATIENT:	[shrugs] *A bit.*
DOCTOR:	*You didn't love her, then?*
PATIENT:	*I wouldn't tell you if I did, would I?*
DOCTOR:	*Why not? She was your wife. It's normal for husbands to love wives, isn't it?*
PATIENT:	*How the fuck ought I to know?*
DOCTOR:	*Was it a happy marriage?*
PATIENT:	[shrugs] *All right, I suppose.*
DOCTOR:	*Not really?*
PATIENT:	*I says it were all right.*
DOCTOR:	*Were there problems?*
PATIENT:	[looks down for a long time]

DOCTOR: *Were there infidelities?*

PATIENT: [continues looking down, then breathes deep and nods]

DOCTOR: *On both sides?*

PATIENT: [nods]

DOCTOR: *How did you feel about that, your wife being with another man?*

PATIENT: [glares at me, then looks down again] *I didn't like it, did I. Would you like it?*

DOCTOR: *Probably not, but we're not here to talk about me.*

PATIENT: *Nah, always me, ennit.*

DOCTOR: *Your wife died in a fire, Royston. A fire at your former place of work. You were charged with her murder, and underwent psychiatric evaluation here at Parpham, which concluded that you were unfit to face trial. Now, did you kill her?*

PATIENT: *No I fucking never. Check your fucking facts before coming at me with your accusations, you...you fucking...I weren't even nowhere near her when it happened. Mad with grief, I were. That's why they brung us in here, ennit. Mad with fucking grief.*

• • •

'Are you Royston?'

'Not to you I ain't.'

'Where's Royston then?'

'Eh?'

'I'm lookin' for Royston.'

He were a weedy little shortarse in a white short-sleeved shirt and shiny black tie that only went halfway down his front, the way he tied it. A nice bald patch were settling in at the back of his head, and he were so short I could see it when he faced us.

'Fuck off,' I says, turning away.

It were half four and nearing the end of me shift, but while I were still on duty I didn't want shortarse cunts like him hanging about, making us look bad. See, I'd noticed I could get away with a lot of me old Hoppers door behaviour, in relation to women in particular. And it's flirting I'm on about here, the smiles and winks and occasional arse-pats that is the right of every pub or club doorman. I'd found—from me observations, like—that these birds going in and out of the Wossname Centre was no different from the pissed-up ones you had later on of an eve, and that they gave out the selfsame signals, about loving it up em and that. So there I were, making a name for meself as the handsome door-man of their dreams.

And along comes Shortarse.

He weren't budging. I could sense him behind us being short and weedy and making us look bad. He took a breath and goes: 'But—'

'I says fuck off, didn't I?' I says, not even turning.

He got the message then, just as a slinky brunette with nice tits, a filthy smile, and high leather boots going right up to her fanny came past.

'All right, doll,' I says, giving her the eye.

'Hello there,' she says, stopping about a couple of inches from us and clocking us upwise and down and quite clearly liking what she found, which you couldn't blame her for. 'I haven't seen *you* before.'

'You ain't been lookin.'

'I assure you I have. I've just not been finding.' She had a right posh voice and it went perfect with the rest of her. Them high boots, leather miniskirt, big black fur coat, loads of slap. Pure fucking class.

'Aye, well, you ever needs any help with yer goods,' I says, looking down her leopard skin top, 'you knows where to come.'

She eyed us, the pointy tip of her tongue sliding along her lips like a pink slug, and goes, slow and low: 'I'm sure I *will* come.'

'F-f-fuckin' hell,' I almost says. What I actually did say were: 'F-f-flippin' heck.' Cos you got to mind your effs and blinds with posh birds. If you wants to shag em, like.

'Not now, Bernard,' she says.

Which struck us as a bit odd, when I thought about it. I mean, for fuck sake, she didn't think I'd jump her bones here and now, did she? You never knew with birds. And where the fuck did she get the name Bernard?

'It's Blake actually,' I says. 'Me name, like. Royston B—'

'Bernard,' she hollers, spinning about and slapping the paws of a littlun off her coat. He were a dopey looking lad of between three and ten, with too much floppy brown hair and an overall soft look about him. And from the way the bird cuffed him round the head, I reckoned him her son.

She turned them dirty eyes back on us one last time, and I could tell the magic we'd shared had gone. 'Excuse me,' she says, like I were just a servant or summat. Then she were off into the place, working them stilettos and yanking little Bernard by the wrist.

'You are Royston, ain't you.'

'I told you to fuck off, didn't I?' I says to the shortarse, who'd managed to creep up on us again, his swede being below me line of view.

'I knows you did, but I been reliably told that Royston Blake is you. Royston Blake is the front-of-house customer flow manager of this buildin', I been reliably told, and that's what you're doin'.'

'What?'

'Managin' flow. At front of house.'

I sparked a fag. 'Don't you understand what "fuck off" means, or summat?'

'You ain't meant to smoke. No one smokes in the P—'

'Ah, for fuck...I ain't even in here, am I. I'm on the fuckin' door. I'm puffin' me fumes outside, like. So *hop it*, before I drops you.'

He huffed and puffed a bit, with his shiny tie and his bald patch, then goes: 'Mr Porter wants you.'

'Eh?'

'Mr Porter. He wants you in his office when you knock off.'

'Who's Mr fuckin' Porter?'

'Mr Porter,' he says all slow, treating us like I'm thick. 'Mr Porter is our boss. Mr Porter has an office upstairs on the third floor. You go in that lift over there and press the button sayin' "3." When it stops, you get out. Then you go over to the door marked "C. Porter (HND, Esq), CEO," and you knocks on it. There's a secretary there and she'll show you in.'

I looked at him for a bit, him looking back. I could tell he were shiting himself a bit. But he reckoned himself safe, being in public like.

Well, he weren't.

I grabbed him by the throat and picked him up.

'You *ever*,' I says all calm, 'you fuckin' *ever* fuckin' talks to us like that again, right, an' I swear I'll...I'll fuckin'...'

I stopped there cos Rache were walking past. I'd been wait-ing all day for her to come back out and tell us how the interview had gone. 'All right, Rache,' I says, dropping the feller. 'How'd the wossname go?'

But she didn't answer. She fucking blanked us, didn't she, sailing on past as far away as she could get, shaking her head and keeping her eyes off mine. I wanted to go after her but I thought better of it. Best to give her some space like as not, to come to terms with failing her interview. And spending all day at it and all, poor lass.

'You'll pay for that,' says the feller, already stomping off.

I couldn't recall who he were for a sec, and I had to look hard at him and rack me brains. It were hard doing that, on account of me brains feeling like old porridge of a sudden. I flexed me fingers and remembered the feel of em around his turkey neck, and the pure fucking rudeness of his words to me. 'Aye,' I shouts after him. 'And you...' But me swede were giving us grief summat chronic now, and I couldn't think for toffee. 'An' you can *fuck off*,' I shouts after him. But the shouting only made the pain worser.

I slumped down on the hard stuff and rubbed me eyes so hard they nearly popped. Then I sat still and waited for the shite feeling to pass.

10

'Come on, son.'

'What?' It were a while later and someone were shaking me shoulder. I didn't feel so bad now. A bit groggy, mind, like I'd been kipping.

'Yer shift's over.'

I looked up and saw an old feller standing over us in the self-same togs as I were wearing, except smaller. Then I recognised him as the old security guard I'd took over from, the morning prior.

'I been asked to tell you the boss is waitin' on you,' he says, me getting up all slow like. 'So you best go on up an' see him.'

I shrugged and walked off out the main door into the street, patting meself for smokes. The fresh air were making us feel ship-shape already.

'He'll sack you,' he says after us. 'An you won't get paid.'

• • •

I couldn't face that fucking lift again, so I had a nose around and found some stairs behind a door marked NO ENTRY and NO SMOKING. I took me sweet time on em, enjoying a fag, humming a nice tune. At the top I came out in that bit again where the feller had honked on the carpet yesterday. You could still smell it. The dirty fucker.

'All right, doll,' I says to the secretary as I went in.

'Oh,' she says, looking at us and biting her lip in a rather fetching way. There was loads of fit birds in the Wossname Centre, and I were well happy with it in that respect. Then she looked over at the feller's door.

I became aware of the row just then. He had a bird in there with him, and she were verbally knocking the shite clean out of him. The walls was thick, so it seemed, and you couldn't make out her words like. But she weren't half screaming.

'Don't fret, love,' I says to the nice secretary. 'I'll wait here with you, eh?' I went over to her desk, taking her scowl in me stride. If a bird ain't hard work she ain't worth the effort.

'Please don't sit on my desk,' she says as I went to do just that, a splash of pink glowing above each cheekbone. I liked that. 'There's seatin' over there.'

She'd pointed over at the far corner, and I looked over there as I parked a cheek on her desk. A big glass coffee table with some mags fanned out on it, two big low sofas the colour of baked beans flanking two sides of it, and a fucking big pot plant between em. A young lad were sat on one of the sofas.

'Who's he?' I says to the secretary. But I recognised him before she answered. He were the littlun with the posh lass, down the stair just now. Which meant the screaming and bawling in the feller's office were her.

'That's Bernard,' the secretary said after huffing and puffing about it. 'Mr Porter's son. Now please get off the desk.'

I looked at her, scratching me bollocks and easing another buttock on. 'Who the fuck's Mr Porter?'

'What?' she says, screwing up her pretty face.

'You oughtn't to do that,' I says, touching her cheek. 'You'll get lines.'

She batted us off and pushed her chair back.

'Make us a cup o' tea eh?' I says, swinging me leg. It were nice enough being in here but I were fucking parched. 'I been graftin' all day long.'

'Who the hell d'you think you are?' she shrieks, though not as loud as her in the other room. 'You want tea—go to a café.'

'Come on, you're a secretary, ennit? Make us a fuckin' cuppa, eh.' I nodded over at the other corner, where there was a tea trolley and all the gear. 'Go on—stuff's over yonder.'

'Make yerself a flamin' cuppa.' The splash of colour were now all over her face and down her neck to the tops of her tits, which you could see. I didn't half like that. And if that's what shouting did for her, she could shout on. 'And get off my desk.'

'Tell you what, I'll get off your desk if you makes us a cuppa. How's that, eh?' I gave her a wink.

She closed her eyes and puffed hard through her nose for a bit, getting on top of herself. I quite fancied getting on top of herself meself, and I wondered if this here moment weren't me big chance, what with her peepers being shut. But I didn't wanna fuck me chances up with her, so I made do with leaning over a bit and peering down her top. 'You bastard,' she says all slow, getting up and going over to the tea trolley.

'Good lass,' I says, getting up. 'See, I'm good as me word.'

The lad were sat on one sofa so I sat on t'other. He were wearing a pirate outfit by the looks of it, if that's what them stripy trousers and black waistcoat and headscarf was meant to be. Bit shite though, cos he didn't have a sword. And he looked too soft and dopey to be a pirate anyhow. I didn't mind him being there though cos he were a quiet pirate, and if there's one thing I fucking cannot stick it's a lippy youngun. So all in all he were the best I could hope for, considering I were stuck with him until I got to see the boss. Mind you, I wouldn't want any son of mine being like him. I'd want mine to be a bit more forward, like, speak his mind and give grief where grief's due. There's nothing worse than a silent youngun.

Mind you, I were fairly taken aback when he pulled a fucking pistol out of nowhere, pointed it at us, and goes: 'Stick em up.'

I don't mind telling you, it put the shite up us just a bit. I ain't a fan of guns. I've had em up close before and I just don't like the look of em. Nor the smell. And this one here, there were no telling if it were a toy or otherwise. I mean, you just never knew with younguns these days. Couldn't be a real gun though, could it? I mean, a lad his age couldn't even lift a real gun. Could they? 'You fuckin' twat,' I says, shaking me head. 'Pirates has swords, not guns. What the fuck's they teachin' you at schools these days. Eh?'

He looked at us odd, letting his gun hand drop to his lap. I preferred it that way, but I still didn't approve of the way he were clocking us.

'Pooey,' he says after a bit, pinching his nose. 'You smell.'

I didn't know what to say to that. Like I says, I ain't got much to say to younguns. I wondered if I could give him a smack, and looked over at the nice lass to see if she were looking. She weren't, being busy with her tea making just then. But to be honest I don't reckon the little feller could take a smack. Instead I waited for the lass to bring me tea, which she did surprisingly sharpish, on a little tray with a couple of biccies, bless her. I says ta and went to give her a friendly pat on the arse as she bent down, but she seen it coming and got out the way sharpish. Mind you, she hid her face from us as she walked off, so I knew she had a smile on it.

Anyway, I sipped me tea and ate the biccies and lit a smoke. Then I leaned forwards, elbows on knees, and says to him: 'Listen you, you cheeky cunt. You oughta be careful what you says to strangers. Some strangers is bad uns. They'll take you away and chop you up into bits, then cook you and eat yer. How'd you like that, eh, pirate? Ain't so bad now, is yer?'

He didn't answer us, so I knew it were working.

'An' who's to say I ain't one o' them strangers? Who's to say I ain't got a big knife in here, specially for slicin' up little fuckers like you? Eh? Woss you say to that, eh?'

The lad started screaming. Took us off guard, it did, and I dropped me smoke, burning a little hole in the cream-coloured carpet. (No one'd notice it though, unless they came and sat where I were sat.) I put the smoke back in me gob and says: 'Hoy, hush it.' That didn't work so I got up and moved towards him. He rolled off the sofa just before I reached him, and hared over to the desk, where he hid behind the lass and went quiet.

'What did you do?' she shouts, all angry. She were trying to get a look at him but he kept slithering away. As she swung around her elbow caught him a glancing blow on the cheek, and he started blubbering all over.

'Go on,' I shouts at him. 'Answer her.'

'Not him, *you*,' she yells. And I swear I felt little drops of her flob on me face from eight yard off. She got the lad cornered at last and stroked his cheek, going: 'Sorry, darlin', I were only—'

Just then the door swung to and the posh bird comes flying out of the feller's office, eyes all over the shop. 'Bernard,' she hollers in a voice that could strip bark. 'Where are you?'

'Here, Mrs Porter,' says the lass. 'He—'

'What have you done to him?'

'She elbowed him in the chops,' I says, looking for an ashtray.

'I *never*. Mrs Porter, I—'

'I asked you to look after him.'

'But I didn't mean to—'

'I don't care if you didn't mean to. A little care is all that's required. Honestly, I can't even—'

'It were him,' she yells, pointing at us. I were just then flicking some ash under the coffee table, so I stopped. 'He hit him.'

If there's one thing I've learned it's to never get involved in the arguments of others. Specially birds. So I sat back and enjoyed me smoke.

'Oh, hello,' says the posh bird, showing us a peep at the other side of her, the side I'd seen down the stair a while back. 'I didn't see *you* there.'

'All right, darlin',' I says, winking. 'I were just tellin' your lad here how he ought never to talk to strangers. You know, on his way home from school and that. Sensible lad, he is.'

'Well,' she says, pulling the lad's waistcoat straight, 'he's not quite school age yet. But I agree in principle. Especially in this town.'

'Aye,' I says, nodding. 'It's a rough town.'

She smiled at us proper now, a full dirty one, saying: 'Full of rough men.'

We looked at each other without words for a short while, and I knew there and then that I'd be shagging her some time soon, all going well. I knew I'd be shagging one of these two birds here anyhow. And, as it turned out, I weren't wrong. (You'll have to sit tight to find out the which, though. Cos I ain't telling you yet.)

'Mummy, that man smells,' says the lad.

'Oh don't be silly, Bernard. There's nothing wrong with a pungent male odour. Come on, bedtime for you.' She yanked him doorward, stopping to say: 'Lovely to meet you, Mr...'

'Blake,' I says. 'Mr Blake.'

'You want me to call you Mr Blake? Don't you have another name?'

I thought about it and says: 'Aye: Blakey.'

'Well, er...bye bye, Blakey. I'm sure we'll meet again...*very* soon.' Then she were gone.

Soon as the door swung shut the secretary lass turned on us. She got as far as 'You f—' before the blower on her desk started ringing. 'Hello, Mr Porter,' she says, all sweet of a sudden. 'Yes, I'll send him in.'

'About fuckin' time,' I says, getting up. 'I got places to go, ain't I.' I stopped at her desk to give her the smouldering fag end, saying: 'There's no ashtrays over there.' She didn't take it so I dropped it in her tea, which were nearly finished anyhow. And you can never be too safe with smouldering butts. She started saying summat but I were off doorward now, getting me business swede on, like.

'I've heard some worrying things,' says the feller before I'd so much as parked me arse. 'Worrying stories from customers, Mr Blake. About your conduct. And I'm a fair man so I want to hear your side of the matter. Sit down.'

I did so and got me fags out. First things first.

'No smokin' in here,' he says. 'This is a no smoking building. That's why you'll have noticed NO SMOKING signs everywhere.'

'Oh,' I says putting em away.

'Several customers—*female* customers, I might add—have lodged formal complaints about you today. They say you shouted and swore at them, and threatened them with a weapon. Also I've heard you've been smoking on the job, and assaulting another member of staff. And you've been seen asleep at your station by three separate parties.'

I wished I could have that smoke. I thought about asking him if I could go over to the window while he went on at us, but summat about his manner told us not to bother. 'I ain't been at no station,' I says instead. 'I been on that door all day. Ask anyone.'

'I know, I know, I meant—'

'An' where's these fuckin' parties? How's I gonna fall akip with all them parties goin' on? Eh? See, it don't make sense.'

He closed his trap and let the air out through his nose, drumming his fingers on the desk a couple of times. Then he says: 'Look, Mr Blake…I took a risk when I agreed to have you here. Your reputation goes before you, so to speak. I've lived in Mangel all my life and I read the papers. I know what kind of town this has always been, and what kind of men it breeds. Well, I'm not one of those men, Mr Blake. I've stayed apart from all that, watching others fail while I marched on. While they mucked around with their girls and their fighting, I pursued my education. I chose to *better myself*, Mr Blake. They mocked me for it at school. Oh, they mocked me all right. I was the quiet one, the little swot who kept his nose clean. No one ever remembers the quiet ones. Well, look around you—see what I get for being quiet. Do you think they'll remember me now?'

I thought for a bit, then goes: 'Mind you, it is possible to go on kippin' while a party goes on around you. Me old mate Finney used to do that sometimes, at Hoppers. Stripper up on stage an' everythin', an' there's him snoozin' away on a chair, right next to the action. Weren't the ale neither. He just liked his kip, our Fin. Ah…' I says, shaking me head at the memory.

He did that thing with his gob and his nose again, the little boss feller, then goes: 'All right, all right. Never mind all that. It's not important anyway, and it'll all come out in the history books. I'll cut to the chase, shall I? You're a rough man, Mr Blake.'

'Aye but I got style an' all. No one can say I ain't got no style.'

'Whatever. The point is you're a man of violence, a man of strong words and strong fists. You're big, and you know how to use your bulk. But you were never a bully by nature, oh no. You could say I've been following your exploits in the papers over the years, Mr Blake. I've read what you've done, and I've imagined the rest, the bits they didn't—'

'I ain't fat though.'

'What?'

'You says I'm big. I'm just sayin' like.'

'Saying what?'

'You know, all muscle, ennit. Look...' I punched meself in the guts. To be honest there were a bit of give there, but I were sat down and there's always a few rolls when you're sat down.

'Right. Mr Blake, do you want me to explain this to you or not? Would you rather I just sack you?'

I thought about the Granada outside. I'd had to park her over on the Strake Hill car park. Double yellers everywhere these day. 'No,' I says. 'Go on an' say yer bit.'

'Thank you. Do you read the papers, Mr Blake?'

I shook me head. 'I don't believe in em.'

'What? Don't believe in em? You ought to read them, then you'd know what's going on around you. You might learn that there's some local opposition to the good work we're doing here. We're bringing Mangel into the future, Mr Blake. And she's kicking and screaming. Only a small part of her, mind. Most citizens are decent folk who want to make the most of their lives, which means having access to the best retail outlets, restaurants, and services. Everyone has a right to those things, Mr Blake. But there is an element who would deny them that right. There is an element who would prefer Mangel to remain stuck in the dark ages.'

The feller were looking at the wall as he spoke, eyeing up the tasteful tits hanging there. I'd got a waft of summat and were looking around, all quiet like, wondering if a rat hadn't carked it under his desk or summat. I couldn't see no rat but I got another waft, and it came from a bit more local this time. I got my head down and sniffed under me arm, wondering if that lad hadn't been correct after all, about us humming. A bit spicy around the pits, truth be told. Maybe I'd spray em before going to Don's for cards. I looked at me watch: gone six already.

'Well, I happen to know that this element—this *Old Guard*, as they call themselves—are prepared to use extreme measures to get their wish. That intruder the other day, the one who put three of my employees into hospital…that was one of them. He must have been scouting for security holes, and turned nasty when my men apprehended him. You know what they've got planned next? Explosives. They want to blow this place up, Mr Blake. Or so they tell me anyway, in the letters they keep sending me. Mr Blake, you've come to me at a good time. I'm upping security at all levels in the mall. I've already got cameras watching every corner of the place, but now I'm hiring extra staff to watch the screens. The entire complex will be monitored in real time, Mr Blake. I'm going to double mobile security in the ground, so we can react on the camera data with only a split second's delay. And I've recruited two sniffer dogs, trained to detect eight different incendiary substances. We cannot take this threat too seriously. All inways to the complex will be manned during hours of business. And finally there's the most dangerous, notorious man in Mangel at the front entrance.'

'Who's that then?' I says.

He laughed and goes: 'A joker, too. I admire that trait, Mr Blake. I've been described as short on humour, but let me tell you here and now: I like a good laugh. I just need a good joke to get me there. Eh? Eh? Heh heh…'

I smiled a bit for politeness sake, then says: 'Can I go now?'

'Aye…of course. But Mr Blake, er…there's something else.'

Oh for fuck sake.

'I'm asking for some advice, really. You can see for yourself that I'm a successful man, but there's one area of life I'm just not schooled in. And you are, Mr Blake. Which is why I'm asking for your advice.'

'Oh aye?' I says. This were all I needed—someone dumping their bird problems on us. 'Go on then.'

'Good, good. It's like this…' He got up and started pacing hither and thither, paws in pockets. 'Did you notice the lady and young child who were in here just now? That's my family, Mr Blake. I'd do anything for them. I'd never let anyone hurt them.'

Ah, so that explains all the shouting just now. My own experience of married life had been much the same as his, and I truly felt for him. Mind you, it were his own fault, getting spliced with a bird like her. She were well filthy. You could smell her a mile off. Plus his boy were a bit of a runt. So all in all I didn't envy him.

'And that's where my problem is, Mr Blake. I've got someone hanging about who's intent on harming them. A pikey little villain he is, no morals in him, just a lot of nastiness and greediness. It's always the same,' he says, stopping by the big window and looking out over the town. 'Folks see you bettering yourself, they want a piece of it for themselves. They want *something for nothing*, Mr Blake. It's bloody ironic, I swear. I'm the bloody *saviour* of this town. I'm bringing jobs and prosperity to a town that's been in the dark for too long. And what do I get for it? Money-grubbing parasites…erm…*threatening* to harm my loved ones. Mr Blake, will you help me?'

I were looking at me fingernails just then, noticing how I'd been biting em right down of late. Never used to, before Parpham.

'Mr Blake.'

'What?'

'Will you help me?'

'Aye. Help you what?'

'Stop him?'

'Who?'

'This parasite. He's a threat to my family, Mr Blake. I just told you.'

'Aye, but who is he?'

'Oh, I see. Well...' Flipping heck, he weren't half slow, this little boss feller. Anyhow, he got a photo out of his drawer and gave it us. It were well blurry and quite dark, but you could just make out half a phone box with a bin next to it, and a long-haired feller dipping into it. 'Name of Baldwin,' he says. 'Kevin Baldwin. Known as Badger to his pikey mates, I think. I want him taught a good lesson, Mr Blake. I want him to stop. For good. Know what I mean?'

He winked at us.

I put the picture on the table and says: 'I ain't doin' it.'

Don't worry, I knew what I were doing.

Watch and learn, mate.

'Why not?' he says. 'You've done this stuff before, haven't you?'

'Don't matter.'

'You want money? I can give you money. However, I was thinking more of it as a fav—'

'I don't want money,' I says. 'I just ain't doin' that aggro stuff no more. I'm buildin' a new life for meself. I ain't goin' back in Parpham, and I ain't goin' in no jail neither. It's like you was sayin' there, about betterin' yerself. Thass what I wants now. I wants the proper stuff, the nice job and bein' respectable an' that. I ain't no thug.'

He were sat down now, clutching his jaw like it were hanging loose, spying us through slitty eyes. 'Hmm,' he says after a bit. 'I can see that, yes. Of course you want to better yourself, to maximise your potential in a legitimate way, whilst gaining the respect and admiration of your peers. I can help you with that, Mr Blake. There's many an opportunity here, and if you help me—if you show me your loyalty—you'll do well here.'

'How well?' I says.

'Sky's the limit, for a man like you. Who knows?'

'*You* knows. Tell us what you'll do for us if I does this.' Cos I ain't thick.

'I can't just name something. There's all kinds of considerations...'

'Right,' I says, getting up. 'I'm off.'

'No, Mr Blake...All right, sit down. How about...' He were looking up into a corner, drumming his little fingers. 'How about I make you chief of security? That's a high-profile position, in an area I don't take lightly, as you know. What d'you say to that?'

Sounded all right, didn't it? Mind you, 'Who's chief of security now?'

'Er...no one, as such. I fill those boots myself.'

'Ah.'

'But, you know, the more I think about it the more I like it. We'd work together closely, of course. With my business brain and your knowledge of local...er, *security matters*, we could have this place sealed tight as a walnut. The Porter Centre could be the leading light of consumer security across the whole country. I can see it all now…Mind you, I'd expect the same kind of loyalty on an ongoing basis. You scratch mine, I scratch yours. See?'

'I wants it in writin'.'

'You want what in writing?'

'This job offer.'

'Come on, Blake. Think about it. You'll get the job offer when you do the job I asked. I can hardly put that in writing, can I? Look, you'll just have to trust me. Like I trusted you when I gave you a job here, eh?'

Which were fair enough. We shook hands on it and I said me bye-byes, not even looking at the secretary bird on the way out. Gotta be hard on them, you have. Gotta make em see how they needs you more'n you needs them. Top birds, top jobs…you'll get em both if you does it my way.

Like I told you, watch and learn.

• • •

DOCTOR:	*Royston, I want to ask you a direct question, and I want you to answer it with a simple yes or a no. Can you do that?*
PATIENT:	*Course I can, fuck sake.*
DOCTOR:	*Do you know how your mother died?*
PATIENT:	[appears uncomfortable and angry, but says nothing]
DOCTOR:	*Yes or no, Royston.*
PATIENT:	*Yes I fucking know. And it's none of your fucking business.*
DOCTOR:	*I accept that, Royston. But I'm not asking these questions for my benefit. These are areas I think we should explore, for your sake.*

PATIENT: *You knows fuck all about it.*
DOCTOR: *OK, so enlighten me.*
PATIENT: *Lighten yourself, you fucking cunt.*
DOCTOR: *Royston, come on.*
PATIENT: *All right, I never meant that. You ain't a fucking cunt. You're a fucking wanker.*
DOCTOR: *How does it make you feel, calling me those names?*
PATIENT: *Not bad. But I ain't saying em for my benefit. These is things I think we should call you, for your own sake.*
DOCTOR: *Very clever.*
PATIENT: *Fuck off.*
DOCTOR: *I meant it. But never mind…Look, Royston—for the record, I know how your mother died.*
PATIENT: *You fucking do not.*
DOCTOR: *Why would I lie?*
PATIENT: *Why's you asking us, then?*
DOCTOR: *Because I…*
PATIENT: *"…think we should explore," oh aye. Listen, pal, you wanna go exploring, get yerself a map and a compass and fuck off to Hurk Wood.*
DOCTOR: *OK, let's forget about that. How do you feel about your mother?*
PATIENT: [appears uncomfortable and angry again, then mumbles something]
DOCTOR: *Pardon?*
PATIENT: *I says I loved her.*
DOCTOR: *Thank you, Royston. I'm glad you could tell me that.*
PATIENT: *Fuck off.*

DOCTOR:	*Why do you find it hard, saying it?*
PATIENT:	*A feller don't talk like that.*
DOCTOR:	*But you said it. You didn't have to say it but you did.*
PATIENT:	*I can't lie about it. Me mam's me mam. I loves her, and that's that.*
DOCTOR:	*You talk about her like she's still alive.*
PATIENT:	*She is alive. She's alive in me heart.*
DOCTOR:	*And do you think she'd still be alive in your heart if she'd died a different way? If she hadn't died in an arson attack, with your own father suspected of—*
PATIENT:	*Fuck off.* [stands up, gestures aggressively] *I fucking told you—you knows fuck all about that and I ain't talking about it.*

• • •

I had a little think as I coaxed the Granada in the Bonehill direction. You can't help but have a little think, when someone offers you a top job like chief of security at the Wossname Centre.

Cos this were it, you know.

This were the good life I'd been craving for so many a year, every one of em spent toiling as a pub doorman and kipping in a cursed house, all the while dreaming of summat else and not knowing what it were nor where to find it. Mind you, it takes the opportunity. You don't just walk into them sorts of jobs when you feels like em. Up pops a chance, you got to swipe him while you can. Well, here were my chance, at long last.

And all I had to do were get rid of Ferret.

Which don't seem so bad, when you looks at it. I mean, the bastard had been poking my bird, hadn't he? I knew where to find him and what motor he drove and everything.

Piece of piss, mate.

Aye, soon I'd be there in me own office, telling folks what to do and shouting at anyone I didn't like the look of. I'd have me own secretary to make tea for us and shag whenever I wanted to. Maybe I'd even get the one out of the little boss feller's office, if I played me cards right.

And all I had to do were sort the ferret.

I fancied some tunes so I switched on the radio. I couldn't find nothing on there besides news, weather, and "The Last Waltz" by Engelbert Humperdinck. I ain't a fan of Engelbert and that song in particular, so I switched the fucker off sharpish and started humming to meself. That didn't do the trick neither, being as I never had been gifted hummingwise, so I stopped. Weren't long before I sensed the black clouds of tunelessness descending all around me ears. Then I thought of summat, and tapped me inside pocket.

I slotted the tape in and the deck started whirring. *A SONG TO MAKE YOU THINK*, it says on the box. I'd had enough of thinking for now and me swede deserved a well-earned, but I were curious to know what this song were. A trumpet piped up giving it a nice and relaxing intro, followed by the unmistakable voice of Elvis Presley, the undisputed king of the rock 'n rollers. *There must be lights, burning brighter, somewhere...*

I'd always liked 'If I Can Dream.' I mean you gotta, ain't you. It's an Elvis song, and where Elvis is doing the vocals you ain't got no choice but to like. But it were a great song on its own steam, and would be even with Nathan the barman singing it. And I'll tell you for why:

Shivers. Up your spine.

And down again.

It's all about that relaxing trumpet, see, at the start. Get em all settled and snoozing, then hit em a bit harder. Then hit em harder and harder until that final note, Elvis going: *Riiiiight nnnnnooooooooow*.

Far as I'm bothered, that's what maketh a great song. If it does the old shivers, they could be singing the fucking footy results and it's still gonna work. And it's for that reason that I hadn't ever really harked what the King were saying here. I mean, I knew the words and that, but they was just sounds, like the parping of that trumpet feller.

Anyhow, the song finished, leaving us tingling all over. I expected summat else to come after it, but the song were the only one on the tape, so it appeared. I flicked off and let the radio come on, a feller telling the weather forecast (he says there's a storm coming). Then I reached out, wound the tape back, and played 'If I Can Dream' again.

I can't say it made us think, but there were summat there all right. Felt like Elvis were singing straight into me own heart.

11

I hadn't been over Bonehill way in fucking yonks. Not to stop anyhow. Being perched just across the river it were somewhere you went
past on your way to Norbert Green. And let me tell you as an expert
on local security matters—Norbert Green is a place best avoided.

Bonehill flats was three big blocks sticking skyward like massive fag lighters. Fifteen or so storeys apiece, and Don lived atop
the middle un. I went in and walked straight past the lift. It were
another one o' them boxy uns, like at the Wossname Centre. I
went up the stair.

Five minutes later I'm ringing the bell.

'Ah, just the man,' says Don, opening up. 'All right, Blakey.'

'All right, Don,' I says, handing him the four-pack.

'Nice one, Blakey. Lift bust again is it?'

'Eh? I dunno. Why?'

'Sweatin' like a slag, you is. Come on.'

I followed him into the flat. They was nice flats, these uns,
with proper hallways and that. You could hear voices coming
out of the living room, and that's where we went. He stopped in
the doorway and says: 'Lads, here's Blakey,' then stepped aside to
reveal us.

'All right, lads,' I says.

'All right, Blakey,' one or two of em says. Others just grunted,
and one didn't even look up. There was five of em in total, seven
including meself and Don.

'Blakey,' says Don, waving at the table. 'You knows Mike and
Tony.'

'Aye,' I says. 'And Pete.'

'All right, Blake,' says Pete.

'All right, Pete.'

'All right, Blake.'

'All right, Blake.'

'All right, Mike and Tony.'

'An' these two lads here is Max and Tommo,' Don says, pointing at em. One of em was the one who hadn't looked up just now. He glanced at us this time and nodded a bit. The other didn't though. He didn't look happy. Neither of em did.

'Woss wrong with them?' I says all quiet to Don.

Don covered his mouth and goes: 'They ain't from local.'

'Ah, right.'

'Anyway, Blakey, you sit here. Tony, deal him in. Hoy,' he shouts kitchenward. 'Giz some more beer, eh.'

Tony dealt a hand. 'So woss we playin'?' I says, picking up me five cards.

Max and Tommo snorted and glanced at each other. I didn't like that. But I'd let em off this once, them being Don's mates.

'Poker,' says Pete. 'You know how to play?'

'Fuck off,' I says. 'Course I does.'

It went quiet for a bit, fellers looking at cards and scratching swedes. I kept an eye open and no one else seemed to be glancing nor snorting, which was all right. 'Here,' goes Mike. 'D'you hear about Berty Fontana?'

'Berty who?' says Tony.

'Fontana.'

'I knows him, I think.' Tony scratched his hairy chin, looking at the ceiling. 'Who's he?'

'You know. Bee Hive.'

'Oh aye?' I says.

'Hoy,' shouts Don again at the kitchen, making us jump. 'Where's the fuckin' beer?'

'S'all right, Don,' I says, reaching for the four pack I'd gave him. 'I'll have one o' these.'

'No, Blake, we got a keg in. Max and Tommo brung it in from the big city. Ain't that right, lads?'

One of em shrugged.

'Here, Don,' I says. 'Who's you shoutin' to out there anyhow?'

'Eh? Oh, the bird, ennit.'

'Oh aye? Who's that then?'

'Fuckin' lazy cow is who. All she gotta do is pull some pints and bring em out here, fuck sake. And her a barmaid an' all.'

'Barmaid, eh?'

'Aye. Well, not no more like.'

'So woss her n—'

'Blakey?' says Tony.

'What?'

'Twenty p in the pot, please.'

'Eh?'

He nodded at the ashtray full of coinage in the middle.

'Oh,' I says, getting me bag of shrapnel out. I had thirty quid worth, and it weren't half heavy.

'You got enough there, Blakey?' says Mike, nodding at me bag. 'I only brung a fiver's worth.'

'Me an' all,' says Tone. 'An' I ain't playin' all night neither, not like last time. Got work the morrer.'

'Where's you workin' now then, Tone?' I says, chucking a twenty in the pot. 'Still at Cullimore's?'

'Nah,' he says laughing. '*They* laid us off donkeys back. Fuckin' outsiders come in an' took it over, put new machines in an' sacked everyone. No offence, lads,' he says to Max and Tommo, who ignored him.

'Oh aye?' I says. 'So where's you workin' now like?'

He shrugged. 'Nowhere.'

'Oh.' I looked at me cards. 'But you says you gotta work the morrer.'

'Nah, I'm helpin' Max an' Tommo. Ain't I, lads?'

'Blakey?' says Tony.

'What?'

'Your bet. Thirty p call.'

'Eh? Oh.' I put 30p in the pot then looked the two outsiders. 'So woss your line o' graft, then? Eh?'

I dunno if they heard us or not, but neither answered. I were getting a bit narked with em now, me only being friendly. I wanted to ask em who the fuck did they reckon they was talking to. Only they wasn't talking to us so that wouldn't sound right. I looked at em instead, waiting for one to return it. They was both on the large side, one of em about as big as meself. His head looked like it had been shaved clean two or three day ago, though you could see he had a big barren patch up through the middle. Under that he had thick black eyebrows and one o' them jaws that makes your bottom lip jut an inch past your top one. The other feller looked a bit like Bo Duke from *The Dukes of Hazzard* (the one with brown hair). A few years older, though. And with tats. He looked so much like him that I started to wonder for a while, until I noticed his eyes was too wide apart. Mind you, I quite liked Bo Duke, in a non-arse-bandit way. Bo Duke were the kind of feller you could be mates with, if you lived in Hazzard, like, instead of Mangel. I didn't wanna be mates with this un here though. Nor the other un.

'Blakey?' says Tony.

'What?'

'Your bet. Thirty p call.'

'I already paid.'

'I know, iss been raised though. Thirty p to stay in the game.'

'Fuck sake,' I says tossing in some more.

Max and Tommo was whispering summat to each other but I couldn't hear it. The one who weren't doing the whispering looked at us and laughed.

'That *fuckin'* lazy bitch,' says Don, slamming his fist down. 'I fuckin' *telled* her...' He looked over his shoulder again and shouts: 'Hoy, you lazy bitch. Bring us the fuckin' beer.'

'*Beer, beer, we want more beer...*' sings Pete. '*All the lads is singin', get the fuckin' drinks in...*'

I hadn't heard that song in ages, and I couldn't help but join in. Couple of verses later we're all singing together, stamping our feet and slamming the table.

'*Beer, beer, we want more beer...*'

It went on for fucking ages, and it were a sweet thing to be part of. There's nothing like a good old singalong to break the ice and forge bonds that will last a lifetime, and I forgot all about Max and Tommo's initial cuntish behaviour.

'*All the lads is singin', get the fuckin' drinks in...*'

After a while the door swings open and a bird comes through it. She were holding a tray laden with six pints of lager. Instead of coming to the table with em she clocked us and stopped.

'Rache?' I says. Cos that's who it were.

And I couldn't fucking believe it.

'Blake?' she says. You couldn't hear it though cos the lads was still singing. She looked fit to drop the tray and I were gonna get up and help her, but Don turned and gave her a look, and she started moving again. The song were dying down now, only Pete still at it. She put one in front of Don, saying: 'I were just—'

'I called you three fuckin' times,' he says. 'Ain't so much to ask is it, couple o' drinks for me mates? Fuck sake.'

'I'm sorry, Don, little Roy woke—'

'Oh for fuck…yer one pint short and all. Go on an' get another for Blakey here. An' take these empties back. A man can't even play cards, what with all the clutter round here. Fuck sake…'

When she'd gave everyone but meself a pint she got the empties and went back to the kitchen, coming back out a minute later with one for us. Not once since first clocking us had she looked my way. She gave us me pint and says to Don: 'Don? Can you all hush up a bit? Little Roy can't sleep with—'

'Can't kip, can he?' he says, winking at Max and Tommo. 'Give him a pint an' all then. That'll make him kip. Eh, lads?'

The outsiders found that amusing, and showed it. All that singing had put em in a good mood, like as not.

Rache went back into the kitchen. I wanted to ask Don about it, how long he'd been with her and that. But to be honest I couldn't get me swede around it.

I mean, Rache and Don?

It just weren't right.

But now were not the time to talk about it. I supped me pint and lit a smoke instead, trying to relax a bit. I were amongst friends here, after all. Except Max and Tommo. And Don, who I weren't sure about just then.

'Blakey?' says Tony.

'What?'

He nodded at me cards. 'Woss you gonna do?'

'Hey? Oh.' I looked at em a bit longer, chewing a thumbnail. 'I reckon I'll stick.'

'Er, but Blakey—'

'No no—I'll twist. Aye. Twist.'

There were a pause, then a lot of cackling. Even Mike were having a chortle, though he were trying not to.

'What?' I says. 'Woss I said?'

'You got the wrong game, mate,' says Mike. 'Stick or twist is pontoon. Iss poker we're playin', an' you—'

'I know iss fuckin' poker. I'm just sayin' I wants some more cards like, you know.'

Max and Tommo was whispering again. Only it were more louder this time and I'd swear blind I heard 'twat' in there somewhere. And possibly 'mong'.

'Hoy, you,' I yells, pointing at the Bo Duke one. 'Woss you just say?'

'What?' He says, screwing up his face. 'Woss the problem?'

'You heard. You just called us a mong, didn't yer.'

'Siddown, Blakey,' says Don. 'Tommo didn't mean it like that.'

'He fuckin' did. I heared him. He called us a twat an' a mong.

Bo Duke—or Tommo as Don called him there—were smirking, looking at his cards. I wanted to smash me pint glass and slash his face open with it, get him smirking for proper. But I didn't do that cos it were a full pint, and I didn't wanna spill the lager all over Don's carpet. I decided on punching him instead.

He looked at us just before I swung for him, and says: 'Look, mate, fuckin' cool it. All right? We're playin' cards here. Cards is an easy and painless way of honin' yer instincts for psychological warfare. You can learn all kinds of things about people from playin' cards, and no one gets hurt. See? Body language, such as. Your body lingo tells me you wanna kill me. Right?'

'Too fuckin' right I do,' I says. But I didn't wanna, really. Not no more. Fuck knows what he were on about, but he'd sucked the wind clean from out of me sails.

'Well, thass cos yer takin' it too serious like. There ain't no real aggro here. Iss just play. Like boxers and their sparrin', yeah?'

'See, Blake?' says Don. 'We're all mates here. Ain't us, lads?'

Everyone says aye except the two outsiders. The one who'd spoke just smirked at us, and his mate was looking at his cards. I unclenched me fist and sat down, picking up me pint then plonking it down empty.

'Blakey?' says Tony.

'What?' I says.

'So how many cards you wanna swap?'

I watched everyone's eyes over the top of me cards. No one were laughing now, but you could tell they wanted to. I knew they just about had to. And I suppose you could say it were slightly funny, when you looked at it. 'All right, all right,' I says chucking me cards down. 'Tell us the rules again, you bunch o' fuckin' cunts.'

• • •

'So, tell us again: two doubles beats a triple, right?'

'No it *don't*,' says Tony. 'Three of a kind always beats two pair.'

'Oh, right.'

To be frank I were getting a bit fed up with it. There were no skill to the game, so I couldn't exercise me superior swede with it. You got dealt some shite cards, you gave some back, and you got some more shite cards. Where's the skill in that?

'I'll have five cards then please,' I says, throwing all me cards down.

'You can't change all of em. Most you can change is four.'

'I'll have four cards then, please.'

'Which one's you keepin'?'

'Dunno. They'm all shite.'

'You gotta choose.'

'Fuck sake…' I picked one up at random. It were king of hearts. Mike gave us four new uns and I picked em up, praying there'd be some more kings in there so I could win a game. I looked at em: queen, ten, jack, and ace. All hearts. 'Fuckin' hell,' I says throwing em down and getting up. 'I ain't bettin' this time.'

'You ain't bet in any of em,' says Pete.

'Ain't my fault. The cards is fuckin' diabolical. All I wanted were a king or two.'

'You can't blame the cards.'

'I can, and I will. Where's the bog, Don?'

'Out there on the right. Tell her to get the beers in, eh. An' give her a slap.'

I gave him a long look as I went past, but his eyes was down. Shame really cos if he'd clocked the look in me eyes, and we'd come to blows about it there and then instead of letting it simmer, things might have turned out a bit better, later on.

But he never.

And you could say it's down to me, not him. You could say I ought to have had him up about the way he treated our Rache the moment I came to an awareness about it. Aye, there's many a thing I could have done and wished I'd have done down through the years, and many a broken heart could have been saved.

But I didn't do em.

• • •

DOCTOR: *You killed your father, didn't you.*
PATIENT: [visibly uncomfortable, but makes no attempt to leave the room this time]

DOCTOR: *It's OK, you don't need to hide anything. You were a minor when it happened, and you were acquitted. But that had nothing to do with whether you did it or not.*

PATIENT: [stands up and paces up and down] *It were an accident. He were...He fucking...*

DOCTOR: *It's OK, Royston.*

PATIENT: *Fucking shut it, you bastard. I just sort of pushed him back, him on the stair like. He were pissed and fell backward, and that were that. I never meant it.*

DOCTOR: *But you hated him, right?*

PATIENT: *No, I never. He were all right, just a bit...*

DOCTOR: *A bit what?*

PATIENT: *Nothing. He had it hard, looking after us, no wife to do the housework. You couldn't blame him for having a sup, of an evening. And if he clipped us now and then, so what? Every lad deserves a clip round the ear, even if they ain't done nothing wrong. He used to smack us for looking at him, or sitting in the wrong chair. Or asking for some scran. He never cooked for us, you know. Best I'd get is a few cold chips he'd brung home, or some beans. I had to open the tin though. The stingy cunt wouldn't even buy togs for us. They asked us why I started robbing, when the coppers first caught us at it. I tell you, they'd be robbing shite and all, they had what I had. Fuck all, mate. That's what me old man gave us. Fuck all, besides a lot of knocks. And you ask us why I killed the bastard?*

• • •

There's a little pantry off the kitchen in them Bonehill flats, which was all identical one to the next, and I found Rache in there, crying into her hands. She stopped that upon my entry and put a hanky to her nose, saying: 'This flippin' hay fever.'

'Hay fever in November?' I says. Cos she couldn't fool me.

'It ain't November, it's December,' she says, dabbing her eyes. 'Ain't you noticed the Christmas deccies in town?'

'Aye, course,' I says. 'Well actually, no. Everythin' in town looks odd to me these days, so I ain't surprised I missed em.'

'Well it's nearly Christmas. An' I wants our Roy to have the best Christmas ever.'

'Aye, I'm sure he will, with you as his mam.'

'Ain't so simple as that, Blakey.'

'It is simple.' I picked a tin of custard powder off the shelf, shook it, and put it back. 'That Roy lad dunno what he's got, I tell yer. He's got the best mam ever. I knows that cos I knows you. You was the best barmaid ever, an' you'll be the best mam ever.'

She smiled at that, which were a joy to behold. 'I weren't that good a barmaid, Blake.'

'Aye you were. Never put a foot wrong. No one could pull pints like you.' I found a little box and opened it. Boiled sweets. I didn't like them but I took one anyhow and unwrapped it, putting the box back. 'Punters came to Hoppers just to get served by you.'

'You dunno the half of it, Blake,' she says, shaking her head. 'I put many a foot wrong.'

'Bollocks.' The sweet were pear flavour and I weren't keen on it. 'Look at that,' I says, pointing behind Rache. While her head were turned I wrapped the sweet up again and put it back in the box.

'What?' she says.

'Oh, thought I saw summat.'

'What? A mouse?'

'No, don't worry about it.'

'I hates mice,' she says, rummaging through the tins there.

'It weren't a mouse. Leave it, Rache,' I says, gently turning her back towards us. 'Come on, you was sayin' about puttin' many a foot wrong.'

'Oh aye,' she says, smiling and shaking her head at the memory. 'You know that feller the once…wossisname? In Hoppers. Anyhow, he tried makin' out he'd gave us a twenty, but I weren't havin' none of it. It were a tenner I says, and I weren't budgin' from it. Remember that?'

'Aye I does. Danny, it were.'

'Danny, that's him.'

'Aye. Funnily enough—'

'Anyhow, you comes up and chucks him out cos he were kickin' up a row about it.'

'Aye I did. It's because—'

'But soon as you was gone with him I realised I'd made a boob, Blake.'

I loved hearing a bird use that turn of phrase, and I tried hard not to look down.

'Danny were right, Blakey. I found the twenty, right there on top of the tenners. But I never owned up to it. And if I were a good barmaid like you says, I would have owned up. I wouldn't of got it wrong in the first place. An' then you wouldn't have had to throw that poor man out.'

'An' ban him.'

'You banned him?'

'Aye, an' he's still—'

'Oh, poor Danny.'

I set me jaw firm and says: 'It ain't "poor Danny." He got what he had comin', twenty or no twenty. See, he called you a cow, Rache. No one can call you a cow.'

We looked at each other. And it were plain as day that summat passed between us that could not be ignored. Aye, we'd gave each other the eye now and then over the years, me being head doorman and her head barmaid, and both of us young and fit. But this were different.

'Hoy,' shouts Don from the living room. 'Where's our beers, you fuckin cow?'

She started past us but I got hold of her. She struggled for a bit then gave up, sinking into me chest. I stroked her hair a couple of times before she pulled away, more calmer this time. And it were right to do that, Don being so near. But I weren't finished with her yet so I grabbed her hand.

'Why him?' I says.

'Leave it, Blake.'

'No, I wanna know. Why's you livin' with Don, fuck sake?'

'He's Roy's father,' she says, looking into the kitchen.

'Aye I guessed that, but why the fuck d'you let him poke...I mean, like, woss he got that...Ah, you know.'

She took a long time stubbing her fag in the tray. 'He asked me.'

'What, to have his babby?'

'He asked me out.'

'But that ain't no reason.'

'Why not, Blake? Askin' out is all it takes.'

'Aye but...*Don*?'

'Go on then—what's wrong with Don?'

'Well, he's like...You know, he's...'

'No, I don't know. Please tell.'

'He's a fuckin' bastard, ain't he.' I weren't enjoying this. No one enjoys telling home truths. But she'd pushed us into it. 'I mean he's all right, like, down the pub an' that. An' I ain't ever had no trouble off him on the door at Hoppers. An' he lent us a tenner the other day. But, you know...'

'I told you—you'll have to tell me. I don't know nuthin.'

'Rache, the way he treats you...' I says, leaning in a bit and touching her cheek. 'You deserves better'n that.'

She looked at us now. Gone were the soft eyes and special look. 'I does?' she says. And her eyes was saying no.

She went into the kitchen.

• • •

When I went back into the living room after me piss I found the poker game to be finished. The cards was nowhere to be seen, anyhow, and neither was the money in the pot. The lads was still in place though, drinking and smoking and looking up at us when I walked in.

'Oh I see,' I says. 'Too good for you, were I?'

'No, Blake,' says Don. 'Iss time to get serious.'

I didn't like the sound of that. Nor the look of it neither. No one were smiling. 'Woss you on about?'

'Business time, Blake. Siddown.'

I sat in me chair and got me fags out. The pack were empty, but Tommo passed us his. I looked at him to make sure he weren't piss-taking, then took one. Embassy Number One.

'Nice one,' I says.

In response he held out his lighter for us. I lit me smoke off it, getting a bit suspicious now. I looked round the table and noticed they was all looking back at meself.

'What the fuck's goin' on here?' I says.

'Don't worry, Blake,' says Don. 'Like I says before, we're all mates here. Right, lads?'

'He's right, Blakey,' says Pete before the ayes had finished. 'We brung you here cos we all rates you so high.'

'Shut up, Pete,' says Don. 'Blake, we got a proposition for you. You might like it an' you might well not. If you likes bein' a nobody, f'rexample, I reckon you'll turn it down.'

'I ain't no nobody.'

Everyone were shifting slightly, breathing or moving fag or pint to lips, or just plain bollock-scratching. Everyone but Don, who looked straight at us and says: 'We're all nobodies. Everyone in this room, everyone in this town. You're born a nobody and you stays it until you makes your mark. Most never does make their mark, Blake. Most don't even know what makin' their mark is. But I does, Blake. An' I reckon you're the sort o' feller knows it and all.'

'Who says I ain't made me mark?' I says. Cos I didn't like his line of thinking. I didn't like him, neither, seeing the way he treated Rache. 'I made more of a mark than any other cunt in this town, in recent years like. Go an' read the papers, mate.'

'Don't need to read em. We all knows what you done, Blakey. Everyone here knows what kind of a feller you is. But you ain't rich, is you, Blakey? You ain't got much to show fer all them battles you won. Riches is what stops you bein' a nobody. An' riches is what you will get, mate, if you joins us in our little project. Untold riches. Eh, lads? Just think: two days from now, you could be a proper somebody…'

• • •

I loves a fry-up.

There is no better sanctuary in life than the one found in a cup o' tea, a plate stacked up with everything the human body needs to get it going, and a little side plate piled up with toast (cos there's no room left on your main plate). If you can have that, you can duck out of all the shite flying around in the world and concentrate on filling your gut.

So that's what I were doing, next morning in the Bonehill Caff.

'Ta,' I says, the bird bringing us over another cuppa. 'Bit more toast an' all, eh.'

'All right, darlin'. You want the paper?'

'Nah. Don't read the paper.'

'No, I don't suppose you do.'

'Woss that supposed to fuckin' mean?' I says, a bit of black pud flying out the corner of me gob.

'Hoy, you,' says the feller behind the counter. 'We'll have none o' that round here.'

'Weren't me,' I says. 'She were makin' out like I dunno how to read.'

'I never said that. I didn't mean to—'

'You fuckin' did. Everyone reckons I'm thick, just cos I been in Parpham. Well I *ain't* fuckin' thick, right? I'm quite brainy, actually.'

The counter feller had been glaring at us all the while, waiting for us to finish before he said his piece and told us to clear off or summat. But instead of that he started laughing.

The bird put a birdy paw to her lips and let out a little titter. One or two behind us had a chuckle and all.

'What?' I says.

A burst of winter shut em up, and I turned round to see who were coming in the door. 'Ah, fuck,' I says, turning back to me scran and forking so much in me gob that I couldn't be expected to speak for a couple of minutes.

'Ah, hello, Royston,' says the Doc, sitting down opposite us. 'I was driving past and I, er...'

He looked at us like it were my turn to say summat. But fuck him—why should I hurry up me chewing for his sake? Like I says, I'd been enjoying a nice bit o' peace and harmony before him barging in, bringing his cold air. If I didn't have me mouth full I'd tell him to fuck off.

The bird came back with me toast, then stood looking down at the Doc.

'Ah,' he says, noticing. 'Just a coffee, please.'

'Coffee?'

'Yes please. With milk.'

'Roland?' she shouts at the counter feller. 'The man says he wants coffee.'

'Coffee?'

'Aye. With milk.'

'Hmm,' he says, scratching his swede and looking around behind there.

The Doc frowned and goes: 'Erm, if it's any trouble...' But the bird were off picking up dirties and didn't seem to hear him.

During all this I'd supped some tea and topped up me gobful.

'Well, here we...er...' goes the Doc, drumming his fingers and looking around. He stopped drumming and leaned in, whispering: 'I need to have a quiet word with you. Outside, perhaps?' Noticing how I weren't replying nor even looking at him, he goes: 'It's important.'

I got a sausage and laid it on a bit of toast, used me knife to get a lot of yolk all over it, then folded the toast over and put the lot in me gob.

Fucking beautiful.

'Look, I don't have much time, so I'll just…' whispers the Doc (though it were more of a hiss than a whisper, come to think on it). 'Anyway, I want to make something clear. Whatever Nathan the so-called barman and his cohorts are planning, I'm no part of it. As I've told you already, he offered to help you out by getting you into a job. And they seemed to be on your side, so I went along with it. But…but…'

The bird came along and plonked a mug in front of the Doc.

He picked it up, sniffed it, then put it down and goes: 'I never knew his true motives, Royston. He didn't mention any of this *Old Guard* business. He gave me to believe that he was an old friend of yours, that you were his most loyal customer and he wanted to see you all right for old times. But now…Well, I don't know what. I can't quite understand what they think they can gain from you working as a security guard at the…er…'

'Wossname Centre,' I says, sucking up a bit of stray bacon rind.

'Yes, the…what? Erm, anyway, what I want to say, Royston, is that I don't like it. It's not a healthy situation. I'm sorry for pressurising you into this job, but I must advise you to resign. Straight away. And stay away from the Paul Pry.'

I only had a bit left. Half an egg white, some bits of sausage, a few beans, and one bit of toast. I piled the lot onto the toast and crammed him gobwise. It's amazing, the way your full English fry-up can work his magic right down to the last scrap.

'Royston, are you listening? I want you to leave your job. I know I said you have to stay there otherwise you could go back into Parpham, but I retract that. I'll see to it that you don't have to go back as a resident. And don't worry about the car…You can drive it for a while—a couple of weeks, say—until you get something of your own. We'll have to get you another job, of course. Something in a factory perhaps. Or there's a vacancy for a security guard at Parpham, if you want to stay in that line of, er… Royston, *are* you listening?'

I stopped licking me plate and picked up the mug to wash it all down. The tea were getting cool and there were only an inch or two of it anyhow. I swigged it and whistled the bird over.

'Hoy, you,' says the counter feller. 'Don't you whistle my Maureen.'

I stood up, opening me gob to give him what for.

'Royston,' the Doc's saying, pulling me arms. 'Sit down.'

I found meself doing like he says, just like in the ozzy. You gets used to doing like the Doc says.

'Perhaps I should explain something to you…' he says all quiet, 'about why I'm getting so involved in all this. Do you remember when you asked me why I became a doctor? Well I'll tell you—because to me the human mind is the deepest well in all of creation, and no matter how far you plumb it, there is always something else to dredge up and examine. It's something I never get bored of, Royston, and something I felt I should devote my life to. Unfortunately, I didn't lavish so much attention on the minds—and hearts—of those who were closest to me. My wife left me years ago, Royston. We had a son, but he left, too. As soon as he was old enough, he disappeared. He just up and left the area, and now I have no idea where he is. And I know it's my fault. I was never there for him. In effect, Royston, my son never had a father. He had no guidance in life, and now it's too late for him.'

I lit a smoke and looked at me watch.

'But it's not too late for you, Royston.'

I'd have to get shifting soon. I had a job to go to, and things to mull over. Like Don and his little proposal last night. (I'll tell you about that in a bit, after the Doc fucks off. Which I assure you he will do, in a little while.)

'You received a letter,' he says. 'Before you left Parpham. I don't know what you made of it, but please let me implore you not to ignore it. Sometimes we get a second chance, Royston. Sometimes our lives veer off course, and we get lost. But sometimes we get a second chance, an opportunity to set everything straight. (In our minds, at least, which is where it counts.) Don't ignore the letter, Royston. And don't be afraid. Sometimes we get a second chance, but there's never a thir—'

The Doc had to stop there cos I blew smoke all over his face by accident. After he'd stopped coughing he got on his feet, going: 'Anyway, you think about what I've just said. I'll see about that security job, all right?' Then he fucked off, leaving a tenner by his mug.

'Yes?' says the bird. She were well grumpy.

I gave her the note, saying: 'An' I wants me change.' The Doc's coffee were still warm, so I drank it. Weren't so bad. Mind you, I weren't so keen on his orders. I'd had enough of him ordering us about, reckoning he knew what's best for us. I were back in Mangel now, and Parpham were in the past. I were stood on me own two wellies and making summat of meself. And the Doc could fuck right off.

Mind you…

• • •

I pulled up on the corner and stopped the motor. The Bee Hive were just along the way a bit, same as always. I watched it for a bit. Dunno what I were looking for, mind. It were early and no one'd be in there yet. Not in the bar anyhow. But there was rooms upstairs and someone must live there. And I could have sweared I'd clocked the curtains twitching just there.

No further twitches was forthcoming, and after a bit I had to shut me eyes and give em a rest. Then I lit a smoke and got the letter out me pocket. It were getting a bit ragged now, what with this and that, and the fold along the middle were turning into a tear. I had a read, again, and then shut me eyes. Again.

12

I were thinking about Don and his project as I stood on me door, watching all them punters filtering past. I'd told him no, course, at the time. I don't mind going for a beer and a game of cards with a bunch of fellers, but I draw the line at risking me neck for em. And for what? Untold riches? What the fuck is untold riches? Wedge you don't tell no one about? I don't like the sound of that. I want folks to see I'm fucking loaded, not hide it from em.

And like I says just now, I'd be risking me neck. I'd done well for meself since coming out of Parpham. I were on the verge of great things. All I had to do were keep me nose clean and do that thing for the little boss feller, and I'd sail into a top job. I'd lose it all if I done what Don had in mind. The door position would go first, even if they didn't find out I were in on the job. Then the car would get taken away. Then the coppers'd do some sniffing and collar me, thereby putting us in Mangel Jail, like as not.

And besides, Don could go piss up a rope if he thought I were helping him. Like I says, no one calls our Rache a cow.

I hadn't forgot about it and I intended on making him pay for it. Just didn't fancy having him up about it at the time, in front of his mates. Be a bit embarrassing it would. For him, like.

'Here,' says a feller going past and shaking me paw.

'Oh,' I says. 'All right, er...' It were one of the many sons of Bob Gretchum the builder. He had five or six in total but they all had the same name, except one of em who were known as Robert. I weren't sure which one this were though. 'All right, Bob,' I goes. Cos I knew it weren't Robert.

But I were talking to the back of his head. He waved an arm behind him a bit, then went on into the crowds, not even twisting his neck at us. I reckoned that a bit out of order, to be frank with you, and I shook me head. Then I noticed the bit of paper he'd put in me paw. There were a typed message inside and it goes:

URGENT: COME TO PAUL PRY THIS LUNCHTIME. DO NOT BUNK OFF EARLY FOR IT THOUGH, DO NOT WANT YOU GETTING IN TROUBLE AND LOSING THAT THERE JOB.

'Hiya, Blake.'

I trousered the paper up and looked up, catching a nice waft of perfume. 'All right, Rache,' I says.

She were waltzing past us and all, like Bob just now. I wished she'd have stopped for a chat, but to be honest I were half glad she hadn't. Talking would be awkward just now, what with the home truths I'd kindly doled her last night, and the way she'd took em. There's a time and a place for sorting out differences with Rache, and half nine in the morning on the door of the Wossname Centre weren't either of em. But she stopped, thought about it for a sec, then turned her shapely arse and came back to us.

'I seen you,' she says, pointing at us like she'd finally found us after half an hour of hide-and-seek during which I'd been cheating and she knew it. 'I seen you this mornin.'

'This mornin'?' I says. From her tone it were like she were telling us off, and I tried thinking of what I'd got up to that morning prior to work. Fuck all that I could recall: get up; wash me gnashers and splash me face using an outside tap I found near some garages; head off for work, stopping off for some scran. Maybe that were it. 'You mean the caff in Bonehill?' I says. Cos she'd like as not clocked us in there, and thought I ought to be supporting Burt's Caff. But I didn't fancy seeing Burt just now, not after having a scrap with him so recent. Couldn't tell that to Rache, mind. 'I fancied a change, like,' I says.

'I don't mean the caff. I means the car. I walked past a car this mornin'—on me way to little Roy's babby-sitter—and saw you fast akip in it. How long you been dossin' in cars?'

I knew summat like this might happen. Before last night I'd been careful to park the motor in a place where no one's gonna clock you. But last night, after all that lager round Don's, I just couldn't be fucked driving back to me usual port. So I'd moved the Granada a few yards into a quiet patch near them lock-ups instead, with dustbins and old tyres for company. In short, the last place you'd expect to get clocked. Let alone by a nice bird like Rache.

Mind you, I didn't see how it were any of her fucking business. 'I don't see how—'

'Never mind that,' she says. 'You ought to be thankful someone's worryin' about you. I don't have to, you know. What's that... Poo,' she says, wafting the air under her handsome nose and standing back. 'You stink, Blake. You can't go on dossin' in cars, you know. Smells like a tramp, you does. And whose car were that anyhow? You nicked it, didn't you?'

I fucking resented all this. What right did Rache have to go on at us? I hadn't even shagged her. And I didn't stink, no matter what she says. I knew I didn't cos I'd sprayed me pits only that morning. 'I didn't fuckin' nick the motor,' I says.

'Oh aye? Where'd you get it from, then? You only been out a few days.'

'Someone gave it us.'

'Someone...? Don't make us laugh. Who gave it you? Father Christmas?'

'Never you fuckin' mind.'

She put hands on hips, tucked in chin, and pursed lips. When she started talking again she kept pursing em again between sentences. 'Oh I gets it. Blakey knows best, eh? Blakey can look after himself. Well you listen to me, Blakey: You don't know best. You thinks you does, but you don't. *I knows* who gave you that car. It's flamin' obvious.'

'Oh aye?' I says. Cos she couldn't know. Could she?

'Course it is. An' don't tell us—he wants a little favour in return, right? You get the car, you does the favour. Am I right?'

She were more clever than I'd thought, were Rache. But how the fuck had she found out? 'Aye, but—'

'But nuthin'. It is what it is and no buts will make it what it ain't. Oh, Blake, why don't you open your eyes? He's *usin'* you. They're all in on it an' they're usin' you. You thinks it's a good deal because it's a nice car, and they're bein' all friendly with you and that. But it ain't a good deal, Blake. You thinks they're being fair but they're just pushin' you around, same as everyone else. You'll end up in Mangel Jail or dead. Guaranteed. You mark my words.'

She stopped pursing her lips and tucking in her chin. She took a step closer, putting a paw on me arm and giving us a look I'd seen on her the other day at Burt's, when she'd said *Oh, Blake, what did they do to you in there?* But this time she says: 'Oh, Blake, do *me* a favour. Will you?'

'Aye, all right,' I says. 'What?'

'Tell em no. Tell em to take their rotten plan and shove it.'

I were nodding. I liked the sound of it. Specially with her standing so close and looking up at us that way, and her tit pressing gently into me ribs. Aye, I could see her point. Nathan and the Doc *was* pushing us around. All the Doc had ever done were push us around, when you thought about it. And I'd always harboured the opinion that Nathan were a cunt of the very highest order. 'Aye,' I says, nodding. 'Aye, all right. I'll tell em to stick it right up their big greasy shite-holes, shall I?'

Rache blinked a couple of times, then gave us another glorious smile and took hold me other arm. Folks was walking past and looking at us funny, but I didn't give a toss about them bastards. I had Rache here, didn't I. And she were holding us and looking right at us with them big brown eyes, and her juicy lips was turning up at the corners and I wanted to stick me tongue right between em. I put a paw behind her back and pulled her to us, aiming to do just that. But just as I got me tongue ready and leaned in, she says: 'And give the car back.'

I shut me gob and let the paw drop off her back. 'No,' I says, firm of voice. 'The motor stays.'

'Blake,' she says, still smiling. 'If you say no to them, you can't keep it. You've gotta return it. You don't need it anyhow.'

'I know but the Doc says—'

'Blake, you're out of Parpham now. It don't matter what the doctors say. It's about *you* now, and what *you* say. Look, what you need to do is sort your life out. You needs folks around you who you can trust. An' you can't go on sleepin' rough like that. I knows what your situation is. I knows about Sally livin' in your house with that... *druggie*. You need to make a *stand*, Blake. That's *your* house, not Sally's. Get em out, Blake. For *her* own good as well as yours. She needs a clean break and all. She's only there still cos she can't be bothered to move. Stand up to her, Blake. It's *your* house. An' you needs it.'

She were right, you know. You couldn't fault our Rache for pushing the right buttons and getting us thinking. It were my house, curse or no curse. Shite might have happened there, but it's where I belonged. An Englishman's castle is like three in the bush. And there's no place like it.

And anyhow, I could always flog the place. Wages I'd be getting soon, I ought to be living out Danghill way, with all them other respectable folks. I'd have a nice big house featuring the following items:

- Gravel driveway
- Double garage
- Pond out back with plenty of them big wossname fish in it
- Couple of bull terriers
- Big living room with a bar set up in the corner
- Games room with snooker table, darts, pinball, and another bar
- Rache

Aye, Rache. Cos why not? She were good for us, it were plain to see. She knew how I ticked and I didn't mind her knowing it. We'd always had a thing for one another, Rache and meself. She'd always kept an eye out for us and I'd always kept an eye down her top whenever she leant over.

And Don could fuck off. He'd had his chance.

The cunt.

'You leave it to me, our Rache,' I says, reaching a paw behind her again. 'Watch and learn.'

She slipped away, giggling a bit. I felt me tadger go hard again like the other morning, and got a paw pocketed sharpish to pin him down. 'I'm proud of you,' she says. And I knew she meant it.

I knew I couldn't let her down.

I watched her into her shop, her turning around now and then to keep waving at us. When she were safely inside I noticed the Gretchum lad sloping back toward the doors. 'Hey there, Bob,' I says, putting a paw on his chest. 'You got a pencil or summat?'

He wanted to go but I weren't having none of it.

'Come on,' I says, holding out me free paw.

'Fuckin' hell,' he says, going through his pockets and coming up with a little bookie's pen.

'Nice,' I says, taking it off him. 'You stand still. Right?' I got the bit of paper I'd trousered just now, turned it over to the blank side, and wrote a little message on it. 'You take this and give it back to Nathan the barman.'

I handed it back to Bob Junior. When he started reading it I slapped him and goes: 'You deaf or summat? Go on an' give it Nathan, you little fucker.'

• • •

DOCTOR: *And what about Beth? You killed her, too, didn't you?*

PATIENT: *No, I told you—I weren't even there.*

DOCTOR: *But you—*

PATIENT: *Finney done it. He put her in Hoppers and torched the place. I went barmy at him when I found out, but do you know what? Best thing he ever done, that were. Finney got a lot of stick for being thick, but what he done there were the best fucking thing…I never asked him to do it, oh no. But he* knew. *He knew me own mind better than meself. Mind you, it were me sent her down there in the first place. Aye, I just had a feeling…And Legsy—I fucking got him, you know. He's the one poking her, you see. But I fucking got him…*

• • •

After work I got changed in the Granada and took her over the Paul Pry car park. I were set on doing what Rache had said, you see, and there were no time like the present. Aye, soon as the motor were dumped I could get on with the real work, namely reclaiming my house. Don't sound such a task to you, like as not. What's so hard about turfing out a bird and a piece of shite like Ferret?

Didn't make it no easier giving up the Granada, mind. Specially with the Doc saying I could have it for a couple of weeks, back there. That motor represented everything I'd ever wanted out of life. It's all about status, see. It's about your standing in the community, the way folks looks at you and talks to you and that. Course, I already had status in bucketloads, as you and everyone else knows. That's how I'd managed to walk into the premier door position in Mangel only one day after coming out of Parpham. But you needs summat to back it up, summat to sway the one or two who might have doubts. And it's transport I'm on about here.

Rache were right, though. I had to make a clean break of it.

The Granada had to go.

A grey Escort van were pulling ahead of us into the car park, and I recognised it as that of the Gromer feller from the offy in Cutler Road. 'Ah, it's you is it?' he says as I opened me door. 'Time d'you call this? You let a lot of folks down this lunchtime.'

I didn't hate Gromer, but I hated the tone to his voice just now. Aye all right, he were a miserable cunt and he'd always sounded that way or thereabouts, though I couldn't recall him ever speaking to us direct. But I weren't having that kind of tone from no one no more. It's like Rache says just there: everyone were pushing us around.

I got the Elvis tape out of the deck and put him in me pocket, then climbed out of the Granada for the last time.

'You fuckin' say summat?' I says, addressing Gromer.

He were stood in a black suit and tie, frowning at us from the other side of his grey Escort van. The frown fell off his face when he seen us coming over to him sharpish, and a look suggesting concern for his personal safety came to it instead. He went to duck back into the van, then thought better of it and stood tall. That showed a fair bit of bollocks, him being twenty year my senior and a foot shy heightwise, and I rewarded his bravery by not knocking him down. Not yet anyhow. 'I says did you fuckin' say summat?' I says, squaring up.

'Aye, I did,' he says, with a bit more respect now. 'I'll admit to you, Royston Blake, I don't expect much of you. The rest of em seem to have planted emselves right behind you. But I don't see it meself. I can't see you comin' through for us, Royston Blake. I think you'll let us down. You done it today already, and you'll do it again.'

'Do you know what?' I says. 'You're right. I will let you down. I ought to have let you down a couple o' day ago when you tricked us into sayin' aye by givin' us that motor over there. Well I'm out of it now. Here,' I says, dropping the keys in front of him. 'Give em to the Doc and send him my regards. An' you can give a message to Nathan an' all, you can tell him—'

'You can tell us yerself,' says Nathan's voice from somewhere in my head. I put paws to ears, feeling a bit of a dizzy spell coming on. Nathan's next words came a bit quieter: 'I ain't in your head, you bloody fool. I'm here, by the back door.'

The dizzy spell didn't happen, and when I turned round I found Nathan to be right there in the place he'd stated, fists on hips, glowering at us. He were wearing a black suit and tie and all.

'There a funeral, or summat?' I says.

'Was,' he says. 'There was a funeral. Now woss this you was wantin' to tell us? Eh? Come on, I'm all ears.'

I didn't say nothing for a bit. It's easy to tell em all to fuck off when they ain't there in front of you, or when it's just Gromer, the miserable cunt from the offy. But it were hard with Nathan the barman.

'Perhaps while yer at it you can explain this, eh?' He held up a bit of paper that looked very much like the one I'd sent him earlier via the Gretchum lad. 'Have you seen this, eh, Bob? Says: "FUCK OFF NATHAN, YOU CUNT." Have you ever heared the like of it? I can't say I have. And truly I dunno what to make of it.'

'It's like I tells you, Nathan,' goes Gromer, 'the feller's no good, like everythin' he lays a paw on. We're best shot of him.'

'An' then what?' says Nathan. 'Eh? Then who's our man? Who will do the work of the Old Guard if not him?'

Gromer didn't know off the top of his swede, so he scratched it and frowned a bit and came up with: 'I don't see why one of them Gretchum lads can't do it. Some of the bigger uns is right dependable. And there's five or six of em, so Bob wouldn't miss—'

'That's enough,' says Nathan in a voice that had all the traffic noises pausing for a moment. Then, a bit quieter: 'You've heard the prophecy as well as I. There's only one it will be, and that one is Blake here.' He turned to me and goes: 'Blake, pick up them keys and come inside here. Our plans are changin' sharpish and it's time to brief you, hence the call for you to come here just now. Things has come forward a bit. The day of reckonin' has come, you might say. And it's tomorrow. So, will you come in please.'

I stood me ground for a bit. I were trying to picture Rache, her telling us, '*You'll end up in Mangel Jail or dead.*' Well, I truly did not want to end in Mangel Jail. Nor dead neither. But like I says, it were hard to tell Nathan to fuck off. I'd always found it easier to go along with him, and right back there in the darkest corner of me swede I harboured the idea that every bit of shite life had tossed our way, every time I'd tried to get summat straight and it had ended up more warped than a pig's cock—they'd all been times when I'd gone against Nathan.

And when Nathan winked and went: 'There's a nice pint of lager in it for you,' I knew he had us.

Mind you, just then another voice piped up behind us, going: 'Hoy, Blakey. You all right, mate?'

I were watching Nathan's face just then and it weren't smiling. He folded his hairy arms and shook his head slow, clocking over my shoulder.

I turned that way meself and found Don there, t'other side of the wall, smoking a fag and giving us a nice friendly smile. 'Fancy a pint, mate?' he says. 'I got a joke for you. You'll fuckin' love it, heh heh. Eh? But not here though. Beer's piss here. Less go down the Why Not. Eh. Why not?'

I didn't look at Nathan again.

Had an idea, hadn't I.

Like I says, watch and learn.

· · ·

'So the feller holdin' the goat goes: "All right, but where do I put it?" He heh. Eh? Heh. D'you not get it?'

'Oh,' I says. 'Goat, aye. Heh heh, nice one.'

'Aye, but it ain't the goat that's…I mean the feller's got his cock out, ain't he. See?'

'Aye. I laughed, didn't I?'

Don had thin lips and a little thin tash above the top one. It were a bit like Nathan's, but Don had to shave some of his off each morning to get it that way, while Nathan were naturally endowed in the thin tash department. I can't say I approved of either of em, if I'm honest. Proper tash or none at all, says I. Anyhow, Don had a thin one, and he licked it just now with his long pointy tongue. 'Summat on yer mind, Blakey?' he says. 'Come on, you can talk to old Don. I'm your mate, is what I am. Aye, you needs mates. Mates helps each other out, you know. Feller can't share a problem with his mate, who can he share it with? Eh?'

The Why Not never had been a favourite drinking spot of mine. It were the kind of place you takes a bird, with lamps and tablecloths and that. Course, I'd always been lucky in the bird department. They'd flocked to us, and I got to shag em most times without having to take em out to places like the Why Not. But I didn't mind being here now, with Don. I had a plan, see.

'Well, Don,' I says. 'You knows how I turned you down last night, about the job an' that?'

He put a finger to his lips, then smiled over me shoulder. A barmaid turned up beside us just then and started clearing the six or so empties off our table. 'All right, darlin'?' says Don, winking at her and patting her arse. She giggled and wriggled and made a show of her cleavage as she picked the glasses up. She weren't bad actually, and I reached round to give her a pinch meself.

She slapped me paw away and looked down at us, the way you looks into a bog that ain't been flushed and ought to have been. Then she went off to the bar with her empties.

Don shrugged and drank his pint.

'Anyhow,' I says, 'you knows how I turned—'

'Don't worry about it,' says Don, tossing a fag my way. 'I asked you and you says no. Thass all right by me, Blake. Yer still me mate.' He sparked us both up and goes: 'Ain't we still mates?'

'Aye, Don, course we fuckin' is.' Was we fuck.

'Well then. Matter's closed, far as I cares.'

'Thass just it though, Don. I changed me mind.'

'You don' have to—'

'No, I ain't just sayin' like. I means it. I wants to come in with you an' the lads. I'm all in, Don.'

He rubbed an eyebrow and goes: 'I dunno. You weren't sure, so maybe you ain't—'

'I fuckin' *is* though. I mean I is, er…What was you gonna say there?'

He puffed his smoke for a bit, then shook his swede and says: 'No, I don't want you doin' stuff you ain't happy about.'

'For fuck sake, Don…I *is* happy. If you don't let us do it, *thass* when I won't be happy.'

He put pint to lips and spied us, says: 'Sure?'

'Course I fuckin' is.'

'Cos iss tomorrow, you know. Kicks off at two in the afty—sharp. You joins up, there's no backin' out.'

'I knows it. Sign us up, fuck sake.'

We shook hands and sank our pints.

'You don't know how happy this makes us, Blake,' says Don. 'Cos you knows how rich this is gonna make us, right? We'll be fuckin' set up, mate. An' I wouldn't want you left out, like.'

It made me happy and all. But not for Don's reasons. I didn't give a badger's arse about Don, his fucking barmy plans, and his wanker mates from the outside. All I cared about were the new life I had coming to us, and the massive kick-start this little plan of mine would give it. I'll explain it in a minute, all right? Just fucking shut up a sec and listen to the master at work.

'But there's summat, Blakey,' he says, leaning in. 'You know Max from last night, right?'

'One o' them outsiders?'

'Aye, he…er…Blake, he ain't sure about you.'

'You what? Him not sure of me? What about me not bein' sure of him? Fuckin' cheek…'

'I knows how it sounds, Blake, but you gotta understand him. Says he were drivin' on the East Bloater Road t'other night an' he seen you roadside with no kit on.'

I looked from eye to eye, trying to suss him. 'You takin' the piss?' I says. 'You must be. Last night yer fuckin' *beggin'* us to go along with you. Now yer sayin'…what? Woss you sayin'?'

'Well, iss a bit…' He looked up and down the pub. One or two had come in, but they was up by the bar chatting with the narky barmaid. 'Blake,' he says, leaning in again, 'he says you was havin' a wank.'

'Havin' a wank?'

'Aye. Pullin' yerself off, like.'

'Pullin' meself off?'

'Aye. Says you was in yer socks and trolleys, bangin' away on yerself, howlin' at the moon.'

'Hang on a min,' I says. 'Thought you says he says I had me kit off?'

'I ain't splittin' no hairs here, Blake. And I won't beat around no bush no more neither. Everyone knows you just came out of Parpham. What Max and Tommo is wonderin'—and I can't say I blames em—is if you ain't still a bit barmy.'

I weren't having this. Plan or no plan, I weren't standing for this kind of talk. Don ought to be licking my fucking boots, me coming back to him and offering me services. And hark at what I were getting from him. I sank me pint and got up, saying: 'I'll be seein' you then, Don.'

Halfway to the door Don's up and after us, saying: 'Come on, Blake. Don't be like that.' He had sense enough not to lay a paw on us. I were boiling inside and I'd have snapped his fucking jaw off. 'They just don't know you, Blake. Not like I does. I knows you, an' I knows you ain't no spanner. You never was, Blake. You just got unlucky is all. There's plenty in Mangel barmier'n you ever was, and no one questions em. But I'll tell you summat, Blake—there's no one round here harder'n you. Nor braver. An' no one with a bigger heart. I truly believes that.'

I turned arse and looked at Don, to make sure he weren't taking the piss. Before I could speak he grabbed me paw and started shaking it hard, saying: 'Thass settled then, right? You're in. If you'll still have us.'

'What about them two cunts?' I says, wrenching me paw away. 'Bo Duke an' wossname?'

'Eh?'

'You know, them outsider cunts?'

'They ain't cunts, Blake. They'm good lads. Just a bit cautious, like. You knows how it is. I'll have a word with em and tell em it weren't you on the roadside there, eh? Mind you,' he says, sitting back down and tossing us a smoke. 'You can't beat havin' a wank in the open air, can you? Eh?' He started laughing.

I joined in. The plan were back on and I wanted to keep him sweet. It weren't funny though.

He hoyed the barmaid for a couple more, then leaned back and says: 'Here, I got another un. There's this farmer's lad, right, and he's out with the pigs one day an' he starts feelin' all...'

• • •

I told you I'd explain it all to you. And now I'm gonna, as your reward for keeping that big fat trap of yours buttoned. It's like this, see:

Picture Royston Blake, newly crowned chief of security at the Wossname Centre. Lower members of staff is looking at him funny, wondering who the fuck he thinks he is, walking into the top job like that. They're scared of him and all, course. They knows his reputation and they ain't about to ask him questions, in case he sacks em. Or boxes their ears for being cheeky. Cos it only takes one look to see he's a pro, and that he don't suffer cunts kindly.

So the backchat starts.

I knows all about backchat. In my time I've known backchat beyond belief, mate. The whole fucking town going on about you behind your arse, spreading rumours and stirring up shite. A lesser feller than meself would have buckled to it, but as it turned out it were the shite stirrers who buckled, the whole lot of em giving way to a superior will. Cos Royston Blake will not be bowed. And he ain't standing for backchat no more. Not now he's chief of security. It needs nipping in the bud. So all he's gotta do is find the bud, then work out how to nip summat into it. Which sounds like you needs special tools for it.

Tools that Blakey ain't got.

Then summat happens. He's only been in the job five minutes and summat happens to test his security skills to the highest hilt. Some bandits has stormed the fucking place, ain't they. They got guns and stockings on their heads and squashed noses and a lot of shouting. Normal decent folks is being told to lie on their bellies and shut the fuck up, else they gets wasted. And who's there to save the day?

Royston Blake is who.

Chief of security.

Cos I knows all about it, don't I.

I'm waiting.

See, here's what Don asked us to do...

13

'There's a little room up on the third floor. You can't get in there unless you got the password, which you gotta plug into a little calculator on the wall next to the door. When you're in you'll see a fucking huge bank of wossnames on your right, buttons and switches and flashing lights and that. Ignore em. It's the other wall you're interested in, the one with the poster of the bird with her tits out on it.

'Anyhow, ignore the bird. Plenty of time for birds with big tits later, when we're all rolling in wedge. Have a quick look at the tits for form's sake and then cast your eyes on the little metal door there, set in the wall. It's got a lock on it but it's a shite one and you can flip the latch easy with a penknife. Inside you'll find a big red button with DANGER! above it and DO NOT PRESS! under it. Fuck that, cos you're gonna press it now.

'So go on, press him.

'Do not fret. All that racket is just security alarms going off. See, what you done there is fire off a secret device what makes special walls come down over the doors and windows and stops anyone coming into the building. And it's coppers we're thinking of here. Cos with the lads downstairs doing the place over, we don't want no fucking rozzers sticking their snouts in. And they won't, not with them walls come down over every place of entry. Quite thin, they is, but solid metal. Special stuff that's rock-hard, and you can't get through it not even with a welding gun. The place were built with them things, though no one knows quite for surely why. I mean, they don't ever bring them walls down at night, so why have em?

'But we ain't worried about that.

'All we gives a toss about is robbing the place blind at our leisure, and then getting the fuck out through the secret tunnel.

'I ain't fucking shiting you here, Blake. There truly is a secret tunnel. Takes you from under the building to a nice quiet spot, well away from coppers and that. And that's how the lads is gonna get away.'

• • •

But they ain't, though, Don.

Cos I got summat else planned for you.

And who's gonna backchat the newly crowned chief of security at the Wossname Centre, after he's foiled a full-on armed robbery single-fucking-handed?

Mind you, I weren't in the job yet.

I had to sort Ferret first.

• • •

PATIENT:	*This ain't the usual room.*
DOCTOR:	*No, it's my office.*
PATIENT:	*Why ain't we in the usual room?*
DOCTOR:	*Because this isn't a usual sort of session. I'm not going to ask you questions today. I'm going to say things to you.*
PATIENT:	*What things?*
DOCTOR:	*Things that I've found, from a professional standpoint. My 'diagnosis' if you like.*

PATIENT:	*Oh aye?*
DOCTOR:	*Yes. Do you want to hear it?*
PATIENT:	[shrugs, but does not take his eyes off me]
DOCTOR:	*Try and remain quiet until I've finished. Will you do that for me?*
PATIENT:	*Aye, course. Fuck sake.*
DOCTOR:	*Good man. I now know what drives you, Royston. I know what the main influence of your life so far has been, the thing that has led you to make all the important decisions in your life. It's your father.*
PATIENT:	[remains silent and motionless]
DOCTOR:	*Your father ruined your childhood. He killed your mother, then refused you the merest scrap of paternal love, let alone carrying out basic parental responsibilities. And it was more than just neglect—he actively sought to give you a hard time. He did all he could to prevent your happiness, your freedom of expression.*
PATIENT:	[remains silent and motionless]
DOCTOR:	*As you started to grow into a man you came up against a block—your father. While he was around, he kept you down. Meanwhile your own ego was growing by the day, bursting to come out into the daylight. And it couldn't, not while your father was there. So you killed him. And then you began to grow. Do you know what you began to grow into, Royston?*
PATIENT:	[trance-like, shakes head]

DOCTOR: *Your father. You killed your father, then* became
*him. You embarked on your adult life with a set
of standards inherited from him. Whenever you
came up against a problem, you simply did what
your father would have done. Even the act of killing him was what he would have done, in your
situation. Can you face up to what he did to your
mother now, Royston? Can you see that he killed
her, even if he was never proven guilty? Not many
people are found guilty in Mangel, Royston, so con-
viction is not the yardstick it should be. He killed
her, Royston, because she was having an affair.
And then you wanted to do the same to your wife,
when you found out she'd been adulterous. You
wanted to, didn't you, Royston? Your friend actually did it, and you've never quite forgiven yourself
for not doing it yourself. You got someone to do it,
whereas your father actually did it.*

PATIENT: [makes an effort to stir from his trance] *N-no,
I never even...I mean I never asked Finney to...*

DOCTOR: *You know, your elaborate fantasy life would have
still been working fine, if you had gone through
with that act. Until then, there was no evidence
that you didn't match up to your father's standards.
But then, in the moment of truth, you failed to act.
You could not make her pay for dishonouring you,
while your simple-minded friend did it without a
moment's thought. And from then on your life spi-
ralled out of control, as you struggled to make up
for this failure. You got involved in one crime after
another, struggling to make up lost ground.*

PATIENT: *But...*

DOCTOR: *No buts. You know it's true. You've been living
               in your father's shoes, Royston. You even live in
               his house.*

• • •

'Right you is, boss.'

It were the bus driver from the other day, the big one who'd
picked us up at Parpham and done that lad for us, and later
turned up at the Paul Pry when Nathan and them lot was trying
to trick us into their nasty plans. He'd winked at us just now, and
now he were waving us away as I reached in me pocket. Seemed
they hadn't told him the news about me resigning. Which stood
to reason, him doing the rounds all day in his bus.

I put 50p in the tray and went to sit down on the back row
before he could argue. I had a little bit of thinking to do, and an
empty bus like this one here were the perfect place for it, long as
Mr Friendly Bus Driver here stayed out of it. See, I had two things
to do here, and I had to get it clear in me head what were what,
like.

The first thing were piss easy: chuck Ferret and Sal out of our
house, thereby taking control of my life, as suggested by Rache.
But that wouldn't do what the little boss feller had asked, which
was to get Ferret off his back for good. No, the two matters had
to be approached separate like, and not as a piece. And being as I
had to get meself into the new job sharpish as can be, the Rache
one would have to piss off onto the back seat while I made the
little boss feller happy.

And then there were summat else to mull over: how best to
sort Ferret.

Now, there's summat I ought to explain to you here. Do you recall back there when I told you about me following Ferret up Danghill way and watching the little boss feller drop an envelope in the bin, followed by Ferret getting it out again? Course you does. Anyhow, what I didn't tell you is what was going on there, behind the scenes like. See, when you're the owner of a large, finely tuned swede, like meself, you gets to see past what your eyes tells you.

You was seeing a feller on the blower, a feller out for a grumpy walk, and the first feller again, scavving out of a bin.

I were seeing a case of blackmail.

Now hold a min, right. I knows what you're thinking. *Don't be so fuckin' stupid*, you're thinking. Or, *You watches too much telly*. But you're wrong on both counts. The first count you knows already. I ain't stupid, and you knows it. You're just saying that cos you don't know what else to say, faced with such superior thinking as I'm showing you here. But don't fret—it's a common reaction and I'm used to it.

And you're wrong about the telly and all. I'd been in Parpham, hadn't I. And they don't allow no telly in there.

Just ask yourself this: who's the local security expert here? Who knows the Mangel criminal fraternity like he knows his own knob? Royston Fucking Blake, ennit. And I knows the things they gets up to.

One of em being blackmail.

The little boss feller hadn't thought to tell us that bit. And he ought to have. 'You'll have to trust us,' he'd said. But he didn't trust us, did he? He didn't trust old Blakey with the full picture. I didn't like that.

Mind you, I knew how to get summat out of it.

A bit of 'job security', you might call it.

The driver grabbed me arm as I went to get off. 'We're right behind you, Royston,' he says, giving us that wink again.

'Fuck off,' I says, shaking me arm loose.

I were fed up with winks.

• • •

No one answered when I knocked. I knocked again.

I were being polite, see.

Just wanted a quiet word.

I knocked for the third time, then stood there like a cunt for a further half of a minute.

Then I started kicking. As I kicked I wondered what I'd done with the key I'd once had to my own house. I hadn't even thought about it before, and it could well be somewhere in me jacket for all I knew. It's only now, shoeing bits of the paintwork off, that I realised how this were my own house and I were fucking barmy for letting Sal and Ferret doss there. I might have gone through a fair bit of shite in there or thereabouts, but it were *my* shite, and I'd fucking well earned the right to treat the place how I liked.

I got a bit knackered after a while and stopped for a breather, lighting one up and looking around. Folks was coming out of their houses behind us, watching us from their doorways. It were just like the other day when I'd had that row with Sal and Ferret in the street here. But fuck em. I didn't care about them cunts, pointing at us and name-calling behind me back. Like I says—this were *my* fucking house.

And then I noticed one of em clapping.

Then another.

Then someone in his upstairs window yells: 'Go on, Blakey. Give em what for.'

'Aye,' says someone else. Mrs Block from Number 29, I think. 'Do us all a favour and get em out.'

'You want a hand, Blakey?' says someone else.

I didn't know what to say, so I turned back to the door and got started on it again. After the first kick I noticed a movement to me left. Summat in the window, through them net curtains. Gone before I could get a good clock of it but there were no mistaking the dull eye and a bit of greasy hair. That were Ferret all right.

'Blakey, Blakey, Blakey, Blakey...'

It gave us strength, hearing me name chanted like that, from folks who not so long previous wouldn't even piss on us if I were ablaze. I felt like Rocky in *Rocky IV*, when he goes over to that foreign place where they all hates him, but he turns em around by beating the shite out of their man. I took a bit of a run-up and put shoulder to wood, feeling the eye of the tiger coursing through me veins.

The door popped open, me falling onto the hall carpet. Ferret bolted up the stair and I heard a door slam. I got up slow, rubbing me shoulder and shaking me swede at young Ferret's lack of judgement. Should have gone out the back door, shouldn't he. I'd tried climbing down from them upstairs windows, and there just ain't no easy way. And you'd be barmy to jump cos it's concrete round front and concrete out back. So all in all he were trapped. And I were in no hurry.

I ain't thick though. I knew he'd try and slip past us, so I shifted that big wood sideboard in the hall over to the front door, thereby blocking his passage. Then I went to the kitchen. Key were in the back door so I turned it and pocketed it. It were still a tip in that kitchen but I found a tea bag and a bit of milk that weren't too bad. Minute or two later I were sat at the table with me feet up, enjoying a nice cuppa. Just like old times, except for the faint sound of neighbours chanting my name out there on the street. Life in a motor's all right for a while, but sooner or later you needs your home comforts. I sparked a fag up and sipped me tea, looking around the old place and having a think. I were wondering if maybe I could live here after all, even with all the wedge I'd be bringing in soon. Lick of paint and a new carpet ought to see it all right, I reckoned. I could have the cellar done out proper, put the snooker table and bar down there. And Rache wouldn't mind living here. Couldn't hardly complain anyhow—she'd have an upstairs here, which you don't get living the Bonehill Flats. And there's a bit of backyard for the youngun.

Mind you, I hadn't thought of that.

I didn't know if I wanted Don's lad living under my roof. Not that Don would be a problem, tucked up there in Mangel Jail for armed robbing. But it wouldn't be right, me having his lad. It wouldn't, would it? I mean, what if they let Don out after a few year, and he came looking for his kin?

I thought about it for a bit, finishing me tea and fag. I found a pack of rich tea biscuits and had a couple of them and all. (Bit damp but not too bad.) Then I got up.

First things first.

I moved some furniture around, then went to the stair. 'Wakey wakey,' I says, taking each step nice and slow. 'Blakey's here.'

The only closed door up there were my bedroom, which Ferret like as not reckoned were his bedroom. I tried the handle and the door opened a bit, but summat were in the way. I applied some shoulder and got in.

I couldn't see no one at first. The window were shut and all, so I knew he couldn't have jumped for it. I checked under the bed, then went to the wardrobe. A noise behind us had us turning, and I got a flash of Ferret's back flying down the stair.

I trotted after, laughing. I knew he couldn't get out in a hurry. Halfway down the stair I thought about what I were gonna do to him in a matter of seconds, and stopped laughing. Breaking heads ain't no laughing matter. Specially if you're like meself and you sometimes goes a bit overboard. Weren't my fault I were so hard, but I had to tone it down here. Time again I'd gone to slap a feller and ended with meat on the floor, sirens blaring after us. But not this time. Not now I'd come so far in bettering meself. All them neighbours out there had seen us come after him, so it wouldn't do for him to turn up dead some place.

No, all I had to do were shite the feller up big time. And to do that, you don't laugh. So as I reached the bottom couple of steps I started growling. I were fairly roaring when I set foot in the hall.

Then Ferret came at us with a samurai sword.

14

'Just my tears and the orchestra playing…la la la…'

That's Engelbert Wossname on the record player. Dad's always got him on. Telly's on and all and he's sat in front of it. Curry sauce on chips on plate on tray on lap. Horses on telly. Fiver on horses.

'Dad?'

'What, fuck sake?'

'I ask you summat, Dad?'

'Fuck off, I'm watchin' telly. Come on, you bastard. Go on, Golden Son.'

He ain't shouting at me now, he's shouting at the telly. Always shouting at the telly he is. Always shouting at me and all. Sometimes I hears him shout and I don't know what he's shouting at. I don't like them times.

'Pick yer fuckin' hooves up, you lazy cunt. Fuckin' goo on. Goo…Ah, for fuck sake.' Shouting at me now. 'Look what you made Golden Son do, you useless fuckin'…'

I lets him eat a few chips and spark a fag. He smokes it and eats a few chips. He chews chips and smokes and sups out of a can.

Seems all right now so I goes: 'Go on, Dad. You never lets us ask you summat.'

It ain't all right. 'Come here, you little…'

I knows I'm all right, mind, cos he's got all that on his lap. Ain't gonna waste that, is he. He takes a swipe with his chip hand and I just steps back. Glob of curry sauce hits me T-shirt. Could be worse.

'Ooh, no runnin' off this time, eh? No scarperin' like a scaredy rabbit? Fair play on you, lad. Might be a man one day after all. I fuckin' doubts it, mind. Go on an' ask us yer little question. Eh? I'm all ears.'

'Iss…iss a bit—'

'Fuckin' spit him out, you dozy cunt.'

'You won't get all angry?'

'If you don't hurry up an' spit I'll go fuckin' barmy, I fuckin' swears I will.'

'Why can't I ever go in the Bee Hive, when I grows up?'

Dad putting chip down and closing gob. Feller shouting the odds on the next race, but the old man ain't listening. Sucks on fag, stubs it out. Puts tray on little table beside him all careful like. Getting up, knees cracking. Moves sharpish, for an old bugger in a string vest.

I moves sharpish and all. Got thirty year on him, I have. You'd think it fifty to look at him. Mind you, it ain't working out proper here. I dunno what it is. It's like a dream. You're pegging it away from a big bastard monster and your legs is wading through syrup or summat. I dunno quite what it is. He gets us in the hall, grabbing an arm.

No words now. Not from him anyhow. I got fucking loads of words, mind. I got em and I says em, honking em out like last week when me and Legs swiped them big bottles of lager from the corner shop. First time I ever tried it, that is. Drank the whole lot before it came back on us. On Legs more like, blasting all over him like a fire hose, him sitting there on the grass not knowing what's hit him. It's words now though, not spew. Words like please *and* sorry *and* don't. *But the old feller stays silent.*

He opens the cellar door and drags us down there.

Dark. Fucking dark. Stinks and all. Old feller never lets us down here. 'Don't ever go down there,' he says long back. 'Else I'll fuckin' kill you.' But I'm down there now. I'm down the stair and getting dragged along the flat, him still gripping me arm like a bastard. Don't like it down here. Wish he'd turn a fucking light on. What's he gonna do? More stairs. More dragging down.

I won't ask him nothing ever again, I tells him. He ain't listening though. I won't even speak ever again, if he wants. I'll be a good boy. Best fucking boy in the whole of Mangel.

Still ain't listening.

On the flat again. Stinks even worser in this bit. Hot and all, like we come down and down and down and now we're in hell, which is a place they told us about at school. Hell is a place, teacher says, where folks goes who tries getting above emselves. Keep atop yourself or below yourself and you'll go up to heaven, which is meant to be a smart place but sounds fucking boring to me, clouds and harps and them white wankers with wings and that. Mind you, better than getting stuck in a big bastard oven, ennit, with a red pointy-tailed fucker poking you with a big fork all day. So I always aimed at not getting above meself, which I took to mean climbing up ladders. But I were wrong, weren't I. Getting above yourself means asking why I can't ever go in the Bee Hive.

I ain't sure if it's hell or not now, cos the old feller's lobbed us on the floor and it's fucking cold. Can't get any darker than this. I scrambles away a bit and finds meself a corner. Spiders and that crawling all over us but I don't care, cos the old feller can't see us. I can't see him neither.

I sit tight and don't even breathe.

He's fiddling about over t'other side. Then a match sparks up and he lights a candle.

He don't look at me. Picks up summat from the far corner. A stick with some rags wrapped around the end. Takes em off and lets us know the bad news, which is that the stick is actually an axe. A big fucking axe.

• • •

I'd seen them samurai swords here and there and they looked all right. All right to put on your wall anyhow. Or muck about with in your backyard. But they weren't all right when they comes whizzing through the air and you gotta move sharpish to stop your swede going two ways.

I pinged off the wall and went down on the hall carpet. I turned over sharpish and swung me leg, aiming to take his legs from under him. Ferret were too fast and swung again before I knew what were what. This time it were coming down on us dead centre, aiming for me guts. I rolled over and banged me head on the cellar door, knocking it open a bit, sword bouncing off the rug behind us. Times like this you ain't got time to use your swede. If you're like me, your reflexes takes over. They're there to get you out of shite and you should let em get on with it, and not question em. Mine had us throwing meself on the cellar door, just as Ferret aimed to pin us to the floorboards.

I'd always meant to tart that cellar up a bit. In recent years it had become my favourite spot in the whole house, what with the telly and vid set up down there and everything. All I wanted were the walls plastering and a bit of carpet put in to make it more cosy like, but I just hadn't ever got around to it. Not that I'm lazy, mind. You knows better than that. I just didn't ever feel like the time were right. And it's the same for the rest of the house: same carpets and wallpaper as my old man had put in many a year back. One time I'd got so far as buying the paper and paint and scrapers and everything, but when it came to it I couldn't go through with it. To be honest with you, it were almost like the old feller would come back any moment and give us a slap for mucking up his house.

So that's how come them stairs in the cellar had no carpet on em, and was therefore fucking painful to be falling down.

I hit the cellar floor, pinging off the stairs three or four times along the way. I knew I'd knacked meself all over but me heart were pumping like a fucker, and I got on me feet sharpish when the door shut and a light came on. Ferret were coming down slow, keeping his eyes on us and holding that sword out in two hands.

'Put it down, fuck sake,' I says in me best doorman voice. It's a voice that few could resist.

'Like fuck will I,' says Ferret, resisting it. He had a smirk lingering around his chops and it flowered into a full grin as he goes: 'I'm gonna enjoy this.'

You had to admire him in a way. He wanted us dead.

No fucking about.

'You won't enjoy it when I puts that thing up your shitter,' I says.

Cos I didn't admire him that much.

'Oh yeah?' he says. 'Come an' get it off us, then. Come on.' He did ten or so swipes through the air, each of em about a yard long and sounding like Bruce Lee in *Enter the Dragon* when he's got them chain things. 'Come on, hard man.'

I reached for me monkey wrench.

Ferret laughed and goes: 'Ooh, I'm shittin' meself.'

But he weren't being clever. See, as he came for us I jumped in the air and swung the wrench, smashing the dangling light bulb and bringing darkness unto the whole situation.

That stopped him laughing.

Mind you, it were a risk. All he had to do were run about, swinging his weapon all over the shop, and he stood a chance of lopping me leg off. But he didn't do that. He just stood still, making nary a sound. I couldn't even hear him breathing. He couldn't hear me breathing neither.

Cos I weren't.

I couldn't go on without puff though, and it were getting so's I wouldn't be able to inhale without gasping and making a racket, like when you've been holding someone's swede down the bog for a bit. I wanted to shift and all, cos the longer I played statue the more I felt like a feller who just toppled down thirty hard stairs, accruing many a knock in the process. So I went behind the telly, sucking air as I shifted.

Ferret heard us and made his move, swinging his sword hither and thither. But he didn't know the lay of the land like I did. You could see that no one else had been down here much, everything being just as when I'd last seen it. So I weren't too shocked to hear Ferret walking into the telly, knocking it over.

As he righted himself I shimmied to the other stair.

See, the cellar in my house were on two floors. First one were for dossing around and watching telly and that, like I already told you. The other un…Well, I didn't like to go down there. It weren't a nice atmosphere, you could say. Me dad had always told us to stay out so that's what I'd always done, still, except the once or twice when it couldn't be avoided. Like the time I'd had to hide a body. Or a couple of year back when I'd had a clearout and dumped some old gear down there.

I had that gear on me mind as I felt me way down, brushing paws off both walls and picking up slime and crawly bastards on me fingers. It were a particular item I had in mind, and I hoped and prayed I'd find it. Cos it wouldn't be long before Ferret were trying to chop us in half again. And if I could choose a place I didn't wanna die in, the bottom part of the cellar were it. No question.

Mind you, it were a great place for some other cunt to die in.

I were onto the ground now and being careful. I didn't know for surely where I'd left stuff, and I didn't want tangling up with that old bike frame and offering up my arse for cleaving. I edged forward, bending down and feeling around. To be honest I think I'd just lobbed the gear down here from the top of the stair, so it were all over the shop. Bit of a clatter as I kicked an old tool-box, but I stayed up. Ferret would have heard it, mind, and as I froze still I heard his blade scraping brickwork as he followed us down.

I were taking big strides, no longer caring about falling over. If I didn't find what I were after I were fucked anyhow. I *had* to find it.

I kicked summat large and metal and clangy, and when I bent down I found it to be the old bike frame. I picked it up and lobbed it stairward. Must have hit Ferret cos he grunted and swore.

But it didn't hurt him.

You could hear him grinning, squeezing the hilt.

I were picking anything up and lobbing it at him now—boxes, tyres, bottles, bits of old metal, a small coffee table... Some of it hit him, but none of it done the job. I could sense him, stood there with an arm over his face and a smirk on his gob, waiting for us to finish so he could chop us up. There were only one thing that I could stop him with, and I couldn't bloody find it.

Fuck all left in that corner, so I moved.

Ferret cottoned on to it and came at us swinging.

The sword whooshed for ages and landed on me back.

I went down, wondering how many pieces I were in. I think he must have hit us wrong cos I could still move me arms, and I used em to feel around for summat. Anything. I found summat.

A paint pot.

All dried up now, family of spiders living in there like as not. I lobbed it hard, hearing it ping off the ceiling.

The blade came down next to us on the stone floor. He'd blunt the blade like that after a while. But I didn't have a while. I felt around again, hoping he wouldn't chop me arm off. I found it.

I fucking *knew* it were still here.

Mind you, I had to get on me feet in order to use it proper. I had one chance, I reckoned.

Left.

Or right.

If I stayed put he'd gut us for surely.

I went right, rolling over and hauling meself up with the help of summat large. Fuck knows what, and to be honest it didn't matter. Not to me anyhow. What mattered to me, down in that filthy stinking pitch black cellar just then, is that I turned around and swung me dad's rusty old lopping axe.

What mattered to Ferret is that I buried it in his ribcage.

• • •

It's all shiny, that axe, glinting in the candlelight.

Dad points at the middle of the floor.

There's summat there and I didn't see it before. Two big bags of cement, one atop t'other. Dunno why he's got them cos he never does no building nor nothing. But I got better things to think about than the old man and his not liking DIY. I'm thinking about the axe and the two bags of cement. The old feller still ain't looking at us.

He holds the axe in one hand and points at the cement with the other.

I ain't telling him nothing now, about being a good boy and that. I can't cos me voice has gone. I ain't crying neither, mind. I don't cry.

The old man points a bit harder at the cement bags.

'Dad...'

He looks at us now.

There's a big feller, so they says. He's one of them little red pointy-tail fellers in hell. But this un's a big un, about same size as a normal person. Maybe a little bit smaller actually. But he don't need to be big. All he's gotta do is look at you, right, and he's got you. You does whatever he wants you to. And it won't be a good thing. No helping grannies across the road with Satan here (which is his name). He'll have you shoving her in front of a bus. You'll do it and all, cos you ain't got no choice. And then he's got you for hell.

I went over to the cement bags.

Dad comes over and tries pushing me head down. I don't like it and I ducks out of it. He tries again, getting a paw on me back and pushing us down hard. I falls and gets up again, stepping back.

'Are you my son?' he says.

Puts the shite right up us, hearing him speak after so long. The words don't sound right down here. Sound like they're in me own head.

'Are you my son?'

'Aye,' I says. Aye.'

Then he pushes us down again. I lets him this time. I got no choice. There's shite in me pants and he'll only get more angry, when he gets a whiff.

I got me face down on the top sack, hand over head. There's dust in me gob and tears in me eyes. (I ain't crying though.) I'm thinking about him bringing that axe down. He might split the bag, which would be a waste of cement. And I'd get the blame for that. I wanna warn him about it. You gotta do that sometimes with the old man, help him out when he ain't thinking straight. Specially when he's been on the beer and spirits.

I cranes an eye up and gets a look. He's stood over us, axe held over his head, scraping the ceiling and sending bits of wet plaster down like hard snow.

'Am I the devil?'

He's still like a statue. The candle's behind him so I can't see his face. Only the big statue reaching up skyward.

'Am I the devil?'

'I…I dunno…'

I got me face down again now, eyes shut tight. I'm trying to think of nice stuff. I wish I could recall what Mam looked like. Her hair were yeller and she smelled of fags.

The axe came down, chopping my head off.

I couldn't think proper with my head not on me body no more. Instead of thinking proper it fills up with black and noise, like someone chucked it in a tractor engine. After a bit you start thinking again though, and you moves your neck a bit and opens your eyes, though you can't see nothing. You opens your gob and it's fucking horrible, the blood. Mind you, tastes more like cement than blood. Then you gets a boot in the kidneys and rolls over, noticing your head ain't been chopped off after all.

Top sack is burst open, cement everywhere.

Dad's by the stair, picking up the candle.

'The devil's name is Lucifer,' he says. 'He lives in the Bee Hive.'

Then he goes up.

• • •

212

'Badger?'

I stopped and looked up. It were a far-off, high-pitched voice, but I'm sure 'Badger' is what it said. I listened for it again, but couldn't hear nothing. I looked down at me work. Most of it were done and I only had a bit left, but the pause had let us know how tired I were, and how horrible the job were. I couldn't leave it off yet, mind. This weren't a job you could leave half-done. I shook the blood off the blade, then got back to sawing Ferret's body in half.

I'd tried cutting him up with the axe first, but there were no sharpness to it and it just broke the bones and made a mess. Plus I only had light from one candle and couldn't see where to aim for. The sword were all right for slicing through meat, but no good for bones. The saw were best, even though it were rusted to fuck and well blunt. Might have a job cutting through wood but it were fine on Ferret. I'd already done his arms, legs, and swede. Bagged up and ready to go they was, soon as I got this big bit into two pieces. I shut me eyes and got me head down, sawing hard until me arm burned.

Like I says, it were a difficult time.

I ain't proud of meself. I'd only wanted to shite the fucker up and scare him off back to the where he came from. But what could I do? He fucking started it. And now he were dead I weren't about to let the coppers find him. So it were Hurk Wood, in ten or so bin bags. And the sooner the better, cos I had a big day tomorrow and I wanted an early night.

I bagged the rest of him and lugged a couple of bags up the stair. The light were glaring overhead in the hall, and I realised what a mess I were in. I only had one bin bag left so I'd have to cram all me bloody togs in there. I went back down, unbuttoning me shirt. Just as I reached the bottom again someone started screaming.

It were a fucking awful sound and it put the shite right up us. Echoed all around the cellar it did, so you couldn't tell where it came from. I fell back against the wall, paws to ears, and closed me eyes. When I opened em the candle had gone out and it were pitch black again. I thought about Ferret and wondered if perhaps I hadn't finished him off proper. His head were in a bag on its own, but chickens can go on running about for a bit after you lops their heads off, so they says, and I didn't see why Ferret's head couldn't go on screaming. Mind you, you couldn't belt one out like that without a decent pair of lungs in tow.

I felt around for the axe and went back up.

Someone just up there, in the hall.

Bird, by the sounds of it.

Screaming and not letting up.

I hooked the axe round the door and pulled it to us, stepping up. Sal's holding her face, looking down at the binbag on the floor, Ferret staring back at her. She looks at us and goes quiet.

'Sal…' I says, realising how it must look.

But she's out of it.

I caught her before she hit the ground.

• • •

I weren't sure what to do then.

I mean, what if Sal grassed? Would she grass? She might, you know. Mind you, we went back a long way, me and Sal.

But she had a new feller now and I'd killed him.

I picked her up, thinking about it. There were only one thing for it really. 'Ah well,' I says, resting Sal on me knees and picking up the axe. 'Soz, mate.' I kicked the cellar door and turned sideways to fit her through. Four careful steps down I changed me mind and went back up, carrying Sal up to the bedroom and laying her on the bed. I couldn't chop her up, see, cos there was no binbags left. And I couldn't be arsed cleaning meself up, going over the shop for some, then getting messy all over again.

I had a look at her. She looked well rough, like she'd not slept or ate for forty days and nights. Plus she had the brown traces of an old shiner round her right eye, and I could have swore her hooter hadn't been so crooked before. She were kipping hard just now, snoring fit to rattle the windows. I left her be and went into the bathroom.

I stayed under the shower for about half an hour. I were enjoying it so much I could have stayed there all night. I dunno how long it were since I'd had a good hosing down, but I made a note to have more of em from now on. Specially me being respectable now, with the new job and that. I'd have to wear a proper suit and everything.

Back in the bedroom I couldn't find none of me old togs in the drawers and wardrobe. Fucking bastards had tossed em out like as not, thinking they'd got shot of us. But I weren't getting narked over that just now. Sal looked to have had a hard time of it, being without me. And you can't argue with the debt Ferret had paid.

I found a pair of old army trousers that didn't fit too bad, although they was a bit tight around my muscular thighs, which for some reason made it impossible to do em up around the waist. A white T-shirt were the only other thing I could find to wear. Bit on the skimpy side but it didn't half show off me muscles, and I admired meself in the mirror for a while. I knew I wouldn't find no footwear that fit, so I went into the bathroom and cleaned me boots up as best I could with some damp bogroll, tossing it down the pan and turning the water red. Then I pissed in it and flushed it, and went into the bedroom.

Sal were sitting up on the bed, waiting for us.

And she weren't screaming.

'Blake,' she says, nice and calm. I could tell she were emotional cos her lower lip were quivering. 'Blake...'

'Sal,' I says. Cos I'd better go first. I had to make it clear from the off that if she grassed us, I'd fucking kill her. If need be I'd take her down the cellar and show her the rest of Ferret, saw him up a bit smaller just to drive it home for her. Cos no bastard were fucking up my dreams of self-betterment now. 'Listen...'

'No, *you* listen,' she says, eyes ablaze.

For fuck sake...I didn't have time for this. I had body parts to ditch and cellars to hose down.

'Just listen,' she says, a bit softer. She patted the bed beside her and gave us a look I knew well. It meant do as I says and shut the fuck up, and if you're a good boy you might get a shag out of it.

I went and sat down, not wanting a shag from her but fancying a sit-down.

'Blake,' she says again, taking me paw. 'I knows what you done.'

I says: 'I know but—'

'But nuthin'. Just listen, Blake. I knows what you done and why you done it.'

Flipping heck. How'd Sal know that Ferret were chasing us with a samurai sword? 'Oh aye?'

'Aye. Iss obvious, Blake. I sees it in yer eyes, in yer voice, the way you stands. I knows why you killed him. And I knows you had no choice.'

'Thass right, cos he had a fuckin' massive sa—'

'Forget about that, Blake. It don't matter how big his sausage were.'

'Sausage?'

'Aye. It don't matter to us, and I knows you knows that. I knows you wouldn't be jealous just cos of him havin' the bigger sausage.'

I scratched me head and goes: 'Eh?'

'Blake, I ain't here to argue,' she says, putting both paws on me shoulders. 'Let me tell you now, I don't hold it against you for knockin' off that bastard. If you hadn't of done it, I'd of paid someone else to…just as soon as I could get meself clean…Which I was gonna do soon, aye…But listen, no one else done it. *You* done it. An' you done it cos you *cares.*'

She were squeezing me arms now, sticking her face in mine. To be honest I wished she'd stay back a bit, her breath being not so fresh. And she were setting us on edge, truth be told. I mean, I just didn't fancy Sal no more. I don't know how anyone could, her looking like that. Plus I had Rache now.

'You're the only one who cares about us, Blake. Thass the way iss always been. I should of known it. I *did* know it. But…but I got weak, Blake. I couldn't handle it after you went inside.'

'I fuckin' never went inside. I—'

'All right, when you was put in the loony bin, I—'

'It ain't a loony bin, Sal. Hospital it is, like any other. Hospital for heads.'

'All right, Blake,' she says, stroking me head just above the ear. 'Iss all right now. There's nuthin' wrong with you, Blake. There's no one like you neither. You're my fuckin' hero, you are.'

She kissed us. To be honest it were about the last thing I would have ordered, if I'd have gone into a restaurant and they'd said, 'You can have anything you wants, but if we ain't got it in you'll have to ask for summat else.' First choice would have been them getting rid of the dead Ferret, a shag with Rache being a close second. Third place goes to pie and chips down the Paul Pry. While not being a spectacular meal by anyone's standards, I didn't half miss that particular dish. But a kiss from Sal…

Keep it, mate.

Anyhow, she's snogging us, and I ain't into it. Then her tongue comes out so hard she near bruised me tonsils. I've never had much defence against that kind of onslaught, and before long I were doing a bit of tonguery meself. I wrestled with hers for a bit, then gave up that losing battle and moved on, counting her teeth and finding one or two to be missing.

'Hey Sal,' I says, gasping. 'Where'd yer tee—'

She clamped her gob on mine like a lamprey on a lake trout, one paw slipping under me T-shirt, the other rubbing hard on the front of me army strides. Finding em to be not done up proper, it weren't more than a second or two before she had me tadger out and up.

I still weren't sure about all this. I mean, what kind of a bird spreads her legs for another feller the minute her man's carked it, even if it is her proper feller? But before I could point that out to her she bent down and started sucking me bollocks. I knew I were on a ride to nowhere, and when I looked down and saw her with a gobful of knacker and me tadger all tangled up in her hair, I thought fuck it.

• • •

'Blake?'

Fuck knows what time it were. After dark and before dawn is all I knew. I knew there was matters awaiting my urgent

attention and all, matters concerning bin bags and bloody cellars and the like. But fuck all them, just for now. Fuck Sal and
all, who was walking her fingers up and down me back and
trying to get us awake. Fuck em, cos I still had one foot in me
dream.

And it were a good un. I were sat up a tree, right, and looking
down at all them folks down below. It were a fucking high tree
cos you couldn't really see their faces down there, only the fact of
whether they was fellers or birds or younguns, or whatever. They
was all going about this way and that, brushing past each other
and never stopping, not even for a chat or to light up a smoke. I
didn't much like the look of it down there, and I knew I were better off up me tree, though it were a knobbly branch and my arse
were aching.

So I stayed up there. And my arse got so I couldn't feel it no
more. Meanwhile them folks down below was getting faster and
faster, and if you looked close you could see em knocking into
each other a bit now, brushing shoulders at first, head-on prangs
a bit later. Plus the odd fisticuff here and there, leading up to what
can only be termed as scrapping.

I were staying up me tree for surely now. Aye, I likes a rumble,
but not when I can't see the whites of his eyes. Only there was
another problem:

My tree were rotting.

It were summertime in this dream of mine, so the leaves was
out in force, like, green and loving it. They'd been green and loving it at the start anyhow, but they was dried up and dropping
like your proverbials now, wafting groundward like brown snow.
Plus the bark were flaking, making it hard for us to keep me grip.
And when you looked close at the wood beneath it you could so
how worm-ate it were. Which all in all weren't such a fine thing,

considering how high up I were and me being out on a limb so to speak.

Then came the creaking and a-splintering behind us...

'Blake.'

'What, for fuck...'

'Blake, yer sweatin'. Woss matter, love? Yer heart's racin'.'

'Eh? Ah, nuthin'. Woss time?'

'I dunno. Don't matter, do it?'

'Don't matter? Don't fuckin'...?'

'Blake, woss you doin'? Where's you off?'

'Out.'

'Where? Take us, Blake. Don't leave us. We gotta stick together now. Come on...' She grabbed me hand and drew it down to her tit. 'Come on. Stay.'

'Sal, you knows I got shite to do. There's Ferret down there. An' I got a big day tomorrer.'

'We both got a big day tomorrer: the first day of our new life together.'

'Sal, I dunno if—'

But she dragged us down proper now and shoved a tit in me face, smothering my words. 'Blake,' she says, bending down and whispering in me ear, 'there's summat I oughta tell you.'

'There's fuck all you can tell us, Sal.' I wanted to say that but I never, being as I had a gobful of tit.

'About the babby.'

I stopped sucking.

'Our babby.'

Her bosom slid out of me gob and dropped down a few inches.

'The one who died at birth.'

'What of him?' I says.

'Well…' Her arms went stiff around my head. She'd stopped breathing.

'Come on.'

'Blake, don't. That hurts.'

'Come *on*, fuck sake.'

'I can't breathe, Blake. Let go an' I'll tell you.'

'Go on then.'

'Oh, Blake. Don't treat us like that. You gotta be gentle with us.'

'I'll fuckin' gently kill you if you don't tell us.'

She took me paw again and squeezed it. She didn't look in me eyes this time. 'He never died.'

15

Elvis on the radio singing 'Jailhouse Rock'. I likes Elvis. I think me mam used to, in the old days. She played it to us while I were in her stomach, or summat, which got us into him nice and early.

Noise at the front door, which is the old feller trying to get his key in the lock. I gets up and flicks the radio off. He don't like Elvis. Elvis makes him go mental. He's in now, dropping chips all over the shop and stinking of ale. Sits his arse down opposite us and looks at us. It ain't one of his mental looks but I looks down anyhow.

'Where's you off?' he says.

'Up the stair,' I says, stood next to me chair.

'Siddown. I wanna teach you summat.'

I do sit down. It's either that or peg it out the door, meaning I'll have to kip rough someplace, and I can't be arsed with that. I done it last night—dossing down by the blower behind the hairy factory—and I been sneezing like a bastard all day. I been down the arky though. They got heating in there and I got meself almost back to normal again, and I ain't kipping rough again tonight.

So aye, I sit down.

But I ain't happy. The old feller wants to teach us summat, and he ain't a good teacher, see. He don't use a blackboard nor chalk nor books nor nothing like that.

'Don't worry,' he's saying. I ain't looking his way but I can tell he's smiling. He's finding summat funny about us, which is all right. Him taking the piss means he ain't about to hit us. I think. 'You ain't done nuthin' wrong. I just wanna teach you about the birds and the bees, little Royston. Time you learned about em.'

Birds and bees. I knows what that is. He's on about lasses and shagging and that, right? The stupid old get. I'm thirteen fucking years old. I knows all about birds. I even fingered Mandy Gibson behind the swimming baths the other week. Said she'd suck us off after she packs in Duane.

'Women ain't what they seems, Royston.'

I hates him like this. He's pissed but he goes all still and clear of a sudden, like he's a fucking teacher having a go at you.

'They seems nice, aye. But they ain't. They're devils, all of em. Says they'll do one thing—summat nice—and then turns about and does the worstest bloody thing they can do. The worst, Royston. And they don't even do it for emselves, you know. They does it for you. To hurt you. To show you, see, show you how they got you, and can make you do whatever they wants. What d'you say to that, eh Royston?'

'What? Dunno.'

'Dunno? Don't fuckin' know?'

'I mean…like…'

'I'll tell you what you ought to know. You ought to know that if yer a man…if you ever grows up to be a man, you won't let em trick you. Do what you gotta with their bodies, but a real man don't fall for their words. They're all the fuckin' same, son. Yer mam included.'

• • •

'You gave him up,' I says.

I were sat on the carpet now, leaning up against the wall. I had me knees pulled up and me arms around em. I were rocking to and fro, just a bit.

'I had to, Blake.'

'You gave him up.'

'I just told you I did, didn't I? You don' have to keep on sayin' it.'

'You g—'

'Blake, think about it, will yer? You was gone. The doctors said you wouldn't likely be comin' back. You was well out of it, Blake. You didn't know who you was, where you was…They told us to look out for meself now. Told us I were on me own. Thass what they said, Blake, when I asked em at the ozzy. Honest.'

She were sat on the bed, biting her nails.

'Anyhow, you knows them pills you took, what made you go barmy? Well, you left a load of em here. I hid em when the ambulance came, told em I didn't know what was wrong with you. But the ambulance fellers seemed to know anyhow. You was passed out in the cellar, blood seepin' out yer nose and gob and eyes and ears an' everythin'. One of em said you was a classic case of *Joey*. I didn't know what he meant straight off, but I asked around. And then I knew what the pills was. Why'd you get into them pills, Blake? If only you'd of steered clear…'

She'd leaned forward to shout that last bit at us.

'Don't matter now,' she says a bit quieter. 'Woss done is done. I had no money, Blake. I had no one. An' all the while a babby's growin' in me belly. All I had was them pills—loads of em. So I asked around again and found someone who gave us summat for em. Thass how I met Badger. But it were too late, Blake. I were already into the pills. Badger were into stuff and all. Other stuff. He were bringin' it in from the outside and floggin' it. But soon he couldn't sell no more cos he took too much for himself. He stopped goin' back to the outside and all. He stayed here, with me.'

She put her face down and rubbed her eyes.

I knew all this cos I were watching her in the long mirror on the wardrobe.

'And then I had the babby.'

She went on rubbing for a bit, then went still, sniffed, and looked at the wall. She glared at that wall like it had called her a slag.

'I couldn't keep him. No way. I weren't no mother. I didn't want him. I wanted gear. And Badger could get gear, so I wanted him. He didn't want the babby neither. So aye, I gave him away. I sent him to a better place. They could give him what he needed, and look after him. What would I have done with a babby? I couldn't even look after meself.'

She went and got her old dressing gown off the back of the door and tied it around her. Instead of going back onto the bed she knelt beside us and took my hand. 'Blake, you understands, don't you? You sees how I had no choice.'

I rocked to and fro a bit more.

'Oh, Blake, I knew you would. You and me was meant to be together, you know. We'll be all right now. We'll have another babby. You and me.'

She kissed us on the forehead and went to the bog. While she were out I started getting meself together. I still couldn't think straight, but I knew that'd come back with time. Meanwhile I could look after me appearance. It don't do to sit there rocking to and fro with no kit on. I got dressed and looked in the mirror again.

I were looking at a dad.

Someone's old feller.

I couldn't fucking believe it. What Sal had said here just about topped it off for us. Not only did I have a top job and all the things coming with it (including Rache), but now I were a dad again. It were like me arm had fell off and growed back again. But it weren't half confusing, and I tried to keep the corners of me gob down and concentrate. Things weren't in the bag yet, and I'd have to work me knackers off to get em there. Only then could I sit back and spark up a nice fat stogie, sitting in me nice new home in the Danghill district, a great film on the telly in front of us (*Rocky IV* perhaps, where his son's about the same age as mine), smell of frying chips coming from the kitchen, Rache pottering about there with a sexy apron on, and little Royston playing horsey horsey on me knee.

I squinted in the mirror, looking for the old Blake—the one who always knew how to get shite done. The one who wouldn't ever back down, no matter who he rubbed up against. The one who turned this whole town upside down in the name of doing things proper. On more than one occasion.

I knew he were in there, somewhere.

Sal came back in behind us, wiping her nose with some pink bog roll. 'Blake, love,' she says. 'Can you lend us a couple o' quid? Only there ain't no food in the house, and—'

'No shops open this time,' I says, still looking at meself.

'No, there's one over town stays open late. I just needs—'

'Sal,' I says, 'who'd you give him away to?'

'What? Who?'

'Our lad. Who'd you sell him to?'

'I never sold him. I telled you—he went to a better—'

'All right all right, but who? Who'd you fuckin' give him to?'

She had her back to us, looking through her drawers for summat.

'Sal.'

'What?' she says, getting narky.

'Just fuckin' tell us who.'

'Why? It don't matter. He's gone. I had to look after him, make sure he got looked after. He wouldn't have growed up proper with me, the way I were. He's all right where he is. Leave him.'

I left it for a bit, half an eye on Sal in the mirror. I watched her stepping into knickers and snapping a bra behind her back, then pulling on old jeans and a leopard-skin shirt that didn't go down far enough, leaving a couple of inches of white skin for all to see. She turned to face us. 'I'm off out for a sec, Blake. I'll be back—'

'You ain't goin' nowhere,' I says.

She tilted her hips and crossed her arms and goes, slow: 'I just needs some fags. From the pub. Won't take five—'

'Pub's shut.'

'No, he... There's a lock-in tonight. Aye, he does one every—'

'I says you ain't goin' nowhere. We got shite to sort out.'

'We just sorted it, didn't we? I told you everythin' and we're back together. Look, if you gives us a tenner I'll buy us a bottle of—'

'Fuckin' *siddown*, will yer?' I says, pushing her on the bed. 'You ain't goin' no place. Now tell us where the lad is.'

She looked at us for a bit, her lying on the bed with her dark hair sprayed out behind her. You could see some of it was going grey now. She slowly got up on her elbows and says: 'I'll tell you for fifty quid.'

I didn't know what to say to that. I had a few notes and I weren't desperate to hang onto em, what with the new job and regular salary and all. And I wanted to know where my lad were, now I knew he were alive. But this were his own mam.

'You're his own fuckin' mam,' I says to her. 'How can you ask for fifty quid like that, you fuckin' slag?'

'I ain't a slag. Just giz the money. I needs it, all right? An' you wouldn't give it us when I asked you. Come on. Forty.'

'Forty fuckin...'

I ain't never hit a bird. You just don't hit birds. There's some fellers who do, but not meself. I thought about that as I tightened me grip on her neck.

• • •

I'm kipping. That's what I wants him to think anyhow. He's just opened the door and come in. I'm facing the wall and I got one eye open. Can't see nothing but wallpaper, but I can sense him. He's standing behind us, swaying. He's breathing hard and heavy, stinking the room up with his beer and fags and the other stink, the one he's always had, and it's getting worser. I hates him for that stink.

'Hoy,' he says, swaying, looking at us.

I ain't playing though. I'm fast akip, like I says.

A boot's what I'm expecting. Or a slap. What I gets is him perching his lumpy arse on me bed. He tries to perch anyhow, but his back's touching mine and it's hot, making us sweat. I don't fucking like this, not one bit. What the fuck is he in here for anyhow? I ain't done fuck all. Coppers told him about me getting caught robbing, but what does he care about that? If he had a go at us about that I'd fucking laugh at him. Honest I would. I've had enough of the cunt lately, I have. And I'm bigger than him now.

'I sometimes…' he says.

I Sometimes? What the fuck does that mean?

He's off again: 'You know…I been thinkin' about…Ah, woss the point. You ain't awake anyhow.' And he's getting up.

I move me head a bit. Fuck knows why I do. I'm calling meself a cunt for it but it's done now.

And he's noticed it, settling his arse back down.

'I been wonderin' about you. As a father, like. I, as a father, have been wonderin' about you as a son. Why have a son? Thass what I been wonderin' about. Why the fuck…knowin' what I knows about you, and where you came…I mean knowin' that you might not even be…'

He's stopped there for a puff. I likes a fag but I hopes he don't spark up here in me room, me having to kip here. He don't, though.

He scratches himself for a goodly while, stretches out a bit, then he's off again.

'But none o' that matters, Royston. You're my fuckin' son, you are. I don't care what the fuck they says—you're my son, an' they can fuck right off. And it is hard, bein' a dad on yer own. I ain't a good dad, I knows it. But you...'

He's turned a bit now, looking at us. He's making little choking sounds, like he can't breathe proper. Go on, I'm thinking. Cark it. Cark it now, on me bed. I don't mind.

'You're me fuckin' son, ain't yer. An' you know what? I wouldn't change that for the world. Cos...cos of the...'

I won't get no more out of him. Dropped off, ain't he. Fallen akip right there on the edge of me own pit, rolling in towards us and making us sick with his breath.

I climb out the bottom of the bed and go down the stair, taking me blankets.

• • •

There is a far and distant land, sheltered by many a treetop and cushioned by many a year's falling of leaf. It is a place where nature thrives and mankind suffers. No one goes there. And if they do, they'll have a spade and a full load in the boot. They calls it Hurk Wood, and it's a fucking top place for burying deadfolk.

I swung a right into the East Bloater Road and took her south.

Usually I loved it down that way. As I've said many a time previous, it's a thoroughfare shunned by the many. There's no reason to go in and out of Mangel, and no joy to be had sightseeing down that way, for most. I says "for most" there, cos there's always your one or two exceptions. And that's where I came in. I cannot explain the peculiar pleasure I'd always derived from lingering on the outskirts of the Mangel area, but nor can I deny it. It's a fact of life, like eating, drinking, pissing, and doing a shite.

But I weren't enjoying it on that night.

I couldn't, with Ferret and Sal behind us.

Mind you, it were interesting to have a go in a Vauxhall Viva.

There's one or two cars on the road I just cannot get along with, and your Vauxhall Viva is one of em. It's well high on the list, occupying a permanent top three spot alongside your Avenger and your Hillman Imp. And your 1.3 Capri. Sometimes you just knows a motor will be shite before you even gets in it. It is so shite you just ain't ever gonna get in it, so your opinion on the matter will never ever be varied.

But then comes a time when you ain't got no choice.

You got dead meat to ferry, and a wheelbarrow just will not do the job. Not even if you had a barrow. Which you ain't.

Anyhow, so there I were, pootling along in Ferret's piss-yeller Viva, finally putting to the test my long-held theory regarding the utter shiteness of that particular model. And I'll tell you what:

I'd been right all along.

I really ought to trust me instincts more. That motor were a true nail. She flew like shite frozen to a shovel. The general rattling in the interior were enough to scare a flock of crows. The gear box whined like a hungry pup, and popped out when you accelerated too hard in reverse. So all in all I cannot recommend it to you. If it's a mid-range saloon you're after, you're better off with a Cortina. Or a Marina. Or a fucking tractor.

Mind you, she got us from A to B.

B being the little clearing halfway along that dirt track in Hurk Wood South. I picked me spade up and jumped out. It were a clear night, the moon high and bright, a full set of sparklies scattered over the rest of the sky. I looked at em for a bit, finishing off me fag and wondering if the dark blue sky up there really were a curtain, and the stars just pinholes in it. I'd heard that theory before. (On a documentary, I think.) And you got to admit—there's summat to it. Them stars truly did look not unlike pinholes.

Mind you, it'd have to be a bloody massive curtain. And I hadn't ever noticed no one drawing it, come nightfall. And what the fuck were behind it, making the pinholes light up so? A big feller with a torch? Had to be summat like that. But you couldn't get that kind of output from no normal torch. You'd need halogen headlights to get brightness to that degree. So, right, it could be a feller sat there in his motor, lights on full beam. He drives out to the edge of his town every night, has a gander at the world beyond, which happens to be Mangel. He gets fed up with it by dawn and fucks off again. I mean, there's only so much staring at a far and distant world you can do.

Right?

So, when you thinks about it, your feller up there ain't gonna be up there forever. Sooner or later he's gotta choose his pot and piss in it. And when that night comes, when he's in his motor and he's cruising down his East Bloater Road and he's fucking sick of it all, he's gonna pull a U-ey and go back townward, never coming out that way not ever again, and thereby depriving us of our stars.

Either that or he's gonna put his foot down and bust through the curtain.

'Is you gonna untie us or what?'

'Oh,' I says, looking at her there on the back seat. 'Aye, well...'

'Cos you can't keep us tied forever. You gotta trust us sooner or later. We're a team now, Blake. Right? Soon as we gets the boy back, we're sailin'. Iss like we said, right? So you gotta trust us.'

I puffed hard on the last bit of fag, saying: 'I'm thinkin' about it.'

'I won't run off again. Honest I won't. I'm with you now.'

You couldn't blame us for tying her up. You'd have done same. After I'd gave up trying to strangle her she ran down the stair. It were lucky I'd blocked both doors, else she would have got away. Mind you, I still don't understand how she'd got in to begin with. But that didn't concern us at the time. All I cared about were finding out what she'd done with little Royston, and stopping her grassing on us for killing Ferret. So I tied her up and got her down the cellar, with the axe and that. We only went three steps down before she blabbed about the babby. I'll tell you about that later.

You might not believe it, mind.

I fucking didn't.

But she were still sticking to her story, even when I raised the axe over her and made meself look barmy, roaring and dribbling and that. And I knew Sal. She only lied so far as it suited her. And getting your head chopped off don't suit no one.

'Please untie us, Blake,' she says again, sounding like the sweet little girl she hadn't ever been. 'I don't blame you for throttlin' us back there. You was right to do that.' She looked like a sweet girl and all, sat there in the dark, with her long hair falling over her face. 'I deserved it.'

So I got her out and untied her. She couldn't get very far out here. Actually it weren't a bad idea, I got to thinking as I opened the boot. If she had a hand in burying Ferret, she'd keep it quiet. It'd be our little secret.

She were stood by the open door, rubbing her wrists and throat. Poor Sal.

I hadn't ever meant her no harm.

'Here,' I says. 'Giz hand.' Cos, say what you likes about her, she were a strong lass.

She tippy-toed over. She weren't wearing the right footwear for Hurk Wood, bless her. And that little blouse couldn't have been keeping her warm. I looked in the boot and found an old blanket in there. 'Here,' I says to Sal, draping it over her shoulders.

'Ta, Blakey,' she says, smiling up at us. 'I loves you.'

I recall thinking how she didn't look right. It were cold and she were shivering, but it weren't like proper shivering. More like trembling from clenching your gnashers so hard. And her eyes looked odd, in a way I couldn't say. Plus she kept stepping side to side.

'You want a piss?' I says.

'Eh? No, I'm all right.'

I gave her two bags of Ferret and carried three heavy ones meself. We'd have to come back for the rest.

It took us five minutes to find the right spot. I'd found loads of possibles, but I didn't want no fuck ups. This one were fucking perfect though. A patch of soft earth surrounded by brambles. There was a pile of rubble someone had dumped nearby so I could use that to cover the ground over, stop yer dogs digging. And Sal were good as gold. Didn't complain once about all the thorns and that, when I'd made her come through them brambles with us. Cried a bit, but didn't say nothing.

We went back to get the other bags and the spade. 'You gone quiet,' I says, walking back to our spot. 'Woss matter with you?'

'Oh,' she says. 'Nuthin.'

'S'what I likes to hear,' I says, winking at her. She weren't so bad, when you looked at her. Actually that ain't true—she were well rough to look at. But she were all right in other ways, like.

Or so it seemed as she lugged Ferret's swede and most of his arms through them woods.

Anyhow, I had work to do when we got back to our spot. I took the spade and started digging. Few minutes later I pulled me jacket off and threw it at Sal, who weren't looking and got a fright when it landed on her head.

'Bit jumpy, eh?' I says.

'Jumpy? Oh, aye.'

'Wan' a fag?'

'Aye, go on then.'

I tossed her the pack and matches, then winked at her and got back to it. I were enjoying meself. I'm well known as a physical man, a man of strength and action. I needs to get a sweat going now and then, work the muscles. I forgot all me sorrows for the time it took to dig that hole. To be honest it were the best time I'd had since coming out of Parpham. And it were a comforting thought, to know I'd be all right digging ditches if the chief of security job didn't work out. I had a big, man-sized hole four foot deep before I tossed the spade up and called for me smokes.

'How's that, eh?' I says as Sal put a fag between me lips.

'Very nice,' she says, lighting it. 'You ought to do it a bit deeper though.'

'Deeper? What the fuck for? Look how deep it is already.'

'It is very deep, Blakey,' she says, wiping the sweat off me brow with the edge of her blanket. 'But you needs it deeper. To be on the safe side, like. About a foot deeper.'

'Fuck sake, Sal.'

She smiled.

I winked at her. Quite pretty she were, just then. The bright moon overhead lit her up just enough to hide her rough bits and show off the nice ones. I could see the Sal of a few years prior, after she'd packed in stripping but before she'd let herself go. It were almost enough to make us wonder if I shouldn't give her another go. Despite all she'd done, she were still the mother of my lad. And perhaps I could keep Rache going on the side. Or maybe I could get hitched with Rache and keep Sal on the side. Only if she smartened herself up a bit, mind.

I spat me smoke out and got going again on the hole. I were down past the subsoil now and it were all clay, which were a fucking pain cos it sticks to your spade. I weren't enjoying it so much now, and I decided I wouldn't try to find work as a ditch digger after all, now matter how hard times got. But I weren't about to give up. Sal had said take it down another foot, so that's what I done. Then I tossed the spade up again and called for another smoke.

'Happy now?' I says, wiping the sweat from my eyebrows with me forearm. When I looked up again she weren't there. I heard a noise behind us so I turned that way, just as Sal swung the spade at me face.

I ducked. I were fucking knackered anyhow, so it weren't no effort to drop to me knees. The spade clipped the top of me scalp, and I knew I'd have a cut there for a while, but there weren't no proper impact. I went to get up sharpish, but the clay were slippery as fuck and all I could do were scramble t'other end and look up.

Sal were coming over for another crack.

'Sal,' I shouts.

But she ignored us, same as she'd always done. She pulled the spade over her head for a good swing downwards, so ducking wouldn't be no good this time. I got a quick gander at her before the moment of truth, and I'll always recall how she looked just then. Not so pretty now, but not bad neither. She'd dropped the blanket and some of the buttons was gone on her blouse, so it were hardly on her. Her hair were all over the shop, shining blue from the moon overhead. Teeth bared, almost grinning. And her eyes…I swear I'd seen eyes like that in Parpham, when one of the more lairy females had missed her medication. So, all in all, I quite fancied her.

Not enough to let her pop us, mind.

She swung the spade, the effort tearing a yell from her lungs. I didn't have time to go sideways, so I lurched forwards, slapping meself against the wall of the grave and brushing her feet with me fingers. The spade whacked us on the arse, which weren't pleasant but I'd had worse there. It were a fucking powerful wallop, mind, shoving us on an inch and letting us get a proper grip of her shoe.

I yanked hard on it, pulling her leg from under her.

She landed arsewise, spade going behind her but not out of her grasp. I still had her foot, so I pulled hard and dragged her into the grave with us, her screaming and bawling the whole while. She crowned us on her way down, but not so bad I couldn't ignore it. After that I punched her in the face and she went down.

She were making a moaning sound, clutching her face and writhing slightly. I picked the spade up and thought about it for a bit, watching her.

The spade weren't one of me dad's. I dunno where it had come from and couldn't recall where I'd used it before, though I knew I had done. Only a few years old it were, and there no trace of rust not anywhere on it. Quite sharp and all. Went straight through Sal's neck and out the other side, lopping her head clean off.

16

I felt rosy next morning. Best night's kip I'd experienced in a long old while. Aye, it were great to be waking up warm and flat for once, instead of rammed sideways and half-froze in the back seat of a motor, or in a skip with a bit of cardboard for covering. I yawned and scratched me bollocks, looking at the ceiling.

My fucking ceiling.

Sun were bright and hitting us straight through the window, me having forgot to draw the curtains last night. It were a fair weather day all right. And I took that as an omen. You don't get many omens. And when you does, if you knows what's what, you'll take heed of em. This were the big day, see. I had things to do. I had matters to attend to what stood to set us up for life, if I handled em proper. Mind you, that's where the problem lay: how the fuck to handle em proper. I thought about that as I traipsed to the bathroom and pissed in the bog.

My fucking bog.

The way forward, as I seen it, were a three-stage affair. The first bit were fucking easy: go along to the little boss feller's office and let him know I done my part of the deal, so now if you'll just give us the keys to me new office and introduce us to my staff, I'll be on me merry old way. Second part were a bit harder: trapping Don and his gang while they tried raiding the Wossname Centre, thereby making a local hero of meself. I'd have to be on me toes for that, but I knew I could pull it off. Third part were the hardest: having a word with Rache and telling her I knew all about her son.

My fucking son.

That's right. I told you I'd fill you in. If you finds it a bit hard to credit, don't worry about it—I felt just the same. I mean—Rache? Why the fuck would Sal have gave our son to Rache? But when you thought about it—like I'd done, as I shovelled in the earth on top of Sal and Ferret last night—it made perfect sense. Rache were just the right sort of mother a son of mine needed. Sal knew that. And setting it all up were the one good thing she'd done in her life.

And then you got to thinking about Rache, and why the fuck had she kept it secret from us. There's me thinking me and her had summat special between us, and all the while she's harbouring the lad I thought I'd lost. She could see how upset about it I were, and she didn't raise an arse cheek to lessen my grief.

But that were all by the by, and it'd all come out in the wash.

I had a shower, brushed me ivories, shaved me chin, then had a root around in the cupboards. A short while later, right at the back of the old trunk in the spare room, I found a load of trousers, shirts, pants, socks, and a nice half-length leather.

My nice half-length leather.

• • •

'What do you mean, you wants bacon, sausages, eggs, black puddin', mushies, tommies, and baked beans?'

Doug didn't look happy. Looked like he had a handful of tacks down his trolleys. I couldn't give a toss about trolleys and tacks, though. All I cared about was me ingredients.

'Aye,' I says. 'And lard.'

'All right,' he says. 'What do you mean, all them vittles I just mentioned, and lard?'

'What do you mean, what do I mean? Fuckin' simple, ennit?'

'Aye, but what do you mean by it?'

'Fuck sake, Doug. Just giz me fuckin' scran, eh.'

'You'll get no scran in here.'

'Oh, for fuck...I'm banned again, right? After all I done for you...'

'After all you done fer...' Doug seemed to have summat stuck in his throat.

I thought about thumping him on the back a bit. I thought about knocking his flaming teeth out. The fucking miserable cunt, though, eh? All I wanted to do were buy some vittles. I had the money and everything. I turned arse. I didn't bother with the thump or the teeth, I just turned arse and fucked off out of it. I'd be moving out soon anyhow, so he could keep his bollocks corner shop.

'Hang on,' he says as I touched handle.

I found meself hanging on despite meself. I weren't proud and I wished it were otherwise, but I looked at him and goes: 'What?'

He looked at us a bit, sucking his lips, then goes: 'Just hang on a minute, please.'

'For what?'

But he were already off out back.

I felt like a dick. I didn't need this. I knew I could get better treatment elsewhere. Specially wearing me leather once again. I knew I ought to fuck off, but I never. I stood there like a dog waiting for his master to come back. And it weren't even like I looked on Doug in that way. Honest I fucking never. I'd be quite happy to break his head, if I could be arsed. But summat had us pinned.

I looked around, noticing how bare his shelves was. I'd seen em that way the other day, but it were worse now. There were hardly fuck all there, besides a few cans of this and that. I couldn't see meself getting the required vittles anyhow, even if he did change his mind about us.

'I'll admit to you,' he says, coming back in and noting my interest in his shelving situation, 'I ain't overburdened with custom at the minute.'

'I ain't surprised,' I says, 'if you treats em like you treats us.'

'That ain't the reason. Anyone with eyes can see what's happenin' to this world. Out with the old order, in with the new. Only the new one is a bad one, and will lead us all unto great sufferin' and gnashin' of ivories.'

'Woss you on about?'

'There's a big supermarket opened in Clunge Retail Park.'

'Oh,' I says. 'Clunge what?'

Doug stood tall, points right at us, and says: 'Verily, the chosen one will be strong in arm, thick in head.'

'Eh?'

'I just been on the blower. Seems there's still a chance for you. Seems there's still a chance for all of us, long as you stops arsin' around and accepts your fate accordin' to the words long written. In actual fact, Royston, your little hiccup yesterday is predicted in the scripture. "The chosen one will dilly," it sayeth. "The chosen one will dally. But, as the sun goeth down and the crows flyeth to roost, the chosen one will kindle the flames of retribution, and deliver us all from the evil one." There might be a word out of place here and there, but that's the strength of it.'

'Oh, right,' I says, scratching me swede. 'So, like, does I get me vittles or what?'

He fixed us with a long hard one, then goes: 'Aye, you will. And so will all of us. *Local* vittles. Vittles from your corner shop, or your local vittle merchant. Vittles like vittles is meant to be, wrapped in grease paper and smellin' of vittles. But first you got to do summat for your town.'

'What?'

• • •

I'd had a bit of a shock the evening prior, when Sal had told us about the piss-yeller Viva. I hadn't really thought about it at the time, being too preoccupied with other matters and that. Sounded like she was trying to soften us up with the news and all, her sat on the back seat all tied up and fretting over what I might do to her. She actually seemed to think I'd be happy about it.

'You owns this car, you know,' she'd said. 'Do you really not recall?'

I thought she were piss-taking us, but she kept on about it, explaining how she'd traded it for the Capri just before me going in Parpham. And then it all came rushing back to us.

To be frank with you, I don't think she done herself no favours in telling us that. I think I might have had that old Capri on me mind as I lopped her swede off.

Anyhow, so here I were, driving townward in the aforestated piss-yeller Viva, pulling up at them traffic lights on Clench Road. As we sat there I recalled being at these selfsame lights alongside Doug only a couple of days previous. I were in the driving seat this time, mind, which made it a bit better. I could turn arse and go anywhere I liked. I could open the shotgun door and push him out. I could drive him out to Hurk Wood and…

Mind you, I did have a little problem.

I'll let Doug fill you in about it:

'I will just say this,' he says. 'I'm disappointed it's come to this. I had high hopes for you, Royston. I hoped you'd be doin' this off yer own back, for the good of yer fellow man. Instead…well, shall I just say you wouldn't be doin' this at all if I hadn't kept a vigilant eye open and spotted you loadin' yer boot up with all them black bags, followed by that lady friend of yours, all tied up like—'

'Her name's Sal,' I says. 'She's been a customer of yours for fuckin' donkeys years.'

'Ain't my customer no more, though, is she? Nor her friend, the scruffy one. They won't be nobody's customers, not ever again.'

'Just fuckin' shut it, right?' I says, bursting through the red light. Actually it were more like trickling, this being a Viva. If I'd had me old Capri 2.8i it would have been bursting, mind.

'Kerb yer bad language,' he says. 'I holds the cards here. I can always go to the coppers, you know. You want us to, eh? Want us to tell em what I seen—'

'No.'

'Well then.'

That were it, far as conversation went. Five minutes later I pulled up in the Paul Pry car park.

For the last time.

• • •

Filthy Stan the Motor Man passed us on the way in. I thought I'd clocked his van there in the car park, and I found it reassuring in an odd way, seeing him there. We'd never truly got on, me and him, but you knew where you stood with him.

'All right, Stan,' I says as he brushed past.

All I got back were a look, them dark eyes probing right into us like poorly thrown darts in a small pub. I noticed how filthy he were and all, and not with the usual motor oil. No, this were more your farmyard muck—mud and manure and that. Odd manure though, going by the stink left behind.

'S'matter with him?' I says to Doug, door swinging shut behind us.

'Been up all night. Doin' good work.'

I shrugged and says: 'Oh.'

The Paul Pry were well dark. Always were a bit dark in here, but normally you could see your way around the place all right, which you couldn't now. The only bit lit up were the bar, with Nathan stood up behind it, reading a paper and shaking his head. 'Bloody bastard,' he says. 'The dirty bloody bastard.'

I knew he couldn't mean me cos he were still looking at the page. Mind you, there were no one else in the pub so I knew he must be addressing us. Or Doug, who were prodding us in the back, going: 'Go on. He won't bite.'

I stood still, deciding that the next time he prodded us I'd turn and snap his finger off. But he never done it again.

'Read it,' he says, folding the paper over and turning it round. He picked up a pint glass and put it under the lager pump.

I went up to the bar, hoping the pint were for us. 'ONWARDS AND UPWARDS' were the headline, and it were by 'Malcolm Pigg, Chief Editor.' That's as far as I got though.

'Do you know what he says, do you?' says Nathan. 'Says there's a certain "element" in this town who won't accept the changes we've seen of late. He's talkin' about that big monstrosity of a market there, and them other outsider shops comin' in. And he's right: there bloody well is an "element" who won't have it. Lucky for him there is and all. Lucky for everyone in this town. Cos if there weren't this "element" as he calls it, we'd be headed for trouble, I can tell you. But do you know what he then goes on to say, and all?'

I were trying to read the fucking thing but I couldn't, with him going on.

'He says it's fear. He says we don't like change cos we're afraid of it. Who the flippin' hell does he think he is? What does he know about anythin'? I'll tell you summat, Blake—that bloody Malcolm Pigg were on our side until not so long back. All over us he were, wanted to help the cause, talkin' about usin' that rag of his to spread the word and stop the rot. But then what happens? Someone got to him, is what. Sprinkle some sugar on a problem and it goes away. All right, ennit, if you got a big bag o' sugar.'

He put a full pint in front of us and wiped his brow with a rag from behind the bar. He were sweating all over and he'd have a lot of wiping to do. I don't reckon I'd ever seen Nathan sweat before. Not even in summer, which this weren't.

'This is our deep midwinter, Blakey,' he says, pointing a finger in me face. 'Make no mistake.'

When he turned around I picked the pint up. I didn't care what he said, long as I had a pint. I got me smokes out and all.

'They don't know what fear is, stupid bloody bastards. I'll show em bloody fear. I'll put the fear up em all right, and then they'll come runnin' back to the old ways…the *proper* ways. And do you know who'll be head of the pack? Eh? Eh? This little bugger here,' he says, stubbing a finger on the paper. He stood eyes closed for a bit, breathing loud through his nose. When he opened em he had a smile on his face. He looked us up and down and goes: 'Lookin' smart, Blakey. You got yer old leather wossname on.'

'Aye,' I says, smoothing it down. 'Found it at home, in the old trunk in the spare—

'Woss you afraid of?'

I stopped smoothing. 'You what?'

'Come on. What is your fear? Everyone got a fear.'

I tapped some ash into the tray and goes: 'I ain't afraid of nuthin.' And I weren't bragging neither. 'Everyone knows that.'

'Nuthin'?'

I shrugged. 'Nah.'

'So what do you think about that?'

'What?'

'That,' he says, half nodding at the paper.

'Oh.' I hadn't hardly looked at it yet. 'Load o' bollocks, ennit.'

'Good man,' he says, beaming, arms folded like two hairy pythons.

'So,' I says, looking in me pint glass. It were empty. 'So why am I here?'

'Cos Doug brung you here.'

'Actually no—*I* brung him.'

'No you never.'

'Yes I fuckin' did.'

'No swearin' in here, if you don't mind.'

'But I fuckin' did though.'

'He's right, you know,' says Doug from somewhere in the dark behind us. I'd forgot about him. 'We came here in a yellow Vauxhall, him at the wheel. I couldn't get him in me van.'

Nathan frowned at one after the other of us. Then he says: 'Well then. There's yer answer.'

I raised me eyebrows and found meself to be nodding. Thinking about it, I goes: 'Hang on...'

Nathan put a paw up. 'I wants you to meet someone.'

'Oh aye?'

'Aye. A very particular someone. Two of em, actually. Two very particular personages who you don't get to meet every day. Not these days anyhow.'

'Ah.' I looked at me watch. Fucking hell. 'I'm a bit rushed actually, Nathan, so—'

'Rushed?' He went to pull another pint.

'Aye. Meant to be at work, ain't I.'

'Work, eh?'

'Aye. Remember? It's you got me in that job.'

'Aye, thass right.' He plonked a full one before us.

'So if you don't mind...' I picked it up and started necking it.

'As I were sayin', I got two folks I wants you to meet. They will help thee to know thyself.'

I put me pint down half-sunk. 'Like I just says—'

'And you will meet these persons. Shortly. You don't even have to go very far for it, neither,' he says. 'Cos they're right here.'

'Where?' I says, looking about. No one here besides him and Doug. Unless there was someone in the bog. 'Gone for a dump, is they?' I says. 'Both of em?'

Nathan blinked slow and goes: 'There'll be no more defecation fer these two, Blake, as you will shortly see. Doug?' he says, nodding at him. 'The light, please.'

A click somewhere behind us and the remaining lights went out, plunging the Paul Pry into a darkness the like of what I hadn't never experienced. I glanced over at Nathan, but couldn't see him no more. I couldn't see nothing, and had to make do with me other senses. I pinned me lugs back and flared me nozzers, noting an odd whiff in the air that weren't typical of the Paul Pry, a sort of earthy, coppery—

'Blakey,' comes a voice from somewhere. I knew it weren't Nathan nor Doug cos it were plainly a bird's voice. Bit raspy though. 'Blakey, my darlin'...'

'Whozat?' I says. 'Hoy, Nathan—what the fuckin' hell's goin' on?'

'Do not fret, Blakey my love. Tis I, Sally.'

I'd had enough of this. I started feeling me way to the bar, hoping to…you know, to…Actually I dunno what I were hoping. Pull meself a pint, like as not. I turned and went the other way instead, aiming for the door.

'It is no use.' This were another raspy voice now, a feller. Still weren't Doug nor Nathan though. 'You cannot get out of here. This is the long-haired feller you slaughtered last night, by the way.'

'Fuck off,' I says. 'You ain't Ferret. You don't sound fuck all like him.'

'Ferret?' he says. 'Who the fuck's F—?'

A thumping sound and then a grunt coming from nearby. I looked around out of instinct, but me eyes wasn't adjusting. Meanwhile I can't find the bastard door. I've got to the wall no problem, but there's no door there no more. And in a way it didn't surprise us one bit. I knew all about Nathan and his ways.

I started feeling me way back towards the bar.

'Oh aye, er…' comes the voice again. 'Yes, I am indeed Ferret.'

'He is,' says the bird.

'Fuck off,' I says. 'You ain't Sal neither. You don't sound nuthin' like her.'

'Tis true, Blakey,' comes Sal's voice again, though it still didn't sound like her. 'We are indeed Sally and Ferret. I knows our voices sounds a bit different now, but that's cos we're dead.'

'An' also we ain't got lungs no more,' croaks the feller. 'You cut our lips off from our lungs, didn't yer.'

I had a think about that, back at the bar now and holding a stool. They might have a point, you know. Sal had always said how she'd come back and haunt us if she carked it before us. And, come to think on it, she did sound a bit like that some mornings, after eighty fags and a bottle of Pernod the night prior.

'Sal?' I says.

'Yes, darlin'.'

'Soz, mate. About choppin' yer head off an' that.'

'That's all right, darlin'. Que sera, sera.'

'You what?'

'Hey,' says Ferret. 'What about me? Ain't you gonna say sorry to me an' all?'

'You can fuck off,' I says, locating me empty pint glass on the bartop. 'Long-haired cunt.'

'Don't you call me a—'

'All right you two, thass enough.' This were a different voice. A louder, darker voice with a lot of echo in it. And I'd know it any place. 'Nathan here, the barman.'

I leaned over and quietly started pulling lager into me glass. Whisky would have done better but I couldn't reach it from here.

'Nathan,' says the Ferret feller, 'we got this under control, mate. I were just—'

'I don't give a monkeys what you was just,' hollers Nathan. 'You've had yer chance and took too long over it. Now go on, back to the spirit world with yer. I'll take this un from here.'

I think I'd spilt a fair bit but I'd managed to get some into the glass. I were back for seconds now and it were proving spot-on for this situation.

'Now, Blake,' says the booming, echoing voice of Nathan from all around. 'Them two there didn't just come to have a chat with you, as might have appeared, they—'

'But I were just gettin' to—'

'I told you to blimmin' *shut* it, Alv...I mean er...you know—wossname... Ferret. Aye, Ferret. Blakey—I must apologise fer that. There will be no further contribution from the spirit world, such as it is. Like I says, them two came along here to ask summat in particular, but had a bit of trouble with a bush and decided it needed beatin' around, which it never. But you won't get none of that from me, oh no. I'm comin' straight to the meat of it, and no veg. I didn't get to be the man I am by...'

Nathan went on for a bit while I supped some of his lager. I were getting the hang of it now, and I'd sunk at least three this way. And it were all the more better for Nathan not knowing a thing about it, him being all tied up in his own voice. After me fourth I stopped for a quick listen.

'...help from no one. Aye, thass right—I did it all on me tod. Everythin' I got has come from keepin' me eyes open, waitin' me moment, and playin' a clever hand. You'll do well to...'

I pulled meself another. Halfway down it I noticed Nathan's tone were taking a turn for the different. So I tuned in for a bit.

'No, it's a serious matter you've been brung here for. We, namely the Old Guard, asked a favour of you before. We presented you with your allotted destiny, such as it is, and you took it. Needed a bit of persuadin' but you came through. And then you went back out again, tossin' it all in our faces for no good reason. So that puts us in a pickle, Blakey, bein' as everyone round here agrees that you are the Chosen One, as they calls him, and there's no one else up fer the job, and the job cannot go undone. So the only avenue left open fer us is arm twistin'. Understand us, does you?'

'Aye,' I says, spilling some lager. 'Er...woss you sayin'?'

'I'm sayin' about twistin' yer arm.'

'What for?'

'To bring you back on board, where you belong.'

I had a think about that. 'On board where?'

'On board the…the flippin'…Blinkin' hell, Blake. Ain't you been harkin' us?'

'I have, I have…I just didn't know what you was on about.'

'Then I'll put him simply, like I perhaps ought to of done from the outset. I…*we* want you to deliver a certain summat to a certain personage, at a certain spot on a given hour. Half three, to be precise. At half three, you will be sat down on one o' them benches near the escalator, on the ground floor of the Porter Centre, and someone will come and take the delivery from you.'

'Half four,' says Ferret.

'No—half three. Had to bring him forward an hour. Received a bit of intelligence about certain nasty goin's on they got planned.'

'Who got planned?'

'Never you mind.'

'Woss this thing then?' I says. 'An' who's I gotta give it to?'

'Never you mind neither.'

'I can't very well carry summat without knowin' what it is.'

'All right, it's a bag.'

'Bag o' what?'

'Never you mind.'

'Never I mind?'

'*If*,' says Nathan. 'If you're still sat there on yer bench at a quarter shy of four o'clock, and no one's come to collect the delivery off you, then…Well, then—*and only then*—can you open the thing up. But not before. You can't open it, Blake, not under any circumstances save those ones I've laid out fer you here. Namely the feller not turnin' up.'

'Oh aye,' says I. 'Oh aye? An' what if I does open the fucker up before time? Woss to stop us, eh?'

He gave us a long look and goes: 'You knows better than that, Blakey. *I'll know.* An' if I knows, I'll punish. I'll throw the flamin' book at you.'

'Look, just tell us woss I gotta deliver. I got a fuckin' right to know, I have.'

He shook his head, saying: 'None of your b—'

'Fuckin' do it yerself then.'

'I can't do it meself,' he says. 'The executor of the act must be a particular person. A *special* person. Namely you.'

'You callin' us a special person?'

'Thass what I'm callin' you.'

'He's right, Blakey,' comes the Sal voice.

'Shut up, you,' says Nathan.

'Don't tell our Sal to shut up,' I says.

'It ain't your...Ah, look—Blakey, the upshot of this is that you ain't in no position to argue the toss. Like I says, you've made it hard fer yerself at every turn, and now I'm twistin' yer arm.'

'You can fuckin' try it, mate. You'll have a job.'

'I don't doubt it, but I'm referring here to metaphorical arm-twistin' such as it is.'

'Fuck's you on about?'

'No swearin' in here, ladies bein' present.'

I were all set to ask him where them ladies was, but then I recalled about the spirit of Sal, who I could still feel flappin' around in the dark. Mind you, Sal couldn't hardly complain about overuse of swear words, the tongue on her.

'I'll lay him on the line fer you, Blakey,' goes Nathan. 'You don't do this thing fer us, we (namely the Old Guard) will deliver these two items here to the authorities, who might well be interested in em.'

'What ite—' I started to say, but the lights came back on just then and I saw what them two items was. Only a yard or so from us they was, laid down all careful on a couple of plates. Two heads, sat up and facing us—Ferret on the one side, Sal on t'other.

• • •

DOCTOR: *We have diagnosed the problem. We've found that your life has been hindered—and endangered—by the overshadowing influence of your father. And, as long as it remains thus, your problems will continue. But it doesn't have to be that way, Royston. When you get back out there on the streets, it doesn't have to be the same pattern as before.*

PATIENT: [silent. Has been silent since our last session. Gestures indicate comprehension, but no response is offered. On the surface, patient appears to have regressed. However, this is not the case. This is patient's way of absorbing, adjusting. Long periods of inactivity punctuated by spells of intense action—this has long been patient's pattern.]

DOCTOR: *It's about accepting yourself, and working out your own values, based on your own experiences and instincts. Your father is living up there in your head, Royston. It's time to kick him out.*

PATIENT: [I am still wondering if this is the best route to take, if perhaps I should just tell him the truth about his "father." But we do not have enough time for that. Patient would not accept it without a long period of adjustment under my supervision—time which we do not have.]

DOCTOR: *We can do this. We can bring out the real Royston Blake. You will find problems, surely. But they will be* your *problems.*

PATIENT: [no, I must leave patient to discover the truth for himself. Or let his real father finally come forward. That would be as traumatic for patient as if I had told him...But it would be natural. It would be beyond my control.]

DOCTOR: *Are you ready for this, Royston? Are you ready to accept yourself?*

PATIENT: [shrugs] *Aye.*

• • •

I stopped for a minute. If I chucked me guts any more I'd have none of em left. I swear I could see a bit of lung down there.

'Now now,' says Nathan, reaching past us and flushing the bog. He patted us on the back and goes 'Now now' again.

A long trail of stringy flob stretched from lower lip to pan. I tried spitting it off but I couldn't. Nathan were patting me back again.

'Why me?' I says.

I heard him fill his lungs, nice and slow. Must have stank summat rotten in that cubicle just then, so you had to give him credit. 'Because you were born to it, Blake. There's one like you born every once in a while, and we've got to guide them as best we can. I've been doin' that for the past God only knows. An' I've done all right with it, even if I does say so meself. But there comes a time…there comes a time, Blake, when…'

I started honking again, drowning out his voice.

17

I were surprised to see an orange Austin Maxi in the Paul Pry car park on me way out. I'd always thought the only orange Maxi in Mangel were that of Margaret Hurge, the hairdresser. Mind you, she might have flogged it. There were a blue Sherpa van here and all. On the side panel the words 'ALVIN'S KEBAB SHOP AND CHIPPY' had been painted over with a brush, though you could still make em out. On top of it someone had painted 'MAN WITH VAN—REMOVALS, LIGHT HAULAGE, ODD JOBS, ANY-THING REALLY.' I looked at it for a minute or so, then rubbed me face and pressed on, trying to herd me thoughts up and have a look at em.

I were well pissed off, I soon realised. Sounded like a piece of piss, lugging a bag into the Wossname Centre and sitting on a bench with it. Sounded like I'd got the better end of it, consider-ing how I'd stay out of Mangel Jail if I went through with it, and Nathan had promised that Doug would dispose of Sal and Ferret in a proper fashion (using his 'vittle recycler', whatever that were). But I still weren't happy.

Cos I'd promised Rache.

Promised her I'd tell Nathan and his lot to shove their filthy plan up their stinking arses. Which I'd done, going so far as to give em the motor back, even though it were the Doc's and he didn't want us doing their bidding neither. And now here I were, donkeying for em again and without even a push-bike to show for it.

'You'll get more than a push-bike fer yer troubles,' comes Nathan's voice from behind us. I didn't turn about. I knew he were stood behind us in the doorway, leaning up against the frame, arms folded. 'You pulls this one off proper, you won't have to touch a steerin' wheel not ever again. You'll have yer own driver, and your name will echo down through the generations. "Royston Blake," they'll be sayin', hundreds of years hence, "Royston Blake—saviour of our town. *King of Mangel.*" How'd that be, eh?'

I walked on out of the car park, trying to think about that. Sounded all right, didn't it? *King of Mangel.* Mind you, that's the only bit I could recall, now I'd left the Paul Pry behind. I tried conjuring the rest of what he'd said but his voice kept slipping around in me swede, words slopping about like soup in a football.

'Hoy,' came a holler.

'Wha?' I says, looking up. Two fellers was walking across the way from us, by the building site there, and it must have been them doing the hoying. The one of em were bent down picking summat up off the edge of the site, and when he stood up I recognised him to be Danny, the lad I'd refused entry to the other day, on the door.

'All right, Danny,' I says, moving on.

I went sideways, summat hitting the back of me swede. Then there was a lot of racket, followed by summat else hitting us, in the back of the pins this time. Felt like a bull running up and butting us, and for a minute I wondered if someone had left the gates open down the slaughtering yard. Then I touched down arsewise on summat hard and metal, bouncing off it and landing in a frozen pond. That's how it felt anyhow, ice cracking under me shoulder but not quite giving way. I braced meself for the cold water, but rolled over instead until someone hit us with a length of road.

• • •

'Do you think he's all right?'

'How should I bloody know?'

'He's your flippin' son.'

'So bloody what?'

'So you ought to know how he is.'

'How?'

I opened me eyes. Two faces was looking down on us, one of em being me mam. I hadn't seen her in fucking donkeys, not since…since…

'Since my husband murdered us,' says me mam. 'Many, many years ago.' Her long yellow hair were falling down onto me face. It felt warm and I could smell the shampoo on it. I opened me gob and let some of her hair fall into it.

'Aye,' I says, sucking and chewing. 'Not since me old man murdered you.'

'Not yer old man,' says the other feller, who were Elvis. 'He weren't yer old man. I'm yer old man, son.'

He took his sunglasses off and rubbed his face hard, double chin wobbling in them big white collars. I noticed a couple of buttons had gone from his shirt, and his hairy belly were hanging out a bit. When he turned his head sideways to crack his neck I saw how beaky his nose were, and I knew there and then that this weren't Elvis.

'No,' I says, 'you fuckin' ain't—'

'He is, Royston,' says me mam, pulling a cool hand to me forehead. I loved the feel of it there and I wanted it to stay like that forever. 'Yer dad weren't really your dad. That's why he murdered me.'

'But…but…'

'Tis true. I had an affair with him,' she says, nodding her head at the feller who weren't Elvis.

'Him?' I says, still staring at me mam and not wanting to even glance at the feller. I could see him in me peripherals though, and summat seemed different about him of a sudden. 'How come?'

They looked at each other. Mam smiled a tired smile. I looked at the feller, who didn't look like Elvis no more. Looked like the devil himself, all red skin and horns and no hair and that. I couldn't see his pointy tail but I knew he had one, round the back. Still had a beaky nose and double chin though.

'He charmed us,' she says. 'He's a charmer.'

I noticed her hand had got hot on me forehead, and I went to touch it. It weren't hers I found there though. It were the devil's.

'Raagh,' I says, rolling away from em. I kept on rolling, finding meself to be on a bit of a slope and not able to stop meself. Felt like grass under us, so I knew I'd be coming to a gentle stop any second as the hill levelled out into a flat clearing, or summat. Mind you, I didn't bank on a tree being there. I hit him hard, knocking the puff out of us and possibly soiling me trolleys slightly. I were all right to get up though, so I did.

There was trees everywhere. Sun were trying to break through overhead, but the trees was holding him off, even though they had no leaves. It were cold.

'Help,' I heard someone shouting.

I stood still and harked.

'Help,' it came again. A bird's voice.

No, a young lad's voice.

'What?' I yells. 'Fuck sake.'

'Daddy,' he comes back. 'Daddy, I'm lost!' And I got a glimpse of him this time, over there where the sun were breaking through—a flash of chestnut hair between them trees up yonder.

'Little Royston?' I hollers. 'Hoy, Little Royston—stay there.'

I went it after him, crashing through branches and kicking up old pine needles. I knew he couldn't get far. I'd soon be with him. I'd learn him about the ways of the world, and make sure he don't get lost in Hurk Wood again. Maybe I'd take him camping out here sometimes. Or maybe I wouldn't. Maybe I'd not let him out of the house.

'Hey, Little Royston?' I says, reaching the spot and stopping. He weren't there. I looked all around, squinting. The sun weren't here no more. It were getting dark. Summat were shifting beneath me feet. I looked down.

Fingers. Hands, two of the fuckers.

Clawing up through the dirt and scratching me boots.

I jumped in the air, making unmanly noises, landing on my arse a little ways off. The hands was out up to the elbow now, sensing victory. I were glad Little Royston weren't here now, cos I wouldn't know what to say to him. I felt summat under me arse cheeks.

More fucking hands.

I scrambled onto me feet and stood by, watching Sal and Ferret dig emselves out of the hole I'd dug for em. I recognised the spot now. Even spotted a fag butt I'd left there the night previous. Sal were half out now and stopped for some puff, looking at us.

'I only ever wanted your babby,' she says, dirt falling off her bare body.

'Hoy, you,' says Ferret to her. 'What about me? What about *my* fuckin' needs?' He were mostly out now and all. His head didn't look right though, like it were set turning Sal's direction and he couldn't make it go no other. As I looked at it, it fell off.

Then his arms fell off.

And Sal's head.

'Blake, love,' says her head, lying sideways in the dirt. 'Lend us a fiver?'

I weren't having none of that. I turned arse and pegged it like Billy-O. I closed me eyes—I'd had enough of seeing stuff, and to be honest I didn't care if I knocked meself dead on a tree trunk. I seemed to be going all right, mind, chugging along at a fair clip and hearing them two carping heads getting quieter and quieter behind us. I were surprised to find the ground getting harder underfoot though. Gone were the soft padding of an honest feller running over nature's soft surface. What you had now were the slap slap of a heavy sole on tarmac, followed by the telltale screeching of a motor about to run you down.

She took us sideways on. I went limp, letting fate take her course and fuck it. I smacked into the windscreen and rolled off, landing on my sorry arse. The motor pulled up a couple of yards on. Looked like a Granada Mk II 3 litre GL to me, or summat like it. The door opened and out climbs the Doc. Only it didn't look like the Doc.

Looked like Elvis Presley.

The proper King this time—collars high, sideburns thick, nose straight, and buttons all shiny. He spread his legs shoulder width, letting his knees go springy, and pointed a finger at us.

'No one gets out of Mangel,' he says. 'Mangel folks is all leaves on the same tree, you see. And...ah, you knows it.' He scratched a sideburn, looking a bit on-edge over summat. 'Here,' he says, tapping his pockets, 'you got a smoke?'

'Aye.' I got em out and flipped the lid for him.

He took one, going: 'Nice one.'

I lit it.

'Mind you,' he says, puffing and squinting at all the smoke around him. 'Mind you, there is one way to get out of Mangel, so they says. It's all about dreamin', see. What you gotta do is go down that East Bloater Road, right…at night, like…and watch out there in the dark for a beckonin'…'

'What?' I says. 'Look out for a beckonin' what, fuck sake?'

I were crying about summat. I dunno when I'd started, but it felt like I'd been blubbing for ages without noticing. And now the tears was spilling down me face, making it hard for us to see. I rubbed me eyes, and when I looked again Elvis were on the move. He headed for them big glass doors over there without so much as a wink. He weren't Elvis no more neither. He were the little boss feller, from the Wossname Centre. And the Wossname Centre's what I watched him walking into, the doors sliding wide as he goes up to em.

Don were on the door, and he tipped his hat to the boss feller as he went past, even though he weren't actually wearing no hat. The boss goes inside and the doors slides shut behind him, a bit too sharpish for my liking.

I look at Don. He's grinning back at us, giving us the wink I'd looked for from Elvis. It ain't the same though, coming from Don. This un here's a bad wink. A wink before slicing you. Summat glints and me eyes goes to it. Sure enough, he's holding a fucking machete. He gives us another wink and follows the boss feller through them glass doors.

Summat's pulling on me arm and I looks down and finds it to be the bag, the one Nathan gave us just now. I puts it down and unzips it, not wanting to but not able to stop meself. There's only one thing in there—a little box wrapped in brown paper and sticky brown tape. I seen it before, a few years back. This is the fucking doofer I gave Nathan back there, after all that aggro with the chainsaw, and Nathan promising to steer us clear of the coppers if I gives him it. I never did find out what were in the box back then. Curiosity's a bugger all right but I finds I can beat it, if beating it suits us. I zip the bag up.

I'm looking at them doors, wondering if I oughtn't to go through em. As I'm stood there, thinking about it, little cracks appears in the walls of the Wossname centre, starting ground-level and working up like bust veins on an old man's hooter. Then comes the blood.

A river of it.

Pouring through the cracks and flooding the street.

Knocking us over.

I floats on the surface for a bit, looking up at the sky. Lightning's zagging all over it, just like the cracks on them walls just now. But there's no blood up there. There's no rain just yet.

Meanwhile I'm washing up on a desert island, empty-pawed. The sun's on me back and the gentle din of seagulls behind us somewhere. I lies like so for a bit, enjoying the warmth of the sand under me back. Then two fellers walks up and looks down at us.

It's Rocky.

And Apollo Creed.

They picks us up, taking an arm each. Rocky's having a bit of trouble at first on account of his gloves, but Apollo helps him out and he's all right in the end. He's always all right in the end, Rocky.

'Ding ding,' says Apollo.

• • •

'You bloody fool,' says some old fucker, standing over us. 'Ain't you got eyes? You'm pissed, ain't you. Bloody pissed at this time o' day—a workin' day an' all. Look what you done to me windscreen, you bloody...'

I got up sharpish, not expecting me legs to hold but finding em not too bad, considering. Hit the back of me swede on summat as I pulled meself straight, mind, but when I looked up there were fuck all but dark grey clouds up there. Mind you, the old feller were lying backwise now with his peepers shut, blood oozing out his gob. I looked up again and wondered if we hadn't been struck by a thunderbolt from them clouds up there. Stood to reason, didn't it, considering how mushy me swede felt just then. I hurried off up the road, trying to think proper.

I've always found that, when you ain't sure what's what, and you got the fog in yer swede, the wisest recourse of action is to think of one thing only—namely the thing you got to do next. If you knows what to do next, you knows where you're going. And that means you ain't going far wrong in your life.

Trouble were, I couldn't recall even that. I couldn't recall nothing, and I couldn't get no thoughts to stick in me mind for more than a second or so. I could just about remember that I were a smoker and that I had some wedge in me pocket. So I went into a shop and bought some fags.

'Ah, it's you, is it?' says the feller there.

'I knows you,' I says, pointing at him. 'You're wossname, the miserable cunt from the wossname.' No sooner was the words out than I remembered that his name were Gromer, and that he were from the offy, and that we was stood here in it. Then I noticed the bag I were holding and it all came back to us, about the doofer inside it and having to drop it off on a desert island, and Rocky Balboa and Apollo Creed appearing before us as ghosts in the dark there at the Paul Pry, and Elvis chasing Little Royston around Hurk Wood, and that. No, I mean…er…

'Aye, that'd be right,' Gromer says, not looking happy about it. Told you he were a miserable cunt. 'Just take yer tobacco and get off my premises, if you please.'

'I ain't paid yet,' I says, getting a bluey out. I weren't gonna give it him though, after him being so rude. I just wanted him to hold his paw out.

'You can pay us by not ever darkenin' my doorway again. I've no time for you, Royston bloody Blake. You had the chance to save this town of ours from a slow chokin' death, and you turned yer fat nose up to it. You didn't fancy it cos you had better things to do. So go on…Hop it.'

'But yer wrong,' I says. 'You got us all wrong, Gromer…I mean miserable cunt…Woss yer name again?'

'*Out*.'

'No, I were just sayin…I ain't changed me mind, like. About Nathan. I'm doin' the job now, savin' the planet an' that.'

He looked askance at us with his gimlet eye. 'You shitin' us?'

'I ain't shitin' yer. Look, I got the bag here an' everythin'.'

He peered over the counter and goes: 'Flippin' heck…Woss you doin' bringin' that in here?'

'Eh?' I goes. 'S'matter with it?'

'Er…nuthin, I s'pose. What time's it set fer? I mean er…what time's he asked you to, you know, *deliver* it?'

'Half four,' I says.

'You sure?' he says, giving us some more of his gimlet.

'Course I'm fuckin' sure.'

'Well, good then. Half four…Gives a while or so to sort yer affairs out.'

'Affairs?'

'You know…ah, never mind. Look—you just keep yer eye on yer watch and do a good job. We're all behind you,

Royston. Tell you what,' he says, reaching under the counter, 'you comes back here after your little job at half four, I'll have a little summat for you.' He waved a big fat fucker of a cigar in front of us, saying: 'Bottle o' summat an' all. Show me appreciation, like.'

'Aye all right. Giz one o' them for now, eh,' I says, pointing at the miniatures behind him.

'No, Blake, I will not. You don't need that stuff just now. Takes yer edge off.'

'Come on, fuckin' giz it.'

There must have been summat in me voice, cos he shook his swede and gave us the bottle. I unscrewed it and necked it and it weren't bad. I felt all right, all in all. I felt strong in arm, and I could hear me brain ticking like a clock.

I turned arse.

'Woss happened to your head?' he says as I goes out the door. 'You got bumps on it size of the Deblin Hills.'

I half turned, thinking about it and feeling around up there with me free hand. Then I shrugged and fucked off.

• • •

I knew what I had to do next, now. Before all that bag-dumping bollocks. To be honest I didn't know how I could have forgot, it being my passport to a life of respectability and everything that went along with it, including Rache, Little Royston, and a snooker table. But what with one thing and another (getting struck by lightning there...and killing Sal and Ferret and burying em and that) I had forgot it. But I remembered now.

Oh aye.

• • •

'He's not in.'

'What d'yer fuckin' mean, he ain't in?'

'I says he's *not* in, not he *ain't* in.'

'Same diff'rence.'

She folded her arms, pushing her tits up and thereby encouraging us even more. 'No it ain't.'

'Is.'

'Ain't.'

'Is.'

'What do you want, anyhow? You're just a security guard. You should be down there on the door, where you belongs.'

'Oh aye?'

'Aye.'

'Aye?'

'Please go away.' Mind you, you only had to look at her to find all the encouragement a feller needs. She were the fittest secretary I'd ever seen. By a furlong. And by that I don't mean to say there was summat horsey in her. If horses has got big tits, round arses, all right faces, and nice silky yellow hair, then she were well horsey. But they ain't got tits, so she weren't. Least I don't think they got tits.

Do they?

And the best thing about it were that she'd be mine in a few minutes. I'd always wanted to rip a secretary's knickers off and fuck her hard on a desk, and now I'd be able to. See, I wanted her as part of the deal. I'd been around long enough to know how to bargain with a feller. When you got summat they don't want you having, you got em landed. You can get what you wants out of em, long as you holds your rod proper. And I wanted this here secretary. And a nice office, with a waiting room. Just like this un.

'Just buzz him, will yer,' I says. I fancied her and that, but she were high-strung and I didn't have time for it. Plus I had a gut ache coming on. 'Ain't got all fuckin' day, have I?'

'I told you, I—'

'Fuck sake,' I says, picking the blower up. 'Hello?' I says, holding her off with me other paw. There were nobody on the line and I didn't know what his number were, so I chucked the blower down, picked me bag up, and went to his door.

'You can't—'

'Shut it, you,' I says, pointing at her. 'I'll learn you respect, I will. Right?'

I opened the door.

He were on the blower, chair swivelled towards the big window and him looking out of it, admiring the fine view of the Mangel skyline. I don't think he'd heard us come in cos he stayed like so, yakking into his handset. I shut the door behind us, parked me arse in the spare chair, and dropped me bag on the floor next to it. All nice and quiet.

'I don't care,' he shouts in his posh telephone voice, making us jump a bit. 'Tell them if I don't get this funding, the deal's off. Believe you me, Simon, there's plenty more investors in the big city. We've got interest from all over. And if Rogers wants to back off because of someone puking on his shoes when he came to visit me, he can go fuck himself. Tell him that. Go on, tell him.'

I were sat right behind him, looking at him. The top of his swede looked like a little hillock against the white sky out there. You could tell he were emotional cos his hairs was sticking up like a frightened hedgehog. Fuck knows what he were on about, mind. I looked at the tasteful tits on the wall instead. Like I says before, she were all right. Not half so good as his own bird, mind, if I recalled her right. I bet she had a fucking nice pair o' lungs on her.

'Look, Simon, I've got plans for this place. I want to expand outwards—an interlinked set of malls stretching across the town, one single development servicing their every consumer need. And it's not just me, I…What?…Personal agenda? That's bollocks, Simon, and you know it. The fact that I was born here doesn't come into it. This could be anywhere. The fact is it's an incredible business opportunity, and if we don't exploit it, someone else will. The town's ripe for the picking, Simon. And it could be anywhere…What? Just tell him what I said. Give him twenty-four hours and then go to Wiseman. I fucking mean it, Simon.'

He spun his chair round and slammed the blower down, not getting it on right first time and having to do it again. Then he put face in paws and stayed like so for a bit. Life were treating him rough by the sounds of it, and if he weren't me boss I'd near feel sorry for the poor fucker. Mind you, I had other things to worry about just now. Me guts had turned chronic, and I'd been dying to drop one for a couple of minutes now. I let it out nice and gentle so as not to disturb him. Must have been that whisky just now.

Ten or so seconds later he looks up, sniffing the air. 'What the…How the fuck did you get in here? And what's that… *pwoar…*' He covered his nose with a hanky and wafted the air around him. 'That is fucking disgusting. How dare you walk in here and—'

'All right all right,' I says. Cos he were going a bit far now, calling us disgusting and that. 'I come for me new job, ain't I.'

He were at the big window now, looking for a way to get it open. 'These stupid fucking things. You can't open em, you know. Bloody air conditioning.'

'For fuck sake, just sit down, will yer. Here, this'll clear it.' I got a fag out and lit it, blowing smoke all around.

He didn't seem happy, but instead of speaking up about it he held his tongue and sat down again. (Wisely so, cos I were getting a bit fed up with him.) He put his fingers together, making a little steeple, and goes: 'What do you want?'

'Woss I want? I wants me new job is what. I done what you asked.'

'What do you mean, "what I asked"? I never asked you anything.'

'You did. Asked us to get rid of Ferret.'

'I never asked you to get rid of anyone.'

'Aye you did. "Sort Ferret out," you says.'

'What ferret?'

'You know—the pikey feller…The cunt who were pickin' on you.'

'No one's picking on me, Blake.'

'Eh? You said Ferret were—'

'I don't remember saying anything to you, Blake. Picking on me? Who'd pick on me? I draw a lot of water in this town, Blake. I've got influence. People off the street can't just walk up and pick on me.'

'But you says—'

'I said *nothing* to you. If you've gone and got yourself into trouble, that's *your* fucking problem. Sort it out yourself. You've got nothing on me, Blake. *Nothing.* So don't even think about dragging my name into it. And let me give you some advice, you stupid piece of shit. You go blabbing about me and they'll find out what you did. And then what? I'll have a friendly chat with the police, which will clear up any misunderstanding about me being involved. Meanwhile, *you'll* go to *jail*. Can you understand that, Blake? Can your puny mind cope with that?'

He were stood up now, side-on so he could look out the big window and keep his peripherals on us. 'I can't be touched, Blake,' he goes. 'Not here. Not after everything I've built up and worked for. Do you know how powerful I am around here? I *own* the fucking coppers. That's what you can buy with money, you know. And losers like you…Do you know, not even an *army* of people like you could get to me. Not here, in this building. If you only knew what I had here, Blake. If you only knew how well protected I am from the dangers of the world, here in my fortress. You know what? I'm going to move in here in a couple of weeks. There's floor space above here, and…it'll be my penthouse suite. Me and my son, we'll be the kings of the castle, ruling everything, and safe from it all…You hear me, Blake? I'm the king of the fucking castle, mate. And what does that make you, eh?'

I looked right at him, working out me best response. I found it hard to consider every little thing he'd said there, but I got the gist of it:

He were angry with us about summat, weren't he.

'All right,' I says. 'No fuckin' about, eh? I just wants me new job. *Chief of security* you says, or summat. I wants a nice big office like this un here. An' that bird out there—I wants her an' all. As me secretary, like.'

He squinted at us for a bit, like he couldn't understand. Then he smiled.

Then he laughed.

He laughed a lot, slapping the desk and spinning round in his chair. His face were going beetroot and tears was dripping down his cheeks, all the while him glancing at us every couple of seconds, topping up the joke and laughing a bit harder.

It were a short walk around the desk and it took us only a couple of seconds. Meanwhile the feller shut up, trying to spin away from us in his chair. He ought to have got up out of it instead and made a run for the door, carrying on down the stair and screaming for help. I don't think even that would have saved him, mind. Not the way I were feeling just then.

It were me dreams, see.

They was all floating away.

I could see em out there, out the window, drifting up into the clouds over them Deblin Hills. I'd tried, hadn't I? I'd tried setting meself up in an honest life with a proper job and that, doing the decent thing and keeping shoppers safe. All I wanted were a family of me own and a means of looking after em, and so that's what I'd strove for. But striving don't get you shite. You can strive all you likes in this life and you'll be lucky to avoid a slap for your efforts. Shall I tell you what striving gets you?

Strife.

Cos of cunts like this one here. Scheming little short-arse cunts who all they wants to do is keep big, honest, hard-working fellers like meself down.

I picked him up.

One hand on the back of his collar, the other on his belt. I swung him like that a few times, getting the feel for him. I had one last look out the window before smashing it. Somewhere, up there in them clouds, was a nice big house with a gravel driveway leading up to it, large executive motor parked in the double garage.

But it weren't mine, and never would be.

It belonged to this laughing fucker here (who weren't laughing no more). Him and his ilk would always end up with the gravel and the double garages. Always had done, always would do.

Well fuck him and his gravel.

He were welcome to it.

I took one last swing backwards and lobbed him at the window.

18

DOCTOR:	*So really, as you can see, it's about marking out your territory anew, for yourself. Same lamp posts, new scent for Royston Blake. When you get out of here, in just a few days, you're going to see this town with fresh eyes. Born again, Royston. Of course, the temptation might be to leave town…*
PATIENT:	*Oh aye, as if.*
DOCTOR:	*What?*
PATIENT:	*Leave town, you says. I mean, for fuck sake…*
DOCTOR:	*That strikes you as a strange idea?*
PATIENT:	*Oh no, mate. Fucking fine idea, ennit. But an idea's all it is, as well you knows.*
DOCTOR:	*I still don't quite…*
PATIENT:	*Fucking hell, Doc…You're meant to be the brainy one. You can't leave Mangel. No one can, see. We're all leaves on the same tree, and…it's a big fucking tree, right, and…the leaves, like— they drops off and…and…I mean, we can't live without the…*
DOCTOR:	*Royston?*
PATIENT:	[appears to be deep in thought]
DOCTOR:	*Royston? What's the matter?*
PATIENT:	*What?*
DOCTOR:	*You were…erm…*
PATIENT:	*Fuck sake, Doc. I were just having a little think.*

DOCTOR:	*Oh yes? What about?*
PATIENT:	*Nosy, ain't you?*
DOCTOR:	*Yes. It's my job.*
PATIENT:	*Well, I were thinking about leaving Mangel, actually. Cos, like, I'm wondering if maybe, you know, perhaps…*
DOCTOR:	*Yes?*
PATIENT:	*You know, leaving Mangel and that.*
DOCTOR:	*Ah, yes. As I was saying, the temptation might be to leave town. It would be easy to move to a new place, start over. But that would be avoiding the issue. You need to fight your battle on home ground. You need to win Mangel back for yourself. This is where you've suffered. This is where you've made mistakes and lived through tragedy. Maybe you will leave town someday. Why not? But you need to conquer the home front first. And you will. If you ever leave, Royston, it will be as king of Mangel.*
PATIENT:	[ponderous again, pulling lower lip] *Oh, all right.*

• • •

I must have broke over hundred windows in me time. Not often on purpose, mind. Most of em was as a youngun, playing summat in the street and always being the unlucky one. It's normally a ball that does it, course. But the one time I send part of a hoover through a window. You know, the long bit you uses for doing cobwebs and that. It's in two hollow metal bits and you sticks the one in t'other. Dunno where we found it but we was playing cricket with it, see. There I am swinging for a six and the end comes off, going right over the road and through the window of Number 22. And guess who lived there at the time?

A fucking copper.

Aye, ain't I the lucky one.

Anyhow, I pegs it. I ain't thick, you know. I knows me rights. Innocent until caught, mate. I thought I'd be all right and all, me being a bit quick over the flat even then, age of eight or so. But I couldn't shake the fucker, and he got us down an alley off Clench Road and pinned us to the ground. 'Gotcher, you dirty little vandal,' he says to us, planting a knee on me back and pressing me face into the hard stuff. 'I oughta put you behind bars right now and leave you there, you little villain. Save everyone a lot o' bo—'

He stopped there cos a plank of wood came swinging sideways into his head, sweeping him off us and knocking him cold.

'Come on, son,' says me dad, getting an arm and hauling us up. He never spoke all the way home, except when we stopped off at the chippy and he gave em his order. In the kitchen, when I'd finished me saveloy, he goes: 'Yer all right, son.' Then he slipped his watch off and put it in front of us. I stopped chewing and stared at it.

No one ever seen the copper again after that. They says he turned mong, and his family moved away.

So aye, I'd broke windows before, all right. But I couldn't break this un here, chucking the little boss feller at it.

I looked down at him. Out cold he were, just like that copper back then. I thought about picking him up again and having another go, but I knew it wouldn't work. Just by tapping it you could tell this glass wouldn't break. Like solid marble, it were, except you could see through it. Hold up against a bomb it would, I reckon.

'Oh my god,' comes a frightened voice behind us.

I turned about to see the secretary stood there in the door-way, hands to gob, knees clamped together under her little skirt.

I looked at her and looked at him, and I didn't know what to say. 'I…' I says. 'He…'

Froze solid, she were. I knew she'd bolt if I took a step in her direction, and that I might not catch her. So I parked me arse in the swivel chair and sparked one up, ignoring her. Let her calm down a bit before I gave her a talking to. Can't put the shite up a bird who's already hysterical.

About three puffs into me smoke I noticed she'd let her hands drop. I still weren't looking direct at her, but I could tell she were more calmer. That's me girl. Now just walk on out so I can chase after you. But she never done that. She came towards us instead.

I looked her way, wondering what were up. She were braver than I'd reckoned, and like as not she wanted to have a look at her boss, see if she could do summat for him. She stopped nearby and had a quick gander, but only enough to see he were out of it. Then it were my turn.

And fuck me, didn't I half get a turn.

She didn't say nothing, just stood before us for a bit. Slowly the colour were coming back to her cheeks and half a smile were making himself known. She were breathing hard and I couldn't take me eyes off her tits, going up and down like that, nipples poking out through her bra and blouse.

'You're for it now,' she says, getting down on her knees in front of us. 'You're for…it…'

She had us out and in her gob before I could say, 'I know.' And by that time I didn't care. I let her bob up and down on him for a bit, swinging me leg over the side to give her better access. You could tell this weren't her main event, but she weren't half keen, going by all them noises coming from her. I let her carry on like so for a while, sucking and moaning, then pushed her back. She wouldn't leave it alone and I had to get a bit rough with her. It were like trying to get a starved lurcher bitch off a raw steak, I tell you. Anyhow, I got her off in the end and bent her over the desk, yanking skirt up and knickers down. She were backing onto us hard and it weren't easy to slot him home, but I got him there in the end and she gave us a little scream for me efforts.

I looked around us, enjoying the moment. I couldn't fucking believe it. Here I were, boning the fittest secretary in the world on a big posh desk, in a plush office, nice painting there on the wall, big window with a top view of the whole town and outlying hills. I were on top of the world, mate. I closed me eyes and enjoyed the run-in, picking up me pace and giving her summat to scream about. My heart were going like a rocket and there was alarms going off in me head, making us go even harder and faster. I grunted and shot me load, then collapsed over her, gasping for puff. I ain't sure how long it were before I noticed them alarms still going off. And they weren't in me head.

'What are you doin'?' she says, reaching back and pulling us back onto her.

'Summat's up,' I says, trying to get off her and falling on me arse. 'Fire or summat.' I got up sharpish and pulled me strides up, looking over at the boss feller and finding him to be not moving. 'Ah, fuck.'

She were getting herself straight and all, pulling her skirt down and setting her hair to rights. The air had turned parky and it were like a stranger had stepped in the room instead of her. Mind you, she were worried about the fire, like as not.

'Listen you,' I says, 'about your boss there...'

'Like I says,' she says, avoiding me eye, 'you're for it.'

'Aye but you was j—'

'No, I meant it actually. I'm tellin' the coppers what you done.'
She were over by him now, kneeling down and taking his pulse.

'Hey?' I says. 'Fuckin' jokin', ain't yer? After what we just
done?'

'We never done nuthin'. Come here and help me, will you?
We've gotta get him out.'

'Fuck him. I ain't gettin' him out so's I can go to jail.'

'We can't leave him to burn, you thick bastard. Are you gonna
help us or not?'

'I just says no, didn't I? An' you ain't gonna change me mind
talkin' like that to us. Good luck, eh,' I says, going for the door.

'Wait…Just wait a sec, will yer. Help me get him out an' I
won't say a word. I never seen nuthin.'

'What about him? He's gonna grass us, ain't he?'

'He's had a bump on the head. I'll tell em you was never here.'

'Promise?'

'Aye. Yes.'

'Go on then. Hand on heart.'

'I promise to say you was never here.'

I had a little think, then goes: 'You lyin' cow.'

'Please, Blake, I ain't. I'll do anythin' for you. We just gotta get
Cecil out.'

'Cecil?' I says. 'Who's the fuck's Cecil?'

'Thass his name.'

'No wonder I never knew it. You'd keep a name like that quiet, eh?'

'*Come on*, Blake.'

'All right all right,' I says, 'Fuck sake.'

I waved her aside and picked him up.

'Here,' I says as we got moving. 'See me bag over yonder? By
the chair…Aye, that un. Pick him up, will yer? Ta.'

• • •

She stopped by the lift.

'I ain't goin' in there,' I says. 'Come on, this way.'

'I ain't goin' down the stairs.'

'Why not?'

'Why ain't you goin' in the lift?'

'Cos…you know…'

'Chicken, are yer? Thought you was a man?'

'I am a fuckin' man. You *knows* it.'

'Come in the lift then.'

'But…'

'Come on. You might drop him if you goes down there.'

'I won't drop—'

'I *ain't* goin' down the *stair*,' she yells.

'Fuck sake,' I says, joining her by the lift. 'You pressed the button?'

'Course I have.' She sniffed the air and goes: 'I can't smell smoke. You sure there's a fire?'

'Aye. Alarms is still goin' off, ain't they? And can't you hear them sirens outside?'

She had a listen and goes: 'Oh aye.'

'S'right. We're high up here though, so you won't smell it if the fire's down there on the ground.'

'How's we gonna get out, then?'

'Dunno. They'll have firemen an' that down there.'

'So you reckon they'll have the fire out by now?'

'Aye. You wanna leave him here now?'

'No. We gotta get him to the hospital.'

'Fuck sake.'

'It's your bloody fault. What'd you hit him for anyhow?'

'I never hit him. I lobbed him out the window and…the window, it like…'

'Why though?'

I could hear the lift coming now. I bent down and picked him up again. 'Cos he made a cunt of us. Thass why.' I carried him into the lift, trying not to think about what I had coming.

She came in behind us and pressed the button. Then she stood in the corner, hugging herself, and goes: 'He does it to me and all. Makes a fool of us. I hates it.'

'Well then,' I says, and we started moving. Weren't so much of a lurch this time, going down, and I couldn't see meself honking. I found it calming to squeeze the backs of the feller's legs, him draped there across me shoulder.

'So he made a fool of you…Then what?' she says.

'Then I learned him a lesson, eh.'

'He never deserved this. You went too far. Fellers like you never knows when to stop. All muscle and no brain.'

'Aye,' I says, winking at her. 'You knows it though, don't yer.'

She'd turned frosty again now and I wished I'd kept me gob shut. I had enough shite flying around in me life without her blabbing to the coppers about us. Mind you, the feller looked like he were coming round a bit now. I'd heard a couple of groans from behind us and clocked his feet twitching in front of us. Must have been me squeezing his legs what done it. I lowered him gently down onto his feet, to see if he couldn't stand.

'Woss you doin'?'

'I'm lowerin' him gently down onto his feet, to—'

I stopped there cos that's where the lift stopped. And it truly did lurch this time, knocking us right off kilter and sending me guts queer. I dropped the feller and retched a couple of times, making a sound like an old guard-dog. As the doors opened I bent down and honked all over him. He opened an eye and goes: 'Hey, woss—'

Then his head popped open.

It's hard to know what were going on here. I were in the wrong state of head for taking in details. There's no fire anyhow. Not the flaming variety. Plenty of gunfire, mind, if that counts. And looks like the little boss feller here took a bit of it in his swede, cutting him short.

I pressed the button sharpish. I wanted the doors shut so none of them mad fuckers running around could get in. They was everywhere, a few fellers but mostly birds, your typical shoppers out on a little buying trip. Except they was all screaming and bleeding and falling over. Meanwhile the fucking door ain't shutting. I slams me fist into the buttons, screaming at em.

The secretary's screaming and all. She's been screaming since the door popped open followed by the feller's swede, and I can't fucking stand it. I wanna get away from the screaming cunts, not have more of em starting up in here. So I shove her out, yelling: 'Go on, run for it, girl.' She trips over the dead feller and goes arsewise on the deck. Another couple of screamers runs into her and goes down atop her, causing a pile-up. It's like on telly when the feller's scored a crucial goal in the cup final.

'Hoy,' someone's barking somewhere. 'There's the cunt over there.'

I can't see em but I recognises the voice. It's a big city voice, lairy and loving it. One of them two from the card game. I hears a pop over there and a crack in here. I looks round and there's a hole in the metal behind us, smoking.

'Don't fuckin' shoot him, you twat!' It's Don's voice this time, far off. 'Get him. Make him shut them fuckin'—'

I miss the last bit cos someone's coming in the lift. Two of em, the one screaming and the other nice and quiet. The doors is starting to close now.

'Bring them fuckin' walls down, you,' Don's shouting. And I knows he means us. 'You do it or I'll fuckin' waste yer meself.'

More bullets. Fucking loads of em going all over the shop, some of em coming in here. Meanwhile I'm getting the screamer and chucking her out before the lift shuts. And I think she took a bullet on her way out there, which is fucking lucky cos I'd have took it else. The door's shut now. Peace and quiet, at fucking last. I press a button and the lift lurches up, but I don't feel sick this time. I'm getting used it. I have a look around and notice the little lad crouching down there in the corner, nice and quiet, paws over ears.

'Fuck's goin' on in there?' I says to him.

He ain't answering. I bend down and pull a paw away and goes: 'I says what the fuck's...'

There's no point though. I've spotted the look in his eyes and I know me words ain't getting through. He's lost it, ain't he. Poor little fucker. Least he's quiet though. I have a glance over him to make sure he ain't been hit, but there's no blood. 'Here,' I says, standing up, 'you're that feller, ain't yer. You know, the pirate lad up there in the office. The one who...Ah, fuck...'

Cos if he's the little lad from the office, that must have been his mam who I'd shoved out just there, her getting shot. I hadn't recognised her in the heat of it all, but now I thought about it I could swear she had on them thigh-length boots and a leather skirt. Shame that, cos I'd quite fancied her and there were scope for a shag at some point. But I just couldn't handle her screaming, so it were her fault.

Mind you, it were hard on the lad. Specially with his old feller lying here in the lift with us, brains leaking out his head.

'There there,' I says, patting him on the swede. (The lad, not the dead feller.)

The lift stopped.

The doors opened.

Two fellers stood there, one pointing a rifle at us, both with the old stocking over the head. The one without the gun goes: 'Everyone has a role in life. Yours was small, but you still fucked it up. And now you must pay.'

Then he swings his boot hard into me bollocks.

19

'Oh...' I says.

Cos it's all coming back to us now. Don and the lads, me helping em out, shutting down the walls and that.

'Oh aye...'

I dunno how I could have forgot, really. Alarms going off, sirens, bullets all over the shop...

'Here,' I says, 'woss you doin' down there, all them guns an' that?'

Another boot for us, this time up the arse. Hurts a bit but not so bad as the one in me plums just now. Mind you, I've known worse in that area. Sal used to kick us harder. Must be them little feet birds have. More accuracy.

'Shut yer face and shift,' says the one.

It's them two from the card game, the one looking like Bo Duke, the other with a shaved swede and the caterpillar eyebrows. You can see em, clear as morning despite them stockings. Just looks like they got nice suntans and bust noses.

'You oughta take a look at yerself, you oughta,' says the other, the one who said I only had a small role in life just now. He's the Bo Duke one. 'You're meant to be in a *team*, you are. People gets angry when you don't do yer bit. The team breaks down and the job don't get done. Then people gets disappointed. *Really* fuckin' disappointed. And that's why I kicked—'

'Shut yer fuckin' face, Tom,' says Caterpillar.

'Hoy—*cool it*. Right?'

'Yeah yeah…Look, we ain't fuckin' got time for that shit. This cunt here had done his bit, we'd have all day to give little pep talks. But he never. So we ain't.'

'I knows that, Max. But you gotta try and be calm in a situation like this one. Havin' a joke is a simple, effortless way to achieve that aim.'

'Don't fuckin' start with all that. All you fuckin' talks about, them fuckin' books of yours.'

'A man who don't learn is a man who don't grow.'

'*Leave* it.'

'I'm just sayin', try and cool it.'

'I am cool. It's him, this cunt here. The bottler.'

'I never fuckin' bottled,' I yells, stopping and facing em, puffing me chest out. I still couldn't stand straight, mind.

'Oh aye?' says Caterpillar. You could see his stubbly pate turning pink under his stocking. 'Why didn't you do your bit then, eh? You know what they're doin' down there, Don and the crew? Tryin' to keep the fuckin' filth out is what. We only got so many shells, you know. An' all you had to do were push a fuckin' button, fuck sake.'

'I fuckin' never bottled. Just got the time wrong, didn't I.'

'Got the fuckin' time wrong?'

'Aye. I got the fuckin' time wrong. All right?'

'No it fuckin' ain't al—'

'I thought you says we ain't got time to fuck about?' says Bo. 'Come on.' He goes off down the corridor.

'No,' says Caterpillar. 'No—I says we ain't got time for *your* fuckin' pep fuckin' talks. That ain't what I'm doin'. I'm…'

Bo ain't listening no more. He's moved off down the corridor a bit, sparking a fag and shaking his head. Caterpillar don't like that, I can tell. But he's turned to me, clocking us up and down.

I don't like fellers doing that, and I wanna smack him.

'Giz yer wallet,' he says, brightening.

'Eh?'

'Yer wallet. Giz yer watch an' all.'

'Fuck off. Get yer own watch.'

'*Fuckin*' giz em. *Now*.'

'Why'd you want me watch?'

He don't answer us. He's puffing hard from his shouting, keeping eyes and the gun on us. I knows there ain't no arguing, so I take off the watch and get me wallet out.

'Cos you're a cunt,' he says, grabbing em. 'An' I can do what I like.'

'Come on,' I says, watching him slip the ticker on. 'Let us keep it, eh? Me old feller gave us it.'

'Old feller eh?' He's looking close at it. I wonder about hitting him here, but you can feel his nerves in the air and all he's gotta do is pull the trigger. 'Did you love yer old man, did yer?'

I didn't answer that. How do you answer that? I don't reckon anyone could.

'Hey, Tom,' he says, holding his hands in front of me face and rubbing em. 'Look at him blushin'. You could dry a pair o' wet boots in this heat.'

But Bo's off again, and Caterpillar nudges us after him. We goes up the corridor and down some stairs. The lad's shuffling on up ahead, in a trance. I'd have made a run for it if I was him, just then when the growed-ups stopped for a row. But he ain't up to it, this un.

'Hoy, you.' One of the fellers, shouting at him. 'Slow down, you little cunt.'

The lad stops and waits, not turning round though.

'Let him go,' I says.

'You what?'

'The youngun. You don't need him so let him go. Lost his folks, ain't he.'

'Who asked you?' It were Caterpillar, sticking a double barrel in me back. 'Keep yer gob shut and yer pins movin'. An' where's this fuckin' security room anyway?'

I knows they'd be asking us about that soon enough. And I've worked out just the answer. 'Down here,' I says. 'Just up there on the right.'

'Shift, then.'

See, I'm gonna lead em into the broom cupboard, the one I got changed in a couple of day ago when I started here. Me knackers is a lot better now and I feel up to a rumble, you see. But I wants an advantage, there being two of them and a gun. So the plan is to get us all in there, flick the light off, then bash em. That's why I wants the kid away. I don't want him getting hurt, see. I thinks about things like that, being a father meself.

'Hold on,' he says. I mean the lad. The lad turns and addresses the three of us, saying: 'Hold on.' Actually it's mainly them other two he's addressing, but all of us is pulling by him at once, like. 'That's not the way to the security room.'

Bo Duke looks at us and rubs his chin and goes: 'That so, is it? Leadin' us up the path, eh?'

'I fuckin' told em,' says the caterpillar. 'I told em he's shit. He's a fuckin' spaz and you can't trust him. Not a good combination, is it, for a job like this. Spazzy and untrustworthy. Shall I just shoot him here?'

'Hold up, Max,' says Bo, putting a paw on the barrel. 'We don't call em spazzies no more. It ain't political. These days you gotta call em…er…mentals, or summat.'

'Oh, Tom has spoken up and we gotta call the mong a "mental." All right then, Professor fuckin' Tommo, shall we proceed to slaughter this here "mental," or what?'

'Hey, look.'

He nods up the way. The lad's off down the corridor, taking a left and disappearing. Bo runs after him, hollering for him to fucking hold his horses else he's dead. The caterpillar kicks us up the arse and pokes us with the gun, making us jog after. I turn the corner and find Bo and the lad stood by a closed door.

'Password,' says Bo, pointing at a little calculator wossname in the wall there.

I says: 'Eh?'

'Come on, spill. Woss the password?'

'I don't fuckin' know,' I says.

Hard poke in the back, Caterpillar saying: 'This was *your* fuckin' job, you prick. You're an *insider*, thass why we let you join in. Insider who knows passwords an' that.'

I shrugs. 'I ain't even been to this bit before.'

'For fuck's fuckin' sake.'

Meanwhile the lad's tapping away on the buttons and making em beep and the door go click. 'It's open now,' he says.

Bo pushes the door open, going: 'Well, fuck me.'

'Fuckin' hell,' says the caterpillar. 'How'd he know that?'

'I dunno, do I? Hey, kid, how'd you know that?'

'Daddy does it.'

'Yer daddy? He goes in here, does he?'

'Course.'

'Yeah? Who is he, then?'

'Daddy.'

'I know that but who is he? Woss his job, like?'

'He goes to work here.'

'What, in a shop, like?'

'No, in a room. With a desk.'

'An office? Where?'

'At the top.'

'You mean he's the boss?'

'Yes.'

'Of this place?'

'Yes. Daddy is the boss. He told me.'

'Fuck me. You hear that, Max?'

'I fuckin' did.'

'Better bring him with us. Insurance, like.'

Meanwhile I'm looking at the youngun. The fuckin twat, is all I can say. There he is, beaming up at a feller with a stocking on his head, spilling all the family secrets to him. And he wouldn't say a bloody word to me when I spoke to him just now.

• • •

Cos I tried, didn't I? I tried having a word with him back there, asking how he is and taking him under me wing like. But he weren't having it. He chose his own path, and there was fuck all I could do to lead him astray.

I often reminds meself of that, waking up all sweaty and out of puff.

• • •

Half an hour later and the alarm's off. Things is a lot calmer now on account of that, and I can finally hear meself thinking a bit. The lad says he's brung down them security walls outside the building and all, pressing that big red button there in the little metal door, just where Don said it'd be. He weren't wrong about the tits poster neither.

'Woss you doin'?' the caterpillar says to us.

'Takin' the poster down. For the lad's sake, like. Bit rude, ennit.' Like I says, I was trying to look out for him.

'Fuck off an' leave it up there. Go on an' have a look, son. The lad's done well, ain't yer, eh?'

He were right, course. A lad ought to see the female form, give him a taster of what he can look forward to if he plays em right. But summat made us want to protect him from it. Instinct, what it were. Me instinct was telling us to cover his eyes.

'What the fuck's you up to now?'

'Protectin' him,' I says. 'From the...you know, the...'

The lad batted me paws away and got back to staring at the poster, gob agape.

'I ain't happy about it,' I says. Don't you fret—I were well aware of how twattish I came across just then. I'd have laughed meself claret if I'd have heard them words come from a feller. But like I says, I weren't happy about it. Things wasn't right, and I didn't know what to do about em.

The caterpillar turns to Bo Duke and goes: 'Listen to the fuckin'—'

I got some moves, mate. Test em any time. Creep up behind us, take us by surprise, jump on us from overhead—I got a move to handle it. And I had one for this situation here—Caterpillar with his rifle pointed off to the side, him talking to his mate from Hazzard. You don't think about it, you just do.

Like I says, it's instinct.

You got to hark it.

I dropped down low and swept his legs from behind. Maybe I'd have chose to grab his weapon instead, if I'd thought about it. But he might have turned and shot us. This way I took him unawares, and I'd ducked out of his range.

He went down. I'd shoed him so hard he sort of spun like a catherine, slamming headwise on the hard stuff and dropping the gun. Bo went for it sharpish. He were a fast and limber shifter all right (which didn't surprise us, considering the way he used to hop through the window of his 'General Lee').

But I can be sharpish and all, when there's summat to get sharp about. And like I says, I were thinking about the lad here. I sensed harm coming the poor fucker's way, and I felt meself stepping in for him.

Bo and meself got a paw to the gun same time. He had a bit more length his side, but I had summat better than length. I had the trigger end.

He yanked the barrel.

I pulled the trigger.

'Uh,' he says, experiencing the unique sensation of his knee-cap going away from him. His leg gave up there and then, refusing to support him no longer without the pivotal player. He started toppling backward, against the wishes of his good leg. Meanwhile his right hand's reaching for his coat pocket.

I point up and pull again, getting him in the guts.

Fuck knows what sort of gun this is. I ain't ever seen one like it. Not close up anyhow. Summat familiar about it though, and I got a feeling it's cos I had a couple of these for me Action Men, many a long moon ago.

'Hey,' I say to the youngun, standing nearby somewhere, 'you got Action Men, have you?'

I don't think he can hear us though, cos Bo's screaming a bit. The poor feller's in pain, and like as not he's gonna stay that way and die a couple of hours down the line. So I get up and put the barrel to his swede. A sharp bit on the end catches the stocking, pulling it around as he tries to move.

'No,' he yells.

I pull the trigger and watch a big red hole appear in the stocking, about where his eye ought to be. His head snaps sideways like I hit him with a lump hammer. He falls back and that's it for him.

'Ooooh,' goes the caterpillar, moving a bit.

'Shut it, you,' I says, booting him in the ribs. I put the gun on the side and crouch down next to him, reaching inside his jacket for me wallet. I go to get the watch off his wrist and all, but as I touch it summat stops us, and I just look at it instead. Meanwhile I got all kinds of thoughts starting up in me swede, going every which way. After a bit I come to and remember the lad. He ain't in the room no more.

It's only a little room and there's no hiding space. '*Hoy, lad,*' I yells, going out into the passage. 'Where's you hidin'? Come out, you silly bastard. I'm *helpin'* yer.'

Summat skims the top of me head and a big chunk of the wall falls off. I think there was a bang there and all, but I can't hear nothing—only that high-pitched note you gets sometimes and can't get rid of. There's a tickling on me forehead and I got to scratch it, finding it all wet and bloody. 'Eh?' I goes, turning about.

The lad's there, pointing the gun at us, tears pouring down his rosies. I can't hear what he's saying straight off, but me ears starts up again a bit after.

'...*am* a pirate. I *am* a pirate. I *am* a...'

He pulls the trigger again.

It's a bit stiff for him and the barrel goes off to the side and up a bit, so I throws meself the other way. The gun goes off and some more plaster and breeze block falls off the wall.

'Hoy, yer fucker,' I says, getting up.

But he's got the gun on us again.

I'm up and off down the corridor. The lad's doing some more shouting behind us: '...pirate I am a pirate I am a...' He fires into the ceiling this time, going by the plaster raining on us. The little tosser. And I'd tried to help him and all. Last time I helps out a youngun.

Except me own.

• • •

I'm sat on the carpet, back against the door. It's the second floor, I think, but I ain't sure. All I knows is I pegged it down some stairs, went through this here door, and flopped down. And I'm having a little think. Me scalp's stopped bleeding now. Still hurts though, and I knows it's only all that plaster dust gumming it up that's stopping it bleeding. But that ain't what I'm thinking about.

I'm thinking about me future.

There's too much in me head, and it's hard to think. What I wants to do, right, is home in on the important bits, tossing all the rest out. Cos that's been me problem of late, as I sees it. I've got meself involved in too much different shite, saying I'd do this and agreeing to help out with that. I ought to have looked out for meself, for a change. I ought to have gone for what's important and fuck the rest. But I never. I fucked around, going after this scam and that scam. I got meself involved in so many scams I couldn't recall hardly none of em.

And now it's all gone to shite.

You know the barmy thing? I knows what's important now. It ain't the top job, with the office and that. It ain't the money from helping Don and his mates neither. It ain't even the motor that Nathan gave us.

It's about family.

It's about Rache and Little Royston.

And it don't matter where we lives, or what I does for a living. You know what I ought to have done, when I got out of Parpham? Gone straight up the Barkettle Road and asked for work in one o' them pubs up there. Don't have to be door work—collecting glasses would have done it. What mattered were getting meself stable, showing Rache I were all right.

Showing the lad how his old feller can graft.

But now look at us. Fucking fucked, ain't I:

Don and his mates after us
Nathan and his mates after us
Coppers after us, like as not
Can't get out—windows and doors blocked off
Don't wanna get out anyhow—nowhere to go
Cuts and bruises all over
No job
Mangel Jail

Mind you, grumbling don't get you nowhere. And I still had me health. And eight fags left.

A noise up the stair stopped us sparking one. I put em away instead and got up, aiming to peg it. But I clocked a latch on the door so I turned that instead and had a peep through the little oblong window. Pair of boots first, clomping heavy. Then a little pair of lad's trainers skipping after him, all excited.

'Oh aye?' says Caterpillar, holding his gun once again. 'An' he killed him, did he?'

'Yes. I saw him.'

'Kill yer dad?'

'Yes. He made a hole in daddy's head. The madman did. Daddy said he was a madman and never go near him. He was in a special jail for mad people who kill people.'

'Shockin.'

'Will you really take me with you? On the pirate ship?'

'Oh yeah. We'll take you with us all right.'

'And you're really pirates?'

'Oh yeah. I mean...*aye aye.*'

'And the captain will let me come?'

'Who? You mean Long Don Silver? Heh heh. Oh aye, he'll go along. You'll love old Long Don.'

'I'm very excited.'

'You should be, mate. You fuckin' should be.'

'What does that mean?'

'What?'

'That word.'

'What..."fuckin"?'

'Yes?'

'Ah, well...'

I couldn't hear no more. I didn't wanna hear no more neither. Like I says, the lad chose his own path. Now I had to choose mine.

20

MALL MASSACRE:
DEATH TOLL RISES

Robbie Sleeter, Crime Editor

A total of eighteen bodies have now been recovered from the Porter Centre, scene of today's horrific raid. One is believed to be a member of the armed gang, as he was found upstairs in a security control area wearing a stocking over his head. Another has been identified as Cecil Porter, chairman of Porter Holdings, who owned the mall.

The thieves escaped before police could gain entry. Unconfirmed reports mention a 'secret tunnel' leading from the basement to a private industrial lot fifty yards away across the Wall Road. As well as personal belongings stolen from shoppers, nearly £7,000 in cash was taken from the bank to the rear of the ground floor, and £4,000 of goods from the three jewellers in the mall.

Police have confirmed that the massive explosion on the East Bloater Road at 3:30 p.m. was the thieves' getaway van inexplicably blowing up, killing all passengers and destroying most of the stolen goods. 'We're having a hard time identifying these corpses,' said Police Chief Bob Cadwallader. 'They are charred beyond belief, and one or two of them ain't got teeth. However, it looks like one of them was a juvenile, of between three and six years. And no, there's no reason to believe this is young Bernard Porter. Our missing persons team is working hard on that case and let me tell you—there's no better missing persons team this side of Felcham. But I'd just like to say here—if anyone sees a young lad of four years wandering around town, give us a call. The usual number.'

Asked if one of the bodies is thought to be that of Royston Blake, the chief said: 'Well, I'll be honest with you and say that I think so. Like I says—we've not properly identified these fellers yet. It's like trying to identify bits of sausage slipped onto the coals at a barbeque. But we know Blake was part of the gang, and one of the carcasses looks about his size. And do you know what I say? Good flaming riddance. I don't care if it's the right thing to say or not—this town is best shot of him. And the world is best shot of all of them. Except the youngster, of course. Unless he was one of them.'

• • •

I rang the doorbell. No one came. I rang again.

I heard someone this time, knocking around in the hall. Then the noise stopped and there were fuck all for a minute or so. I rang again.

A shout this time, a bird. You couldn't make out the words but I knew what she meant. 'Keep yer fuckin' hairpiece on,' she were saying. But in her own way, like. Rache wouldn't use bad words like that.

Not with the youngun about anyhow.

I pulled me wig straight and righted me glasses, which had gone a bit wonky. I had a whiff of the flowers and all, making us sneeze.

The door opened

'All right, R—' I started to say.

She screamed and slammed the door, just as I were leaning in on her. Not to cop a snog, like—just a friendly peck on the cheek. If a feller can't get a peck on the cheek off the bird he's aiming on marrying, he ain't got no hope. Mind you, this were an odd scenario so you gotta judge it different. I mean, she didn't know who I were, with me disguise and that. I could be a rapist. Or from the council.

'Rache,' I says, leaning doorward to make up for how quiet I had to be. 'Iss me, ennit. Blakey.' I had to say it quiet cos I didn't want no beaky neighbours hearing us and calling the coppers. I knows what neighbours is like, and I hadn't heard nothing different about the ones in Bonehill flats. 'I'm in disguise, like.'

I got fuck all from that, so I pressed me lughole against the wood and harked.

Whirr. Stop. Whiiiiir. Stop. Whiir. Stop...

She were on the fucking blower, weren't she.

Dialling the coppers.

'Silly tart,' I says, stepping back for a run-up. The door gave first time, which I found surprising. I'd always heard them Bonehill flats doors to be quality pieces of workmanship, and I'd been up for two or three shoulderings at least. I weren't complaining, mind. Rache were right there in front of us, blower to ear, going: 'Help.' And if I'd not got in so fast I'd not be able to slap the blower from her paw. And pull the cord out the wall, just to make sure, like.

I think I might have caught some of Rache there when I slapped the handset from her. She were on the carpet anyhow, skirt up and legs askew in a most unbirdlike manner, considering this were me future bride. I reached down to pull her up sharpish, before I went off her.

She scrambled away, staggering up and flying off into the kitchen.

'Fuck sake, Rache,' I says, traipsing after her. I clocked meself in the hall mirror as I went by, and took me disguise off. Didn't wanna frighten the poor lass no more. Mind you, she'd seen us in a similar get-up before and recognised us straight off. Must be the wig I had this time, which were ginger. Didn't look too bad actually. You'd be surprised.

Rache were in the little pantry across the kitchen there. I could hear her panting like a cornered fawn. On me way through I got a couple of biscuits from the tin on the side and stuffed em in me gob. I were fucking starving, and I'd have ate em even if they was dog biscuits. I think they was custard creams though.

'Come on, Rache,' I says, spraying crumbs all over her nice clean floor. There were one of them flimsy divider wossnames shutting off the pantry. I thought I'd leave it shut for now, let her calm down like. 'Me ennit, Blake.'

'I know,' she says. 'I knows it's y-you. The police'll be here soon, s-so you'd best—'

'Didn't you fuckin' hear us?' I were losing it a bit now. I'd been through a fucking lot, and I didn't need this on the end of it. Specially not from Rache, who were meant to fancy us. And her getting to look after me son all these years. I mean, I didn't *have* to carry on letting her. By rights I could take him back, look after him meself. Wouldn't take long to prove he's me own. All you gotta do is wank into a tube, or summat.

Losing it wouldn't help though, so I leaned back on the wall and counted to fifty. When I reached forty or so I noticed summat on the side and went over. It were the local paper, evening edition. And fuck me with a trowel if that ain't my old mugshot there on the front. MALL MASSACRE: DEATH TOLL RISES, the headline went.

A few minutes later, after I'd read all the writing, I felt a lot more sympathetic towards our Rache.

'All right,' I says. 'All right. So you thinks I'm a zombie, right? You thinks I'm dead an' I turned up here on your doorstep. Eh?'

No answer. I pulled back the door a bit and had a peek. She were stood up against the corner, by the tins of beans and peas and that, holding a bread knife out with two hands.

'Woss you gonna do?' I says, laughing. 'Slice us?'

'You get back,' she says, voice all wobbly.

'Come on, Rache. I ain't a zombie.'

'I knows you ain't. You're worse. You're a killer. I always knew you'd killed before, but that was when you was forced into it, I thought. You wasn't this time though. This time you killed em all for money. And one of em was your own s—'

'Eh?' I says, cutting her off. 'I never killed no one. I mean, like…Woss you sayin'?'

'I'm sayin' you blew up that van, you bastard.' She were crying now, but holding on. Tears was streaking her cheeks, but she were a strong un and she kept the blade steady. 'An' don't say you never. I knows you was in on the job. You switched the bag with the money at the last minute, or summat, and done a runner while they went into the van. You killed my Don, you bloody bastard… An' you killed your own flesh and—'

'Fuckin' shut it for a min, will yer?' I says, holding me head. All a bit much for us to take, this. 'I weren't even in with em, in the end. I never went through with it. I couldn't, you know, cos I turned a leaf. I ain't doin' none o' that shite no more, robbin' an' that. If you thinks about it, right, if you thinks about it I ain't done none in yonks anyhow. I ain't robbed no one on purpose since I was a nipper. And I ain't started no fights neither. It's always other cunts, aimin' to take you down and keep you where they likes you.'

The bread knife were dipping a bit now, the tears slowing down.

'I ain't havin' it no more, Rache. I'm keepin' me swede down from now on. You know what I'm gonna do? Get a job in a pub, doin' glasses or summat. I ain't proud no more, Rache. I been a proud man all me life, and woss proudness ever done for us, eh? Eh? I don't need to tell you what, do I. You knows it. You knows us better'n any of em, Rache. You watched us crashin' into one shitestorm after another, and you always spoke up about it. But iss *me*, ennit. Iss *me* who don't listen.'

She dropped the blade and came over to us, looking close into me eyes before giving us a big hug. It didn't half feel good. I never been one for hugs and that (unless I got me knob up her) but it were different here. Felt like I'd come home, after many a wilderness year.

'Oh, Blake...' she says into me chest.

I stroked her hair and moved a paw down her back, stopping short of poking me fingers down her jeans. This were a special moment, and I didn't wanna spoil it. 'I'm done with all that, now,' I whispers into her ear. 'I wants a normal life. A quiet life. Just you, me, an' our Little Royston.'

'*Roy*,' she says. 'His name's Roy. After me dad.'

'Ah,' I says, laughing a bit. 'Yer right there, an' I does apologise. I just calls him Little Royston though, to meself. You know, cos he's me son, like. I knows it ain't his real name. Roy's an all right name though.'

I noticed it in her back first. I had a paw down there, stroking a finger up and down her spine, when the whole carriage went stiff under us. Then her arms dropped from me sides and she pulled back and says: 'You what?'

'What?' I says.

'You said "your son." How can he be your son if you an' me never—'

'Look, I knows about the little arrangement. Sal told us all about it. She told us about how you can't have babbies, and how you offered to bring ours up when Sal hit hard times. An' I'm fine with it, Rache. Honest I is. Suits us perfect. I'd have chose you over Sal as the lad's mam any day. An' this way we can all be...'

I stopped there cos she were putting us off, shaking her head slow, looking at us that way.

'What?' I says.

She were two steps away now, hand to mouth, letting herself fall back until the shelves propped her up.

'What, fuck sake?' I says.

She glanced down, seeing where the knife were on the floor. But she didn't pick it up. 'Blake,' she says, taking a deep one. 'Sally lied to you. I'm sorry, but none of it's true. Not a word. Roy is my own son. Don is his...*was* his father. Sally did have a baby, yes. But...'

'Fuck off. You're just sayin' that cos...cos...'

'Blake, it's true. Roy's not yours. I've got nuthin' to gain from sayin' that. He's just...*not yours.*'

I looked down, trying to think.

'Oh, Blake,' she says, coming forward again and touching me face. Her hand were wet from where she'd been biting it just now. 'Oh...Blake...'

'Just shut up a min, right?' I were stepping back into the kitchen, clutching me swede again and trying to get it working. 'Why...I mean, why the fuck would she...'

'Please, Blake. Please…just leave it. You need to think of yourself for a while, get back on your feet.'

'No, I'm all right. I'm fuckin' all right. I just…I know Sal were a lying bitch an' that, but why would she lie about her lad? *My* lad?'

'I dunno, Blake. There's just no tellin'. But…'

'But what, fuck sake?'

'I suppose she wanted to protect the boy. I mean, give him a better chance of…you know…'

'Hang on,' I says. I were already onto summat else. My mind were raging, digging deeper and deeper. And with every shovelful of shite I found a new question. 'If the lad ain't mine, right…if your lad ain't Little Royston, who the fuck is?'

'He's…he were…' she says, eyes welling up again. She looked in both of me eyes, one after t'other, like a punter with two bets on at the bookies. Both nags came nowhere, going by her face. But you could tell they weren't her own bets.

She had em on for some other poor fucker.

'Sally gave him to an outsider,' she says, brightening slightly, like they'd declared her horses non-runners and she could have her money back. 'A good man. And a woman. From the big city. They'll be lookin' after him well, Blakey, so there's no need to…'

Her eyes went behind us and down. I heard summat and turned. A young lad were stood there in the kitchen doorway, holding a teddy. 'Who's he, mam?' he says.

She slipped past us, ushering him away and saying: 'You should be in bed, Roy,' in a stern voice. You could tell she'd turn out good in the mamming department.

'I heard shoutin',' he says before his bedroom door shut.

I waited a bit while she tucked him in. There were no ale in the fridge and fuck all to drink in the pantry. Odd that, her being a barmaid by trade. I waited a bit longer, feeling the cut on top of me scalp. It were scabbing over all right now, though it hadn't been there more than a few hours. I looked at me watch.

• • •

I dunno why I went there. Not to Rache's, like—I knows why I went there. I might get confused sometimes but I ain't thick. It's the place after that I'm on about. I seemed to just wake up there after a long kip, sat on a stool, pint in hand.

I looked up and clocked meself in the mirror behind the bar. I weren't even wearing the disguise.

'Woss you shakin' yer head fer?' comes an all-too-familiar voice.

I looked sideways to find Nathan stood not five paces away, polishing a tankard. I looked behind us: no one else in the Paul Pry. All the lights off and all, besides the ones behind the bar. I looked at me watch.

But I didn't have a watch no more.

'Iss good that you came here,' he says, hanging the tankard and picking up a clean glass. He went to the pump and pulled us a pint of lager. 'Saves me comin' after you.'

I got me fags out. One left. 'Nathan...' I says, sparking up. 'Nathan, I knows it looks like I fucked up...with the bag and that. But it weren't my fault. I—'

It weren't like he'd interrupted us. Nathan hadn't said a word. But I just became aware of summat in him at that moment. Summat that I didn't care for and put the shites right up us. And I couldn't talk no more. I couldn't even pick up the pint he'd set before us. I smoked me fag and watched the bubbles rising. I wished I were one of them bubbles, in a way. Cos then I wouldn't have to be out here, facing the wrath of Nathan the barman.

'Ain't so bad,' he says after fucking ages. 'We've had a word about it, and I've come to realise a couple of things in the wake of it.'

I drank some lager.

'They don't like it, course. Them who calls emselves the Old Guard. Do you know what, though? You won't ever please them. No, they got their sights set all wrong, I says. Course, I went along with em. They was correct in spirit, and they was makin' a point needed makin', what with the current way of things. But the point's made now, and iss time to get on with things. What d'you say, Blakey? You ready to get on and all?'

'Oh aye,' I says, putting me empty down. 'So you ain't grassin' us to the coppers, you mean? About Sal and Ferret?'

'I means just that, Blake. An' not only that—I'll also arrange it so's you don't go down for them other matters neither. And iss recent events at the Porter Centre I'm referrin' to here.'

'Flippin' hell, Nathe,' I says. 'Nice one.'

'The name's Nathan. You oughta know that.'

'Aye all right. I were just—'

'You also oughta know you don't get summat fer nuthin'. Not in the Paul Pry anyhow. So you'll be payin' fer that.'

'Oh,' I says, looking at the empty. I reached pocketward and says: 'Put another in there then.'

'Not that, you flamin' pranny. The coppers. You're payin' fer me smoothin' you out with the coppers. Don't cough up and you knows where you'll be headed. Right?'

'How much?' I says. Cos I still had a few notes on us.

'Put yer wallet away. There's nuthin' you can do fer me mon-eywise. No, summat else I'm after. Summat quite specific like.'

'What? I ain't got nuthin'. Me house? Come on, Nathan, I gotta live some—'

'Not yer house. There's enough homeless scroungers in this town without addin' another to em.'

'What then?'

He leaned in, plonking another full one under me nose. 'Your most valuable possession,' he says. Then he walked off to go on about his barmanlike affairs. 'I see you rackin' yer swede there,' he says after a while. 'Yer thinkin' "woss he want, then?" Yer thinkin' "woss I got thass worth summat?" And you'd be right in both cases. But there's summat I ain't said yet. Summat that'll make it all clear to you in time. See, I wants the thing that will be most valuable to you *in one hour's time*. Not now, but an hour hence. Understand? No, I don't suppose you does. But you will. Now go home. And put yer disguise back on first. You'll not be needin' it the morrer, after you hands over my fee and I sorts things out with the coppers.'

• • •

The Viva were still there in the Paul Pry car park. I'd lost me car keys somewhere so I had to spark her. She started first time though, which were all right, and sailed home like a very slow sailing boat. I didn't see a copper all the way. I didn't clock no one at all. It were sometime in the middle of the night, though I couldn't tell you for surely when.

Instead of turning into our street I pulled up on the main road. As you know, I had on a good disguise. But I still didn't want no nosy fuckers seeing us go in. Not that I gave a toss what they thought. I'd had it with Mangelfolk, and they could say what they fucking wanted about us. But I didn't wanna go to jail. And I didn't feel squared on that score yet, Nathanwise.

I got into the house through the kitchen window round the back. There'd always been a way of prying it, ever since I were a youngun. Mind you, I used to be a bit more lighter on me feet them days and I didn't smash so many plates clambering over the sink and draining board. But I got in, is all that counted. Plenty of time for sweeping up broken china. Or maybe I wouldn't bother.

I made meself a cuppa and sat at the kitchen table, looking around at the old place. 'You here?' I says. But no one answered. 'Dad?' And I knew no one would answer. Least of all that particular feller.

Mind you, I felt chilly in there of a sudden. I got up and took me tea into the hall, noticing a letter on the bit of carpet where the doormat used to be. I put me mug down and had a look.

Wigram, Markle & Pucker Solicitors Ltd
5 Sheepcote Lane
Mangel

Dear Mr Blake,

I have been instructed to execute the final will and testament of one Berty Fontana (formerly Albert Malcolm Fountain), who died recently of a long and drawn-out illness.

In short, Mr Fontana has left you the freehold of The Bee Hive public house in Spencer Road, Norbert Green, Mangel. Mr Fontana also passes on to you the business attached to the site, namely that of a fully licensed public house, including all fixtures, fittings, and stock. Your are of course free to do with the property as you wish, but my client suggested only that you might think about selling it, and using the money to start again in a better place. What he meant by that, I cannot interpret.

Please arrange an appointment to see me at your earliest convenience, so that all relevant documents and contracts can be signed. And please accept my condolences.

Yours,
Grayson Pucker

• • •

After a while I noticed the phone were ringing.

'All right,' I says.

'That a yes, then?' says Nathan.

'Eh?'

'Does 'all right' mean yes? Or not?'

'You what?'

'Your most valuable possession, I said. Do I get it, complete with all fixtures, fittings, and stock? Or do you go to Mangel Jail?'

• • •

I started up the long hill on the East Bloater Road and put me foot on it.

Summat always made us floor it when I started up that hill. I wanted to keep on going and smash through the barrier and come out the other side, battered and bloody but somewhere else. Normally it were only ever a brief urge, gone by the time I were halfway up. And there were no barrier up there to smash through anyhow. Not one you could see, anyhow. But just cos you couldn't see it nor smash through it don't mean the fucker weren't there. It were there all right. It had always been there.

But it weren't stopping us this time.

Mind you, by the time I reached the brow of the hill the Viva were feeling it bad and I pulled in, letting her have a quick breather. I planted her left tyres on the grass verge and got out.

I says grass verge, but there weren't much grass there now. Just black, it were. Black scrub and a few scorched larches nearabouts. The tarmac were black just there and all. Normally a sort of tired grey, it were, but under the bright full moon you could see the soot all over it quite clearly. And the bits of broken windscreen and twisted plastic and that piled up against the verges, swept there by the coppers only a few hours previous.

The fucking twats, though, blowing up their van.

I sat on the warm bonnet of the Viva and looked out at the world beyond. You could see lights here and there. Some I knew to be East Bloater, but there were a definite glow coming from just beyond them Deblin Hills over there to the west, like the sun were rising just beyond it, though I knew it to come up in the east by habit. That's where our Little Royston were. And that's where I were headed. Cos he needed his dad.

And I needed him.

Out there in the dark, I heard Elvis sing. *There's a beckoning candle...*

So I sat there, warming me arse, looking at that beckoning candle and listening to Elvis as he got them shivers moving up and down me spine. I thought about the youngun who I'd never played with nor seen nor so much as spoke to on the blower. I thought about me old man. I thought about Nathan, the Bee Hive, and the way I never seemed to get nowhere in me life, though I always seemed to scrape by somehow. And I thought about how I never seemed to have a fag when I wanted one most.

Then I got back in the Viva and turned her around.

THE END

About the Author

Charlie Williams was born in Worcester, England, in 1971, where he still lives with his wife and two children. His novels include *Deadfolk*, *Booze and Burn*, *One Dead Hen* and *Stairway to Hell*, and have been translated into French, Spanish, Italian, and Russian.

Photograph by Lisa Williams, 2010